NED 7

BY

Jim (Jimmy) Smith

Leader Of The

MIGHTY AVONS
SHOWBAND

HI SIOBHAN,
HOPE YOU ENJOY THE
STORY.

A VELVET BOOK

Hi Siobhan,
Hope you enjoy the story.

Jim

VELVET Publishing
Tel: 00353 91 792853 / 00353 86 2491027
E-mail:
velvetbooksandmusic@gmail.com
mightyavon@eircom.net

Published by Velvet Publishing

Pub Prefix 0 953 7210

This book is sold subject to the condition that it shall not, by way of trade or otherwise, be lent, resold, hired out or otherwise circulated without the publisher's prior consent in any form of binding or cover other than that in which it is published and without a similar condition including this condition Being imposed on the subsequent purchaser

Copyright © 2004 Jim Smith

ISBN: 1-4392-2635-0
EAN13: 9781439226353

First Published 2009

No reproduction without permission
All rights reserved

The right of Jim Smith to be identified as author of this work has been asserted in accordance with

Section 77 and 78 of the copyright

Designs and patents Act 1988.

This book, along with his last one called Animal Mountain, a hilariously funny story about animals, in show business and politics plus three ORIGINAL CDs are also sold directly by getting in touch with the above contacts.

Front cover photograph and design idea by Jim Smith.
Model supplied by Legs Inc.

Artwork: Bridget Flynn
Word Processing: Melissa Smith

Typeset, printed and bound by BookSurge an Amazon.com company.

Book Sponsored by, Apex Travel, Dame St Dublin & Tractamotors, Dublin Rd, Cavan.

COMMENTS FROM SOME FOLK WHO HAD A QUICK SQUINT…

"The most visual piece of fiction I have ever read…"

"Read it and you'll get involved…"

"I found myself dancing to the Novas Showband…"

"The fictional Ned Brady is so real, you'll be convinced you've met him…"

"There's a bit of Ned in all of us red blooded guys…"

"The Novas Showband-the consummate package…"

"Ned the Bed is a rogue with class, could you blame us girls?"

"Sandra Boyle was bold long before she met Ned, but Susan Prunty-now I'd Love to meet her, she could fiddle around with me anytime!"

"Ned may have laid a lot of women, but I still think he's a good egg…"

"This is fiction, *Real Life Style*…"

The author would like to thank the following people:

Shane Connaughton, author and Movie Maker, for suggesting that I change the book title and for adding the slogan, in the same Breath.

The owner of the fabulous bedroom on the front cover.

Oliver Burns, Oldcastle, for the trombone.

The Book's Sponsors. APEX TRAVEL. DUBLIN. & TRACTAMOTORS CAVAN for their support.

…And, to everyone who was patient with me during the four years and two centuries it took to write this story.

Chapter One

Back in the Sixties and Seventies in Ireland, being a member of a Showband was a dream that lurked somewhere in almost every young fella's mind and in a lot of cases spreading to the female of the species as well. It was the one industry back then where you didn't need to look like a movie star or a fashion model. As long as the dancers thought the Singer had a 'great auld voice' and the band had 'the beat' to dance to, then you were on the pigs back so to speak. Ned Brady came from Ballypratt in the Midlands and he had what you could call the good fortune to be the Leader of one of these outfits, known simply but far and wide as The Nova's Showband. He was not I hasten to add, the Lead Singer of this outfit and seeing that he was the Band Leader you might wonder why. Well, there were a couple of reasons, out of the seven musicians already in the band, four of the others were as good or better singers than he was and reason number two, the Lead Singer who had joined about a year earlier, wouldn't like it. They had robbed him from another local outfit that seemed to be going nowhere and he had agreed to the move on the condition that he would be the only singer to record. They all took this idea on board (for a while) as they said, the bottom line being, everyone was doing well financially so they didn't want to rock the boat, but if you happened to have a large ego (which the singer had) then you were laughed at behind your back and called, 'A big eejit.' They basically got on with entertaining the huge crowds, and banking the proceeds.

Another very important aspect of the whole scene which took their minds off recording, was the 'Shafting!' Yes you've guessed it, looking after the more tender needs of the opposite sex. Ned would admit he was a bit of a lad in this area and had a neck like a jockey's bollix, which earned him the nickname of Ned the Bed even though not all romancing was carried out in bed. Quite a lot of lovin' happened in the good old knee-trembler fashion and quickies were in great demand, mainly because the ladies had to be in by a certain time. Another band had a well known drummer called 'Back Seat Pete' and you'll know from his handle that he was not into knee-tremblers, but a few of his conquests missed curfew never the less. As a result Pete had the odd visitor looking for him when they were around that area again, causing the band members to chorus. 'Sorry sir, Pete has left the band.' Then they would point at another member and say 'meet our new drummer, his name is Dick.' Showbands always had a big problem getting insurance, because the companies had the opinion that the band members were on the roads at all hours of the night driving while half asleep, or racing each other in overloaded vans and buses at ninety miles an hour, while still trying to get a court. Not so! They may have got up to some strange antics but where safety was concerned and the safety of others in particular, the greatest of care was always taken. Anyway, in most cases a well-rested roadie would be behind the wheel guaranteed to be sober, so if he had had the good fortune of scoring, that deed would have happened during the gig in the van and he would be over the moon for the remainder of the night as a result. Certain bands had a few mooners and they would lay in wait for some other orchestra, then line out across the road flashing their bums, this was never attempted while moving. Of course there was the odd egg ambush, one band would flag the other down faking a breakdown, then attack with a couple of dozen eggs and make their getaway while the unfortunate ones were cleaning their windscreens screaming.

'We'll get you wankers the next time.' They usually did.

The part of the business they enjoyed best was the actual gig, the buzz of taking a crowd who looked like they didn't give a shit and tranform them into mad people. The one thing that really cracked them up was the fact that every couple had their own way of performing the same dance. Some of them jumped up and down, some did the jive, some did the twist and a few couples always tried to impress by doing some fancy steps while keeping an eye on the band to see if they impressed anybody. The musicians always made it their business to notice, giving their efforts the thumbs up while shouting to each other.

'They think it's come fuckin' dancin' they're on.'

Mickey Joe was currently trying to launch new lingo on the Showband scene, so his very loud reply to suggestions like that would be just one word. 'Bollixolutely.'

Another interesting thing was the din on stage. You could talk about anybody; even the band members and they could hear nothing over the noise. It also gave great scope for farting and this would only be noticed if you had a curry or some other big feed, where you would have eaten far too much the night before.

In most Dance Halls and Carnival Marquees, you would have to go to the public toilets before going on stage. This visit had many funny sides, especially in some situations where the toilets had no sides at all. You went through a flap in the canvas, which in a plush carnival tent would bring you into another smaller one, but in the less glamorous surroundings, the flap brought you out into a field where you would do the business behind a sheet of corrugated tin, otherwise known as galvanise. The best fun of all was listening to the young brash lads talking about their would be conquests for the night, big shirt collars out over their beige jackets, each one trying to piss higher up the corrugated sheet then the other.

Lad1. 'Did you see the one with the wee black dress and the high heels?' 'She's fuckin' mad about me and I'll give her a fierce ridin' tonight.'

His mate usually answered with. 'You haven't a fuckin' hope, because I've been there and she doesn't do the bould thing.'

'Shite,' says Brash Chap No.1. 'I'll bet a tenner she'll do it for me.'

Then the surprise answer of the night comes in the form of a question. 'Where the fuck would you get a tenner?'

Suddenly, the Guitar player attempts a last minute tune up, so all the remaining eve's dropping band members' rush to the stage. Ned picks up his trusty trombone and gives it a couple of quiet blows while scanning the floor for the young one in the black dress and high heels. There's a couple of them and they're both gorgeous, but then our hero with the tenner comes out of the loo, so you don't have to wait long to find out which lady is the object of his lust. He's standing about three feet away from the nicest one of the two and Ned bets another tenner on the outcome. The Drummer counts 1.2.3.4 and they go into their signature tune. The crowd lurches forward, the gig is on.

Ned has been singing this song since the band began, so instead of concentrating on the words he's watching Casanova, as he goes about the chore of going a tenner up. He makes a great effort to propel himself the few feet to his quarry but fails and the young lady has noticed, so she moves away. Don-Juan's doubtful friend begins to give him a hard time for which he gets a box and while all this drama is going on, a very positive guy sweeps the same young girl in black on to the dance floor. Everyone is laughing except the guy with the beige jacket, as the band moves to song number two sung by the Lead Singer. The now less brave young man moves back, because he has noticed that he is in the way of progress and is getting walked on. You can see he's cooking plan number two.

The Guitar player sings some rock-and-roll as song number three in the set. The crowd changes all their dancing patterns and you come to the conclusion that the young would-be dancer has done the prudent thing by moving off the floor. Ned says, next dance please and most of the men take up brand new positions, with the still unsuccessful suitor now standing behind his would be partner. Ned gets as far as, 'and the next dance is,' when he sees the dancing gambler boldly tapping the shoulder of the girl in the black number and heels. She turns around and smiles thinking it's her last partner lose the smile while saying politely. 'No thank you.' The Bandleader has become quite good at lip reading and he's beginning to feel sorry for the chap, but things go downhill for him as he moves back to the side.

'Where's my fuckin' tenner?' asks his friend.

'Fuck off,' came the answer. Ned is lip-reading again.

The people are still teeming into the venue, it gets hotter, the two young guys who are now rowing over the bet, have lost the jackets looking ready for business again and the would be stud has shifted his attentions to maybe four different young ladies. Here's hoping he has stopped putting on bets with his friend, who seems to be doing no better. By now Ned has noticed that the nice young lady in the black dress and heels has great legs. By now the band members have noticed that he has noticed and the Trumpet player asks out of the side of his mouth

'Will you be able to get her into the bed Ned?'

'I'm hoping she'll tire of Mr. Suave,' he answered, also from the corner of his mouth.

The set ended and the nice young one who has by now tired of her partner, thanks him profusely, refuses to stay with him for the next dance, then sits down. Guess where she parks herself? On the stage of course! The Lead Singer smiles broadly to himself, gives Ned a sly wink, then while the raffle is being announced the Singer drops down on one knee, buries his face in her long hair and has a word in her ear. She smiles at the attention, knowing quite a few people are watching and then to the Singers horror she shakes her long black tresses, this bit of lip reading was easy.

'No Thanks,' she said again.

A couple of girl friends join the young woman siting on the stage and it seems they have decided to take a well-earned rest, so Ned picks up his trusty trombone again and what he did next never fails to break the ice. Standing about three feet behind this collection of ladies, his eyes are riveted on the zipper of the little black number. The trombone slide goes out, in again, out, then snake-like, it runs down the zip on the black dress.

The girl turns to her friend on the right and says. 'Stop trying to open my zip.'

The other girl looks at her in horror. 'I'm not trying to open your zip,' she answered.

During the song he did this dastardly deed three more times and last time around he made sure he was caught.

'You're bold,' she shouted.

'Yes,' he agreed.

She seemed pleasantly surprised by his nonchalance and issued a threat, grinning.

'Don't do that again,' she said trying to look tough.

'I'm not doing it, it's the trombone's fault, it seems to like your zip,' he answered.

There's one in every band. 'Get the fucking thing going again or we'll die,' hissed the Bass player.

Ned stuck the mike up to his mouth and said. 'Go on, you tell them what's next.'

The Bass man was pissed off with that plan and went back to his patch, while Ned got a prompt from the Piano player as to what he wanted to sing next.

'You're losing it,' said Mickey Joe, still using the corner of his mouth, then Ned had a fleeting thought. The mouthpiece must be sealing the remainder of the Trumpeter's gob; he can only talk out of one corner. Laughing at this idea as the Drummer attempted to count he shouted to the nice women in black.

'Will you be annoyed with my trombone if it does it again.'

'I'll give you a severe ticking off afterwards if it happens any more,' she laughed.

'I'll tell it that,' he shouted, as the band swung into action once more.

Hardly anyone on the stage was talking to him by now, especially the Lead Singer, but you win some you lose some. He was happy. He hadn't missed the meaning of the veiled threat issued earlier by the nice young lady in the black dress. She and her girlfriends were now dividing their time between sitting on the stage and jiving with each other, giving the odd glance at different members of the band. Maybe some of the lads would have something to thank him for before the night came to an end and the Singer looked a bit happier as the time went by. He had made eye contact with a big bird they had seen him slither out after a few times before and the, (I'm all right on the night) look, was forming on his face.

Luckily, Ned had worked out the approximate number of times you could get away with a trombone zipper attack and he always made sure not to overdo it. As you will agree, too much of anything is good for nothing, so just before the dance ended he asked the young lady to confirm his telling off and she said it could definitely be arranged.

As usual they hit them with everything they had for the last half-hour and the dancers were having a right old time. So also were the bouncers. During that same 30 minutes there must have been six rows around the door started by lads with a few jars, who always insisted on getting in free.

'I'll not fuckin' pay at this hour of the night.' the straggler would say.

'Then why didn't you come earlier, we're here all night to let everyone else in,' was the standard answer in a situation like this.

'We wouldn't pay good money to listen to that bundle of noise,' the reluctant spender would say, edging in another couple of feet. 'Anyway, we only want to get in for the last few minutes to see if we could pick up an auld ride.'

'In the state you lads are in, I don't hold much hope for you in that area,' was the usual reply the bouncer would give, pushing the wags back out through the door and from the stage could be seen the retreating fists flying for a minute. Who would want to be a bouncer?

At last the music dies and the hum from the crowd makes you wonder how they could hear the band in the first instance, also from fifteen hundred people in a venue with no air conditioning, there is usually another hum but now is not the time to talk about that. Finally he's face to face with the young lady in the little black number, the high heels, the gorgeous legs and he's holding her hands as if life itself depends on it. She's beautiful.

'I'm not going to get into a wagon full of strange fellows,' she said for openers, after agreeing that he could take her home.

'But they're not strange at all,' he said, 'anyway you have been looking at them for over two hours now, isn't that true.'

'Sorry,' she said, 'that's the bottom line.'

'Don't worry, I've got a car and some of your friends can have a lift if they need one,' he offered.

This went down well, causing her to tighten her grip and send his pulse racing. The young woman was making a serious impression on him as the moments pass and the lady from the kitchen informs them that a cup of tea waits. 'And you can bring your young lady too,' she said.

Dancers are getting the bands autographs and saying how much they enjoyed the night. The Lead Singer is lapping it up while his big bird parks herself a little bit away, unable to take her eyes off him for a second just in case he throws a shape at someone else. On the whole, she seems happy with her lot knowing what's in store for later. The two would be gamblers are at the stage for band photos which they seem keen to get, then leering at Ned while giving him the fingers they shout in unison.

'Wanker.'

He laughed back at them and shouted. 'Not tonight anyway lads.'

'Your band is shite.' they said

'Give him the tenner and go home,' Ned advised.

They were not pleased that he seemed to know their business and showed their feelings by ripping the pictures to shreds, throwing them in the air. They now looked extremely happy as they bounced out into the night. It wasn't the first or the last time band members had seen that happen and his 60/40 grins returned as he planned his visit to the bank the following day.

The Roadie has had the tea earlier and is now busy packing the van. He hasn't clicked tonight so he's going around asking some of the lads if they will travel back with him, but to no avail. The fella's are too busy checking out the available talent to consider spending four hours in a van, so the Roadie gets on with the job swearing under his breath. Ned's new friend says her name is Susan.

'It suits you.' he replied and then he told her his name.

She burst out laughing and said. 'Nobody gets called Ned.'

'I was christened Edward Seamus Brady,' he answered, 'but everyone called me E.S.B. thinking I was the man from the electricity supply board who kept sending them the big bills, so that had to go, now Ned it is.'

'I suppose you were always blowing a fuse,' she joked.

'You see what I mean, you're at it also, trying to be a bright spark.'

'Sorry,' she said with a chuckle. 'I won't mention anything unless it's current.'

'Do you know Susan, you're a bit of a live wire yourself, thank God I was fitted with a good voltage regulator which keeps me calm, but for the remainder of the night no more shocking jokes if you don't mind.'

They both spilled the tea with the laughing and he felt he had known this young woman all his life.

'Tell me a bit about yourself,' he queried, as he came to the conclusion that this young lady was not going to become a notch on Ned's bedpost.

She told him that she lived in the back of beyond, at the wrong end of a potholed thoroughfare called the Fiddler's Lane, so known because of three generations of the Prunty Family who mostly all played the fiddle and who's music was legendary.

'I'm a member of that family and I'll give you three guesses what I play,' she said with a grin.

'You play the fiddle,' he said enthusiastically.

She shook her head.

'The flute.'

Her head kept shaking.

'The piano.'

Her head is still shaking and he thinks he's falling in love. 'You'd better tell me, I give up.'

'I play the violin Ned,' she said, bursting into fits of laughter once more.

'What's that like,' he asked with a straight face and for a moment she thought he was serious. It was then he decided, that if this young woman continued being smart with him she would soon deserve a rub of the relic and no better man for the job than himself.

'It's time to take you home to face the music,' he quipped.

'If my brothers hear the car it'll be you who'll be facing the music,' she said, as he helped her wriggle into a gorgeous knee length coat and for a second he slipped an arm around her.

'There must be money in music,' he said, giving her a little kiss on the cheek.

'You should know!' She answered.

Later in the car park, he briskly guided her to the oldest, rustiest car and tried to insert his key in the lock. Glad to see she was still laughing and not a bit phased by the banger he realised his mistake, then led her over to the big car he had spent all his money on a couple of weeks earlier. Up until then he had been driving a similar rust bucket, which he had had for years, and was still having problems getting used to this gleaming new machine, purchased on the spur of the moment you could say. Passing through Cavan town one day on his way to a gig, he had stopped for petrol at Tractamotors and there it was, winking at him from the showroom window.

As he looked at it longingly, a friendly voice brought him back to reality. 'That's what you should be driving young man,' was the garage owner's opening comment, as he strode towards Ned with outstretched hand.

'She'd be nice Sir, if I could afford her,' came the reply.

'No bother to you affording her,' was the morale boosting answer. 'Aren't you in that famous Nova's Showband that I'm hearing about all the time and anyway, here at Tractamotors you'll get a deal of a lifetime.'

In about half an hour the said deal was done, leaving only the paperwork to be dealt with and after a hot cup of tea our hero headed off to the gig with a full tank of petrol (on the house), in the knowledge that he would be picking up his new car one week later. Now he was holding the passenger door open as Susan climbed inside in the most alluring fashion, flashing quite a bit more of those beautiful legs in so doing.

Just then he looked back at the rusty car and guess that was getting into it? Yes, the two guys from the dance with the shirt collars still out over the jackets.

'It's a good job they didn't come back when I was trying to get the key into the lock,' he was thinking as he asked. 'Do you see yer-man Susan?' Drawing her attention to the two blokes. 'The driver had big plans for you tonight, would you believe.'

'I'd believe you all right, that cod, sure his parents were first cousins and all the neighbours thought the kids would be born with two heads or worse, if that's possible.' Her answer came as she pointed down to their right and added. 'I live out that road and by the way, watch out for the potholes.'

It looked like there would be very little courting for Ned tonight, even though all of Susan's friends had spurned his offer of a lift seemingly having other plans. He drove very slowly doing his best to spend as much time in her company as he could, with unknown to her, one eye on the potholed road and the other one glued to a beautiful knee which had popped out through the opening in her black coat. He had

Radio Luxembourg playing softly in the background while they talked about things in general, then he felt her hand on his leg and his blood pressure went to max.

'Go left here,' she said softly, removing her hand much to his disappointment, as he realised she had only put it there to bring his attention to the famous Fiddler's Lane.'

'My God,' he exclaimed, in lieu of 'For fucks sake,' (which would have been the reaction if he hadn't been trying to impress). 'These are caverns Susan, not just potholes.'

'I know and I'm sorry,' she said and really sounded like she meant it. 'I hope you don't break a spring, but I suppose in this big strong car that wouldn't be easy.'

He had an answer for that but he bit his tongue, realising that now was not the time for innuendo.

'Take the next right and our house is the first on the right,' she said. 'I hope you'll come in and meet my brothers, they were all at the dance and they'll all be here with their girlfriends, anyway, they told me to bring you in or else.' She saw the quick look of concern on his face and said. 'Don't worry, they are looking forward to meeting you and they'll probably play a few tunes seeing there's no work tomorrow, you can join in if you like.'

'The auld trombone is not the best for the reels,' he said, 'but I'll have a go on the bones instead.'

'That's what you think,' came the reply and she was grinning all over her lovely face.

He wanted to kiss her just then and she knew it, so she opened the door and with another quick flash of gorgeous legs, she was out of the car waiting for him.

'This is some mansion you've got,' he said, gobsmacked. 'There is definitely money in your music, so I think I'll learn to play the spoons as well.'

Her four brothers were very pleasant chaps and so also were their girlfriends, but as time went by he realised he was very tired. Calling Susan aside, he explained that he had to work that night about one hundred miles away and he would need to be on the way. She had a quick pow-wow with the family and announced that if he wished, he could have her brother John's bed. It took about ten seconds for him to say yes and he said goodnight to everyone as this gorgeous creature ushered him from the room. He could hardly believe his eyes; here he was walking up the stairs with his eyes riveted from this new angle on her lovely legs.

'You're having bad thoughts even though you're tired,' she said, just as they reached the landing.

This was the moment, he was going to wait no longer, so he slipped his arms around her and kissed her on those beautiful full lips. Fighting hard to keep his tongue under control as they kissed, he could feel the promise in this young woman.

'Thanks for a lovely night and for taking such good care of me,' she said, 'if it wasn't a hundred miles to your dance tonight, I'd be there.' Then pointing a well-groomed finger she continued. 'You're in this room, there's the bathroom and I hope you don't snore.' With that request she ran back down the stairs.

Kissing Susan made it difficult to get his underpants off that morning and he knew for sure, there was one chore he would have to perform before sleep would take over.

At three in the afternoon, he awoke to a knock on the door and Susan's message that lunch was ready. Thinking he couldn't wait any longer to get another glimpse of his new love, he almost fell down the stairs to be greeted by the nicest, neatest, tightest blue jeans he had ever seen any lady poured into. He had to be careful how he looked at her, because not alone were her four brothers seated at the table, so also were Mammy and Daddy and she was being helped with the cooking and serving by another nice young girl who he could swear he had seen before, then the penny dropped. She was the other girl in the second black dress from the dance the previous night and was now introduced to him by Susan as her sister Mary. He was having a problem but it didn't show. Who took Mary home last night? Was it one of the lads from the band and if so, where had he taken her as he surely didn't take her to her own home? Had she spent the night with him in the car and if so, why was everyone so calm about it?

He decided to take the bull by the horns and find out. 'You missed a great night's craic here last night Mary,' he said, hoping he wasn't opening a big can of worms.

'So I believe,' she replied. 'I'm a Nurse and I had to go and keep an eye on my cousin who's expecting a baby, so that's why I wasn't here, but at least someone missed me,' she said, scanning the room.

He hadn't the gall to say he didn't miss her either, because he hadn't known she existed, but he was so glad the other scenario was wrong. Being weak at the knees with worry didn't stop him noticing the fact that Mary could get the same results from a pair of blue jeans as her sister, not forgetting the matching frilly aprons they were both sporting, then an hour later he said goodbye to this lovely family and Susan walked with him to the car.

'I want to make sure you take nothing with you,' she said with a laugh.

'There's only one thing I'd like to take with me Susan,' he said, as he turned and took her gently in his arms.

'Can I have three guesses?' she asked.

'Yes,' he replied.

'My fiddle?'

'No.'

'Rosin for my bow?'

'No.'

'Is it me then?' She asked.

'Yes,' he answered, looking her straight in the eyes. They just looked at each other without a word, both feeling the vibe of something special going on.

Then she said. 'You'd better go or you'll be late, but I'll expect a call from you soon, so don't lose my number.'

They were standing in full view of the house so they gave each other a peck on the cheek, then he jumped into the car and drove away. Just imagine what would happen if he followed his urges and tried a knee-trembler right there on their street. That would be the end of that, he correctly concluded. With lots to fill his mind he drove the long journey, suddenly there was the sign, which read, Carrickbay 2 miles. Jaysus, this is it, he thought as he drove up to a big building just outside of town, with the usual collection of cars in the usual kind of car park and the usual big mobile chipper parked in the middle. He wondered what Susan was doing as he asked around for a phone box.

'There's one up the town,' said a greasy fellow from the chip van, 'but it doesn't always work.'

'That's all I need,' he thought as he checked his watch, scanning the small town for the other band members. This is one gig I'm not going to enjoy.'

Chapter Two

Some months previously, the then little known Nova's Showband had had a major hit across the water and it launched them into the big time here, with bigger venues, crowds and money. Big heads for some of course and groupies, plus the odd drink or two.

They got their big break by covering a very successful single from a big star in The States and there were a few reasons why it worked so well for them. Number One being, it featured a lot of brass which the lads took off to a tee and the Lead Singer's voice sounded just as good as the original. Also, the lyric referred many times in the chorus to a famous bandit called Pancho Villa and it seems the British took him to their hearts, possibly because his deeds reminded them of their hero Robin Hood.

Probably the main reason for their success with the song Mexico City was, the hit American version was not released in Britain, leaving the way open for their recording to do the business. The B-Side of the single was an instrumental called Tattoo for Horns, which the Trumpet player had found on an obscure album of instrumentals by a lesser-known American outfit and this tune turned out to be one of the most requested numbers in the bands repertoire. The Nova's Showband had their record label to thank for getting the deal with a small English company and everyone believed their first release Till The Sun Comes Up, would have been a number one here if they had had the first hit already. The old story of (everyone loves a winner), would have sorted out the airplay situation, which was almost non-existent at the time.

Sax man Conn was heard to say. 'Rome wasn't built in a day,' and everyone agreed.

After the hit, an International Promoter snapped them up for an English tour, and he supplied a luxury fifty-two-seat bus, so now they could bring their favourite girls from city to city and some of them availed of the opportunity. It was on this bus that the nickname of 'Ned the Bed' was given to the Bandleader.

Being the Boss, he got away with claiming the big back seat, which was better than any bed and it was here that he took his conquests. That experience stopped him from complaining about a two or three hundred-mile journey and the gentle swaying of the coach plus the rumble from the big tyres could lull you into a very romantic state.

They had just acquired a new manager, who in many ways including stature was larger than life. Ned had been the band manager before and during the successful single, but things became so busy they decided to get a full time manager and Mike Johnson was the man. He took to the job like a fish to water and was brilliant with figures having studied accountancy in America, but he was homesick, so he came back to Ireland for good.

On their return to base one morning after one of these marathon trips in the rain, Ned and his partner for the night failed to exit the coach and sooner than disturb them, the driver locked the bus and went to bed. They slept through until three in the afternoon and as this was departure time for the next gig, the band and its entourage got back noisily on board. The comments were ripe and it's a good job that his girl friend wasn't easily disturbed.

'Where the fuck is Ned?' 'He never went to bed, he must be to the maker's name in her all night,' said one of them.

'Don't be bold,' said his bird giving him a thump.

'Fuck off, I'll say what I like,' said yer-man.

Just then Mike the manager got on board and looking to the back of the coach where the lovers were looking the worse for wear, he shouted.

'Everyone take note, on this very bus we are all witnessing a marathon, between this young lady and our virtuoso of the slip-horn/ trombone, our own Ned the Bed.'

'Jaysus, that's a great name for him,' said the Trumpet player, using the front of his mouth this time. Then he continued. 'Ned, you and your friend have three minutes to pay a visit, unless you both want to hold on to it.'

Ned's lady friend looked at her watch and let off a scream. 'I'm supposed to be at work since 9 o'clock, about five miles away from here,' she sobbed.

'I'll get you a taxi,' he offered, saying to the others. 'Stay away from my fuckin' bed.'

'It's that all right,' growled the Bass player, who hadn't scored so far on the tour.

Ned got his friend into a taxi, gave a sigh of relief and had the quickest wash and shave of all time, happy in the thought that he could sleep soundly all the way to the next gig without having to perform. Anyway, as people say. A change is as good as a rest. When he got back on the bus feeling refreshed, the lads started asking him how he got on with his last love encounter. To most of the girls on the bus and the new manager, the language they used sounded very strange and Mike (who didn't mind committing sin in other ways but not by swearing) spoke up.

'In the name of God lads, what kind of lingo is that?' He asked, looking bemused.

'It's the Ben-Lang,' answered the Drummer, 'and you're right, it is a lingo which is used a lot by the Showbands.'

'And could you not speak English?' Mike asked.

'Tell him Ned,' advised the Drummer who had been working on the Ben-Lang for years, but had failed to master it and would say some words that would give the game away by not using enough abbreviations.

'The Ben-Lang is English Mike,' said Ned. 'The only difference is that you must put the letters EG into every syllable to cause the confusion, Krupa here only uses them the odd time and most people know when he's talking about them.'

'Who's Krupa?' The manager asked.

'Oh, he's a famous American Jazz Drummer,' came the answer. 'It's a nick-name we loosely use on our man sometimes.'

'*Neged gegot ega regide legast negite,*' yelled the Drummer, laughing his head off.

'What did he say Ned?' asked Mike, looking mystified.

'I know what he said,' said one of the girls grinning. 'He said that Ned got a ride last night, which is probably only half of the story.'

Ned loved the lingo, so he abandoned the idea of sleeping in lieu of talking the Ben-Lang to this well informed lady, much to the annoyance of the Guitarist who's plans included an afternoon session with this quite nice willowy blonde, who had picked up 'The- Ben' as it was often called, in London's East End.

Mike and the Drummer started talking about the big money they hoped to make in the not too distant future and the Manager talked about the strokes he intended to pull to get another hit for the band, not all of them legit it must be said. It was plain that a stroke wasn't just an affliction that came around and paralysed your body. According to Mike, it came in many shapes and sizes, providing a much used tool in this new world of drink, sex and rock & roll, not forgetting the odd cowboy song or two.

Ned learned a lot from the blonde and after an hour or so they called it a day. He consigned himself to his big bed in the back of the bus, the blonde having agreed at last to join the Guitar man in a sexy session, if he was lucky. The Bass man sat in the front with the Driver and he had a permanent scowl on his face.

'We'll have to take him around to Soho soon if this mood carries on,' thought Ned as he flopped down on the big bench seat, covered himself with a blanket and slipped into the land of nod.

The three girls and the remaining band members started playing poker, firstly for small money which eventually moved to bigger stakes, then about one hundred miles up the motorway someone suggested strip poker. This was taken on board and it was soon evident who was getting the bad cards. In about twenty minutes the Sax player was down to his underpants and socks but they had never seen him so happy, yes, there was a reason. The little dark haired Dublin girl who kept saying 'Jaysus' this and 'Jaysus' that, had said she would 'Go Down' on the first man to lose all his clothes.

As she led the Sax player towards the back of the bus he whispered to the Trumpeter. 'I never got better fucking cards in my life, but who wants to win a stupid game of poker if there's a chance to poke her instead and she has confirmed a speed wobble as well, lead on Mc Beth,' he shouted.

'Don't wake Ned or the Piano man,' hissed the Singer, or we'll tell Cynthia Rose.'

'Who is Cynthia Rose?' Asked one of the girls, who as yet, was not interested in any kind of sexual activity? The Lead Singer was enthralled by her Brummie accent and wanted her to keep talking. The Trumpet player had worked in Birmingham for years and wanted her to shut up to fuck.

'The aforementioned Cynthia Rose is yer-man's girlfriend at the moment and if she finds out about today, she'll put the sax where it will be hard to find.'

'What do you mean by that?' Asked the dimmer of the two ladies.

The other one gave her a dig; then leaned over and whispered in her ear, causing her to blush.

'It would be almost impossible to get it out from there,' she said, with a pained expression.

'You could leave out the word almost,' said the Trumpeter, 'but he knows the story about her.' 'I was talking to one of her Blue Dots Showband the other day and he said, the one thing about Cynthia Rose is, that she (rose) every morning from a different bed.'

Ned was awake by now eavesdropping and he was surprised at what the Singer had to say. 'No matter whose bed she's been in, she can definitely sing, to be honest, I think she looks and sounds like Dolly Parton, every bit as good.'

'Good on you,' thought Ned. 'Imagine him paying another singer a compliment.' He also considered her to be very good and he'd suggested to her once that she should have called herself Dolly Rose, but she had asked why suspiciously. 'Because you look and sound like Dolly Parton,' was his answer.

He got a shock when in a real common voice she said. 'I just want to' be meself,' so he excused himself and went to talk to another musician instead. Later he glanced back at her and she was now wrapped around the Sax player from his own band. He remembered thinking. 'Better you than me mate.' Just then the big bus pulled up at the entrance to a very large ballroom and they all looked in awe.

'You won't get the birds in here free,' leered the Bass man, speaking for the first time in about three hundred miles.

Mike gave a big grin, straightened his jacket and said. 'Hold on folks, I'll sort it out by pulling a few strokes, OK!' He hopped off the bus, strolled slowly up to the uniformed doormen and began talking to them. About two minutes later he walked back shouting loudly through an open window.

'Alright, members of the Orchestra this way, but make-up ladies first so don't forget your brushes and combs, the lads must be looking well tonight.' He gave Ned a big wink and led the way past the doormen into a real luxurious dance hall.

'That was some stroke Mike,' said Ned admiringly.

'Ah sure they loved the idea of you having your own hairdressers and make-up people on board, it's what they're used to here.'

The Bass player looked even more pissed off now.

'Which of them do you want to do your make-up John?' He was asked and with his usual hiss he replied. 'I'll not let any of that fucking riff-raff touch me.'

'You wish,' said one of the girls.

'Quiet and don't blow it,' Mike said, in little more than a whisper. 'I'm fresh out of strokes at the moment until I get some shut-eye.' Because of his time spent in The States he always began to sound quite American if under pressure and Ned had been trying since he joined the band, to work out if the manager was a bull-shitter or not. So far he couldn't make up his mind.

'The jury's still out on that one,' he mused as they went backstage to the most fabulous dressing rooms imaginable.

'A far cry from Mullymore Ned,' said a voice.

He looked in shock at the Bass player who had decided to speak at last and seemed on the verge of cracking a smile.

'Are you taking the piss?' Ned inquired.

'No way,' he said. 'I think I'm a bit overwhelmed by it, that's all,' then he lapsed into his morose mood again.

Mike came in all excited and said there was a big meal laid on for the band and it's entourage, in the large hotel across the street. Then they had two hours to enjoy the scenery, after that back to the ballroom to get ready for the gig and he also informed them that their relief band for the night playing the first two hours, was none other than a sixteen piece orchestra, the venue's resident band.

'Oh Jaysus,' roared the Sax man, 'they're gonna cop on to us eight 'Omies' when we hit the stage later on.'

Not to worry,' said Mike, 'they haven't got a record in the charts like you guys and by the way, what's an Omie?'

Ned left it to Conn to finish what he started. 'The Nova's Showband are the Omie's Mike, we're from the arsehole of no-where, we may have a record in the charts, but the resident band will be reading their music from charts and laughing their arses off at our feeble effort later on.'

'I think your last two words 'later on' are the key to who are the 'Omies' and who are not, you are the 'later on' band they are the support outfit, it doesn't matter whether they read dots or not you guys are the stars.'

'Stars!' quipped Ned. 'The one and only time I saw stars was when I headbutted the boot lid of the car one windy night.' 'Anyway, I think you're all looking too deeply into the situation, who cares if they read, I'm gonna watch the Bone player closely and try to pick up a few tips, meanwhile, I'm gonna do some real reading.' So flashing a brand new copy of Playboy, he headed for the hotel. 'At least the women of this town will be safe from me tonight,' he bragged.

During the meal, the Brummie lady decided she would be head make-up person and she asked Mike what exactly he wanted them to do.

'Just go through the motions girls, a little parting here, a little wave there, but don't cover them with powder or you'll have the lads at the gig chatting them up instead of the girls.'

The dim one asked. 'What do you mean by that?'

The little dark haired one from Dublin butted in with. 'Jaysus, have ya never heard of fellas chahhin up fellas, or whah planeh are ya from anyway.' 'I won't let any fella near my Sax player, no matter how much powder ya puh on him.'

One nice young waitress seemed to be showing an interest in Ned, a fact that wasn't going un-noticed by the man himself. Then the Sax man shouted across the big table. 'Ill bet your sorry now, for spending the last half-hour with that Playboy magazine.'

Ned blushed for the first time in years and gave a fierce dirty look in the direction of the loudmouth, and then they all shouted. 'Ned's blushing, Ned's blushing, look, Ned's blushing.'

The nice young waitress copped on what was happening and just stood looking at his red cheeks and she asked him. 'Why is your band called a Showband?'

'Go on, tell her,' they all advised, laughing their heads off.

'How long have you got,' he asked, 'or maybe I could explain to you after the dance instead.'

'Just tell me now, we can always talk about something else after the dance.' she said.

The other band members were really pissed off at the results of their attempted intimidation and they sat quietly as Ned did his best to describe a Showband. He decided to send up his description to annoy some of the lads, so this is how he began to paint the picture. 'The criterion for the title of

Showband is.' That's as far as he got. Everyone at the table went into convulsions.

'Criterion my arse,' said one, 'you didn't get that big word in Mullymore National School, who are you trying to impress?'

Ned just ignored them and carried on. 'You must have at least six members, you dress loud and each member is expected to smile non-stop during the night. You have to know a minimum of three chords and to most of this orchestra the fourth chord is an adventure, you will agree they don't look an adventurous lot. Last but not least, you must stand up and kick out one leg as you move in and out, that my good woman is what a Showband is and by the way my name is Ned, what's yours?'

"I'm Gloria and I'm pleased to meet you Ned,' she said, as she made no apparent effort to remove her hand from his.

'How does the ugly fucker do it?' Whispered the Trumpeter in a pang of jealousy.

'I heard that,' his Boss said. 'You know it takes one to know one.'

The waitress excused herself, feeling the tension build around the table and she went back to the kitchen.

'If you ever say anything as rude as that again while I'm chatting up a woman, I'll put the trumpet where the sun won't shine on it.'

The dim one looked at her friend, her friend nodded and said. 'If everyone keeps putting the instruments up each others arse, you'll soon have no instruments left to play music on.' They all looked at her and when they realised she was serious, they fell about the place laughing.

Just then Mike strode into the dining room looking really business like. 'I hope you all enjoyed it,' he said, 'it's over, duty calls so everyone up and out and remember girls, look professional.'

The Bass player was even laughing and he said to the dim lady. 'I'll let you do my hair if you let me do yours on the way home.'

'I think you've scored,' said Ned, 'but it was a crap chat up line and you called her riff-raff earlier.'

'I've had a closer look and I think she's fuckin' gorgeous,' said yer-man.

They headed back across the street and there was a new spring in the Bass man's step.

'He'll be really driving the band tonight,' mused Ned.

When they got back to the Ballroom, the big band was playing Glen Miller's, in the mood. 'It's as good as the record.' said the Trumpeter.

'I think it's better,' said the Lead Singer, 'even though I'm not into that kind of stuff.'

The crowd was lapping it up and dancing like mad. With tangos, mambos, rumbas and of-course, the slow waltz.

'Jaysus, you's are gonna die here tonight,' said the wee Dublin girl.

Her boyfriend the Sax player added. 'If you say that again, you'll also die here tonight.'

The Trumpeter said to Ned. 'If we tell Cynthia Rose, he'll be dead a week from now anyway.'

The make-up and hairdressing idea went down a treat, then they heard the orchestra announce their last number and one by one they lined up behind the big curtain as they heard the M.C. saying loudly. 'And now let us have a big welcome for the chart topping Nova's Showband.'

While the Guitar men were putting on their instruments, Ned got a big hand for the resident band and he added. 'I hope you're in the mood so for the next two hours, it's dancing all the way, A, 1.2.3.4.'

They couldn't go wrong, lots of punters were singing their songs along with them as they danced past and from the reaction their records must have sold well in this area. Ned was going to town as usual, but the stage was too high for the girls to sit on it, so he couldn't get up to his old tricks with the slide of the trombone. Then he suddenly remembered. He hadn't seen the nice young waitress from the hotel yet.

'What's keeping her he thought?'

He didn't have long to wait, there she was beaming up at him from the front of the stage and she looked gorgeous. Now there's one thing about Ned that you've got to know from day one. He's a legman. Faces yes, bodies yes, hair yes, if they're okay he's happy, but legs, they must be perfect. He had gone to too many Marilyn Monroe/ Betty Grable/ Lana Turner/ Susan Hayward movies in his day and if a girl didn't have legs like those ladies, they were out.

He had failed to see this girl's legs in the hotel earlier and now he was trying to get a glimpse, as the huge crowd swirled around her on the dance floor, but no luck. Then the set came to an end and as she walked across a piece of empty floor to her friends, his heart almost stopped. She was wearing the shortest white dress with beautiful matching high heels and he sounded like the wee Dublin girl for a second, all he could say was 'Jaysus.' She had the thinnest, most shapeless legs he had ever seen on a girl in his whole life. As the next set began, the other band members started playing unaware of his state of shock. He tried to blow the trombone but nothing would come out and as luck would have it, they were playing a traditional jazz tune in which the trombone should feature quite strongly. The Trumpeter noticed the shortfall and followed Ned's gaze to the young woman. Suddenly there was no trumpet in the tune either. He detected what silenced the Trombone and broke down laughing.

The young woman was oblivious of what was going on and flashed a big smile at Ned just as Mickey Joe roared.

'Hi lads, have you seen the scotchpegs on Ned's Richard the third, they're like fork handles.'

'Who gives a fuck,' said the Bass man, 'let's keep her lit for fuck's sake.'

By keeping her lit, he meant to keep the music going and that's what they did for the remainder of the gig. Ned was in trauma, but he knew he had to pull some stroke that wouldn't offend the young girl.

The dance came to an end after three encores, then the crowd surged towards the stage to get autographs and talk to the band members. Some of the lads knew quite a few people from home and Ned was hoping that someone he knew would materialise, saving him the embarrassing task of talking this nice young woman out of him. No such luck, she's standing at the stage with all her friends and they're giving him real knowing looks. Their approval to this liaison is obvious.

'Whegat egis thege stegoregy neged,' roared the Trumpet player, knowing well that they could hear him clearly.

'Nanty, Nanty, Thege Shegams Cegould Bege Wegide,' Ned appealed.

'Whegat Stregoke Egare Yegou Gegoeging Tego Pegull Negow Shegam,' the other guy persisted.

'Yegou Feguck Egoff,' said Ned, as he hopped down from the stage and took the young lady by the hand, leading her gently to a seat at the side.

Before he could get a word out Gloria asked. 'Do you have to go back with the lads tonight?' 'I've got my own room in the staff quarters and you can stay if you wish.'

'Gloria, I've a confession to make, you're such a beautiful lady and it would be so easy to fall in love with you that I must tell you my situation. I just got engaged a month ago to a girl the image of you and when I saw you earlier I could have sworn my Patricia had turned up. I'm sorry, but you'll agree it wouldn't be fair to you or Patricia, now would it.'

He could see the look of disappointment sweep across her face as he delivered this load of crap and for a moment he thought she was going to cry, but she picked herself up and smiled weakly instead. 'I suppose there's some consolation in the thought, that you fell in love and will marry someone the spitting image of me, so I want you to promise me something.'

'What is that?' He asked.

'Promise, that every time you make love to her you will think of me for a moment, could you manage that?' She enquired.

'I think I could manage that Gloria,' he lied and felt awful, fooling such a lovely caring person in that way. 'You'll go to hell Ned Brady, for things like this,' he thought to himself, but the bottom line was, he could never get it up for girls with matchstick legs, so what would be the point in trying. 'Its Playboy for me again tonight,' he was thinking, as he gave Gloria a big hug before she rejoined her friends who had got all the autographs, plus a fully signed picture for her.

'Will you sign them for us Ned?' She asked, 'and will you put a few extra kisses on mine. We'll come to see the band the next time you're here, then I'll want to know if you've kept your promise to me.' With that, she and her friends headed for the exit, leaving Ned not feeling too proud of himself.

'I'm an awful Bollix.' he said out loud.

'Why are you talking to yourself Sir?' Asked the Trumpeter, 'and by the way, I'm sorry for shouting so loud earlier, but I was using the lingo.'

'You can't trust the lingo Mickey Joe and you know that well, how often have we been caught out talking about people, who have let us go on and on before they let us know that they're wide.'

'Christ.' 'I'll never forget what happened while we were having the tay and hang sangwiches before that carnival in the west last year, we were slagging everyone including yerman's wife and they knew every word we were saying.'

'Yeah, we were lucky we weren't killed,' said Ned. 'Anyway, let's get on the road as soon as possible, tomorrow night looms.'

It took ages to find everyone that night. They had all clicked, some with the girls in the bus, the remainder including Mike went off with the girls from the hotel.

'How come you guys didn't walk down the hall with them?' Ned asked.

'We arranged to meet them at the staff quarters instead,' said Mike, 'some of them have boyfriends, so they didn't want to be seen and that includes Gloria by the way.'

Ned began to feel a little better about his lies when he heard that. 'There's one promise I don't have to keep,' he thought, 'especially considering my not having the said Patricia to keep it with.'

At that moment, they walked into the band room and there they found the Bass player, halfway through a knee-trembler with the dim lady from the bus. He wasn't aware of their arrival in the beginning, so he kept going while she combed his hair singing an aimless tune. 'I did a lovely job on your hair tonight, Oh, I will do a lovely job on your hair tomorrow night Oh.'

After every line she went Oh, to coincide with the long leisurely strokes she was getting from the Bass man. They never heard him use the Ben-Lang before, but now as he became aware of their presence, to their surprise he said. *'Feguck Egof, Feguck Egof.'*

They got out of there fast and from the sounds they heard, only just in time. The three hundred-mile journey back was quiet, mainly because everyone was tired apart from the Roadie, who talked to the driver all the way. The lights were out at once, which meant that Ned didn't get a glimpse of Playboy until the next day and to tell the truth he was glad. The remainder of the tour went without a hitch and the following Monday found our heroes at the Airport minus the girls. The numbers had dwindled as the week went by, so the only thing they were going to miss was the fifty two seater coach, with its big back seat and all it's recliners.

'We've got to get another hit and soon Mike.' They chorused as they boarded the plane.

Mike was smiling as he asked. 'How would a tour of the U.S. grab you?'

'We could definitely handle that.' they all agreed.

They were already up to high-doh with the thrills of this, their second time to fly and now the news of the American tour. 'Wow.' They could hardly wait to board the plane. Just before the first flight to London the mood was a lot different though and when Mike handed out the plane tickets booked through 'Apex Travel' of Dame Street, Dublin, there were a few shakey candidates.

'Jaysus, I'll get air sick.' moaned the Bass man.

'So will I,' chorused a couple more, followed by a question. 'Why can't we go by boat?'

'Look,' said Mike. 'I had the same problem before my first flight to The States, then, after a few Internal trips and my flight home, I forgot all about it, it's chicken feed.'

Back at Dublin Airport they all smiled at him and said in unison. 'It was chickenfeed.'

Chapter Three

Back home, the band members had Tuesday and Wednesday off for a breather, while the Roadie had to confirm that the bandwagon was serviced during their absence. For Mike, it was straight into the office to check his diary and make sure he could clear all the dates requested for the U.S. tour, which would be in two months time. The planned trip would be geared towards emigrants, plus whoever else cared to turn up, and the old Ballad, the homes of Donegal would definitely be resurrected.

'Don't forget to bring a few records and tapes of ours for sale when we're there.' Ned reminded him on the phone the next day.

They had had the newest in radio and Hi-fi fitted to the wagon, so he took along some of the latest chart hits to be listened to and absorbed over the weekend, for a planned rehearsal in their local Parish Hall the following Tuesday. Rehearsals usually turned into pandemonium of some kind and regularly, threats of violence would be issued. The Piano player was the musical director of the band and that often caused hassle, with different members placed under pressure by a riff or line. He would become impatient with the pace of the musicians and sometimes suggested that the particular fellow should take up a different profession. That chap usually came back with.

'Hold your fuckin' horses now, or I'll wrap that fuckin' piano around your neck.'

The Bass player, who was scared stiff of the band breaking up because he loved the money, would try to ease the tension, so he would be told that the large pegs on the bass would make it extremely hard to swallow and it could even be worse from the other end. How they got through a 'Practice' as it was known, was often the cause of wonderment.

The weekend flew, the gigs were good and so were the chicks. The Bass man went mad altogether, scoring every night but as the Sax player said. 'His eyes were in his arse when it came to women.' The Bass man heard this and was not a happy camper, causing him to keep the band waiting an hour after the gig on the Sunday night.

'Next time you'll have three minutes to get your hole,' said the Sax man, 'or we'll be gone without you.'

'Is that true four hands,' answered yer-man. 'You can talk, that's all the time it takes with Cynthia Rose, or so all the lads tell me,' he continued.

The Sax man made a swipe at him and connected with the seat frame, which caused him to double up in pain. Everyone laughed.

'What did you mean by calling him four hands?' Ned asked later.

'Well, if he leaves me behind, he'll have to play the sax and the bass at the same time, that will take four hands,' he said.

'Do you know John, you haven't been the same since you screwed that dim bird across the water last week, something has rubbed of whatever in the name of God it is, but you've got a new lease of life, long may it last,' said Ned, just before he went to sleep.

Each musician was supposed to tape the numbers for rehearsal, but didn't always get around to it, and then the singers would take turns in the wagon and write the words of their number down. Lyrics, (which were usually shite) as Ned would say, were often hard to decipher so help would be solicited. This was often the cause of more trouble. You would hear 'Obla fuckin what?' and 'Lucy in the sky with Desmond?'

'That's not what the fucker is saying.'

'Well Einstein, what the fuck do you think he's saying?'

'With diamonds, not with fuckin' Desmond, that's crap.'

'It may be crap but it's number one across the water.'

'Big fuckin' deal, they'd buy anything over there, we proved that.'

'Shut up lads,' said Ned. 'I need some help 'big time.'

He switched on the tape once more and they listened.

'Is he saying Antelope Eyes?'

'Play it again Sham,' said someone, trying to sound like Bogey.

'You won't fuckin' believe it,' said Mickey Joe. 'I think he's saying Cantaloupe Eyes.'

'What the fuck is a Cantaloupe and how do we know it has eyes?' Were the Trumpeters six and eight pence?

At last they all agreed it was Cantaloupe, then the Trumpet man questioned the title. 'Judy in disguise, with glasses, some fuckin' disguise a pair of shaggin glasses, why didn't she get an ape suit and really go to town!'

That put everybody in good humour, so they all agreed that if it sounds right it's right. Roll on Tuesday to put them to the test. Inevitably, Tuesday arrived and all the orchestra members turned up on the dot of 1 o'clock, that is all except the Sax player, who to be fair to him wasn't often late. He had been given the nickname of Conn by a band member because he was always bragging about the very shiney, very costly Saxophone he had, which was made by that world famous company of the same name, hence the double nn.

Now Ned's trombone was made by those very people, but this was in no way important to him so he never mentioned the fact, especially as he knew he would possibly be known as 'Conn two' or 'Conn the second.' The Sax man welcomed his new handle much to the surprise of the other band members and it was some time before they found out why. He had been christened Bartley Murphy and over the years he had been finding this a problem while chatting up girls. Not the Murphy bit, it was the Bartley bit which was causing the problem and he smiled from ear to ear the day the Piano player re-named him Conn, after listening to him going on and on about his Saxophone at a rehearsal.

The Roadie had all the gear up in the little hall in the middle of nowhere and as the lads assembled their own instruments, the Piano man noticed that the Sax player was missing.

'Where the fuck is Conn?' He enquired.

'Dunno,' answered Ned.

'I may be able to throw some light on that subject,' the Bass man suggested.

Everyone stopped what they were doing and turned their gaze on him. 'I was at a gig in town last night, which was on after a celebrity football match and Conn was there.'

'Who was playing the gig?' Ned enquired.

'I'll give you one guess,' came the reply.

'I don't want to fuckin' guess,' said Ned. 'I want you to tell me.'

'Cynthia and The Blue Dots Showband,' replied John.

'I should have guessed.' Ned grunted.

'But you refused when I asked you.' The Bass man ground to a halt as everyone was glowering at him.

'Well, his song is up first,' said the Piano man. 'Let's start breaking it down, yer-man is probably still to the hilt in Cynthia, so lets show him what pressure is really like.'

'He was on stage last night harmonising with her and I swear her tits have got bigger, because he couldn't get any closer than three feet, we'll probably not see him for a month!'

Ned was about to suggest that they should work on some other number, when the door of the hall burst open and Conn ran in complete with his pride and joy, no, not Cynthia, but his saxophone and he gave a frantic wave in the direction of the road. Before he could apologise they all chorused. 'Did she give you a lift?'

Then one voice asked. 'Did she have a car?' It was the sarcastic Keyboard man. The Sax player gently put his case down, walked over and took the Piano man by the lapels, yanked him from his seat and said. 'You know I love my Conn saxophone, but if you don't shut-up, I'll sacrifice it by shoving it down your throat and we can either do it here or outside, just in case something else gets broken.' That sorted that and in a couple of minutes they were ready to begin.

'By the way,' said Conn. 'I'm sorry for being late, I was just catching up on some lovin.'

There were no smart answers just in case and they got on with the work in hand. By 6 o'clock they were three chart songs up and their only problem now was, what three do they drop? Before they left the hall, Ned told them to dig out any old ballads they had, as that would be the content for the next practice, then he gave the Roadie a hand and as they were about to leave, the latter said. 'After what I saw today I'm sure of one thing.'

'What's that?' he was asked.

'Its money that's keeping this band together you know, not your love for each other.'

'I agree,' Ned replied. 'Things will only get worse in that area, I knew a band once where none of them spoke to each other for four years and that was while they were at the top.'

'That's fuckin' amazin,' said the Roadie, as he headed off down the road.

Ned was curious about something. What does the Roadie do on nights off? He's very seldom seen in the pubs and he's never at home when you ring. 'He must have a bird stashed somewhere,' he thought, as he locked the little hall and took the key back to the lady who looked after the local church and when she met him at the door, he had this outrageous thought. Could it be possible that she might be the one, as the Roadie often spoke about her in fond terms, but he dismissed the idea at once? She had been the Priest's housekeeper for years, living in and to be honest, you wouldn't throw her out of the bed. Ned was always curious about 'their' situation as they had come to this parish together and the understanding was, that she had worked for him for many years elsewhere. He was wondering about their sleeping arrangements while he handed over the key and then she said.

'Thank you Ned and wasn't that a lovely day.'

He thanked her and answered with. 'I find it a bit hot in the bed these nights and it must be worse for two.' It was only when he saw her blushing that he realised what he had said and for once the gift of the gab forsake him, causing him to go red also. He mumbled something incoherent as he reversed away from the door, wishing that the ground would open up and swallow him. 'Jaysus, I'm the right Bollix,' he hissed, as he put his foot to the boards.

The band was off on the Wednesday, causing a decision by our hero to give his only suit it's yearly outing, so he decided to break some new ground and head for a dance in Belfast. 'I'll cut a dash tonight he thought,' as he looked in the wardrobe mirror, following with, 'who's that hunk looking back at me?'

'Are you talking to yourself Edward?' His mother shouted from outside the door. His mum never accepted the Ned tag and bluntly refused to use it.

'Oh. I'm just running over some words from a song we learned yesterday,' he tried.

'Is that so Edward,' she said, and then followed with a subtle put-down. 'Well it must be a song about someone on an ego trip.'

'Bloody hell,' he said in barely a whisper. 'She was listening to my bullshit, I'll have to be careful in future.'

His mother was grinning when he went downstairs. 'I hope you'll have at least one early night tonight, where are you off to anyway and by the way, I agree with you, you are looking well.'

He could feel the colour coming back to his cheeks as he said to her. 'Which part of that last epistle would you like me to answer first?'

'Oh, don't bother, it'll only be a pack of lies anyway, but hold on a minute.' She took her hand from behind her back and doused him with holy water. 'That'll keep you safe son, just take it easy on those roads now.'

He gave her a big hug; kissing her on the cheek and in two shakes he was speeding on his way North. Ned found a parking space about one hundred yards from The York Ballroom, paid his money and walked inside. Nice ballroom, nice birds lined around the sides, with more pouring in.

'I'm gonna have a ball here tonight,' he mused. Then he turned his attention to the band. 'Fuck me, they can play and that Trombone player, he's excellent, that guy's playing on his instrument, I'm only playing with mine, big difference.' He waited until the crowd grew just enjoying the band, while trying to imagine the Trombone man running his slide up and down girl's zippers. This guy was reading the dots and he probably hadn't even smiled in years.

Ned checked his watch. 'It's time,' he thought to himself, 'and she looks lovely.' He had picked out a beautifully dressed dark haired girl, so he strode across the floor already measuring the tempo of the song. 'Would you like to dance?' He asked.

She started with his shoes, moved up past the seldom-used charcoal suit and looked him squarely in the eye. 'No thanks,' she answered, turning back to her pals in fits of laughter.

If he had had a tail, there was only one place it could have been as he turned and walked back across the ballroom. It seemed to take forever and he kept bumping into dancers on the way, before throwing himself on a seat in the corner. He would have to re-think the whole situation and then to add insult to injury the band began playing, do you wanna dance? With the trombone player on vocals.

'The fucker can sing as well.' Ned thought, as he sat licking his sores.

'The next dance will be the Foxtrot,' said the Announcer.

Ned had been watching this cute wee blonde, he was going to ask someone totally different from the last one and she looked like a girl whom would be nice to 'lie up to' as he liked to do in slow dances. He composed himself and strode across the room, then with a flourish he said to the blonde. 'Can I have this dance love?'

'You can if you like, but not with me,' she answered, 'and by the way, I'm not your love, OK!'

'Jaysus, I've got to turn and go back now,' he thought, panic taking over.

He kept walking around the hall, made a quick decision to ask another one who could not have witnessed his two failures, she grunted 'No' and without breaking his step he was back in the seat in the same corner. Next, the band called a 'Ladies choice'. In seconds the floor was full but Ned was still seated, then out of the corner of his eye he saw this mountain of a woman bearing down on him.

'Will you get up?' she asked.

'Why?' he answered, 'do you want to sit down here?'

'Very funny, I'm asking you to dance!' She growled.

'What the hell,' he thought. 'I've had it here anyway.'

That set must have lasted fifteen minutes and she talked all the time. Ned was pleasant to her and thanked her profusely, but he had a horrible feeling she wanted him to stay. He hid for about half an hour, in which time he paid a visit to the gents just to check his flies and make sure his shirttail wasn't hanging out. In total, he asked nine girls to dance that night and they all said no, later, as he drove home along the motorway he came to the conclusion that it was retribution for his evil deeds. He had the heater on full causing him to become a bit drowsy, so remembering his mother's advice; he decided to pull over on the hard shoulder of the motorway for a rest. Leaving the heater running, thinking he would only stop for a couple of minutes, he let his seat back, locked the door and closed his eyes. Now he must have been more tired than he thought and in the cozy atmosphere of the big car he drifted off to sleep. Next thing he heard was a knock at the window and when his eyes opened he could see a crowd of hooded men, staring in through the windscreen.

'Jaysus, I didn't think we had the Cu-Clux-Clan up here,' he thought, then while getting ready to rev up and make a run for it, he noticed that the men were dressed in yellow. Slowly he turned his window down and asked the nearest one. 'Is there something wrong gents?'

In a kind voice, which he was glad to hear, the man answered. 'No there's nothing wrong with us, but are you alright?'

'Yeah, I felt drowsy,' he said, so I stopped for forty winks before I'd go any further.'

'Good idea,' said yer-man, 'when we heard the engine running, we thought you were committing suicide, but then we failed to find a hose.'

'Thanks for that and will you look at the time.' Ned said thankfully. 'By the way, why are you dressed in yellow?'

'We are a motorway maintenance crew who work at night and it has been raining for the last hour, so these are our waterproofs, anyway, take it handy for the remainder of your journey.'

That episode gave him food for thought, some bad things had happened in that area and he realised how foolish he'd been in stopping. The word suicides bothered him also and just imagine if they had been someone else, he gave a little shudder at the thought. So it's been raining over an hour, my god my mother will think I'm dead. That reminded him of the holy water and he grudgingly gave it ten out of ten. 'Thanks mum and thanks God,' he said to himself.

Neither of his parents heard a thing and thinking he was home early they called him for breakfast. His mother cooked a great meal as usual, so he decided to come down to eat and talk to them both. His dad who he resembled greatly, was the one who passed on the 'bit of music' as he called it and his name was the same as Ned's only different. His mother (who hadn't a note in her head) would always say proudly, Edmond this and Edmond that. To her, Edmond was the bees-knees and he wasn't too keen on his son's shortened version either. Ned would panic every time he considered the possibility of them finding out his nickname.

'Why do they call you Ned the Bed son?' His dad would ask. His prepared answer was going to be based on the fact that he spent so much time travelling, it was a must that he would spend all his spare time in bed sleeping.

His father always hoped he would join him running the pub, but being a musician himself he knew the pull of

Showbusiness, even though he had only ever touched on it in the odd old smoky bar. 'I'll need you there when I'm not around son,' his dad would say wistfully. 'Those fuckers are trying to rob me blind, but I'm making it hard for them.'

'Good for you dad, as bad as the music business is, at least the fiddlers are fewer and further between, I'm speaking of the non musical type.'

'I was talking on the phone to another publican recently and I asked him, how are things? His answer was a novel one. I'm like Ali Baba and when I inquired as to what he meant, he said. I'm here with my forty fucking thieves.'

'Stop swearing Edmond, you'll give your son a bad habit.'

Ned looked at the innocence on his mother's face wondering. 'How have I misled this lovely lady for so long? I hope it lasts.'

Chapter Four

Ned had to lie a lot about his visit to Belfast and painted a rosy picture of the fun he had in new surroundings. 'You've gotta see the birds,' he enthused. 'They're fuckin' gorgeous, I had to literally beat them off me,' he fibbed.

'It must have been the charcoal suit,' someone slagged.

'The poor suit, it will never be the same again, they nearly ripped it off me,' he was going further out on a limb and the piece he was clinging to was being sawn off as he spoke.

'I'd say you put the trombone in your pants for a bit of bulge,' said the Sax player.

'Auld jealousy,' said our hero, 'just wait and see, we're playing up there when we come back from The States and they'll all be there,' he lied.

The mention of The States took the pressure off immediately and suddenly they all wanted to fantasise about 'New York'.

'There's a big black one over there with my name on her,' bragged Mickey Joe.

'Fuck off, you'd run a mile if one of them came near you,' the Bass player added and the buzz was even getting to him.

They had met in the chipper, before visiting Mike in the office to get the itinerary for the trip and if there was ever overkill on a word, it was happening that day with itinerary. They were all trying to say it differently, so much so that

Ned said it sounded like they were talking about travellers most of the time.

'We'll be travellers big time when we come back, won't we lads?' Said someone.

They filed into the office and sat in a semi-circle across from the desk, which housed their manager who, after formalities, reached for the paperwork on his labours.

'Is that the itinerary Mike?' John asked foolishly.

The fellas roared in unison. 'If you mention that word again, we'll make you stand outside, OK!' There were other words not as nice so the Bass man stayed quiet.

Ned could see Mike's secretary through the glass door to the inner office and couldn't help wondering if their manager was mixing business with pleasure. 'Wouldn't mind myself,' he was thinking, when suddenly he heard the magic initials L.A.

'What the fuck is L.A?' inquired the Drummer.

'Jaysus, your some fuckin' bog man!' said Mickey Joe. 'It's California you eejit!'

'Well Mickey Joe, it's not all of California, it's just the city of Los Angeles which is part of the region,' the Manager explained.

The lads gasped as they listened to the names of the places they would be visiting. 'San Francisco, Philadelphia, Boston,' that barely got a murmur. 'All our cousins are there so carry on.' 'Chicago, the windy city,' said Mike.

'It'll be winder when Ned gets there, he's always fartin' on the stage,' it was John taking a chance on being expelled again. They just ignored him.

'We're also going to New York, but the real big deal there, will be Carnegie Hall.'

'I believe that's huge,' said Ned, in little more than a whisper, the enormity of the plan starting to sink in.

'Now, the bad news,' said Mike, 'you all have to be inoculated.'

Ned had gone to the Seminary and knew what it meant, but that was a word the lads had not been taught in Mullymore National School, so he gingerly said to Mike. 'Maybe you should fill us all in as to what it entails, if you don't mind.'

Mike hadn't been in the last shower and copped on straight away that he was dealing with a bunch of ordinary country lads who had probably missed school as often as they had attended. They knew lots about music, a bit about sex and just the minimum about knowledge, yet they were paying the bills so he would have to take them easy. He cast his memory back to before his trip to The States and he remembered how green he had been himself.

'You have to get injections to protect you against different fevers and diseases that you might come in contact with, I had it done and it's no big deal,' he said.

The Bass player had gone very pale and when asked if he was all right, he mumbled something about having a problem with needles.

Now Mickey Joe is not the brightest spark, so he thought he would make the poor fellow feel better about the problem and he added. 'I can't sew or knit either John, but I don't think needles are anything to be scared of.'

Everyone including Mike glowered at the Trumpet player but said nothing, he in turn noticed something wrong, and then slowly he began to look quite healthy looking as the conversation continued.

'One more thing I would like to emphasise lads.' Mike took a quick look to make sure the door to his secretary's office was shut tight, and then he continued. 'To be certain that no one gets a dose and I don't mean the cold, I want you all to stock up on Condoms, alias Rubbers, alias French letters, OK!'

He had suspected correctly that everyone hadn't heard the word Condom before and that is why he was so specific. 'As to where you can buy them, they're available in every chemist or drugstore, twenty-four hours a day and theres no need to buy a comb instead in case theres a lady serving, it's the good old U.S.A.'

'That happened to me in London,' Conn volunteered, only I ended up with five combs and still no rubbers.'

'It could happen to the Bishop,' said Ned.

'God forgive you,' said someone.

'The mention of God reminds me of clouds, heaven and Aeroplanes,' said Ned, looking skyward. 'Have you done anything about the flights to The States yet?'

'Yes.' Mike answered. 'Our good friends at 'Apex Travel' Dame Street, Dublin, are dealing with all that as we speak and they're booking all our pre-planned internal flights as well.'

'What happens if some of us miss flights, or want to go to certain places at the last minute?' Queried the Guitar man.

'Well, each individual will have to deal with those situations, if or when they arise,' said Mike.

'Just one question,' it was the Piano man. 'How did you make contact with Apex Travel in the first place, why not a local agent?'

'Simple,' he replied. 'I worked in Dublin with a firm of accountants before I went to America and everyone there used their services, so when I decided to fly I chose Apex Travel, does that satisfy you?'

'What you may not know lads,' said Ned. 'The owner of Apex Travel is a local man, he comes from a couple of miles outside Mullymore, his father and mine have been friends for years.'

'I hope that makes you happy,' was Mike's comment, directed at the Piano player.

During the remaining weeks gigging at home, all the lads could think about was the American tour. At that last meeting in the office it was decided to bring the Roadie to the States, because they would have to pay him anyway, plus the fact, he was one of the gang and they'll never forget the look of pleasure on his face when he was told the good news.

'There's one thing I must do when I get to New York,' he gushed.

'Do you want to spend the night in Harlem?' Someone asked.

'No, fuck Harlem, there's a street in New York where you can go to the pictures twenty-four hours a day and that's what I want to do, but I won't go on my own.' Then looking around he asked. 'Will you go with me Ned? I'll pay.'

'OK.' Ned agreed, 'but we'll have to be careful, because that's the street where all the prostitutes hang out.'

'I'd love to shag a prostitute,' the Sax man volunteered, trying to look the hard man. 'I believe there's nothing they won't do for you.'

'There's one thing they'll do for you if they get a chance,' said Ned.

'What's that?' asked Conn, his enthusiasm boiling over.

'They usually rob you,' the Bandleader informed him. 'They will bring you back to some room somewhere and while she is relieving you of your lust, her partner will be relieving you of your loot, that's before you get badly beaten up and dumped.'

'Jaysus Ned, you're a fierce spoil sport,' the Drummer cut in. 'Why don't you leave the poor fellow to his fantasy?'

'All right lads, but don't call me from the hospital, I won't want to know,' he said.

'I think you might be right Ned,' said Conn. 'I got carried away by the idea so I'll just shag some lonely little immigrant instead.'

His Boss felt like giving him a box, but decided to ignore his stupidity instead. How come sex is all he can think about, if he went to a few dances in Belfast that might sort him out, let him see that all women aren't easy. He had to smile when he thought about Belfast, imagine if we didn't play in a band none of us would ever score, an opinion which became stronger when he had a good look at himself in the mirror on the band-room wall that night.

The time flew; the working visas came through and the injections weren't too bad in the end even though that's where they got them, but when the plane tickets arrived excitement was at fever pitch, this was it, L.A. here we come.

The Roadie got the job of checking the instruments into the wagon and out again at the Airport. 'It would be a fuckin' disaster if we forgot my sax,' claimed Conn, not for one moment even considering what the situation would be like if any other instrument was left behind.

The Roadie, who didn't like being doubted for his thoroughness, whispered to the other lads. 'When we get there, I'll hide his saxophone and let him sweat for a while.'

'Don't tempt fate.' Ned advised, 'just grin and bear it.'

The trip to the Airport was noisy, with everyone shooting questions at Mike and they all began with. 'You were there before, so what's it like?'

He advised them not to go out alone especially at night and not to wander too far away from the hotel. One block in Manhattan looks the same as the next to a stranger and by turning the corner you could be in uncharted territory. The solution of course is easy, if you can count it's hard to get lost as most avenues and streets go by numbers and you just watch out for north, south, east or west.

'Where are we staying?' came the question.

'We're booked into The Woodlawn Hotel in Manhattan,' said Mike. 'It's fifteen stories high and is sort of OK, not the best or the worst place I suppose, it's got Bars, Restaurants and a Diner so you won't go hungry or thirsty.'

'Why is it called a Diner Mike?' Asked John.

'Because people dine there!' He answered.

There was a bit of a giggle and John shut up. The lads had organised that a friend living in the city would take the wagon away and before they knew it, they were waving the chap good-bye.

'Are you sure my sax is on the plane?' Queried Conn.

Nobody answered him so the penny must have dropped. Having arrived at the Airport early, they took their time doing some shopping for their cousins in the States, cousins that they had never seen.

'It's gonna be strange meeting relations who probably look the spitting image of us, yet we hardly knew they were there,' John said wistfully.

'For their sake I hope they're not the image of you,' said the sometimes-sarcastic drummer, while ducking a swipe from the offended one.

'Lads,' said Ned, realising it was time he showed them who was boss. 'If there's any more messing we won't be let on the plane, so who wants to take the blame for that, plus it's not allowed in-flight either.'

The musicians promised they would behave as they made their way on board, anyway, with all the lovely airhostesses strutting up and down; they were back to talent spotting. As the flight got underway the other passengers started drinking like it was going out of fashion and while the members of the band let their errand be known it wasn't long before they were being asked for a 'butt of a song.'

'Ah, come on lads, what will ye have and have ye ever sung this one be-dad?'

Conn had brought his Clarke C tin whistle, which meant he was the centre of attention and the Drummer joined in with two mineral bottles on the frame of the seat.

'Make sure you don't break those,' the Air Hostess said to him.

'Why, can you not afford to lose them?' he quipped.

Looking a little crossly at him she answered. 'That's not the problem, they might shatter on impact and fly all over the place, cutting people on the way.'

'Sorry,' he said. 'I'll hit them easier, but are you not enjoying the craic?'

Him and Conn were now laying into a reel and the place was humming. Soon the interested passengers found out about their hit song so they insisted on waking the singer and he had to sing it right there, without any backing.

Ned cringed, thinking. 'How the fuck did he get the job as Lead Singer?' Now he realised at long last how bad they would all sound without a band behind them. Just as he was coming to terms with that, a tipsy woman, or would it be fair to say a very nice tipsy woman, asked him to sing The Haunted House.

'Who told you I sang that?' he asked.

'Your friends,' she answered, gesturing towards the front of the plane. 'They're waiting.'

Ned was going to say he had no friends on this flight, but the plane lurched a little and the nice tipsy lady fell on him. She felt good spread all over him so he thought.

'Why be a spoil sport, let's go up there and do it, but the lads will have to sing backing.'

As they approached, the orchestra had already started sounding like a brass section and the lady joined in. After they had gone through the song a few times they ground to a halt and the woman asked.

'How come you guys know that song?' 'It's been a big hit in The States and I've met the guy who recorded it.' Then taking him by the hand she said. 'Come with me, I've got an empty seat next to mine where we can get to know each other.' Seated comfortably she told Ned all about herself, that she was an Irish woman who had lived in New Orleans for years and was on her way back there. 'This is my number if you would care to call me sometime,' she offered.

'Next time we're on tour, we must get a gig in your town,' he said, 'by chance are you staying in New York tonight?'

'Yeah,' she answered, 'but I've got to book a hotel yet.'

'You can always stay at our hotel,' he bluffed, not having a clue what the situation would be there, but the one thing he knew was, don't let this woman go, if you do you'll be kicking yourself.

'I've got a nice bottle of Irish Mist we can share.' She offered.

'I love sharing things,' said Ned, as he followed her gaze to the overhead bin.

He had vaguely heard about the Mile High Club, but wasn't sure whether or not you had to be a member, also whether it was for passengers, staff or both. The Irish Mist tasted good with Ned lying about having had it before.

'I'd say that's not all you've had before young man,' said the slightly more tipsy lady, 'by the way, what age are you?'

'If I tell you it might put you off,' was his cagey reply.

'Not at all young man,' she said, repeating the term. 'I love young men, so pray tell me.'

'I'm 25 next birthday,' he answered, 'now, would you mind telling me your age.'

'I'm forty this year, but I feel 25 and at this very moment I want to feel someone who's 25 in me.'

Ned's mouth was full of Irish Mist when she said that, but not for long. Her comment made him splutter and he sprayed the Liqueur straight into her face.

'Jaysus I'm sorry,' he said, 'give me a tissue and I'll dry you off.'

'No tissue for you young man, you've got a tongue haven't you.'

'I can't start licking you in front of everybody and anyway, I still don't know your name,' he stuttered.

Her mouth was only an inch away from his when she answered. 'Kiss me and I'll tell you.'

He didn't believe in backing down in a situation like this and anyway, he had been dying to kiss her big red lips for ages now. They both leaned forward that last inch and began nuzzling each other, their mouths touching, then parting fleetingly only to touch again. He was so horny in seconds, he could have beaten an ass out of a sandpit, then he felt her tongue flashing out and in so he just opened his mouth and she almost choked him with the first thrust. By now even the revellers had gone to sleep and she had noticed, so she whispered in his ear.

'Let's go and make love in the bathroom.'

'Jaysus, there are no bathrooms on an aeroplane,' he said.

'We call them bathrooms but you guys call them toilets, let's go to the bathroom young man, I want that hot rod inside me,' she insisted.

Ned always considered himself as possessor of the hardest neck in the business, but now, when he was faced with entering an aircraft toilet with a sexy woman he was forced to back down, for lots of reasons he felt. There's an old saying in the country that a standing cock has no conscience, but this was one time when that old saying had to bite the dust.

'There's no way I'm gonna' do that!' Said Ned. 'I'd love to when we get to New York, but I don't want to get arrested for having sex on an aircraft, I think there's a severe law against it. I'm sure if you've been in a toilet like that before, you'll realise there isn't room to swing a cat.'

'Oh honey,' she said, 'who mentioned swinging a cat, I'm talking about a pussy that's swinging already so we'll compromise. You stand up and get the blanket from the overhead bin, I've got a thrill in store for you, but be careful and don't wake that old lady in the isle seat.'

He got up very carefully, glancing around furtively in case a hostess might see the bulge in his pants and when he leaned over, he noticed that his aroused equipment was about one inch away from the woman in the next seat. 'Better not hit her with it,' he thought, as he gingerly removed the big blanket from the bin. 'What the fuck does she want this for anyway? I hope she doesn't intend going to sleep on me in the near future.'

He had a lot to learn about women and he was about to get the biggest lesson of his life. His still unnamed lover took the blanket, opened it slowly and putting part of it over her head she literally dived on his privates, spreading the blanket on the way. He heard the noise of his zipper being pulled down and then she began to wrestle with his very tight underpants, which he had luckily changed that morning. Suddenly he felt her taking his prize possessions, triggering something he hadn't experienced since a feebler attempt made by a young Madge Gilpin some years earlier. This was the real thing, the complete ball of wax, he was always telling the lads about getting a speed-wobble but from now on he could be more graphic, it was now taking place for real. It's all the better it didn't last too long or he would have caused a multiple awakening on the plane. Holding both his hands over his mouth and biting his lip at the same time, it happened. He was going to warn her of the state of play when he realised that she had no intentions of stopping until the job was done, then he let out a groan, which caused the other lady to stir a little in her seat. If he was to be honest, at that moment he didn't care as his lover continued to pleasure him, much to his joy. Then he could feel her replacing everything and he heard the zipper travel back up slowly, as she made sure he wouldn't get a zip nip. A well-manicured hand drew back the blanket revealing the happiest pretty face you could find and she really looked like the cat that had got the cream.

Kissing him on the cheek she nestled down on his shoulder and whispered. 'It's your turn when we get to New York.'

He didn't know whether to panic or not, knowing what her last comment meant.

'I'll never be able for this one and do you have to kiss your lover after it happens?'

He would have another few hours to decide on that one, but then he thought. 'I'll go with the flow and I'm sure she will teach me, anyway, I think she has worked it out that I'm a beginner.' 'Jaysus I hope the lads don't tell her that my nick-name is Ned the Bed, because she'll just call me Edward the Backward.'

With about two hours of the flight left to go, he eased himself out from underneath his now sound asleep lover and propped her head comfortably on the blanket, which he had folded as a pillow. Looking at her pretty relaxed smile he wondered, where does this go from here? The one thing he had to check was whether or not he would be allowed to bring this woman to his room in The Woodlawn Hotel. To be able to do this, he would need a room to himself, so he headed down the isle in search of Mike who was just waking up.

'How's it cutting Ned,' Mike asked, rubbing the sleep from his eyes.

'It's cutting mighty Mike,' he answered, 'but I'll need your help I think.'

'What's the problem, or would it have anything to do with a glamorous Irish American lady a few years your senior?' came the double-pronged question.

'You've hit the nail on the head, but how did you know?'

'A little bird told me,' was Mike's reply, 'in fact you might say it was a flock of them that put me in the picture.'

'Well Mike, this is the situation, her and I have had round one earlier and she's willing to come back to the hotel with me for the remaining fourteen rounds, but I don't know if I'll be able to bring her to my room, that is if I've got a room of my own in the first place.'

'Most of the band lads want single rooms, so just make sure that you get one of them, as for getting her in, this is New York we're talking about so I can't see any problem, just don't make it too blatant. Anyway, I'll give you any help I can as I'll be getting a room also but I think I'll be staying with friends, so it will be vacant. By the way, who won the first round?' He asked with a grin.

Ned could have hugged him but it would not have gone down too well with Mike, maybe causing round two with a difference, so he thanked him profusely and headed back to the seat. Nestling in again beside his woman, his head spinning with thoughts of what was to come, he dropped off into a deep sleep. Sometime later he woke up with someone's tongue in his ear and for a while he thought it was part of the most wondrous dream he was having.

'Wake wakey,' she whispered, 'we are about to land so you've got to fasten your seat belt and put your seat in an upright position.'

Her having messed with his ear had him in an upright position also, so he grabbed a corner of the blanket and covered his latest bulge.

'I can't be getting hard-ons every few minutes from a woman whose name I don't know,' he said. 'My name is Ned, what's yours?'

'I'm Patricia Kramer, I'm married to Doctor John Kramer from New-Orleans who I met on a flight high up in the clouds one day when I worked for American Airlines and some poor lady collapsed with a heart attack. Luckily for her he was on board, so both he and I worked on her until we saved her life and we have been together since, trying to work out what would have happened to us if that lady had not had her attack.'

'That's fate,' said Ned. 'I'm a complete believer in fate, what's for you won't pass you by.'

'Quite the philosopher,' she said and with a grin she continued, 'there are times like now when I wish that piece of fate had passed me by.' He was about to ask her what she meant by that but his thoughts skipped back over the past few hours and there lay the answer.

After touch down in New York, it wasn't long before they were through emigration and Mike had met their contact that was in charge of the transport.

'Welcome to New York guys,' said an Irish-man with a perfect American accent. 'Follow me, I've got a stretch limousine outside to take you to Manhattan, it shouldn't take long.'

When the lads laid eyes on the car there were loud gasps and lots of swear words. Ned stifled a gasp also, but as he was trying to impress Patricia he just sung dumb instead. There were some choice comments from the orchestra.

'That must be my cars mother,' roared Conn who drove a mini.

Then it was the Drummer with. 'Maybe they ran short of wheels and had to weld two cars together.'

John stuck his oar in next. 'Maybe it was engines or steering wheels they ran short of.'

'I'm not sitting in the back of that fuckin' thing,' said Mickey Joe, 'if I can't see the driver, there's no fuckin' way I'm getting in.'

Panic wasn't far away. 'I can't find your sax Conn,' said the Roadie.

'Stop bull-shittin,' said Conn.

'I swear to fuck,' repeated the Roadie, 'it's not on the trolley.'

Ned, who thought the Roadie was doing what he said he would do by hiding the sax, had a quick look at the equipment and to be sure, no saxophone.

'I'll murder the fucker,' Conn promised.

The Roadie was very pale. 'It's not my fault, I thought you picked it up yourself,' he whined.

'OK,' said Mike, 'put the remainder of the stuff in the stretch, Ned, Conn and I will go back and have a look.'

With the help of security, they traipsed back to the baggage area but no one had seen a sax. Then Mike suggested that staff should look again in the hold of the plane. This got results. There, tucked in behind baggage now bound for Florida was the Conn saxophone. They all got religion for a few seconds and chorused 'Thank God!' Then with his prized possession firmly gripped in his hand, Conn went back to the limo beaming.

'Where was it?' They all asked.

'Heading for fuckin' Florida!' He answered.

'Maybe it was trying to escape,' ventured John, who this time failed to dodge the swipe Conn made with his free hand.

'I must apologise for my mates.' Ned said to Patricia. 'They can be real bog men at times.'

Patricia shouted 'Hello all,' followed by. 'I'm Patricia and I'm hard to shock,' then she said. 'You've heard the old adage, you can take the man out of the bog, but you can't take the bog out of the man.'

That died a bit of a death so it was let go by everyone except the Drummer, who proved her point by asking. 'What's an old adage Patricia?'

'It's just another word for an old saying,' she replied kindly.

As the stretch car headed for the hotel, the gasps began again. The Lead Singer started singing the old hit Downtown after seeing a sign with that on it, someone shouted. 'Brooklyn Bridge, 'Jaysus!' Further in they saw a sign which read 'The Bronx. Christ, all my cousins live there!' Said Mickey Joe.

'I thought they all lived in Boston?' countered the Drummer.

'I've got loads of cousins in both places you eejit,' Mickey Joe answered, in a voice loaded with sarcasm.

Suddenly they were in Manhattan and the stretch pulled up in front of the Hotel. After various comments about the size and colour our heroes teemed into the lobby, then, while both porters and receptionists were dealing with room allocation, Patricia went to the lift, got in and pressed floor one. This was Mike's plan, she would wait for Ned on the first floor by the lift and he would find her there when he got his room. Unknown to the other band members, Mike informed Ned that himself and Patricia could move to his room after 8am, as he had just phoned friends and they were picking him up. The plan was to knock the other fellows off the scent and because of past experience, it was a foregone conclusion that when the lads got up, they would go straight to Ned's room to hear how he was getting on, romance wise. Sure enough, four of the band surfaced early and after meeting in the lobby, Mickey Joe went to the reception desk where he asked if they could tell him the number of the room that Mr. Ned Brady was in.

'Of course Sir,' the nice lady said, 'he's in room 344.'

'Thank you,' said the Trumpet man with a wide grin, which he lost when he was asked if he had found out what floor that was on.

A porter overheard the dilemma and offered some help. 'It's on the thoid floor,' he said.

The lads looked at him as if he had two heads. 'If you were over in Ireland, what floor would that be now?' asked the Drummer.

The Porter wasn't too happy with the sarcastic reply, so he held up one hand and counted his fingers in front of the Irish man's nose. He said, 'Feist, Second and Thoid, it's on the Thoid floor, OK you guys.'

The Drummer went a little off colour as they headed for the lift. 'I was at a Mafia movie before we came here and they all talked like that,' he whispered, as they stepped inside. They all looked at each other for inspiration when the door closed and it was Conn who acted by hitting button three. 'Well he did count his first three fingers,' he said in a superior tone.

They walked on tiptoe along to room 344 and barely breathing, they each pressed an ear against the door. 'I can hear nothing,' said one. 'Me neither,' said another. 'Maybe she has screwed him to death,' was another verdict, but he was advised that it was a bit too soon for that to happen, then someone came around the corner and took a very strange look at them, their ears glued to the door.

'We'd better get out of here or we'll be reported,' said the Drummer, 'we could be done for loitering.'

'Oh I love the big words your using, next you'll be saying paraffin oil,' said Mickey Joe, as caustic as could be, then, 'come on we'll go down to this diner, they have massive big ice creams.'

'Poor Ned, he's probably dead in bed.' John said.

Just as they walked into the diner Conn was saying. 'John, you're a poet and I don't think you know it.'

A surprise lay in store for the four house detectives. At the corner of the counter sat Ned and Patricia tucking into two large steak sandwiches with fries, (the new name which our heroes had discovered for chips) and they were having a big laugh at something.

'Where were you two?' came the quadraphonic question.

'We just got here from my room,' said Ned. 'But where were you?'

'You weren't up there at all,' said the Drummer, putting his foot pedal in it.

'How would you know, because you're not on my floor,' parried Ned. 'Can I take it you were all up there having a listen?'

'They wouldn't do that, so stop trying to make them look foolish.' Patricia said, giggling.

'Foolish my arse,' hissed Mickey Joe under his breath, while he got as red as the ketchup on Ned's chips.

The four lads grabbed the shiny two sided menus, their eyes getting wider by the second at the selection.

'I'd love to have the lot,' grunted the Drummer, causing Patricia to glance at Ned and roll her eyes up to heaven.

The waitress was in shock as she wrote the order down. 'Are you guys going to eat all this stuff?' she asked, a look of genuine concern on her pretty face.

'No, some of it is for Vincent-De-Paul,' roared Conn mirthfully.

'Are those two guys going to join you as well?' she asked.

'Jaysus,' said Conn, then quick as a wink he came back with. 'Before you ask if he's joining us, the answer is no.'

The girl, who hadn't heard of the charitable organisation called Vincent-De-Paul before, didn't get the joke, shook her head and went off to get the huge meals. Patricia whispered something into Ned's ear giving him a quick kiss on the retreat, and then they paid for their food, slipped off the high stools and headed for the lobby. As they left the diner, Mickey Joe slid off his stool to follow them, then stood and watched the lift climb to the fifth floor. 'Gotcha,' he exclaimed, and then he strolled over to reception and asked.

'Could you give me the room number for our manager Mike Johnston on the fifth floor please?'

'Yes of course, but I could ring his room for you if you like,' she said.

Mickey Joe panicked. 'Oh no don't ring him, it's too early yet, we'll go up and call him when we have finished our food.'

'OK,' she said, 'your manager is in room 555, have a nice day y'all.'

He went back to the diner beaming and muttering. 'Have a nice day y'all,' he hollered to his mates.

'Have you eaten a Yankee dictionary?' Conn asked, in an unimpressed fashion.

'Where were you?' the Drummer asked.

'I've been finding out where the afternoon's riding is going to be,' he grinned. 'Room 555 which belongs to Mike, who is not in the building.'

Just then the Singer, Piano man and Roadie came in to order their food. 'Where's Ned?' The Roadie asked, 'he's supposed to take me to the movies in 42nd Street and it's our last night off this week.'

'In about ten minutes after you've eaten that food, you will have as good a show on the fifth floor as you'll get in 42nd Street.' 'The only difference will be, you'll have to work out the action from the sound track, but at least you'll know the stars.'

'Will Ned the Bed be in action?' asked the Singer. 'You know I wouldn't mind a crack at that Patricia myself and she'll make a man out of Ned.'

'He thought he was one already,' mused John, not too sure what the Singer meant.

Mickey Joe took control. 'When we get to the fifth floor, five of us will go to the room door and the others will keep look out at both ends of the corridor, to make sure we're not caught by guests who might report us, then a different two will be the lookouts, OK!' 'So have a nice day y'all.'

They were tittering at Mickey Joe's overused new greeting as they poured out of the lift, almost knocking down two stunners who were about to get in. The Drummer quickly grabbed Conn by the collar as he did and about turn to follow the two ladies.

'Fuck off you,' said Conn, 'one of them winked at me.'

'Winked at you my arse, they're two prostitutes plying their trade and you'd end up not having a nice day when they'd roll you for your few dollars, remember what Ned said.'

As quick as lightning, Mickey Joe whistled a few interwoven bars of the soundtracks from the Clint Eastwood movies a fist-full of dollars and a few dollars more, then he said. 'Shush this is it.'

As if he was Clint, he grabbed two of the gang and pointed to where they had to take up duty and they hadn't long to wait. The moans grew to yelps, the yelps grew to screams and then they could clearly hear Patricia giving instructions. 'Put it in a bit further Ned darling and don't you dare come for another hour.'

The five lads immediately looked at their watches. 'It's a good job we're not on tonight,' said one.

'Maybe so, but Ned is,' said another.

Then loud whistles from one end of the corridor announced the arrival of company. A young couple came around the corner arm in arm kissing and nuzzling each other, stopping outside room 557 they produced the keys. In answer to their enquiring gaze, Mickey Joe blurted out that they had forgotten their keys and someone had gone down for them.

The couple went into the room and the Singer said. 'I wish them luck getting to sleep with the noise next door.'

At that moment in room 555 someone was going down for real. 'Go down on me Ned.' Patricia was screaming and the audience outside considered knocking on the door, to stop them making a spectacle of themselves in front of the young couple. Before our heroes could intervene, they heard the young female's screams in 557.

'Fuck me now Bill.' 'I've been dying for it all morning during the ceremony and that stupid reception, come on Fuck Me!'

The noise from 557 was now much louder and much more inventive than that of 555, so the lads called in the outriders. John and the Roadie had been on watch so they listened for a minute, then John said.

'It sounds like they're also having a nice day.' With that, they all burst out laughing and ran to the lift.

When they got to the lobby the Roadie begged to be taken to the movies in 42nd Street, so they all agreed to go after they got instructions on which bus there and which bus back. That info logged, not I might add from the porters whom they were a bit afraid of but from the head receptionist, they bravely set forth with the intention of going to the steamiest picture they could find. They were again awe-struck with all the flashing lights and the scantly clad girlie pictures outside the cinemas as they walked close to each other, like a herd of zebra being stalked by lions. The Roadie kept walking two steps forward then two steps backwards taking in the sights, when suddenly he let out a yell. When the others saw what had happened they didn't know whether to help or run. The Roadie was standing like a statue, his balls firmly in the grasp of a big black prostitute who was asking him.

'Would you like some fun baby?'

Mickey Joe knew, that when Ned wasn't there, it was up to him to solve this problem and the memory of a bad experience he had had in the public toilets in Mullimore when he was fourteen, came to the rescue. He took the bull by the horns, (pardon the pun) and in a desperate effort to look and sound feminine he ran over, put his arm around the Roadie and said.

'Leave my boyfriend alone you bold woman, nobody touches him only me.' Then to the terrified Roadie he said. 'Are you alright darling?'

The prostitute let go and jumped back screaming. 'You faggot, you piece of shit, I'll get someone to take care of you.' Then she roared. 'RASTUS.'

While she was busy looking for Rastus, the lads made a run for it. 'Stay together, Stay together,' shouted Mickey Joe and then to the black woman he roared. 'Have a nice day!' They ran for about four blocks, only slowing down when they thought they had enough space between them and 42nd Street.

'So much for the pictures,' ventured the Singer, as they climbed gladly on a bus. 'That happening reminds me of a yarn I once heard,' he continued, 'this fellow was groping a girl outside a dance hall and she asked him what he was doing so he said. I'm looking for my hole, the girl breathed a sigh of relief and replied, Thank God, for a moment there I thought you were looking for mine.'

There were a few nervous laughs and Conn said. 'Very funny, but that happening back there wasn't very funny, we could have been killed.'

When they got back to the hotel they made their way to the diner, where they found Ned and Patricia having coffee as they gazed into each other's eyes.

'We had a close shave this evening,' volunteered Mickey Joe, as he told the full story.

'You're lucky she couldn't find Rastus,' said Patricia, 'he would be the Pimp and he would be either carrying a big knife or a gun.' Then looking at the vacant look on the Drummers face she continued. 'A Pimp manages prostitutes and they are not nice people.'

'Mickey Joe told her to have a nice day and that seemed to piss her off big time.' Conn stated, before continuing with a question. 'How did you and Patricia get on Ned?'

'Well lads, we were putting on quite a show for a full house in the corridor, when all of a sudden a couple went mad riding in the room next door and they were ten times louder than us,' he said. 'We spent the evening listening to them and their phone kept ringing, when we came down the receptionist apologised to us, hoping our manager wasn't kept awake by them, I believe they got married this morning. By the way, before we split for the night, everyone has got to be in the lobby at 1 o'clock tomorrow to go to the dance hall for a sound check, the stretch will pick us up here and you can all say goodbye to Patricia now gents because she's leaving in the morning. I don't want you cluttering the corridor tonight, anyway it's not lucky as you all found out today.'

Everyone said goodbye to Patricia and on the way upstairs they agreed that she was a nice lady, making Ned a lucky fucker as usual.

'I think there's a little more than luck involved,' the Drummer opined, 'we're a bunch of morons and we could do well by taking a leaf out of his book.'

'Speak for yourself,' were the multiple answers to that.

They were all tired and there was music to be made tomorrow night, now The Nova's Showband needed rest. At 1 o'clock the next day everyone was relaxed, fed and watered, that is all except Ned who was walking around as if he was lost.

'Are you missing her already?' He was asked but he ignored the question.

There hadn't been much sleeping done in room 344 the previous night and when the cab drove off with Patricia this morning, he knew that a short but memorable episode of his life had drawn to a close, maybe never to be repeated. Yes, there had been a lot of lust involved, but there had also been much tenderness as well, leading to quite a few tears being shed for the last hour or so. Promises of phone calls were made and of visits to New Orleans being reciprocated by visits to Mullymore. Patricia said that she would stash Ned in the Hotel of a friend on his visits, failing that there was always Florida where she had a home. He wasn't sure where he would stash Patricia in Mullymore, but I suppose they both knew that it probably would never become a real problem, as Patricia was going back to her family and she knew it would be ages, before she got back to Ireland again, maybe never.

Chapter Five

He went for a quick cup of coffee and as the hot brew made it's way down his throat, he made a conscious decision not to let the memory of Patricia ruin his life.

'Find another lady soon.' Those were the words she had used to Ned this morning when she advised him to pick a girl at the dance tonight and replace her at once. 'Just make sure you don't call her Patricia unless that happens to be her name,' she'd said.

They were booked into The City Plaza Ballroom for the Friday, Saturday and Sunday nights and they were told at the sound check that they would be on stage from 10pm to 11pm, have a one-hour break, and then back on from midnight to 1am. The resident eight-piece Showband would provide the music for the remainder of the dance. They met some of the house band members, made up of four Americans and four Irish and they discovered that they knew the Irish members as they had all been in bands back in Ireland. The Lead Singer was an Irish lady who had almost made it back home and was an excellent exponent of the Irish ballad.

'Our few shite ballads are going to die a death with that one around,' stated the Drummer, after catching them in rehearsal.

'Just because you can't sing a note, you're always putting down our efforts,' complained the Lead Singer. 'Wait until you hear the Yankee drummer in this outfit and you'll have enough to worry about.'

The P.A. and all the stage gear was top class so the sound check took no time. Ned would be in control of the knobs, but he was familiar with the make and model so there should be no problems. They all went back to the hotel and Mike arrived with the Promoter, a big Irish American guy with gold dripping off him everywhere, not leaving out the bare hairy chest plus the medallion.

'I bought a comic yesterday,' said the Bass man, 'and yerman's the image of the fucking incredible hulk, I wonder if he goes green when he's vexed?'

'Shut up John,' said Ned. 'If he hears you we'll find out soon enough and some of us will be a funny hue when he sends us home.'

The band got back to the Ballroom at eight to give a final touch up to their tuning and get a feel of the venue with a crowd. It was a huge place with a balcony at the back and both sides, so you could have full view of the punters. The lads were getting more excited by the minute, saying things like. 'Did you see such a one or such a fellow, they used to live beside me?' Some of them saw girls they swore they shagged back home after gigs around the country and they were deemed to be spoofing. The resident band was great at everything, including the girl singer who was massive at Irish ballads and country songs, spurring the crowd to dance for the first hour non-stop.

So far Ned had not seen any girls he knew or even liked. 'Now I need a woman I'll probably fail to get one,' he mused.

The Nova's Showband always preferred having a good band on first, because the dancers were always happy when they took the stage and this was one of those times. They started their set with some fast numbers and the floor was full at once, people waving in welcome as they danced by. During the second fast set the Drummer let out a yell, then began playing on his tom-tom's which was something he rarely bothered doing unless he was trying to get somebody's attention. Ned looked around expecting to see the guy crashing to the floor, instead he shouted 'Left hammer' and pointed frantically with one of his drumsticks, much to the annoyance of the band members who felt that the misused stick would have been useful to keep the tempo.

The Trumpet and Sax men were glad to once more have the Trombone aiding their efforts and our hero felt this vibe so he concentrated on the job in hand, not daring to glance to the left. While he was announcing the next number, he could hear the Drummer being told off by the other band members and you ought to hear some of the places they were going to put his sticks.

The Guitar man played the intro, the rhythm section swung into action, the other musicians began clapping their hands and now playing the tambourine, Ned knew it was safe to take a slow careful glance to the left hand side of the ballroom. The music drowned his loud exclamation of shock, which started off with.

'Where the fuck has she sprung from?' And then, 'of course, that would explain why she disappeared from home, but somebody told me she got married.'

There smiling sweetly, not a hair out of place in her usual neat bun, was the subject of multiple frustrations for Ned in the past. This lady, Brenda was her name, had refused every advance he made over the years and he was about to give up on her, when a friend told him she fancied a stranger who had moved to Mullymore recently. This really annoyed him as he had asked her so nicely so often, making no secret of the fact that he liked her a lot but to no avail and now she wanted a total stranger. He heard that this fellow was from England and decided on a plan of action. He would ring Brenda, put a handkerchief over the phone, and then ask her out using an English accent he hoped would sound like the man of her dreams. Now he shuddered as he remembered the day, an old coin box in a local pub as he carefully covered the mouthpiece, inserted the money and dialled her number.

Her lovely voice said. 'Hello, can I help you?' The sound caused him to panic and he quickly hung up, visibly shaken.

'This has got to be done,' he convinced himself, so picking up the phone again he reached for another coin and almost repeated the process when she answered, then the chancer in him took over. 'Is that you Brenda?' he asked, in a voice alien to him, but one he hoped she would react to.

'Who's calling?' she asked. 'It's a bad line.'

He was glad to hear that as it would be a plus in this scam, so he continued. 'This is Frank, I met you last week in the Ritz Bar and I was wondering if you would meet me on Wednesday night in the Tower Ballroom? The Nova's Showband are playing there and I could make it at 10.30.'

Without the slightest pause for thought she'd replied. 'OK Frank, I'll see you there at 10.30, I'm looking forward to it.'

He remembered saying as he hung up the phone. 'You bitch, that's one date where there's a surprise in store for you.'

He remembered telling the Drummer at the time, so as the band played both chaps had their eyes glued to the door. At 10.30 on the dot she walked in all on her own looking only gorgeous, then she scanned the crowd for her fellow and went to the ladies. Ned and the Drummer gave each other a wink and waited. A few moments later they could see the bun gliding around amongst the dancers, just like the periscope on a submarine as she searched for her date and as time went by they could see she was peeved, as she shot down one suitor after another.

'*She's gonna Pepul the Pleplug,*' the Drummer shouted in his bad Ben-Lang, in between two numbers.

'*Egi thegink sego,*' Ned answered, '*Egill Hegave Tego Megove Segoon.*'

The Drummer had just suggested she was going to pull the plug and he agreed, saying he would have to move soon.

He wasn't performing in the next number, so he caught her eye and beckoned her to come to the stage. With evident displeasure, she made her way through the throng while Ned bent down to talk into her ear.

'What do you want?' was her curt request.

'Did your date not turn up?' he asked, continuing with. 'I thought he was supposed to be here at 10.30, but after all it was a bad line.'

She looked a picture when vexed and he must have been the closest ever to being hit by a woman, as all her usual good manners went to the dogs. 'Fuck you, it was you,' she fumed. 'I've got a good mind to give you a box, smart Alec.'

'Don't be angry,' said Ned, 'it just proves how much I like seeing you, that I would go to such lengths to bring you here.' She had looked at her watch and he could remember that she was almost smiling. 'A go on,' he added, enjoy the remainder of the dance and I'll walk you to your car afterwards.'

'You're a fierce chancer,' she said, but the laugh is on me so I may as well stay, see you after,' then she gave him a little slap and walked into the crowd. She could have had about ten men that night, but Ned still walked her to her car getting a quick peck on cheek for his bother.

'I shouldn't talk to you at all,' she had said.

Now after a couple of years, she's standing only yards away from him with the bun still in place, looking totally stunning and believe it or not, she's smiling at him.

'*Whegat's the Stegory,*' asked the Drummer, his lingo not having improved.

'I'll check it out when the other band comes on, meanwhile I'll watch her antics, maybe a man will appear and that will be the answer,' he replied.

Ned had glanced her way a few times and she had smiled back, but she had not stirred. He wondered was she getting flashbacks from the night she'd turned up in the Tower Ballroom? The last song of their first set came to an end and as they vacated the stage to make room for the other band, he beckoned at her as before to come over. They both shook hands and he immediately felt the old thrill he always got on seeing her.

'If you're not busy maybe you might have a drink with me, as we're not back on for an hour?' he asked, not knowing what to expect.

'Well there is one thing for sure, I don't have a date tonight,' she said, trying to sound scathing. 'For a change I'm available, but maybe you're not.'

As they headed for the balcony bar he put her in the picture with. 'If I wasn't, I'd make bloody sure I became available, what have you been up to?'

'Well,' she paused for a few seconds. 'I was supposed to get married but it didn't work out.'

'Glad or sorry?' was his question.

'Glad now, but it was messy at the time, just like all men you can't rely on them.'

'That's a bit hard on men, seeing you were never particularly sensitive towards them yourself.' Ned said and he meant it, because of his treatment or lack of it at her hands in the past. By now they had found a table and he also found out she was on Southern Comfort.

'I'm sure she never took a drink,' he was thinking, as he went to the bar. 'Being jilted does strange things to some people, I'd better not say that to her or I'll be fucked in the wrong sense of the word.'

In the past she had been very quiet, some would say stuck up, a country snob, but now she was wound up. He wanted to ask her if it was Frank whom she was supposed to marry, but decided against it as it would only open a can of worms, anyway, he thought Frank was married back then whether she knew it or not. They got out to dance a couple of times and he made sure they were the slow ones, dancing so close that all kinds of funny things were happening to him. She felt his hard-on and pressed herself closer, using her leg to make sure it wouldn't go away, then he had a worrying thought. What if she was setting him up, turning him on just to drop him in it later in lieu of the Tower Ballroom episode? That made him decide to kiss her right there on the dance floor and if she was acting she was good. She opened her mouth even wider than his taking his tongue as far as it could go, and then in a flash her tongue pushed his back and almost choked him.

'Jaysus,' he thought. 'I'm in for it tonight.'

When the kiss ended and they seemed even closer, he went for it. 'Are you taking me home with you later?' he asked, as he made an effort to eat her ear off.

'Yes,' she replied. 'I can hardly wait so we can catch up on what I foolishly missed over the years.' This time she led the kissing and he swears he saw tears in her eyes.

Ned suggested they sit down for a little while after that, because he couldn't go on stage with a big root like this and as the other band finished their set; he made his way back wondering what had hit him.

'Has her body been invaded by something from outer space?' 'It's some transformation,' he mused, his head spinning.

As he picked up his trombone the Bass man asked. 'Have you forgotten Patricia already?'

'I'll never forget Patricia,' he answered civilly. 'But you know I've been mad about this woman for years and I finally find her in the mood, what would you do John?'

'I'd fuck the arse off her Ned and make sure you do the same!' He advised. The Bass man loved the idea of being asked regarding such an important subject and it brightened him up for the remainder of the gig.

The Roadie's arm was tired giving out souvenir pictures of the band, but he loved the attention he was getting from the girls even though he got a huge slagging re: his episode in 42nd Street. He was talking to a nice American girl and the jealous Drummer went over and asked him.

'How are your balls?' It was the best thing that ever happened to the Roadie.

She asked him to explain and the girl was almost crying as he told the story. 'Oh you poor Irish guy,' she enthused, 'you come all the way to New York and the American girls let us down, if I could be of any help to you in getting over your trauma, I would love to.'

The Drummer was pissed off at this result, but it didn't stop the others as the night went on and because he had scored he didn't care, or neither did his friend. He was called 'Smash and Grab, Nuts, The Ball-breaker, Mushy Peas, Rubber Balls and The Handful' plus many more, but he smiled through it all. Another talking point with the lads back at the hotel was Ned and how he had found his new old love again.

Brenda hailed a taxi and as they climbed in he had to stop himself from grabbing her private parts, which for a second, were only inches away from him.

'I'll hold on,' he thought, 'we'll be even closer later.'

She made herself comfortable while giving her address to the driver and then she turned and melted into his waiting arms.

The cabbie made several attempts to start a conversation leading with. 'Was that your feist time to the Plaza Ballroom?'

Ned was in the middle of a juicy kiss and a very bad thought when the interruption came. 'Jaysus, he's another one of the Mafia men,' he thought, but he was unable to answer, because his mum always said that it's bad manners to talk with your mouth full. When they came up for air he decided it would be good manners to answer the driver so he said.

'Yes it was my first time, but my girlfriend has been there before.' It was like wine to his palate calling the elusive Brenda. 'His girlfriend.'

In the glow of the bright streetlights, he could clearly see her magnificent breasts beautifully enhanced by the coral blue of her lovely dress. Oh how often had he sinned thinking of those breasts over the years and now was the time to partake, so gently he eased one out of its snug habitation. As he was deciding whether to leave well enough alone and be happy with one, she reached into her dress to produce the gorgeous twin, then with her free hand she gently brought his head down and placed the nipple in his gaping mouth.

The cab driver's timing was perfect, as he chose that second to ask Ned a question.

'Are you guys over from the old country?' He considered answering but Brenda wasn't having it, so she thrust her nipple further into his mouth and decided she would hold the conversation with this insensitive fellow herself.

'Yes, they are over from the old country with a Showband and they played in The Plaza all night, now if you don't mind, we would like the opportunity to catch up on what we couldn't do earlier, OK!'

'Sorry lady,' he answered, as he carefully re-sets his mirror on their new position.

'So what', she thought, 'let him enjoy it while it's lasts.'

When they got to her apartment he was going to be the perfect gentleman and attempt to replace Brenda's boobs, but she beat him to it by quickly buttoning her coat over them, leaving things as they were internally. As he paid the Cab driver, Ned could see his eyes riveted on the top of Brenda's coat and he could almost hear his thoughts. 'I know what's behind those buttons.' Our hero had the same mental vision while he watched the frustrated cabby speed away, then he said as he stepped inside.

'It's a nice place Brenda.'

'It's not bad I suppose, but it's all I can afford on a Restaurant Manager's wage, excuse me, I'll be back in a moment.' She disappeared through a door and the still nervous Ned; half expected her to return with a man demanding his money. Minutes later, she came back minus the coat and her lovely breasts were once again back where they belonged. She followed his gaze, smiled and then pointed to the bathroom saying. 'I'll make the tea while you pay a visit.'

The bathroom was spotless, with loads of soft fluffy towels and a huge shower, which helped conjure up all kinds of ideas, and then when he came out she had the table nicely set.

'I've used my best china to welcome you to Queens,' she said, offering him a chair.

He looked her up and down as she walked about the room with one thought uppermost in his mind. He was going to enjoy taking that blue dress off her later and seeing he had been so busy above her waist earlier, he was wondering if she was wearing stockings so he decided to ask.

'No, not at the moment, but I'll put some on later if you wish.' Brenda replied.

He couldn't get over the change in this woman, if he had asked that question back home he would have had a thick lip and now during the tea they just sat looking at each other.

'You wash up and I'll be back in a moment,' she said and with that she disappeared through another door.

His head was spinning as he washed the cups and saucers, then he heard the door open. He wasn't going to get the thrill of taking her blue dress off tonight, she had done that already and was framed in the doorway swathed in full-length pink satin. His pet word 'Jaysus' slipped through his lips as he looked at her, one lovely hand high up on the doorframe, the other one on her hip. She gave a little wiggle while the now stocking clad leg popped out through a slit that went up all the way and looking down he could see she was wearing pink high heeled slippers with a woolly bobble on the front.

'You're a picture Brenda,' he gushed, 'that outfit is beautiful and even though I was looking forward to taking your blue dress off, that more than compensates.'

'Don't worry, you'll get another chance.' Then reaching out her hand she led him into her big, dimly lit bedroom with an enormous double bed against the left-hand wall. They began kissing just inside the door and it must have been five minutes before they both collapsed on the bed.

In his excitement he hadn't noticed that the bun was gone, now he realised that he was running his fingers through her beautiful fair hair. 'This is the first time I've seen you without your bun Brenda,' he ventured.

'This is the first time you're going to see me without a lot of things, does that bother you?' she asked.

He kissed her as his answer and unable to wait any longer his roaming right hand began to do its rounds. She offered no resistance as it slid up between her legs, pausing for a moment at the sexy lace on her stocking top. Then his fingers found her suspender, so to take his mind off the high he felt he took the suspender between his thumb and finger, pulled on it gently then let it slap against the lovely smooth skin of her thigh.

She took her mouth off his for a moment asking. 'Are you OK?'

'Brenda, I'm so OK I'm about to pop my cork and while I'm cooling down I'll tell you a wee story.' He put his hand firmly on her leg just above her stocking top and asked her a question. 'What do you call that piece of bare skin just above a girls stocking?'

'Would it be my leg,' she ventured.

'No,' he replied.

'Is it my bottom?' she asked.

'No,' came the grinning answer.

'I don't know so tell me, I want to get back to what we were doing,' she was almost scolding him now.

'It's the giggling-gap,' he said real smugly, not letting her know that he had found out this piece of information just two days ago from Patricia, the lady from New-Orleans.

'So what's a giggling-gap pray tell me?' she asked.

'It means, when a man gets past it, he's laughing.'

He was glad to feel her laughter as she tried to keep a straight face, just then he put his hand on her and she melted into him again, still trying not to laugh. Moments later they were thrashing around on the big bed, clothes flying in all directions, until all that remained at his request were the stockings, the suspenders and of course the giggling-gap but nobody was laughing. All that could be heard were moans and groans and the other sounds that go with full-blooded love making. He awoke to bright sunshine pouring in through a crack in the curtains and couldn't help wondering what time of day it might be, in fact for a second he wondered what day it was. Then turning around quickly as if to check who owned the bed, he was pleased to see it had not been a dream. Sleeping soundly with a happy smile on her face was that girl he could never get a date with back home, the elusive Brenda.

'I wonder why she puts that lovely hair up in a bun?' he mused. 'I must ask her to leave it down when we go out to lunch today.'

All the shafting and the lack of sleep was taking its toll on him, so he lay back down and drifted off into a nice deep sleep, awaking later to a very pleasant damp feeling in his nether regions. He lay quietly, resisting the inevitable for as long as he could, but it was a foregone conclusion that the sexy Brenda would get what she was after.

'Jaysus,' he thought again. 'What's the story here, would it be possible that he had been too local for her years ago and that was why she wouldn't go with him in case he would tell someone?' 'That would explain why she would perform for a stranger, because he would know none of her friends or neighbours and no one would find out if she had sex with him.' 'She's had lots of practice with somebody,' he concluded.

He was in bits after this session and must have dropped off again, and then some time later he heard her call his name.

'Ned, get out of that bed and come in here like a good chap.'

Like a zombie, he walked towards the voice, which was coming from the big shower. 'Are you in there,' he asked.

'No, it's the Queen of Sheba,' came the answer, then the frosted shower door slid back and there she was, naked as a jaybird apart from a cute little shower hat, with the powerful jets pelting her gorgeous body. 'Come in here Ned, I want you,' she demanded quietly.

As things became complicated he had a funny thought. 'Now Patricia loved sex in the shower and it looked ditto for Brenda, if the lads find out, they'll be changing my name from Ned the Bed to the Power Shower.'

Brenda was a very fit woman and he had to remind her of the fact that he was working again tonight.

'You're going soft on me Ned,' she said, and then going crimson she continued. 'Oh I'm sorry darling, but you know what I mean.'

'Yes I do and it's all right, with you around, I needn't worry about ever going soft.'

He was admiring her elegance as they walked to the Restaurant for lunch, the same one that she managed.

'Why are looking at me so?' she asked.

'I'm trying to work out the changes in you since I knew you and it doesn't add up.'

'I was badly hurt by a man who took advantage of my innocence, then dumped me,' she said, with a faraway look in her eyes.

Then he asked a foolish question. 'What do you mean by your innocence Brenda?'

'You were all smart with your giggling-gap, yet you don't know what a young woman's innocence is, how naive Ned, I'm talking of my virginity of course.'

They were now seated at the table so he decided to risk a thump, knowing she couldn't get up and walk out because everyone knew her. 'I always wanted to be the one to do that,' he stated, looking her straight in the eye, while he wondered at her story about being a virgin which would knock his previous theory on the head.

'I know and I wish you had,' she answered, a touch of sadness in her voice. 'But anyway, after last night we'll probably have to get married so you'll still have the best of me.'

His stomach lurched, but he couldn't let her see the turmoil that statement was causing him. 'That would be nice,' he said, smiling thinly, 'we can have a house-full of babies.'

She leaned over the table and kissed him, laughing loudly. 'I'm glad you took it like that,' she said, 'but not to worry, I'm safe for the moment, you know I wouldn't take chances with something as serious as that.'

He began to breathe again. 'She's nice, telling the truth like that,' he thought, 'she could have kept up the facade and was only getting on to him for being smart.'

The food was good and the staff really took good care of them, almost pandering to Brenda. 'Is everything to your satisfaction Miss Walsh, can we get you more wine Miss Walsh.' Then the Boss came over with a complementary drink and Ned was sure it was just to find out who he was.

'This is my boyfriend Edward, from Ireland,' she said with a flourish and he could detect a little bit of pride in there as well. Then they talked some small talk before the man excused himself and went back to his till.

'I see he's looking after the loot today,' said Ned, 'and by the way, why are you calling me Edward?'

'I wanted to impress him and I think Edward sounds nicer than Ned, don't you?'

'It's Ned you've been making love to, were you not impressed then?' he asked, yet fully understanding what she meant. He could see that she was a little surprised at being told off, so he smiled and said. 'Sorry Brenda, I know you meant well, but the only person who calls me Edward is my mum, my dad even calls me Ned but I'll tell you what, the next time we make love you can call me Edward and we'll see how it sounds.' He was glad to see she was laughing again and he asked why she was checking her watch.

'Within the hour Ned Brady, I'll be calling you Edward,' she promised.

With that veiled threat they left the restaurant holding hands. As he hailed a cab later on, he had to agree that the name Edward sounded OK, especially when it was being screamed at him in the throws of orgasm.

'You can use it in those circumstances anytime pet,' he told her, in between their final kisses.

Brenda would not be going to the City Plaza Ballroom that night because she had to work, but he would be catching a cab to the address she had stuffed in his top pocket, the moment the dance ended.

'Just think of a lady dressed in blue, waiting to be disrobed,' she had promised. 'And away with you now before you get horny again.'

They had another great gig that night and the place was wall-to-wall chicks. He knew quite a few of them and especially one lovely bird he had given a seeing to a couple of years earlier back home, or was it her that had given him the seeing to. Anyway, she was giving him salubrious looks and he began working on a good excuse that would tide her over, so trying to keep his mind on the job as well, he reached two possible conclusions. One, take her for a quickie in the band room warning the lads to stay out. Two, bring her back to the Hotel where he would ask her to wait until he got back from a party being given by the sister of his girlfriend back home and tell her. 'I can't take you, because if I do she'll tell her sister by letter the next day.' 'We can't have that now, can we?' As the night passed he decided on the second option, so at their first break he took the young lady out to dance and during a getting to know you again session, he suggested the idea.

'Oh, that's not a problem,' she said. 'I can stay until 4 or 5 tomorrow evening, my boyfriend is not coming around until 7.'

Somehow that made him feel better, but for one horrible moment he made a mental check. 'Did Brenda say she was going to work at 8 am?' Then to his dancing partner he said. 'I hope you understand, I've got to dance with a few girls from home who are here tonight, so I'll talk to you later.'

'OK,' she replied, 'but it's a pity I can't go to the party, could I not go with one of the other band members as his date?'

Panic-struck. 'I'm sorry Helen, all the lads have girlfriends back home and they would be in the same situation as myself, so that wouldn't work.' Just his luck, at that very second Mickey Joe was convincing a girl that he would see her later and he was using the good old tongue to the tonsils technique to do so. Helen was not impressed.

Ned probably told more lies that night than he had told so far in his life. He used the party story a couple of times plus more inane stuff and just before they went back on stage, he bounced up to the balcony where Helen had strategically placed herself, to watch the goings on.

'You've got a lot of good friends living in New York Ned,' she said, in a slightly scathing tone.

'It has to be done,' he assured her. 'If we didn't talk or dance with those girls, they would write home and destroy us.'

She saw logic in that somewhere and seemed to think she was lucky.

'Of course you're lucky, getting to spend the night in the hotel while I go against my will to a silly old party.' She was smiling again. 'Good, the moment this session ends I'll take you to the hotel, then I'll get a cab to the party and be back as soon as I can, just be sure you don't answer the door to anyone,' he warned.

He had a bottle of Seagram's Whiskey in the room and Helen got stuck into that, but not before she gave him a right good going over, reminding him.

'The last time you screwed me was in the back of a VW beetle, so you're not getting off the hook tonight seeing that we have this big bed at our disposal, anyway, this will stop you shafting some silly bird at your silly party.'

His legs were like jelly as he headed to the lift. 'How the fuck am I going to perform when I get to Brenda's? I hope she's asleep,' he wished out loud.

Brenda was not asleep, as promised; she was dressed in blue even down to her lovely high heels. The moment she opened the door she put her arms around his neck and began kissing him, then she stepped back.

'Do I get a whiff of cheap perfume off you and a strong scent of soap?' she asked.

'Yes you do,' he agreed, 'and the reasons are, I had to dance with a few girls from home who almost got up on me (hence the perfume) and they wanted us all to go to a party afterwards which some of the lads did. When I eventually got away much later, I went back to the hotel and had a quick shower because I was covered in sweat and smelled to high heaven.'

'All right, you're forgiven I think,' she said. 'I was giving up on you and as you know I'm at work in a few hours.' She stood back from him smiling and asked. 'As promised I'm wearing blue, but tell me Edward, what am I not wearing?'

That question got rid of all his tiredness because it was obvious that nothing outward was missing, that could only mean one thing. 'No knickers Brenda, give me a quick look.'

She did just that and he was glad he hadn't got as far as lying about the flu he thought he was getting. He moved forward quickly, not letting the dress drop down and he gently eased it over her head to discover that she had no bra on either. Then drawing strength from his desire for this woman, he picked her up and carried her into the still dimly lit bedroom. Before leaving for work in the morning, she suggested he should stay and she would nip home after lunchtime, but he remembered his prior arrangement and felt awful as he lied to her.

'Sorry Brenda, but we're all booked on a sightseeing trip of the city today, Mike booked it so I'll have to go.' They kissed as he hailed a cab and she promised that she would make her own way to the dance that night.

'Jaysus, what will I do later?' 'I'll have to keep Helen away from Brenda at all cost or she'll blow the lid.'

As the taxi sped back to Manhattan, he had mixed emotions. He was becoming a 'fierce' liar and he thought it was only a matter of time till he slipped up. Did he love Brenda? If so, why was he lying to her, then he remembered the way she treated him back home and that made him feel a little better, but in a few minutes he had to face Helen and tell more lies.

'I got drunk and someone put me to bed.' 'Yeah, that would do for starters and he could build on it if needed, but he realised none of that would be necessary when he walked into the brightly lit bedroom. Helen was lying as he had left her, dress still around her waist, her legs as far apart as they could go and the empty whiskey bottle gripped firmly in her left hand. She was snoring loudly he was glad to hear and kept on doing so as he slowly removed the bottle from her clenched fingers. Lifting her gently he eased her underneath the covers, then stripped silently and slipped into the bed beside her. He awoke a few hours later to Mike banging on the door, reminding him of the sightseeing trip, which was really on.

'I think I'm getting the flu Mike, I'll stay in bed and be ready for tonight instead,' he said, using the excuse he had prepared for earlier. It worked.

'OK,' said Mike, the job is more important, I'll bring you a souvenir from China-Town and you can always say you were there.'

'You know me Mike,' he shouted, glad the latter wasn't coming in. 'I don't tell lies so I can't be saying that.' Mike chuckled and went on his way as Ned was thinking. 'I hope he doesn't tell those other fuckers that I'm not getting up, or I'll have them all banging on the door.'

'Where am I?' Came a high-pitched wail, as Helen sat bolt upright in the bed.

'Here I go again,' he thought. 'You're in my bed in my hotel room, you came back with me last night and we made mad passionate love, I nipped out to my girlfriend's sister's party for an hour, rushed back hoping to repeat the deed but you were sound asleep, I was disappointed.'

As he was planning to grab her she screamed. 'Where's the bathroom?'

He pointed to the wide open door and within seconds she was making the oddest noises, as she got rid of the whiskey plus whatever else she had on board. About five minutes later, she re-appeared minus the dress, but looking a lot better.

'Will you excuse me while I have a shower?' she asked.

'Go ahead,' he answered, listening to the sound of the shower on her body and to the little tunes she was humming as the jets brought her back to life, and then he heard.

'Would you like to join me Ned, I owe you one.'

He could have pole-vaulted into the bathroom as a result of the obvious enjoyment she was getting from the hot water, but the real decider was that sexy invitation that could not be ignored. She reached for his protrusion with her soft soapy hands and propelled him into the shower, then she turned her back to him and reaching between her legs she guided him inside her body.

With a little moan she said. 'I had forgotten how big that thing could really get.'

That was a great promo for the still inexperienced Ned, as he began to build up-tempo. He had used his last contraceptive with Helen the night before and she was very aware of the consequences of going without in her present condition. He soon noticed that she was helping herself towards orgasm with her free hand and this drove him crazy altogether, but she was also monitoring progress carefully so she laid down the law.

'I'm absolutely lethal at the moment and you must not let any of that stuff inside me,' she said, 'just tell me when you're ready and I'll look after it.'

His head was about to explode; in fact he was all about to explode. Was she saying what he thought she was saying and was this what he wouldn't let Patricia do to him a few days ago because she was (too nice)?

'I'm ready,' he shouted.

This was one fit lady. She pulled away from him, spun around going down on both knees in the same action and yes; it was what Patricia had suggested. Now he was wondering why he had stopped her, it was wonderful. You've heard of the Lords name being taken in vain, well it was happening now in multiples and Helen who was halfway through a climax was treating Ned's equipment as if she was eating steak. Like the old saying, it was the moans from her and the bawls from him. As with all good things it had to end and now she was looking up at him with a big smile on her face.

'Nice huh,' then before he could answer, she jumped up and kissed him full on the lips.

It's a good job Patricia had convinced him a few days ago that this was a regular happening and if the lads in the band knew, they would never let him live it down. Kissing after a speed-wobble, no way Jose. The lads had a lot to learn. They both washed and dried each other and when Ned came out of the bathroom, Helen was sitting up on the bed in her birthday suit leafing through the copy of Playboy he had bought on his arrival, thinking things might be quiet. He had been lusting after this particular copy for ages and had failed to get it in London but saw it the moment he got out of the limo, now he stood and watched her with interest. She was as good looking as the model on the cover and he had just had his way with her.

'Wow, she must be mad,' he mused.

'Do you buy Playboy for hard times Ned?' she asked grinning.

'Yeah, there's no better way to get over hard times,' he answered.

'You're just a dirty get,' she said, flinging the mag at him in mock disgust.

Afterwards, they sat on the bed for ages picking their favourite models until he said.

'You're a woman, you shouldn't be picking out your favourite girls in a magazine, that's only for us men.'

'Maybe I'm a bit like that,' she roared laughing, while hitting him over the head with her fists.

They began wrestling that moved to kissing, then the inevitable happened with all the trimmings and as they lay back on the bed he said. 'How am I going to play music for two hours again tonight and talk to people for another two? I'm wrecked.'

'It will make sure you have an early night instead of chasing young ones, or maybe your girlfriend's sister,' she said suspiciously.

He felt the dig in her voice as he thought of his date tonight with Brenda and the fact that she may want to dance for the two-hour break with him. He got a cab for Helen, then hurried back to the room so he could get a couple of hour's sleep before the gig. Even though he was hungry sleep was more important, so he put the do not disturb sign on the door before passing out and when the phone rang later it was Mike.

'How's the flu?' he asked.

'Am I supposed to have the flu?' Ned asked himself, then on autopilot he answered.

'I'm OK I think, I got a marvellous sleep and now I need food.'

'The stretch is leaving in ninety minutes,' said Mike, really sounding American again. To the lads back in Ireland that would be an hour and a half, but as the Manager would say. 'This is the good old U.S.A.'

All the musicians were in the diner when he got there, so he wasn't surprised to hear them all say. 'We think you were riding all day.'

'Yeah,' he answered, 'but tell no one ya-hear.' He was now trying to sound like Mike.

'Come on head, who is the latest conquest for Ned the Bed?' It was Conn trying to make it into a song.

Ned smiled and took the slagging, because he knew it was the best way to make it go away. 'Tell me about the tour lads?' he asked.

They all tried to answer at once but Mickey Joe shouted. 'Shush, I'll tell him, it's fucking unbelievable, you're driving along in the bus and you can see all colours, then you turn a corner and everybody is fucking black, that's called Harlem, a little bit further on you turn another corner and you think you're in fucking China!'

Someone butted in with. 'And that's called China-Town Ned!'

'Shut up to fuck,' said the guide, 'there was a man lying on the footpath in China-Town with a million flies on his bandaged leg, but nobody was passing any remarks. Then we came to a part called The Bowery and the bus driver said that the people lying on the streets could have been Bishops, Lawyers, Doctors, or from any walk of life, who hit on bad times through drink, drugs or gambling.'

'Did you see any Showband members on the street in The Bowery?' asked Ned.

'No, we're all too fucking mean to ever end up there,' said the Singer with a sarcastic laugh.

'Speak for yourself,' said John the Bass man.

'Did anyone get grabbed by the stones?' Ned asked, looking at the Roadie who blushed readily.

'Don't you start,' the Roadie answered. 'I'd say there was a better chance of that happening in your room.'

'I swear the guy is physic,' Ned thought and smiled.

Their third gig in the City Plaza Ballroom was even bigger than the previous two. Ned was feeling much better after the food, but what was making him feel a lot calmer was the fact that Helen would probably not be there. Her boyfriend hated dancing and was jealous of her dancing with anyone else, but of course there was the slight possibility that he might go home early and if so she would rush around to the venue having said she would like a repeat performance. He decided to deal with that if and when it happened, but for the moment he would get on with the gig and keep an eye out for Brenda who he could hardly wait to see. He wondered what she would be wearing, having said that she would wear her blue dress to give him the opportunity to remove it, but seeing he had done that in her apartment the night before he had a feeling she would be in some creation he had not yet seen. Sure enough, halfway through their first session to the left of the bandstand she stood in all her glory, dressed in a beautiful red trouser suit no bun, her lovely fair hair cascading over her shoulders. She gave a little curtsey to get his approval, then turned and made way to her vantage point on the big balcony.

'You must behave tonight,' was Ned's foremost thought as he crossed his fingers and hoped that Helen wouldn't show. The last note of their first session was still in the air as Ned prepared to jump down on to the floor, then from somewhere he got a tap on the shoulder.

'Sorry to cramp your style sham,' said Conn with a big smile, obviously enjoying doing just that as he handed Ned a list of future gigs in the Plaza and on the end a very important one for the lads themselves.

'The Manager of the Ballroom wants that done now and several times during our next session,' said Conn, as he jumped down and made a beeline for a young lady he was having relations with.

Ned looked up ruefully at Brenda and pointed to the note, and then he began to announce the list, which covered all the functions in the venue for the next two weeks, ending with. By special request, the return of The Nova's Showband, after an earlier appearance as special guests in the famous 'Carnegi Hall' and he felt a thrill run up his back at the mention of that awesome place.

'I wonder will Brenda come,' he thought, as he read out the list again, almost saying her name into the mike as his thoughts fused with the written words. He wondered what the lads would say if he had read out. 'And appearing two weeks from tonight at the amazing Carnegi Hall, the one and only, the sexy Brenda!' Jaysus, he'd never live that down, or she wouldn't be too crazy about it either he was thinking, as he jumped off the stage and headed for his love. They greeted each other with open arms like they hadn't met for years, as people milled around them going to and from their seats. The resident band had started playing a slow number so without a word he led her down to the dance floor and during the three-song set they moved approximately four feet, oblivious of all the other dancers.

'We would have been arrested for dancing like that at home,' he said to her in the taxi going back to her apartment in between kissing and groping, whilst this new cab driver feasted his eyes on Brenda's bra-less breasts, bared for the world to see. If the word gets out among the cab drivers, they'll all be queuing to pick up this Irish couple long after the Band has gone home.

'I didn't care if we were arrested,' she said. 'I was getting my rocks off on your leg and I was out of it.'

Ned learned even more that night about the many ways of lovemaking and as she skilfully moved from one position to the next she kept saying that she loved him, while sounding like she meant it. Then she asked, 'Do you love me Edward?'

'Of course I do,' he answered, but as the lust wound down doubts began creeping in. He started thinking again. 'How does Brenda know so much about making love, was she more experienced than she led him to believe years ago, why did she change so greatly towards him and how come she's now telling him she loves him?' While he was wondering they both fell asleep exhausted, Brenda waking only ten minutes before she started work.

'I didn't hear the clock,' she gushed, as she ran around getting herself ready. 'You can lie on, just pull the door after you when you leave and I'm sorry we'll have to wait ten long days for our next love-in.'

'I'm looking forward to it already,' he answered, as he watched this lovely woman slip into her attractive uniform. His doubts of the previous night began to slip away and he realised how real this lady was. Even without any make-up she looked a treat. Next he witnessed the creation of the bun and was fascinated as she wound her long fair hair around and around not one out of place, then she pinned it up and finished it off with a velvet ribbon to match her uniform.

'That's lovely,' he said from the bed.

'If you say any more I'll be back in there like a flash, meaning no work done today.'

As she said that she sat down on the side of the bed, gave him a quick hug coupled with peck on the cheek, then she was gone out the door leaving him nothing but the scent of nice perfume wafting through the air. He decided he would think a lot about her during his travels, and then drifted back to sleep and God knows he needed it. He got back to the Hotel to find most of the lads had headed off to their cousins in different cities and the only one left feeling very lonely was the Roadie.

'Am I glad to see you,' the latter shouted across the lobby. 'Amanda, that's my Italian American girlfriend has gone home to buffalo and I thought I was on my own in this big city.'

'Poor you,' said Ned while looking at his watch, 'just about now there's an invasion of the Bronx, Boston and Chicago, but you and me are off to Niagra Falls in the morning, via Buffalo.'

'You're coddin,' said the Roadie.

'No I'm not coddin, I've always wanted to see the falls and theres no time like the present.'

Chapter Six

The first bus to buffalo was at 5 am, so they got a cab to Grand Central Station and bought two tickets on Greyhound.

'Jaysus, this is a rough place,' said Ned and then he asked. 'What did Amanda say when you told her we were coming to Buffalo?'

'She was over the moon and told me she would organise a friend for you, if that's OK?'

'I don't think I'd be able,' said Ned ruefully. 'I told Brenda I was off to my two aunts in Philadelphia because we're gigging there on Thursday and even though I need the rest, I feel bad about lying to her, I miss her you know.'

Each band member had to bring his instrument to and from every gig and today was no different. Ned put his trusty trombone under the seat of the bus, because it wouldn't fit in the overhead bin where they had both put their travel bags containing the band uniform and a few shirts. The Roadie had to carry and look after the hand-outs/pictures and he commented on how lucky the Drummer was, as he only had to carry a snare drum and his sticks.

'It would be some problem for me if he had to bring the whole drum kit,' the Roadie was thinking out loud.

His girlfriend had booked them into a cheap Hotel which wouldn't eat into their funds and Ned proceeded to tell his mate all he had read about The Falls, including the Marilyn

Monroe movie he had seen back in Mulllymore a few years ago. The buzz was on. They both agreed it was a pity to leave all the empty rooms in The Woodlawn Hotel, which were available to them in case they were staying in the city, but the episode in 42nd Street had scared them off and they were glad to get out of town. The big reclining seats were like beds so our heroes slept all the way, arriving refreshed at the bus depot where they got a cab to the address given and were glad to see that it was really quite a nice place.

They took their bags into the reception area and began to book in, suddenly Ned roared.

'Jaysus, my fucking trombone, I left it under the seat in that bus, I'm fucked!'

The young receptionist looked shocked but asked. 'Can I help in any way sir?'

'Only if you're a trombone player,' said Ned, explaining to the girl what had happened?

She picked up the phone, dialled a number and when they heard the word police being mentioned they both panicked.

'Jaysus, we're in trouble now,' this time it was the Roadie robbing Ned's pet word.

'Did I hear you mention police?' Ned asked hesitantly.

'Oh, don't worry,' she replied, 'my boyfriend is a police man and he'll take you both to the depot where you'll find the bus you came up on.'

'That's very nice of him,' Ned said, 'but we're putting him to a lot of bother, with us being strangers and all.'

'Amanda is his cousin,' she continued 'and she thinks your friend is cute, so let's say he's doing it for her.'

Just then a police car roared up to the hotel siren blaring and a young cop got out. Running into the lobby he began talking to the receptionist, who in turn pointed to Ned and his friend.

When he came over he said. 'I guess you guys lost a horn on the bus, lets go git it.'

Ned did his introductions when they reached the car and as they got into the back the driver shouted.

'I'm Randy, this is Skip, welcome to Buffalo.' They barely had the doors closed when the driver put the pedal to the metal and screamed off down the road. 'We'll go to the Greyhound depot first to see if the bus is still there and if it's not, I guess we'll just chase it to where it's at,' said Skip.

Luckily the lads had the stubs of their tickets to prove which bus they were on and after about two miles straight out of a gangster movie; they pulled up to the Greyhound station.

'Thanks-be to fuck.' Ned whispered. 'I hope that fucking bus is still here, if it's not, these fellas are going to kill us in this fucking car.'

'Hold on guys,' it was Skip again. 'I'll go and check if that bus is still here, don't go away ya-hear.'

'I never thought my auld trombone would be the end of me,' he whispered to his friend, 'but if I don't get it back that will be the end of me anyway because I can't afford a new one. Aw fuck it, these lads are doing us a favour so don't complain or look scared.'

Skip came out shaking his head. 'The bus has gone to another town one hundred miles away, but the guy in there said they checked the overhead racks and found nothing.'

'I didn't put it on the overhead rack in case it might fall,' said Ned. 'If that happened it could bend the slide, so I put it underneath the back seat instead and sat over it all the way up here.'

Randy was revving up the car again and his partner was barely in when they took off after the bus. One thing the passengers noticed was, they were now going much faster than before with lights flashing, siren screaming and everyone scurrying out of their path, a look of bewilderment on peoples faces as the cop car didn't seem to be chasing anything.

'We gotta make up four minutes,' Skip said to Randy and the driver put the boot down further. The lads from Mullymore took one look at each other and slid down all the way in their seats until they could no longer see the road or any of the near misses they were having, as the engine noise became louder.

'I think I'm gonna shit myself,' said Ned.

'I think I have shit myself,' answered the Roadie. 'You know when a fart's not a fart, if you get what I mean.'

Ned was hoping this was not true when he heard both cops shouting. 'There's our God-damned bus guys,' then Skip turned around and he couldn't see anybody in the back seat, so his eyes moved slowly down to the two pathetic blokes who were grinning stupidly at him from floor level.

'Gee, were we going too fast for you guys?' he asked.

'Just a little, but we're OK now,' volunteered Ned.

The slightly shocked bus driver was now slowing down at the cop's request and the passengers were all talking like a gaggle of geese.

'They probably think there's a drug dealer on board, heading for the Canadian border,' Randy, the man of few words had spoken.

'You gotta come on the bus and identify this horn of yours,' said Skip, as he jumped out of the car and got on board with Ned close behind, the Roadie a tight third.

Just then, Ned remembered something that almost made him abandon the whole idea. 'Jaysus, my fucking copy of Playboy is in the bone case and it's unwrapped, I could be put in jail for carrying that kind of magazine here in Buffalo.'

At that moment, Skip was taking this long, grey, shaped, case from underneath the seat and the passengers panicked.

'It's a machine gun,' one lady whispered to her friend, 'and those two men are Irish, I've just heard them speak.'

'Everybody please calm down,' requested Skip, 'it's only a trombone and this good gentleman from Ireland is going to play a tune for y'all, just to prove it ain't a shooter.' Then under his breath he said to Ned while he thrust the case into his arms.

'Take the fucking thing out and play it or we're gonna have a problem with these people.'

Luckily the back cover of the magazine was towards them, so he quickly slipped it underneath the bone and grabbing the mouthpiece he rapidly assembled the instrument, then slamming the lid he put the trombone to his lips. The only tune he could think of was, 'When the saints go marching in' and over the noise he could hear the lady saying. 'Oh Thank God it's not a machine gun.'

'It's twice as dangerous,' the Roadie shouted into Ned's ear.

He gave him a dirty look and kept blowing, then as he finished his 'solo' the doubtful crowd applauded. He gave a long over the top bow and said. 'Thank you, Thank you,' then he turned his back to everyone and put the instrument back in the case.

Just as he was thanking God, Skip winked at him saying. 'You must give me a look at your Playboy magazine, they haven't got that issue in Buffalo yet.'

'I suppose that's why they're called cops, they cop everything,' those were his thoughts as they went back to the car.

On request, they drove much slower back to the hotel and used the time to get to know each other. As it happened, both men were jazz musicians, one a Drummer, the other a Clarinet/Sax player and unknown to our two heroes, Amanda had booked a table for that night at the Jazz Club where they were playing.

'You gotta get up tonight and join our band,' said Skip. 'We don't have a regular bone player so consider yourself hired, anyway, Jane your blind date will be impressed.'

They dropped the two lads at the hotel telling them to be ready by 8, as they would be back to pick them up along with Skip's girlfriend the receptionist.

'You got your horn then,' she said, when they came into the lobby.

'Oh yes, thanks to you and the two police men, only for your quick thinking I probably would have lost it forever, I owe you one,' he said.

'Not at all,' she bantered, 'keep it for Jane.'

Ned and his mate went to their rooms and on the way he couldn't keep from wondering what this Jane would look like. He also found himself looking forward to playing a bit of jazz with some strangers, as the opportunity seldom arose around Mullymore. They had a few hours to kill and both agreed that the best place to do just that was in bed, after they had asked for a call from reception. The two Irish guys as they were now known, got to the lobby at 7.55 to be greeted by a host of smiling faces and Ned did a quick scan in an effort to pick out Jane. He could see Amanda whom he had met in New York, Skip was there with his Girlfriend and Randy the cop plus two lovely strangers, one a blonde, the other auburn haired. I hope the latter is Jane he was thinking, as he held out his hand to the sound of Randy making the introductions.

He introduced the blonde first. 'Ned, this is Jane.'

She smiled and pumped his hand as a little bit of disappointment struck him.

Then Randy said. 'Ned, this is also Jane.'

He took the bull by the horns and thumped his chest asking. 'Me Tarzan, which is my Jane?'

Amidst howls of laughter, the auburn haired girl stepped forward hand outstretched and said. 'Me your Jane, do you approve?'

'Me approve big time,' he said, 'but how do I know you guys are not pulling my leg?'

'This is all the proof you need,' said Randy, as he took the blonde in his arms and gave her a big kiss.

'That's good enough for me,' said Ned, kissing the back of his blind dates hand.

'Oh how gallant,' she said, smiling shyly and he thought he got a hint of an English accent in there somewhere.

Skip took over arrangements for travel and there were two huge cars outside, no lights flashing, and no sirens. As they were about to get in Randy asked.

'Where's your slip-horn Ned? Your not getting out of jamming with us tonight.'

'Jaysus,' came the reply. 'I've forgotten it again.'

Then Skip addressed the company. 'Ned always forgets his horn, I wonder how many more times that will happen before he gets to Philly on Thursday?'

They were laughing loudly as he ran back inside to get his trombone. 'She's nice,' he was thinking, as he carefully removed Playboy from the bone case and put it in his travel bag. 'If I hadn't bought that magazine, I wouldn't have met a single bird,' he mused, then. 'I wonder does she wear a leopard skin leotard like Tarzan's Jane? Yummy, yummy.'

He held the back door of Skip's car as the gorgeous Jane got in and as usual, his eyes were glued to her legs. 'I think they're the best pair of legs I've seen for a while and look at the style.' 'I'm a fierce lucky so and so to be in a band, otherwise I'd never get a woman.' All these thoughts were flooding his mind, as the big car headed off down the road with loads of chitchat passing between the others.

'You're very quiet Ned, has the cat got your tongue?' she asked, looking concerned.

'If I told you what I was thinking, you'd laugh at me,' he replied.

'Try me,' she answered, putting her ear over to his mouth so no one else would hear.

'Here goes,' he thought, as he blurted out everything that had gone on in his mind since he saw her. How he had hoped the auburn haired girl was Jane, how beautiful he thought she was including the legs, how elegantly she was dressed and how he couldn't resist a good looking woman in high heels. The truth always works. He could see from the streetlights that she was smiling and he decided to behave with this lovely lady so he didn't try to kiss her.

Then they heard Skip's voice again. 'We're here.'

The deep drone of the engine ceased just as he was thinking. 'You're in deep trouble here old son, your falling in love again but this lady is out of your league, so cop yourself on now, OK.' He helped her out of the car and they walked hand in hand into the club where a four-piece band was already playing.

'I'm in more trouble now,' he thought, as he listened to a band, which sounded like the Dave Bruebeck Quartet, so he tapped Skip on the shoulder and said. 'I can't play this kind of jazz, I've only ever jammed in Dixieland type outfits.'

'Don't panic,' said Skip, 'we only play Dixieland ourselves and we just jam, you didn't leave your trombone in the car again did you?'

'Yeah, I didn't want to bring it in until we're ready to start, anyway, my mind is not on music tonight,' he addressed the last part of the sentence to Jane.

'Come on lets join the others,' she said, as she strode to a table up front.

'All the drinks are on the house,' Randy informed him, 'that's how they pay all the musicians who play here, we just do it for practice so what's your poison Ned?'

The drinks came and the jokes were flying. Then the band played Take Five and Randy said. 'I've got a joke about that, what did the cab driver say to Dave Bruebeck's roadie?'

'We don't know,' was the basic answer from everyone.

'He said I'm sorry, I can't take five.'

Everyone laughed and Ned wondered if Randy had made it up on the spot. Just then four men came over to the table and they were introduced as the other members of the band. Trumpet, Bass, Banjo/Guitar plus Piano and three of them were also cops, so when the first band introduced their last number they said.

'In a few moments you will have on stage 'The Bobby Stompers' and tonight, they've got a trombone player from three thousand miles away, all the way from Ireland, so we're all looking forward to that!'

'There was loud applause from the room, and then a spotlight settled on Ned who had to get up and take a bow.

'How did that happen?' asked the Roadie, thankfully leaving out the word fuck.

'I told the guys in the band earlier and I also pointed Ned out to the guy on sound and lights, nobody from that far away has played here before,' said Skip proudly. 'I'll go git the trombone.'

Ned was wondering how he would gel with these strange musicians, so he decided to take it handy and not try to be a hero. He was also hoping that he wouldn't screw up in front of Jayne, who he now knew spelled her name with a Y.

'Jayne, Jayne,' he kept saying it over in his mind. 'I like it with a Y,' he said, after finding out.

'Oh go on, you're just a flatterer,' she answered.

Randy was the M.C for the band and in his intro he said. 'The first number will be Ned's choice, a tune this guy really loves, he likes it so much he plays it at all his gigs and has been known to play it on the bus without accompaniment, much to the delight of the passengers. I know, I was there, and folks the tune is. When the saints go marching in, hope you like it.'

The entire band knew the story of the bone on the bus and they were breaking their sides laughing as they started playing. They all took solos as the tune continued indefinitely, but these guys were great musicians and the old number took on a new identity. For the third solo they pointed at Ned shouting.

'OK Irish, do your thing!'

He went for it as best he could, while thankfully everyone seemed happy with his effort, but he himself could hear the difference in the flow and he was glad when they shouted.

'OK, take it Loaf,' and now they were pointing at the Piano player.

It was unbelievable what this man could do with a piano; he must have incorporated every chord that was ever written into that old standard and the crowd got to their feet, applauding all the way through.

'The Loaf is a mean dude,' said the Trumpet player, as he clapped along with all the others.

'Why do you call him The Loaf?' Ned asked amid the din.

'Cause he's a baker by trade and makes the best loaf in town, piano playing is just a sideline.'

Ned felt like quitting music that night. Even though he enjoyed himself immensely, he felt real guilty at the fact that he was the only professional musician there, yet they could all play rings round him and to top it all you had The Loaf, he was something else.

'You were all great,' chorused the girls afterwards.

'You did well Ned,' said Jayne and your singing was good too.'

'Honestly Jayne, those musicians are in a league of their own, I'm only trotting after them I'm afraid.'

The club was really a big friendly pub where everybody seemed to know everybody and they talked for ages after the gig until Skip announced.

'OK, work tomorrow guys, we've gotta go home now but we're all off to The Falls tomorrow evening.' 'We can't have these Irish guys travelling by bus on their own again, God knows what might happen.'

Ned took Jaynes hand while he asked her if she would come on the trip to The Falls and she willingly agreed, but he knew she was different. There would be no shafting with this lady and to be honest he was glad for a change. The Roadie had a quick cuddle with Amanda, Ned got a hug and a tiny kiss from Jayne, then Randy took the girl's home leaving Skip to bring the lads and his girlfriend back to the hotel where they went at once to their rooms.

On the way up the Roadie asked. 'Well, what do you think?'

Ned thought for a moment. 'We're getting away with murder in The Nova's Showband, because we can't play skittles compared to those fellas. As long as my arse looks down, I'll never be able to play like that trumpet player and he's a cop, not even in Show Business, then where do you leave The Loaf?'

'He was something else,' volunteered the Roadie. 'He would eat our fellows like one of his own loaves.'

'They may call him The Loaf, but you couldn't call him a loafer,' said Ned, 'so lets hit the hay then we can get up early and have a look at this town.' 'Goodnight.'

'Goodnight,' said the Roadie, with a loud yawn.

Ned drifted off to sleep trying to work out his womanising problem. The question being, was it becoming a problem and if so what repercussions would it have. Then he remembered Belfast and came to the conclusion that he may as well avail of ladies being interested in him on stage, because they would be few and far between when it was all over, anyway a drink problem would be worse. The next he knew he was being called for breakfast and his last thought came back as he was shaving, prompting comments like. 'Jaysus, the Belfast women were right, you are an ugly fucker and you're perfect for a Showband, just like the back of a crashed bus.' Then he grinned, thinking out loud. 'Thank God for that auld trombone.'

After a nice breakfast, the tourists bought a pair of sightseeing tickets and headed off on the bus, full of the joys of life.

'I'd say theres a lot of cousins pissed off with each other by now, in the Bronx, Boston and Chicago,' volunteered the Roadie.

'Yeah, and my two aunts in Philadelphia are really pissed off with me by now I'd say, seeing I was supposed to be there yesterday. My dad made me promise to visit them, because they never married and he says they're both loaded.'

'If that was me I'd be there,' said the Roadie.

'And what would you tell your Amanda,' countered Ned. 'You told me you were getting your Nat King Cole off her, it didn't look much like that last night.'

The Roadie got very red and blurted out. 'I had to put on an act in front of the lads, the fact is, she won't let me do anything only kiss her but I think she's on a turtle with me.' (Turtle in the lingo meaning, Turtle Dove, i.e. Love).

'That's great,' said Ned. 'I wish Jayne was on a turtle with me, she's very nice and I'm wondering what she does for a living?'

'She's a trainee Lawyer,' he answered. 'Amanda told me that's how Skip and his mates know her, they have all met in Court.'

'That explains it,' he said, 'after all I could be better off with her company than my two aunts, because one day she'll be loaded and she's a lot better looking than my aunts.'

'Fuck me Ned,' was the reply, 'that's the most stupid thing I've ever heard you say, you only know her a wet day and you're living off her already.'

'Having heard those part-time musicians play last night, I've realised I'll probably need someone to live off in the not to distant future.'

Then they said in unison. 'I can't get over that fucking Loaf.'

Something of interest cropped up on the trip, so they stopped talking and started listening to the courier instead, who told them there had been a shooting earlier during an attempted robbery, but there was no more information about it on the radio. The bus went all over the town and they saw some nice parks and some awful places, then the Roadie nudged Ned in a real rough part of town and said.

'I think this must be the Buffalo's arse, because it smells like it.'

They had a mid-day snack on the tour and at 4 on the dot; they got back to their hotel. Jenny the receptionist was waiting for Skip all dressed up and she told them that her lover had been shot at earlier that day during a Post Office raid, but he was OK.

'We heard that news earlier on the bus, but they gave no names,' the Roadie enthused.

'Skip's friend is coming along and he's taking his mini-bus.' Jenny informed them. 'We'll have a wonderful time.'

Later, a big red mini-bus nosed up to the hotel with everyone else on board and the last three passengers climbed in. Ned was thrilled to see that Jayne had kept a seat for him next to her and as he sat down they both pecked each other on the cheek.

'Did you have a nice day?' She asked.

'Yes we did thank you and how was your day Jayne?' He loved saying her name and she had noticed.

'Oh, the usual Ned,' she answered, and then she leaned over and whispered in his ear. 'Can I call you Eddie or Edward instead of Ned?'

'What's up here?' He was sussing as he put his mouth over to her gorgeous ear. 'Only when were alone,' he answered with a grin. 'Love the perfume and the ear.' Realising she might be a bit surprised by his answer, he set about explaining the situation one more time. 'It's not the first time I've had that request, but the only person who calls me Edward is my mother and anytime my mates hear it they go, Mama's boy or even worse, so that's why it can only happen in private, I'm really sorry.'

'OK,' she said, 'but it may take a while before I get the opportunity of calling you Edward.' She just whispered the last word in case anyone heard it.

Her last comment gave him food for thought and then he heard the conversation going on about Skip's close call earlier that day. 'It whistled past my ear,' he was saying, 'but I stuck a couple of slugs in him and he was no trouble.'

'Did you kill him Skip?' queried the Roadie.

'No, I just put one in his gun hand, the other one may create problems next time he tries to make love.'

Ned pre-empted the Roadie's next question so he cut in with. 'We did a Freddy Weller song about that one time called 'The Ballad of a Hillbilly' and he gets shot there! The words are, (the bullet didn't kill him, but it made darn sure he'd never love no more). We recorded it one time and the studio engineer just called it. (Shot in the Balls' take one, two or three).'

'Did you record it Ned?' he was asked, then he had to explain why not and Randy said. 'If that guy was singing with us he'd get shot in the balls instead.'

'I do attempt to sing it though and if you all join in the chorus, I'll warble it for you,' Ned offered. They gave him a big hand to get him going and he said, 'You won't be clapping when it's over.'

It was a beautiful evening for travelling and everyone was singing at the top of their voices. Randy's girlfriend Jane was a marvellous country singer, equal to any voice in Nashville and as the time passed she was the main attraction. The lads noticed that instead of saying cheers, they all shouted chug-a-lug when they were handed a can of beer before raising it to theirs lips and it had become apparent that the blonde Jane was known as Mabel, so Ned decided to ask why.

'Yeah,' said Randy. 'She drinks Black label all the time so we christened her Mabel, do you like her singing?'

'She's great,' said Ned and the Roadie was busy nodding his approval.

There was a short silence after Jane's song, then Ned could hear someone else singing. 'Drink chug-a-lug, chug-a-lug, chug-a-lug, Drink chug-a-lug, chug-a-lug, and as he scanned the mini-bus he realised it was the driver.

'Are you making that up as you go along?' he asked.

'No, I ain't,' came the reply. 'Some guy from Buffalo had a minor hit with it a couple of years ago, but he failed to get a major record deal so it died, I think he also died probably from disappointment.'

'That's a pity because it sounds good. Jaysus, that was a sign for Niagra Falls, we're here!' Ned exclaimed.

Sure enough, over on their right were the famous roaring rapids, with white churning foam leaping into the air.

'Just imagine, a baby went over that in it's pram one time and survived,' said the Roadie.

'You're full of surprises,' said Ned, 'who told you that?'

'Oh, I read it in a paper once,' came what sounded like a well-informed answer.

Skip confirmed this to be true and the Roadie looked as proud as a dog with two pricks.

'I'm not as stupid as I look,' he proclaimed, realising his mistake as he spoke. The foolhardy slip up went unnoticed in the excitement, as they piled out of the mini-bus and ran over to the perimeter wall, which was fortified with mesh wire being held in place by steel poles.

'My God they're beautiful,' said Ned. 'Just imagine anything so fierce being so stunning.'

'Do you like beautiful things?' Jayne asked.

She was standing beside him, her lovely nose protruding through the mesh when he saw the opportunity; so moving behind her he slipped his arms around her waist and pressed his cheek against hers.

'I think you know the answer to that already,' he replied.

He could have stayed like that forever, smelling her perfume, feeling her body breathe with him and the touch of her hands as they moved on top of his. His brain was in turmoil knowing he could have said anything to her at that moment and meant it, and then someone shouted.

'OK you two, less of that, would you both turn around until we take your picture?'

The cameras were out even though the light was failing and flashes were going off all over. Jayne didn't seem to want to break free, so they both turned around together.

'OK everyone, say Chug-a-lug,' ordered the amateur photographers.

'What ever happened to cheese?' Ned wanted to know.

They all decided not to go down into the tunnels as Ned and the Roadie were a bit daunted by the idea, anyway it was much nicer up top, especially after dark when all the lights started flashing. Their multi-coloured beams were cutting through each other and on to the torrent cascading over the edge. The two Irish lads agreed it was by far the most sensational sight they had ever seen, and then Jayne said.

'When I came to Buffalo first I came here every weekend for ages, but I'm still fascinated by the sight.

Ned was in like a flash. 'Where was it that you came from?' he asked.

'Oh, I'm from Surrey in England which is just outside London, my dad is with the British Government and he was posted here ten years ago, it only seems like yesterday.'

'Do you miss Surrey?' Ned asked.

'Not anymore,' she replied. 'I love it here.'

'I was thinking I got a hint of an English accent when we met yesterday,' he said. 'It's nice.'

'I thought I had lost it all, but living with my parents who still sound like they never left Britain, probably explains it,' she answered. 'Anyway, enough about me, I like your brogue Ned.'

He wondered if she had ever heard of the Ben-Lang but he decided that now was not the time to unleash that on her, it might make him look foolish so he'd leave well enough alone for now. They headed for a nice Bar/Restaurant overlooking the falls after all the photographs and spent the most enjoyable couple of hours he had ever had. The Roadie was having a ball with Amanda; they had paired off with the mini-bus owner George and his girlfriend Hilda. George was a luxury coach driver and him and the Roadie were matching journeys they had driven in one night, then when George mentioned a one thousand-mile round trip the Roadie gave up the ghost.

'I wouldn't be able for that.' he admitted.

After the meal, they moved to a lovely bar giving them full view of the falls, which matched every colour in the rainbow as the spotlights penetrated the thrashing foam. The singing started again after the mini-bus owner had brought his acoustic guitar in and he played with ease. Jane began with the latest Dolly Parton hit and if you closed your eyes you would think it was the great lady herself.

'I wonder what Cynthia Rose would say if she heard her?' asked the Roadie.

'I'm sure she would feel the same as I did last night after jamming with the lads, she'd want to quit,' said Ned.

Everyone in the bar loved her and someone from Norway requested a song by The Brown's, called Little Jimmy Brown. 'Ve are wery big country music fans in Norvay,' he offered.

The coach driver struck up the song and Jane began to sing harmony, and then from somewhere in the bar came the tightest third vocal line imaginable. Everybody looked around in the direction of this latest blending voice and Ned was agog when he saw it was emanating from his friend Jayne.

'Jaysus,' he muttered to the Roadie. 'Even the lawyer's are outsinging the professionals, the bus driver sounds like Jim Ed Brown and he's great on the guitar, Jane and Jayne sound like his sisters Maxine and Bonny and I still can't get over The Loaf.' The applause was huge for the song and suddenly all eyes were on Jayne, who shyly agreed to sing the latest Emmy-lou Harris hit.

The Roadie was next, but with both hands in the air shouting no, he pointed to Ned saying. 'He'll sing 'The Haunted House' for you, he sang it on the plane on the way over and it went down great.'

'Ned played the trombone on the bus and it went down great as well,' they all shouted.

His version of the song must have made everybody aware of the time, so reluctantly they all traipsed back to the minibus to head home. The Norwegian's got and gave phone numbers to everyone and promised to call or write and as they walked to the coach Jayne said.

'I've enjoyed our time together and I want to say that you are a real gentleman, so I hope we can stay in touch if that's OK.'

He felt like telling her the truth about all his women, but knew it would be a mistake and he realised that it would be another kiss on the cheek night tonight.

'By all means, lets keep in touch and I think when a man meets a lady he should always behave like a gentleman.' he said.

That last comment worked and there was some kissing on the journey but nothing heavy, and in no time at all, they were in front of the Irish lads hotel where Ned remembered something he had wanted to ask all evening.

'I've got a question,' he announced, 'can anyone tell me the name of Marilyn Monroe's co-star in the black and white movie Niagra?'

'I know that,' Skip enthused, it was a guy called Joseph Cotton.'

'Oh Thank you Skip,' said Ned, as he pumped the other mans hand. 'That would have kept me awake all night.'

While they were saying their farewells, Amanda and the Roadie ran around the corner for some privacy and Jayne (who had got out to stretch her legs as she said) walked with

Ned to the door holding his hand. They looked almost shyly at each other as they stood face-to-face hands outstretched and it was he who broke the silence.

'I'll never forget these two days and I promise I'll never forget you, you beautiful woman.'

'Just make sure you don't,' she said, as she put her arms around his neck and kissed him softly.

This was one of the many times he could feel a stirring in his loins since he met Jayne and each time he fought it, but not this time as he unashamedly felt his hard-on grow against her tummy. It was a long kiss with Ned keeping his tongue in check, proving the respect he had for this woman. He knew that she knew the condition he was in so he would let that do the talking, then taking her lips from his while still holding his body close enjoying the feeling, she said.

'I'll remember these two days also Edward, there, I've said it and it sounds good.'

'It's the way you say it that makes it sound good and I hope it's not too long until you call me that again,' he said, as his voice blended into another kiss which they both knew would be the last one for now. She stood at arms length smiling, then turned and strode the few feet to the coach. At that moment, the Roadie came around the corner with Amanda having said their goodbyes, she gave Ned a quick hug before running to the bus and they all waved while the vehicle drove away.

The grinning Roadie looked Ned up and down as he said. 'I'd say your glad now that you bought a copy of Playboy, which by the way I want to borrow in the morning and from what I see, you won't be able to blame Joseph Cotton for keeping you awake tonight.' Then he got another brainwave. 'You know the way you're always talking the Ben-Lang, apples and pears, barley and wheat, daisy roots, well from now on a hard-on will be known as a Joseph Cotton, OK!'

'That's funny alright,' said Ned, 'now I'm away to shake hands with Mr Joseph Cotton, Goodnight.'

'Goodnight,' said the Roadie, in fits of laughter.

The aforementioned gentleman obviously got by without borrowing Playboy and was in a happy mood at the breakfast table when Ned got there. 'Amanda has just phoned and asked me back next Monday, Tuesday and Wednesday, will you come?' he asked, and then he continued with. 'I think next week might be the time to introduce Joseph.'

'You're going to kill your new saying if you keep going on about it,' said Ned. 'Anyway, I'll have to wait until I'm asked and next week is planned with the cousins in Boston.'

They talked mostly about The Falls, also of the fantastic talents they had witnessed, then Ned's thoughts drifted back to Jayne and how gorgeous she was. He decided he would give all his girlfriends marks from one to ten and when he was settled on the flight to Philadelphia he began, after he had re-checked that his trombone was on board. The Roadie was surprised when he didn't forget it.

'When I went to my room last night, I stood it behind the door so I couldn't get out without it, that's my new strategy.'

Never having tried this ratings idea before, he was having great fun with it so he created a great sex category, another good kisser degree, one for the worst court on the face of the earth and a most beautiful turtle dove class, the latter which Jayne kept winning with Brenda a close second. In fact he had to give Jayne eleven as Brenda always seemed to be getting ten. Helen kept winning the best sex section because of the get-together in the shower, with Patricia close behind for her performance on the flight over and The Woodlawn Hotel sessions. He couldn't help wondering where he would feature if it were the girls who were grading him.

'I probably wouldn't feature at all,' he groaned, just before falling asleep.

They got to Philadelphia by noon and Ned made sure they had all their bits and pieces off the flight before hailing a cab to take them to their hotel for the night. On arrival they discovered they were first so they went ahead and booked in, explaining that the members were coming from all different directions so they must be sure and hold the rooms.

'You bet we will,' said the receptionist. 'The rooms are all paid for in advance, so even if you guys didn't show we would still hold them.'

Both lads panicked for a minute. 'What would you do if the lads didn't make it?' the Roadie quizzed.

'Well,' said Ned. 'I'd lock the door to my room, drag the biggest piece of furniture behind it so that no one could get in, then I'd stay as quiet as a mouse until tomorrow morning and make a run for the Airport. Why, what would you do?'

'I'd be mouse number two and make sure you didn't go to the Airport without me,' he answered.

'You hold the fort here and I'll go to my aunts, just make sure you bring the bone to the gig when the transport comes later,' said Ned, 'this is the phone number I'll be at.' He noticed that the Roadie looked a bit lost outside the hotel as they called a cab, so he continued with. 'Ring me if there's a problem,' then he got in and sped away.

His aunts were glad to see him, only giving him a minor telling off for not showing sooner.

'Oh Edward, you've got so big since we saw you last in Mullymore, how is that brother of ours, and your poor mother? She's a saint for staying with him you know, because he's never at home with that bloody pub to look after.'

They both sounded like they had never left home while they got all the news from him, but he made loads of things up just to satisfy their hunger, later, he had a lovely dinner which both ladies cooked and it couldn't have come at a better time.

'We didn't bother getting any wine in Edward, because your mother told us in her last letter that you don't drink.'

'Yes, that's true.' 'I never got the taste for it so I don't miss it,' he lied, wishing there was a big bottle of wine to wash down that lovely grub.

At 6 o'clock on the dot the phone rang and it was the Roadie. 'Bad news Ned,' he said. 'No sign of Mike or the Singer, you'd better get back here soon, a few of the lads are shittin' bricks!'

The aunts knew it was bad news and the older one offered. 'We'll say the Rosary, it never fails no matter what the problem is.'

Now Ned really panicked. Even though his mother tried hard, it had been some time since he had been involved in saying the Rosary and he knew he would be caught out if that happened, so he said.

'Auntie, you go ahead and say the Rosary by all means, but I'll have to get back to the hotel to hold things together, thanks for looking after me so well and I'll ring you later.' As he got in the cab, he was thinking of the Holy Water his mother splashed on him the night he went to Belfast and he felt terrible about dodging the Rosary, but it would be much worse if he had joined in and messed up the words.

Imagine the letter that would go off the next day. 'That son of yours is a heathen, he wasn't able to say the Hail Mary and we're surprised at you his sainted mother, for letting him forget his prayers. The Holy Water worked though, I may have failed to get a woman in Belfast, but I got home safely.'

The Roadie was waiting for him outside the hotel door and he looked really happy when he saw Ned getting out of the cab. 'They're up in Mickey Joe's room and the fucks out of them are fierce,' he said.

As Ned passed the desk the receptionist shouted at him. 'Your manager is on the phone.'

'Is everyone there?' Mike enquired.

'No, that wanker of a Singer hasn't shown and where the fuck are you? There's gonna be a lot of brown trousers tonight and I'm heading up to Mickey Joe's room now,' said Ned.

'Well, the answer to your question of ages ago is, I'm at Philly Airport and I'll be there in an hour, you all head to the venue, I'll go to the hotel.'

'All right, you can try to track him down from here,' he said.

When he walked into the room, they were all sitting around with long faces like they were blaming him.

'Where the fuck were you?' Asked Conn.

'I was here before you,' he answered caustically, 'then I went to visit my aunts but you knew that already, did the Chanter mention any plans to any of you?'

'He said he might go to Nashville,' offered John the Bass man, the only member the Singer really confided in.

'He's probably doing duets with Loretta Lynn instead of Conway Twitty,' said the Drummer, real sarcastically.

'Did you ever consider that he might have been run over by a bus somewhere?' Ned asked. 'That would be a lot worse, he could always get away from Loretta for the weekend, but not from under a bus.'

Some of the lads looked like they hoped the bus scenario might be true and he thought that was very 'Alan Ladd' as he would say.

'Mike is on his way from the Airport and our transport is due about now,' he added, 'so lets get to this venue and do a sound check, Mike will find our Lost chord.'

'That's a good handle for yer-man,' said the Drummer. 'From now on he's the Lost Chord.'

'He won't like it,' said John.

'Fuck him,' they chorused, 'if he doesn't show we'd better dig up some old songs to fill the gap.'

The lads did their sound check and said nothing to anyone about being a man short, then with half an hour to go, a call came from Mike to say that the Singer was at the Airport and would be making his way to the venue.

'What went wrong Mike?' Ned asked.

'It seems he bought a ticket from New York to Nashville and instead of getting one from Nashville to Philly he got one back to New York, then he had to find a connecting flight to get here and there was only one, so he had to wait until now.' Mike answered.

'Jaysus, he cut it fine,' was the opinion.

The resident group played an extra number but it wasn't enough, so The Nova's Showband had to go on.

'He'll probably bounce on later like Elvis and try to make it look as if it was planned,' said Conn with venom. 'I hope he doesn't get any ideas from it the Bollix.'

The band was playing it's fourth number, not yet feeling the pressure when Ned noticed the late arrival in the wings and he looked as if he was waiting for a big introduction.

'That's what he thinks,' he opined, as he announced the Guitar man to sing.

The Singer got the message and stepped in beside the Drummer who immediately attacked him verbally. He didn't wait for much of that, so he came to the front and began moving with the band to the tempo of the song. Ned called an end to the first selection of numbers and to save a battle on the stage, he announced the next dance with the Lead Singer starting off on vocal.

'They can't harass him when he's singing,' he concluded sensibly.

The gig was great and Ned was so keyed up by what he sensed would happen afterwards; he failed to check out the female situation.

'I've got to be around to stop a possible riot in the changing room afterwards,' he judged, then while he was still talking to punters he heard the roars coming from out back, so he excused himself and ran through the curtain. 'Not in public lads,' he hissed. 'Keep whatever it is until later.'

'Whatever it is my arse,' said Conn. 'I want to know what kept him now, not later.'

'I'm afraid it will have to be later,' said Ned, 'there are people out there who are aware of this fracas and if you don't shut up I'll fuck you out through the back door, just try me.'

The sax player calmed down on hearing the leader's remedy. He had seen Ned in a few scrapes and he took no prisoners, things would be sorted quietly later. It was like a morgue in the mini-bus on the way back to the hotel, so much so that the driver asked.

'Did someone die who was related to you guys, or is there a bust up in the band?'

Ned was sitting in the front passenger seat so he decided to answer. 'Well, you're close on both counts, there's a bit of aggravation going on at the moment which could end up with someone belonging to someone dying, but it's nobody outside the band and few will care.'

The driver looked surprised at Ned's off hand explanation so he decided to leave it alone and dead silence closed in again. As they climbed out the leader said loudly.

'OK, everyone to room 505 and we'll sort this out now.'

They had brought a few beers back, so for a minute of two all that could be heard were popping sounds and as they called it in Buffalo, the Chug-a-lug of beer flowing down gullets, then Ned eyeballed the Singer and asked. 'Where were you?'

'I went to Nashville,' he answered, flashing the used return ticket as proof, and then he began to spoof. 'I was on the Grand Old Oprey, sang three songs and I went down a bomb.'

'Is that the American version of going a bomb? Because if it is, that would mean you bombed, alias flopped.'

'That's auld jealousy, just because you'll never be on it, you don't want me to be able to say I done it.'

Ned saw red at that and felt like telling him about his bad grammar, but decided not to bother.

'I may never be on it,' he answered, but I know for a fact that most of the big stars only sing one song each night as there are so many trying to get on, plus all the commercials.'

All the lads were listening closely saying nothing, because Ned seemed to be doing fine and the Singer was about to put both feet in it.

'What do you mean by commercials?' He asked.

'Now I know you weren't even at the show,' said Ned, 'after almost every song someone reads a commercial because it goes out live on W.S.M. Radio, I thought you knew that, it's been like that since the year of dot!'

The Singer went purple and they all thought he would hit his inquisitor, probably hoping he would, instead he roared at them all. 'I can tell you fucker's nothing,' then he turned and stomped out of the room.

The bandleader beckoned to John and said. 'Go and bring him back, we've got plans to make for morning and no more mention of Nashville, OK!' The Bass player came back with a very subdued Singer and they sat down on the bed Ned continued.

'Mike, will you run over the plans for morning which is only a few hours away, then we must get some sleep.'

'The flight to L.A. is at 8am,' said the Manager, 'so we've got to leave here at 6.30, there can be no mishaps on this one and I believe some of you plan on going to Universal Studios on Saturday morning. We have a flight to San Francisco at 4pm Saturday and we can't fuck with that one either, so see you all 6.30. Goodnight.'

A very bleary eyed bunch struck out for the Airport that morning in the same mini-bus, with the same driver.

'I see you're still alive and together,' he ventured, but there was no reply.

The Roadie made sure Ned brought his trombone and someone asked Mike where were they staying in L.A.

'We're booked into a posh Motel on Sunset Boulevard with it's own pool and the lot,' he answered.

Guess what the Roadie asked as the driver looked at him in disbelief?

'What's a Motel Mike?' He was totally ignored.

The flight was smooth, so they all slept most of the way which was a godsend and when they arrived, another big limo was waiting. Ned was thinking that this Airport seemed to be the biggest so far, but after all this is Hollywood U.S.A. home of the big movie stars and what could you expect.

As they headed into town in the blazing heat Mike nudged the Roadie, pointed at a building and said. 'That's a Motel.'

The recipient of the knowledge was chuffed and said. 'Thanks Mike, those other arseholes are as thick as bedamned, they think they know it all but they're pure Paddies every one.'

'What's this about us being thick?' asked the Drummer.

'Oh, nothing, nothing,' answered the Roadie, realising he had had a close one.

Then the Drummer, who had been taking in the big movie billboards along the way, shouted at Ned. 'How do you like the *thrupps* on the *richard* on the poster Ned?'

'*Vegeregy negice,*' said Ned, eventhough he had seen nothing. Now you might wonder what the drummer was talking about in his last Ben-Lang offering, so let us explain. He was asking the Band Leader if he had seen the 'Treepenny (Truppenny) Bits, (Tits) on the Richard the third, (Bird) on the poster. Very nice was the answer.

The limo was at their disposal while they were in L.A, so the driver parked it and went to the bar. The lads got into the swing of things with some of them being really adventurous by dangling their feet in the pool, but Mike and the Lost Chord were the only ones with swimming togs so they got in and messed about. Ned couldn't find his togs before he left home and he concluded that his mother had probably hidden them. She didn't want him doing any of that dangerous swimming in America, where she couldn't sprinkle him with Holy Water like she used to in Whiterock, were they went every summer for the fortnights holiday. He lay on a poolside seat, his mind running over the happenings since they began the U.S. tour. So far it had been great, with all the horny women and the lovely serene Jayne to cap it all. He hadn't fully heeded Mike's advice about the rubbers so he hoped things would be OK and he also wondered if the Rosary had any bearing on the Singer making it on time for the gig.

'Ah, God's good,' he was thinking, as a pure apparition strolled past in a scanty bikini heading for the bar at the end of the pool and he started singing the old song 'Itsy bitsy teeny weeny, yellow polka dot bikini' as he hopped up to follow her. She had by now joined four men of different shapes and sizes at the end of the bar and was kissed by each one in turn.

The limo driver made his move and got to him before he got to her. 'Hold on amigo,' he said in a guttural voice, as he placed his hand gently but firmly on Ned's chest. 'You just come with me and we will have a conversation,' he said, as he propelled our misguided hero to a stool at the other end of the bar. 'She ees very nice yes, but she ees a gangster's moll like in the movies so you must stay away from her, comprende!'

Ned was quite shaken by events and for a moment he thought their driver was attacking him but it was worse when he was told of his close shave.

'My name is Juan and I come from Mehico, when I am very young, many time my hide has been saved by strangers before I know (what you say) the score.'

'Thank you Juan,' said our hero in a shaky voice, 'let me buy you a drink, my name is Ned.'

'Tequila,' Juan said to the barman, who immediately filled up three small glasses with a slightly golden liquid that Ned had not seen before, and then the Mexican had a pinch of salt with each drink.

'I won't try that,' he was thinking as he ordered an old reliable beer.

The four men at the other end of the bar seemed to be getting louder, so he took a quick glance in their direction. The big greasy one in a light shiny suit, who appeared to be called Big Joe, was trying to maul the bird in the bikini and she seemed to enjoy it, much to the displeasure of a thinner guy called Max. Then there was a fellow in a heavy suit sweating profusely as he egged Big Joe on and laughing at them all was a little guy without a jacket sitting on a high stool, his feet dangling six inches from the floor.

'You no look at them senor,' said Juan, the big one ees local Mafia, so ees the little one, the thin guy and the woman are Vegas Mafia and the man in the heavy suit, he ees in for the day from Chicago, they come here every week running drugs and prostitutes and they are very dangerous hombres.'

'I'd better warn the lads,' thought Ned, 'some of them might try what I tried, with no one around to do what the driver did for me.'

They were all using the Mafia lingo, calling a bird a *Boid*. One guy said, 'If you don't leave my *boid* alone, you're gonna get *hoit!*'

'*Soives* you right Big Joe,' said the little fellow.

'I don't think you *hoid* me,' said the thin man from Vegas.

'You're a nasty guy Big Joe,' said the sweaty man in the heavy suit.

'Let's go and see the stars hand prints,' Ned said to the driver, 'and the old Chinese Theatre.'

'Yes,' said Juan, 'it would be much safer than staying here.'

Mike booked them into the restaurant at 6 o'clock so they would have a little break before going to the gig. When the Singer came into the dining room he made a beeline for a vacant seat beside Ned, who was busy telling the lads about what he saw and heard earlier.

'If they come in here don't look at them, you could get shot,' he advised.

'That's fierce altogether,' commented the Roadie, followed by a shiver.

'Can I have a word?' Said a voice, which turned out to be that of the Lead Chanter.

They all waited thinking he was going to give his notice, and then he said. 'I'm sorry for being late last night, also for blowing up after the gig, but I was only kidding to see if I would get away with it and have one up on you fuckers for a change.'

'OK,' said Ned, 'apology accepted, now tell us what you really saw.'

'Well, I was in a couple of famous recording studios on Music Row as part of a sightseeing tour. We also went to the Earnest Tubb and Conway Twitty music stores, then at night, I went with two guys from Wyoming to Tootsie's and later we toured all the other famous bars in Printers Alley.'

'Did you sing in any of those places?' Enquired the Drummer.

'Yeah,' he answered. 'We made out we were a country group called The Whispers because one of the guys, Dave, was a fan of whispering Bill Anderson and they loved our Mexican songs that I sang. Till the sun comes up and Mexico City went down a treat, then they made me promise to send both singles to them when I go back home, but guess where I was as well Conn?'

'Where?' Conn asked in a voice void of interest.

'I was in Boots Randolph's Club in Printer's Alley and I've got the photos to prove it,' came the reply.

Conn came to life at the mention of his hero. 'Jaysus, I nearly tore my hair out while I was learning that fucking tune Yackety Sax. What was he like?'

Before the Singer could answer Mickey Joe the Trumpet player butted in. 'But you always had too much fucking hair anyway Conn, Bollixolutely.'

'More than Boots has,' replied the Singer, 'he's got a sliding roof you know and quite a bad one at that, but he can play yon sax even though he seems to be a fierce show off.'

'We've got a couple of those in this band as well,' quipped the Drummer, and at least four suspects told him to fuck off.

'If there was a competition on shit stirring you'd win it,' said a very quiet Piano player to the Drummer, who seemed to be enjoying his role of causing a stink. Just then the four Mafia men came in with the moll and sat at a table on the other side of the room, still talking loudly.

'Can I look?' asked the Roadie.

'Yeah, if you want concrete boots,' the Drummer answered, still grinning.

'Well I know where they can find someone to mix the cement, you could use those old bent drum sticks,' said the Roadie, chancing his arm.

Those were fighting words. Ned sung dumb waiting for an onslaught from the Skinner and he was surprised when it didn't happen, so he winked at the Roadie in a 'Good on you' style. After the fabulous meal they had half an hour in their rooms to freshen up, then back to the lobby to catch the limo to the venue. On the way the questions were hot and heavy to Juan about the strange guests in the Motel. He explained that they always meet there on Fridays; sometimes more than four would turn up with many more birds who are all prostitutes and travel to keep the guys happy. They come to pick up or drop hot money from gambling, girls, and Bank jobs, which can be very scary.

'One night a guy get shot in one of the rooms and I see hees body being taken away next day, the story eet never make the papers.'

Ned, who was dumbfounded by what he heard said. 'Imagine that beautiful bird being a prostitute, I really fancied her.'

'She could have been the last girl you fancy yes,' said Juan, as they pulled up to the venue.

Chapter Seven

They all got a great buzz when they saw the big poster outside the Dance Hall. For one night only, the first visit to L.A. of The Nova's Showband and there they were, grinning down at themselves from the huge billboard.

'Next we'll have our hand prints on the pavement along with Bob Hope, Bing Crosby and Grace Kelly,' said Conn.

'Keep dreaming,' growled the Piano player, 'we won't mean a thing here and I'm sure there can't be many Irish people in Los Angeles.'

'Let's wait and see,' said someone.

The venue belonged to some religious faction and was hired for the night by the Promoter, who was sitting in the cash box all sun-tanned, with the big medallion hanging on his hairy chest inside a floral open necked shirt just as he had looked in New York, only a different shirt.

'You're very welcome to L.A lads,' he beamed, 'we're gonna have a big one tonight.'

The Piano player couldn't take any more of this crap as he called it, so he gave the Promoter his opinion. 'I'll bet fifty dollars with you that she'll be empty sir, OK!'

'Why not make it five hundred?' Came the confident reply, as the Promoter took a ball of money from his pocket and began peeling big notes from it.

'All I can afford is fifty dollars,' said the Piano man, 'take it of leave it, if there's any more than one hundred people you win.'

'Right,' said the Promoter, sporting a confident grin. 'I'll give you ten to one if that's OK,' and the happy smile on the musician's face was all the answer he needed. Mike agreed to hold the stakes as the Piano man went off rubbing his hands in glee.

'Now we know how to make him smile,' said Conn, 'but he may not be smiling later tonight, because that Promoter is no fool and he must know the score.'

There was a three-piece support group on for the first two hours and the crowd looked non-existent much to the joy of their own (Liberace), who was still gloating.

'What did I tell you,' he said, 'as well as getting paid tonight, I'll make an extra five hundred dollars plus my own fifty back, Wow!'

Around 10.30, just half an hour before The Nova's Showband were due on stage, Ned counted the dancers and the tally was seventy-five.

'Looks like Mr. Ivory will win,' said the Roadie. Ned just laughed at the new nickname and was inclined to agree.

'Let's look on the bright side,' he said. 'God is good.'

The Roadie knew that was a two-fold wish as nobody wanted the piano player to succeed, but more importantly they didn't want a bad gig on the tour. They were all ready as the MC announced them and you could hear the loud roar from the Piano man over everything else as he stepped on stage.

'Aw fuck no!' He exclaimed, his hands clutching the top of his head as if it was about to burst.

Over the past thirty minutes, about two hundred patrons had filed into the hall and it looked quite a good crowd, much to the joy of all but the Piano player. Ned quickly announced the band, got a hand for the support group, then the Drummer counted and away they went. It was one of the best gigs on the tour and they were having a ball, that is, all except Mr. Ivory. Even when he was singing he looked like death warmed up, then Ned heard the very excited Drummer shouting in a slightly different lingo.

'Ned, have a butchers on your left hammer, the Richard from the Jack tar and the four omies, they're at the fucking soldier.'

Sure enough, there they were, (at the soldier of France, the Dance) waving madly at the band, the four Mafia members and the moll, grinning from ear to ear, directly at him. He managed a weak smile in return as his stomach churned, and then he got a bigger surprise when he saw their Promoter joking and laughing with Big Joe, the fat really dangerous one. He caught the Piano man's gaze and you could see the situation dawning on him, as he managed to get even paler. One o'clock came and the crowd, which had swollen to approximately five hundred, didn't want to know about going home. Quite a few had acquired their records by one way or another and some had heard the band while at home on holiday, tonight they were reliving that experience and they didn't want it to end. Luckily, the band members were able to blame the owners of the hall and the dance came to a halt with almost everyone trying to get near them at the same time. The Roadie was in his element giving out the band pictures and he was throwing some like Frisbees into the crowd, just to see them jump. Ned was busy talking to a fan when he felt a squeeze inches above his knee and glancing to the left he saw the object of his early evening interest. She was holding out her hand to him and saying in a sexy voice,

'Have you got a picture for me honey?'

He panicked and pointed to the Roadie. She shook her head and her long hair danced around her bare shoulders as she said.

'No, I want you to give it to me honey,' then licking her lucious lips she added, 'and you can put your room number on it too, I'll be free around 4am.'

'Jaysus,' he thought, 'that beautiful bitch will get me killed, so I'll ignore her.'

He was busy talking to other people while still kneeling on the stage, when suddenly he felt the hand again and this time it was about two inches away from his tackle. She smiled, knowing he was under pressure, and then beckoned to him to bend down so she could whisper in his ear.

'I promise you, I'll get your undivided attention in a moment if you try to ignore me,' she said. 'All I want is your picture signed and your room number, no one will know if I pay you a visit at four in the morning.'

The words of Faron Young's hit song drifted through his brain. 'It's four in the morning and once more the dawning, woke up the wanting in me,' and he thought. 'If she visits me at four in the morning, I'll never see the fucking dawning.' Now he could see where her gaze was targeting, so he blurted out. 'I'll get one for you immediately.' When he came back, she was sitting on the stage pointing to the space beside her and grinning at her four friends, who were busy chatting to women a little way down the floor.

'Put love to Marilyn on it, along with some of the kisses you wanted to give me when you saw me earlier today,' she said. 'I saw you, you old coward, being warned by your driver, there's no need to be afraid of my friends regarding me. They will only shoot you if you try to take their money so I hope you will join us in the bar later and by the way, your band was great!'

She gave him a big kiss on the cheek with lips like damp velvet, then as she went back to her friends he noticed that there wasn't much more fabric in the dress, than there had been in the bikini earlier. But she was one fine bird and maybe he would find a use for those lips later on. It would save him digging out Playboy and anyway, the bit of danger was an extra turn on.

The Roadie was glad to be able to walk away from the gear these nights and he spared a thought for what it would be like when they got back home. 'Ah, we'll worry about that when we get there,' he thought, 'but the worry tonight is, what's that blonde bird up to?'

'She'll get you killed,' he was saying to Ned, when they saw Mr. Ivory skipping up the floor, a big smile on his face.

'What's the story?' they both asked.

'He wouldn't take my fifty dollars,' he answered, 'he told me he had made money on the gig and wouldn't spoil my night, I think that was sound of him, don't you?'

'Yeah,' they chorused in answer.

'Tell me,' said Ned, 'was there any sign of that blonde and her gang down at the office?'

'Yeah, they were all there when he gave me my money back, he seems to know them well.'

'I wonder are we on tour for the Mafia?' The Roadie asked.

'You took the words right out of my mouth,' Ned answered, 'maybe that's why the bird thinks she has a hold on me and wants to shag me at four in the morning.' He knew he had made a mistake mentioning that fact and hoped he'd get away with it, so he went to find the driver. Juan was in his favourite seat in the front of the limo and as Ned got in he said.

'Tell me Ned, are you gonna what you say, fuck her later, cos eef you are, maybe eet ees safer that you do eet in the back seat of the limo while I drive you around, No?'

Now that appealed to him big time. Imagine the stories he could tell back home, it would last for years. Him shafting a gorgeous gangster's moll in the back of a stretch limo, as he was being chauffeured around L.A. in the middle of the night and all the lads would have to back him up, because it would be true. 'That sounds mighty,' he thought, but what about the chase when the four gangsters find out and come looking for me with their guns blazing, as Juan makes a desperate but futile attempt at getting away. Perhaps it will be one of the lads telling the story, about this Showband man who was shot dead for shagging a gangster's moll, as they careered through the streets of Los Angeles. He shivered at the thought, as all the lads piled in to go back to the Motel.

'Where's Mike?' he asked.

Mr. Ivory spoke up. 'Oh, he's gone back to the Motel with Richard and the people from Vegas.'

'So it's Richard now,' Conn jibed, 'and the people from Vegas, are you going to work for them?'

'No!' 'They were talking in the office about the bet and I heard Marilyn saying to Mike, that she was planning on paying Ned a visit in the middle of the night.

'At four in the morning to be precise,' piped up the Roadie. 'Oops, sorry Ned.'

Our hero knew then that he had goofed by mentioning it earlier and he realised he would have to kill off this rumour if possible.

'That's great,' said the Drummer. 'We haven't had a good ear to the door session in ages.'

'We've got to be up early tomorrow to go to Universal Studios,' said Conn, 'so I won't have my ear to any fucking door at four in the morning,' and then he added. 'Wasn't that a song?'

'Yeah,' the Singer answered. 'I sang it in this band for ages, do you not remember?'

'You've just explained it,' came an even more sarcastic answer. 'It's because you sang it that I've forgotten it, you've got that effect on songs.'

'If it was some crap tune on that piece of bent tin you'd remember it alright, maybe it's because it takes you so long to learn them, that they stay in your mind forever,' the Singer's sarcasm had reached a new low.

Ned copped what was about to happen, so he told them to grow up or they would be fucked out of the limo at two different places and they could find their own way home. That prospect brought silence.

Back at the Motel, Juan said to Ned in little more than a whisper. 'You let me know eef you need limo later, yes?'

'Yes Thank you Juan, but I think I'll go straight to bed and not answer the door to anyone, but first, let me buy you a Tequila for all your help.'

As they walked into the bar, they could see the four mobster's playing cards with the Promoter and Mike, but there was no sign of the blonde.

'Thank God!' Ned said, 'we'll have a quick drink and off to bed, would you look at the time, it's almost 3 o'clock.'

Juan had the three small tequila's, with salt, while Ned and the Roadie had a couple of beers. Mr. Ivory pulled a chair over to the card table but he was being ignored and the other three band members were having beer at the counter. The Bass man and the Guitar player had left after the dance with relations they didn't even know existed, on instructions to be at the Airport for 3 o'clock the next day. Ned drank the beer real fast and excused he, then the Roadie joined the other three further up the counter.

'Well, is it on or off?' They asked.

'What?' The Roadie queried.

'Is he shagging yer-one at four, or is he not?'

'I haven't got a clue, but I get the feeling we should keep an eye on the situation anyway, to be sure like,' the Roadie was enjoying being at the core of things.

'OK, we'll wander around there at about four and see what happens,' they all agreed.

It was a long corridor so they took up positions at one end, hoping anyone approaching would come the other way and they didn't have long to wait. On the dot of four, a door opened about twenty feet away and as they retreated, they got a flash of the blonde as she swished from her room and headed down the corridor to Ned's room. They stuck their heads around the corner at different levels, the Roadie going down on his knees and they watched as the moll tapped lightly on their Leader's door. The tapping got a little louder and it looked like she was calling his name quietly, but to no avail, then to their horror she turned and headed back towards them. They fell over each other to get out of the way and then they heard her voice real close. She was on the wall phone a few feet away, talking to the porter.

'Yes that's right Pedro, I have locked myself out of room number 133 and I couldn't be mistaken so hurry, I haven't got many clothes on.'

'133, that's Ned's room, the bitch is going to get the porter to let her into his room, we should warn him but the only problem with that is, he would think it was her and wouldn't answer us either, there she goes.' said Conn.

By now she was back tapping on Ned's door and the sexy black negligee was very transparent indeed. Ten seconds later, a Mexican porter came around the corner with a bunch of keys and she was well prepared for the situation. Before the porter could check if it really was her room, she produced a number of dollar bills from the palm of her hand, which she pressed into his, then he quietly opened the door and like a panther, she disappeared inside. As the porter walked away, the lads ran to the door in question and began to eavesdrop.

'No Marilyn, I'm not able,' they could hear Ned appealing to her.

Then they could hear her sexy voice saying. 'All you've got to do is lie there and I can promise you'll enjoy it, cause I give the best head in L.A.'

'What does she mean by that?' the Roadie asked real innocently.

'Haven't a clue, it must be something new, shush!' Some poet replied.

There was total silence for a couple of minutes, then the moaning started. First the blonde, then Ned and it got louder and louder.

He was shouting, 'Yes, Yes, Yes' and she kept moaning, then the Roadie was asking more questions.

'How come she's not shouting Yes, Yes, Yes?' He asked.

'Because you can't talk with your mouth full,' hissed the Drummer, who had by now worked out what head meant, 'now would you shut up to fuck or I'll hit you!'

Suddenly they heard the phone ringing in Ned's room, next the banging started on the adjoining wall to the left and then it started on the right.

'We'd better get out of here,' said Conn, 'all hell will break loose for sure any minute now and we'll be the talk of the town if we're seen.'

With that bit of good advice they split, each one heading for their own room. Breakfast was at 11am and anyone going to Universal Studios had to be in the dining room no later than that and to everyone's surprise they made it on the dot. Ned was the last and he headed for a different table, but there was no way he was getting away with that.

'Over here,' they all shouted and at a glance he knew they meant business, so he quietly took a seat with the others.

'No sign of the blonde this morning, I wonder where she might be?' Enquired the now smiling Piano player.

Ned tried to change the subject. 'How come you're smiling, you must have got your hole last night or is that what saving fifty bucks can do for you?' He bantered.

'No, but at four this morning we heard you getting your hole, or what was that she called it, 'HEAD.' Mr. Ivory continued.

Ned was about to lose it with yer-man, but when he saw the smug looks on all their faces he knew there was no point. 'So you were all listening,' he suggested.

The Drummer gave his usual count like he did to start a song and they all went Yes, Yes, Yes, Yes, Yes, Yes, Yes, getting louder each time. Right on cue, he could see the blonde standing in the restaurant door fully aware of what was going on and loving it. Then he came up with an idea to put the lads off the scent, so he called her over.

'Good morning Marilyn, did you notice anything unusual in the corridor at four this morning?'

'Not really, apart from a gang of young men resembling The Marx Brothers, peering around the corner thinking they had not been seen,' she answered.

Ned was grinning evilly, thinking this approach would put the lads off, but he lost the grin when she said.

'We should have asked them in for a Gang Bang and that would have saved me doing all the work, perhaps next time guys,' she said loudly, as she walked away to join her mobster friends.

'Not another fucking word about her now,' hissed Ned, 'if they think we're talking about them they could 'Take us out' to use one of her phrases, so let's eat and stay healthy.' The warning worked and the noise of knives and forks took over, but he knew he hadn't heard the last of it.

Juan arrived to take them on the Studio outing and as they put their stuff in the huge boot they were making all kind of jibes at their leader. It was the Lost Chord who came up with the title for his escapades of the previous night.

'Seeing it happened at four in the morning and Faron Young had the big hit with the song, this episode in Ned's love life will be known in the future as, 'The Faron Young Affair!'

Even Ned had to grin at the comparison, so he decided to laugh with them. Several times that day the Drummer counted while the lads went into a stream of Yes's and they even did it on the little train that was carrying them around the Studio Set, much to the joy and confusion of other people on the trip.

One woman said. 'I guess you're a bunch of funny Irish guys, are you from Dublin?'

Some of the lads said yes, some said no, so the Drummer gave the count and they all shouted 'Yes Yes, Yes, Yes, Yes, Yes, Yes.'

They had a ball for two hours watching Cowboys being shot from Hotel roofs, Indians riding Piebald Ponies and of course, you had the Fake Mountain. The tour guide told them that film directors preferred using the man-made mountain, as it looked better on film than the real one. They were allowed to go around behind the fake and see that it was built with wooden beams covered with a type of canvas.

'We'll keep an eye out for that back in the cinema in Mullymore, next time we go to see Clint,' commented Mickey Joe.

'Jaysus, don't mention Mullymore,' Ned begged, 'things will never be the same after this trip.'

The Drummer counted once more and this time they all chanted, No, No, No, No, No, No, No.'

They checked in at L.A.X. on the dot of three and the other two lads were already there, telling about the fabulous time they had at Disney Land, also about meeting Mickey and Minnie Mouse plus all the other Disney characters.

'We met Clint Eastwood,' said Conn, with a straight face.

'Go to hell, you didn't,' said the Guitar man and for a second his face looked like he missed something, and then he bounced back with. 'Who cares, we saw Mickey.'

'Yeah, we almost saw Ned's Mickey and we nearly got an invitation to a Gang Bang,' the Drummer informed the two Disney fans.

'Nanty The Horses Hoof,' hissed an unhappy Ned. *'Degont Bege Spregedeging Scegandegal Egabegout Mege Shegam.'*

'What the fuck is he on about?' asked the non Ben-Lang Guitar man and the Drummer who just about understood, explained.

'What he's just said was, don't be spoofing and spreading scandal about me sham.'

Nobody made any comment as they made their way to the plane and Ned was looking forward to catching forty winks on the flight to San Francisco. He was so tired he kept drifting off to sleep, then, in his subconscious he could clearly see and feel what had happened to him that morning, which in turn made him wake up with a jolt.

'Are you alright young man?' Enquired the lady in the adjoining seat.

'Oh yes Thank you,' he answered and each time he nodded off he would wake up in similar fashion.

The older lady, who was by now quite concerned about his health, suggested that he must have suffered some trauma or other and should have himself looked at on arrival, so he conjured up a story a little on the lines of what happened, but not the full truth. He told her he had met up with this lovely lady in L.A. and they were having a drink in the bar when her Mafia boyfriend came in and threatened to shoot them both.

'He even opened his jacket and showed me the gun he would use, he had it in a shoulder holster,' he added.

'Oh My God, you poor guy, no wonder you're cracking up, did you report it to the cops?' The woman asked.

'No way,' said Ned, almost believing it. 'She told me not to, as he would surely shoot us both if I did.'

'Those guys,' she said. 'They should all be gathered up and locked away for life, along with their Molls who are to blame for most of it. Half hanging out of their clothes, they have no shame,' added the older woman.

'You're right,' he answered, as he tried to slip off again, this time replacing the sex scenario with the new gun theory, which to his surprise, he found easier to handle. 'A gun wouldn't be half as dangerous as that woman let loose,' he thought, as he drifted into a deep sleep.

The plane touched down quietly in San Francisco in the hot sunshine and as he headed for the exit, the Roadie shouted from the window seat.

'Hi Ned, welcome to Frisco.'

'What's wrong with the full title?' He enquired. 'Or is it taking too much effort?'

Conn spoke up. 'He's been annoying our heads for the last hour since the hostess said it to him, but if he says it once more I'm gonna smash his gob.'

By now I suppose they were becoming spoiled and hardly looked at the fifteen-seat coach that awaited them outside the Terminal, that is, until they got a glimpse of the driver. She was a tall blonde with huge breasts and a real happy smile.

'Jaysus look at her,' hissed the Singer. 'I saw her first so she's mine.'

His mate John came to life with. 'Don't you think she might have a say in that?'

She stepped from the bus and they all gasped when they saw the short, short hot pants she was wearing. To complete the outfit she had a plunging open neck shirt and a rhinestone studded waistcoat with cowboy boots to match.

'Hi, I'm Jenny,' she drawled, 'you must be the guys from The Nova's Showband.'

The Singer was in front and he almost crashed into her as he stuck out his hand to introduce himself. 'Hi, I'm Steve and these are the lads in my band, I love your cowboy boots.'

'Well actually, they're not cowboy boots, they are cowgirl boots,' she answered.

The lads as he called them, were about to rip him limb from limb for the 'My band' bit, but when they heard the put-down about the boots they couldn't stop laughing.

'My band my arse,' the Piano man managed to say under his breath.

When the introductions were complete, Mickey Joe made a statement that he hoped might enhance his chances with this good-looking woman.

'Gentlemen,' he said. 'I don't want to see this lovely young lady lifting any equipment while she is looking after us, OK!'

Everyone shouted. 'OK.'

'Oh thank you guys,' she replied, 'you are the most chivalrous bunch I have met in a while and by the way you're welcome to Frisco.'

Realising he had an ally, the Roadie piped up with. 'Jenny, the lads won't let me call it 'Frisco.'

'Ignore them,' she said, 'you and I will call it anything we like.'

Everyone laughed and just as the Roadie thought he had cracked it he asked.

'Jenny, what do you mean by Chivalrous?'

Whatever chances he might have had evaporated in seconds, then Mike spoke. 'She means, the age of Chivalry is not yet dead and that's a good thing.'

Jenny smiled at Mike, concluding that he at least knew what she was talking about, so now it was the Managers turn to switch on the charm, while Ned watched and listened as the band members vied for the attentions of this lovely woman. The Roadie had died a death by now, but he was still working feverishly to load the gear in the back of the bus trying to impress and not really aware of the clanger he had dropped.

'He's a real silk purse from a sows ear job,' he thought, 'you either have it or you don't, but if he had a little bit of it at least, it wouldn't be too bad.'

He had shaken hands with the blonde driver and discovered that she had a good firm grip, which forced him to wonder how her grip might be on other parts of the anatomy. She was nice, but he decided to leave it to the other fella's so they could make fools of themselves and she was behaving like she had no interest in any of them anyway, apart from being pleasant.

They were booked into the hotel but there was no time to go there, so they set out for the venue, which was another biggie. The band was off on Sunday, but the hotel was booked until Monday to cover any member who wanted to see the city or visit friends and relaxing was uppermost on their agenda. They had another Jammer in 'Frisco' and all the band's songs seemed to go down well, but when the gig was over, a man around forty years old came up to the bandstand looking for the leader and he was duly pointed in Ned's direction. He told him his name and that he was Irish, then he put a proposition to him in a roundabout way.

'Are you guys working tomorrow night?' He asked.

'No, we're off tomorrow night, but most of us are booked on flights to visit our relations all over the country, why?'

'Well,' the stranger began. 'We've got this big gig on tomorrow night and I thought you might want to help The Cause.'

Ned thought his story about the morning flights would solve it, so he mentioned the fact again.

'There's no problem changing those,' the man said. 'I'm a travel agent and I can have it sorted by 9 o'clock. My friend owns the Irish music store in this town which sells your records and he has had them played on local Irish radio programmes, you must have seen the reaction here tonight.'

The Bandleader decided to pass the buck, so he said. 'I'll have to hand you over to our manager, hold on here please.'

Ned could see Mike standing halfway down the hall, so he tapped the microphone to see if the P.A was still switched on and as luck would have it, it was.

'Could the manager of The Nova's Showband please come to the stage,' he said, then he went over to the side of the bandstand waving at him to hurry and they both met at the top of the little set of stairs where he put his colleague in the picture.

'I know about that already,' he answered, much to the surprise of the other man.

'How?' He questioned.

'That guy on stage is a mate of the Promoter and they both asked me earlier, in the interests of promotion and future gigs, I would suggest we do it,' Mike was looking at Ned expectantly.

'I've already told this man that we're all flying out to different places in the morning, how will I get around that?'

'Don't worry on that score,' said Mike reassuringly. 'I've already said the same, but the Promoter says there will be no problem changing the flights and we can phone whoever we like from the hotel to change any plans we have made. It will cost us nothing.'

'Jaysus', said Ned, for the first time in a long while. 'My two aunts in Philadelphia will fucking kill me for sure this time, if I don't show tomorrow.'

'Just tell them why you're being delayed and they will be OK with it I'll bet,' said Mike.

'There's no way they'll believe that,' he said, sounding really panicky and telling the manager about The Rosary and The Holy Water.

'You'd be surprised by some of those real holy ones.' 'The Cause is uppermost in all their minds, but tell them something else if you have to,' was his suggestion.

'Where's the gig?' Ned enquired.

'Where you're standing,' was the reply.

'Holy Jaysus,' Ned moaned. 'We'll have nobody here tomorrow after being here tonight and how come we didn't promote it earlier?'

'One of the reasons is, they have two thousand tickets sold already and we're only one of the bands playing, you'd better tell the lads it's all being filmed for posterity, four cameras.'

'You can imagine the showing off when they see the cameras, or maybe they'll be shitting themselves wondering if the people who see it will think they've joined up.' Ned's voice tailed off dubiously.

Mike called the travel agent and record shop owner over, telling them that the job was oxo. Two quite serious faces broke into grins and they pumped both men's hands firmly.

'You won't regret it, the place will be full, but we needed one high profile act from home to make it a real success, thanks guy's,' they said, as they headed down the hall to give the Promoter the good news and there was a bit of back slapping as they made their way to the office.

The Singer was getting nowhere with Jenny, which prompted him to slide over to the two lads and make the following statement.

'I'm getting up at cock-crow and catching a flight to Nashville, so the next time I see you guys will be in Boston, don't worry, I'll be on time I promise.'

The two recipients of this statement looked at each other and laughed.

'You tell him,' said Mike.

'I've got bad news for you in the form of good news, if you know what I mean,' Ned said.

'Well,' was the answer, as the guy waited?

'We're playing tomorrow night,' was the reply.

'Where?'

'Here!'

'How the fuck can we play here when we've just been here tonight?'

'That's easy, we just come back tomorrow night.'

'You're taking the piss, just because I've got plans,' the Singer whinged.

'That's not it at all,' said Mike. 'There's two thousand tickets sold for tomorrow night, so we must do it!'

'Jaysus,' gushed the Chanter, 'we must be fucking huge here, do the lads know?'

'The lads in your band don't know,' said Ned sarcastically, bringing a high colour to the Singers cheeks, then he leaned over and in little more than a whisper, told yer-man the story.

The blush faded from the listener's face and he went quite pale, while he whispered into Ned's ear.

'Don't give any of them my name,' he said. 'My father was a member when he was a young lad, but he ran away and hid before an ambush one night, they were looking for him for years but he was in Glasgow on the run.'

'Now, that explains the fucking Scots accent you had when you were at Mullymore National School, but you managed to get rid of it alright, we called you Scottie and you used to say you were the son if the fella in Star-Trek, that's a good one!'

The Promoter brought everyone to the bar but the Roadie was missing, so Ned went to see what had befallen him this time. Good job he did, yer-man was beginning to dismantle all the gear and he nearly asked Ned for a signed affidavit before he would stop.

'I'm supposed to be in Buffalo tomorrow evening,' he whined, 'and I thought you were coming as well.'

'There'll be none of us in Buffalo tomorrow,' Ned told him, 'so you'd better ring your girlfriend and tell her, all the calls are on the Promoter.'

He brightened up a bit with this news and reluctantly followed Ned to the bar, where drinks were flowing freely and the Singer was surrounded by a bevy of lovely girls who said he was the best thing since the proverbial sliced pan.

Mickey Joe came over to Ned and said. 'I've just been listening to Steve introducing himself to that bunch of girls and he's giving them all the wrong name, he even told them his first name was Barry, until one of them read his real name on the band photo and took him to task, what's up?'

'How did he get out of that?' Asked Ned.

'Well, he hummed and he hawed, and then told them that Barry was his real name, but he used Steve in the band. When one of the girls hugged him and said he was named after her hero Kevin Barry he went as pale as a ghost. What's going on?' Asked the Trumpeter.

'I'll tell you tomorrow,' said Ned. 'Meanwhile, tell the lads not to contradict anything they hear Steve saying or we'll have a corpse on our hands.'

Mike told the remaining band members about the next gig and the Piano player asked him how much they were getting for it, but he put him off by saying that it hadn't been discussed yet, so he swallowed that. He was to find out sooner than he thought and when the Promoter got a few jars in he started to get loud, so standing up on a big armchair he began to address the people in the bar.

'I would like to thank the members and management of the fabulous Nova's Showband for agreeing to appear at tomorrows gig on such short notice. As you all know it's for The Cause and being stout patriots like ourselves, they would like to see the last Brit soldier out of Ireland.' He paused for a moment while all the people clapped.

Ned applauded loudly and Conn shouted into his ear. 'Did you hear that?' He asked.

'Yes,' Ned answered, clapping louder, only this time under Conn's nose. '*Clegap Legike Feguck!*' He said.

Conn got the message and looking a bit surprised he began to applaud. Ned scanned the room looking for the band's reaction and was glad to see that the penny had begun to drop. The Roadie was standing beside Jenny the sexy driver and he was clapping loudest of all, then Ned saw him whisper into the blonde's ear, she in turn whispered into his ear, he seemed to swallow hard, miss a few claps then continue. The Promoter's speech came to an end and he got the record shop man on another chair to take over. Before this guy was finished he had almost given a date for the troops out of his country and Ned could see the band members giving him strange looks.

'How come you knew and none of us did?' Would be their first question at the earliest opportunity.

The band members were the only sober people in the bar, so Jenny told the Roadie to put the word around that she would drive them back to the hotel 'NOW.' On the short trip, Ned was barraged with questions from all the members of the orchestra and then the Roadie caused a hush when he asked the pretty blonde.

'Are you a member Jenny, I mean, are you a involved in The Cause?'

They all waited quietly. 'I guess I am,' she replied in her soft West Coast drawl, and then she continued with. 'Just wait until tomorrow night and you'll get quite a surprise when you see all the folk you know from back home who are involved.'

Jenny fixed a pick-up time before dropping them off and there was hardly a sound while they made their way to bed. As he got ready for slumber, Ned remembered the couple of times he had been approached to join back home and the lads who had mentioned it to him were all in the U.S. now. 'God knows who we'll meet later at the gig.' He was right, the venue was thronged when they got there and as he expected there were loads of faces that he knew, including quite a few of his old schoolmates from Mullymore.

'We didn't come to see you last night, as we knew we would hear your band tonight,' they told him.

'Good job we didn't refuse,' he mused. 'Someone must have known we would agree, PHEW!'

He had begun to assemble his trusty trombone when he got a tap on the shoulder and a voice asked. 'Who plays that yoke?'

Without turning around he laughingly answered. 'Well, it belongs to me and I take it most places I go, as for playing it, I'm not sure.'

While he turned around the voice continued with. 'I thought you'd be a Sax player, I remember you starting on the Whistles.'

He was now eyeballing the owner of this voice and he couldn't put a handle on him, so he kept the banter going with. 'I also own a Sax but I don't bring that with me, the main reason being, I get as much money for blowing the one horn as I would get for the two, I can't put a name on you boss.'

'I'm disappointed,' said the stranger. 'I played Cowboys and Indians with you for four years until my family moved here, I'm Larry Kenny or La, as you guy's called me.'

'Jaysus, how are you?' Ned asked, pumping his hand. 'Your full nick-name was La, Ti, Doh you know, back in Mullymore High.'

'Yeah, and we all called you Mi, Fah, Soh,' said La, laughing.

'You were always a bit of a smart-arse or as the Yanks say, (smart-ass),' added Ned.

As quick as a panther yer-man came back with. 'Are you suggesting that I'm an intelligent donkey?'

Both men began reminiscing about their four years as pals at Mullymore School while Ned put his instrument on its stand. Then he asked his long lost friend what he was working at in 'Frisco' and more importantly, why was he here tonight?'

'Well, first things first, I'm studying Law, playing Trad music on Flute and Whistles twice a week and I'm here tonight to support the drive to set our country free from oppression, so what's your story?'

Ned put him in the picture as to how they got the gig, to be told that the word was out for ages they would be playing tonight.

'There has been huge publicity on your band here for months now,' La informed him.

'Are all the people here involved in some way?' Ned asked.

'You can bet your bottom dollar they are,' replied his friend. 'The word here is that there's going to be an escalation in hostilities soon, to try and bring it to a head.'

'It's a pity,' said Ned, 'those bombs are ripping the country to pieces and if it gets worse I don't know what we'll do, there must be another way.'

'The other way has been tried but the Brit's don't want to know, let me ask you one question and it's a yes or no answer. If we didn't have British rule in Northern Ireland, would we still have the bombings?' The sincerity on the young immigrant's face was evident, as he put his beliefs into words.

'Now that you ask, the answer would have to be No, sure we'd hardly go around blowing our country to bits if they would leave us alone. I don't think it's about religion as much as it's about money, property and power, they just use the church as the catalyst to drum up the hatred,' said Ned. Then he continued wistfully. 'Is there not a Universal law which states, that you must have a receipt for something before you can claim it as your own, have the British got one I wonder and if so, who has seen it, or where is it stashed?'

'Well if they have, I'm sure they would have shown it to someone before now, anyway, they'll have to leave us alone soon, now that they're being chased from all the other country's they've raped and pillaged. As you know, they helped to run the poor Indians off their land here as well,' said La.

'Yeah, they have a lot of sins to answer for alright' said Ned. 'It's a pity there's no hell for people like them to go to after death, hell and heaven are here on earth you know, because I'm in and out of both regularly.'

'By God, you wouldn't say that in front of your mother I'll bet, or has she gone soft on you by now,' said the budding lawyer.

Then Ned had a wry thought. 'You told me earlier that you're playing Flute and Whistles, how come, cause you never played a note when I knew you.'

'Quite simple really, there's a huge Irish culture growing all over The States, with Trad music and dancing being and integral part of it.' 'I started playing in High School and loved it, plus I also do the Irish dancing as well, but we do it a little differently.'

'Jaysus,' gasped Ned. 'You must look a right puff in an Irish dancing uniform.'

'Well, you'll get your chance to judge that later on tonight and our Trad group will be playing as well,' said a proud La, and then he continued with a similar question. 'How come you're in this famous band? I remember when you could play sweet fuck all.'

'Long story, it all started when I was seventeen.' he answered. 'I went to a Carnival Dance one night and got talking to the Trombone player in the band, he told me it was a great way of impressing the ladies and he was right, so I thank God for giving someone the ability to make Trombones, it's a pity he didn't make them a bit easier to play though.'

Ned and his friend went for a drink while some other band took the stage and he was introduced to endless beauties including La's twin sisters, all sporting American accents whilst chanting 'Brits out!' Then he introduced his new friend to Jenny their driver and it was the most immediate exhibition of enchantment he had ever witnessed. As he shook her hand he curtseyed, then without taking his eyes off hers he asked if he could kiss her and laughingly she replied.

'If you want to, be my guest.'

'This guy is not shy,' Ned was thinking, as his friend took Jenny in his arms and kissed her. First of all gently, then slowly he gripped her more tightly and it was plain to see she was also enjoying it, because she wrapped her arms around him pressing her body to his. As far as they were concerned, Ned or the crowd didn't exist any more, next, they picked up the tempo of the band and slowly began to dance. Our hero had enough, so he headed off in search of the twins, murmuring to himself.

'The first one I bump into will do, it will save trying to choose as that wouldn't be easy.' Then he saw one of the girls wrapped around some guy and he thought. 'That makes it even easier.'

The remaining sister was all smiles when she saw Ned heading for her so she met him halfway, immediately wrapping her arms around him and he thought he was in for a good session tonight until she started talking directly into his ear. He had intended using some of the tactics employed by her brother earlier, but he soon forgot that when he discovered the main thrust of her conversation was The Cause. He listened for a while, and then he said.

'But I wouldn't kill a fly Catherine.'

'I'll bet you eat lots of chicken, but you probably couldn't choke one,' she maintained.

'You're right,' he answered. 'The only time I choke the chicken, is when I'm reading Playboy or Penthouse.'

He could feel her body freeze, as she stood back and gave him an almighty slap across the face.

'That's how I treat cowards, especially smart Alec cowards,' she roared, before storming off into the throng leaving him standing, feeling quite taken aback.

'I'd better be more careful the next time around, I might not get off so lightly,' he mused.

Two more groups took to the stage playing all kinds of music, including some heavy rebel songs which most of the crowd joined hands for, singing at full volume. Then it was

LA's band swinging into a set of reels, with the man himself playing directly into the microphone at full blast.

'Jaysus.' Ned shouted to no one in particular. 'The fucker can really play.' He stood in awe as the group including his friend put down their instruments and began to dance a jig as the remaining members played. 'He's fucking good at that as well,' he exclaimed aghast. 'Is there anything the bastard can't do?'

It was then he noticed Jenny; she was standing clapping and screaming in front of the stage, very obviously out of her tree with excitement, so he decided to move up and ask her how things were going. She hugged him.

'I'm in love,' she screamed into his ear, 'thanks for introducing us, I want to have his babies.'

'Well, as long as you don't start before you drive us back to the hotel I won't mind,' he answered.

Then she asked. 'I saw some nice bird slapping you earlier, what was that all about?'

'Well that nice bird happens to be one of your future sister's in law and she has a twin, you'll need to be a real rebel to make it in that family,' he said smiling.

He told her what had happened and she said. 'Serves you right, you'll be more careful the next time.'

The dancing ended and next was a big ballad, sung by guess who?

'Isn't he just great,' she grinned. 'You'd need a couple of guys like him in your band.'

'I agree,' said Ned, 'but I'm afraid we couldn't afford him, he'll be a lawyer soon.'

'Gee, I didn't know that,' she proffered. 'Of course it's difficult finding out things when you're French kissing, but thanks for telling me.'

The Nova's Showband were on last and as usual brought the house down.

'The proceeds of this gig will probably bring a lot of houses down,' he thought and even though he wasn't a real rebel, he did agree it had to be done, but he was in favour of talking not bombing. He always said. 'I'd rather live for my country than die for it, you can be more effective while alive and ditto for religion.'

That reminded him of his two aunts in Philadelphia. Decisions would have to be made tomorrow, how he would spread himself around between Monday and Friday when they took the stage in Boston. 'I must ring Buffalo first, then New York.' He was miles away thinking, when suddenly he heard the Singer introducing him to sing The Haunted House and there was no way in the world he could remember the opening line, as the Sax and Trumpet kept repeating the intro riffs. He was completely blank, firstly trying the mike's not working lark until the Bass man thrust another one into his hand, which was working. So with the sweat running up his back, he turned around in despair to the Drummer who didn't sing but knew all the song words and copping what was wrong he roared the opening line at him. 'I just moved in my new house today.' That did the trick, the words came flowing back and with about thirty seconds of intro gone which was like forever, Ned began to sing and not having noticed the panic, the crowd started singing along with him.

Suddenly they were playing their signature tune and it was his job to introduce the band members, which he did with the usual bit of bowing and scraping, pointing to each individual as he called their name. Then it was time for The Irish National Anthem. Everyone in the big ballroom held hands while they sang at the top of their voices and it was obvious that these people meant business, then when the band seemed to be stopping the crowd roared for more, making them play it again.

Later during the signing of the autographs, Ned was aware of one of LA's twin sisters in the queue for his signature. 'Am I in for another wallop,' he thought, as he tried to work out which one she was. They were dressed identically, apart from the fact that one was wearing a black velvet choker that he had admired earlier, then, as she got closer she gave him a big smile and he thought. 'She must be Mary, the twin with the beautiful black velvet band.' The first time he'd seen her, she had been wrapped around some bloke, but then Catherine did the same to him just before she hit him, so you never can tell.

'To Mary with lots of love,' she volunteered, not knowing how relieved he was.

He decided to go for the jugular at once, having picked up the tips from her brother.

'How can I give you lots of love on the back of a piece of cardboard?' He asked.

'Well,' she began, 'you can start with that, and then you can take me home and continue from there.'

'Jaysus,' he thought, 'she must have been watching her brother as well.'

'Will you wait for me so?' He asked.

'Till Hell freezes over,' she replied, grinning.

Just then the twin from Hell appeared. 'Are you going home with that wanker?' She shouted.

'He's not a wanker and the answer is Yes,' the nice one said. 'Why?'

Catherine loudly related the scenario that went down earlier, Mary just laughed and made a rude sign at her sister. Now Ned knew that both girls understood what choking the chicken meant.

'They're gorgeous and the fucking image of each other,' he mused, 'this will be good.'

LA was so busy with Jenny; he passed no heed on the fact that his old mate was just about to transmogrify one of his twin sisters. You may wonder at the use of this big word to explain what Ned had in mind for Mary, but he had picked it at random one night, hoping to explain a steamy session he once had and it caught on, especially as none of the lads had a bull's notion of what it meant. They hadn't got as far as transmogrify in Mullymore National School, but it sounded great. Seeing that Monday was a free day and the rooms were booked in the Hotel, Ned decided to ask Mary to spend the night there with him. She wasn't phased in the slightest by the request and gave him a big hug to prove it. Every member of the band clicked that night and they all seemed to be on the same kick as Ned, everyone was going back to the Hotel. The Roadie dismantled the equipment, but it was all left in the ballroom, that is all except Conn's saxophone.

'No fuckin' way am I leaving that behind,' he said, 'we'd be bollixed without that yoke.'

Then the Drummer put a question to the Sax player. 'Does that wee bird know she has to deal with two horns, later tonight?'

'Yeah,' he answered. 'I'll blow one, she can blow the other one.'

There was a big guffaw from the lads and the lady in question asked if they were laughing at her.

'No way,' Conn assured her, 'they would have to deal with me if that happened.' Then he held his knuckles under his latest girlfriends nose and asked. 'Can you smell dead men off that fist?'

They all laughed happily as they climbed on board the bus, Ned hoping that the twin from Hell would not be accompanying one of them and he was glad when she wasn't there, but he noticed there was a change of driver. When they were all on board, the new driver said.

'Hi everyone, I'm John and I'll be driving you all back to your Hotel, Jenny is busy, she's courting.'

There were all kinds of hoots and catcalls, plus a few very rude remarks mostly from the girls, and then the interior lights went off. Ned was thinking of the wild night they were going to have when Mary jumped on him, sticking her tongue down his throat as far as it would go. A song title summed up his immediate thoughts. 'Let's take it to the limit, one more time,' as his hand began to slide up her bare thigh, to be stopped before reaching its goal, much to his disappointment.

Another song title took care of the scene back in the bedroom. It was, 'Anything goes.' Mary let him remove all her clothing except her scanty pants, while she kept insisting that she had a special surprise underneath and could only take them off when the time was right. He took a look at his tackle and suggested that as far as he was concerned, the time had been right for sometime now, but still no go. Then he had a horrible thought. Maybe she has balls, he had heard of people like that but 'Thanks be to God,' as his mum would say, so far he had not met one.

'What's wrong with you?' She asked, 'you're miles away.'

She was waiting for an answer while he was playing for time as he pressed his leg all the way between her lovely pins and to his delight, could feel nothing unusual.

'To be honest, I'm at the end of my tether trying to work out what you've got stashed away under those pants, come on please, end the suspense,' he begged.

In a flash, she hopped off the bed and struck her cheerleader pose as she explained it. Suddenly, she turned her back to him and slid the pants all the way down, kicking them to the other side of the room. Ned faked a drum roll and a movie he had seen in Mullymore Grand flashed before him. He could see Joe Friday in 'Dragnet' and suddenly he copied the music from that picture. 'DA, DA, DA, DA, DA…' She must have known it too, because on the last long note she slowly turned around and he saw it. Smiling roguishly, mostly at the look on his face she asked.

'Well, what do you think sweetie?' Then using a very good Mae West accent, she moved her hips from side to side saying. 'Do you wanna' come up and see me some time?'

'Thank God for being a movie buff,' he thought, 'otherwise I wouldn't have a fucking clue what she's on about.' He was in shock but managed to say. 'It's beautiful, please get back into bed and tell me all about it.'

Without another word she got in and snuggled up to him, then she began to talk.

'It's known as a Shaven Haven and my twin sister and I both have one, it always gets the guys attention just like now. Some blokes even think theres something wrong with us, but they always enjoy it 'in the end.' She emphasised the last three words, then took Ned's hand and placed it firmly between her legs. He had just been given the green light, but before things went too far she told him he had to use a Condom.

'Oh Thank God for the late night drug stores in New York,' he reflected.

They awoke many times before the next afternoon and on each occasion, the 'Lovin' continued. He couldn't get enough of his first 'Shaven Haven' and he knew that a few girls back home would be asked nicely to comply, in the future. 'The lads will never believe this,' he thought, 'but then who's gonna tell them?' 'Not Ned.'

At around four in the afternoon they began drifting into the Restaurant/Bar in the basement of the Hotel and obviously very little sleeping had been done by anybody. The fact that the lift went all the way to the basement was handy, otherwise they would have had to get out of it, or come down the stairs directly across from the reception desk. There probably would have been no problem doing that, but the sheer volume of the entourage might cause suspicion and cost a few bucks extra. The girls still seemed the more boisterous of the bunch, causing them to head for the bar for a little tipple as they said and the big question among them was, would they be able to stay with their heroes tonight? They had told their parents they were staying at the Promoter's mansion on the coast and he was acting as Chaperone, but would that work again? Some of the lads had a quick pow-wow to find out how many of them were up for a repeat performance and they all voted in favour, then the Singer came up with a great idea for a change, after hearing about the house at the seaside.

'Why don't we ask Mike to ring the Promoter and suggest spending tonight at the beach house, instead of the Hotel,' he said. 'We could spend the night on the sand, instead of in bed.'

'That's a great idea,' enthused Ned, his heart beating with excitement as he pictured moonlight, surf, sand and of-course a certain Shaven Haven.

'Jaysus,' he exclaimed, 'this will be fuckin' massive.'

'What'll be fuckin' massive?' They all asked in unison.

'Oh nothing,' he answered. 'I was just thinking of having a skinny dip seeing that I forgot my togs.'

The Singer went to find Mike and the other lads joined the girls at the bar, passing on the plan. The consensus was, that there would be no problem sorting things out with parents or jobs, the latter which some of them had missed already.

Mike came in with the Singer and he was smiling. 'It's on for the beach, the bus will be here at 7 o'clock, so let's party!'

They all had hearty meals supplied by the Promoter's of last night's gig, washed down by a variety of liquids and the only worry the girls had was, they would have to wear the same outfits again. The lads put them at ease by suggesting that there might not be a great need for clothes, especially as the festivities progressed. They were as one on that. The beach house turned out to be everything they had expected and more, so parking at the back they entered from the rear. Their host ushered his guests into a huge open plan lounge full of very soft settees and matching arm chairs, but the main feature of the room was the large well stocked, semi-circular bar complete with a lovely blonde lady who was ready to serve. The blonde introduced herself as 'Vickey' to the revellers, as she calmly saw to everyone's needs and eventually everybody had a full glass in their hand. Mike quietly put the word around that the lady behind the bar must be treated with respect, because she was the owner's bit of fluff and he was just in time to stop the Roadie asking what that meant.

Mary had just introduced Ned to Margaritas, so after a couple of sips he guided her to what he correctly presumed was the front door. It was breathtaking, the moon shot it's beams over the calm sea and the cool sand was like silk under their bare feet. Mary was accustomed to this stunning scene and quickly sensed that he considered it awesome. Quietly they finished their drinks and put the glasses on the windowsill, then like people possessed, they ran hand in hand towards the silver moonbeams. Mary seemed intent on plunging in fully clothed, but he brought her to a standstill and began to disrobe so she followed suit as they stood looking at each other in the moonlight, then he moved close and held her tightly. She knew exactly what he was thinking as their excited bodies pressed against each other, so she gently kissed him and said.

'It's the sea for you first my boy, lovemaking later and be sure to stay close seeing that you're not the best swimmer in California.' Then laughing loudly, they both ran into the balmy ocean.

That was a night to remember. As dawn broke, many wet glistening bodies could be seen trying to swim, or just running around in the shallow water. The Mullymore lads wouldn't win many swimming trophies, but the girls who were all good swimmers were having a ball and venturing much further out. As the sun crept over the horizon, Mary slipped into her clothes that she had some trouble finding on the vast beach and Ned was pleased, because he didn't want all his mates to know their little secret.

'I'm keeping it for you honey,' she whispered, as she led him off over the sand away from all the others. He was hoping he'd be able to perform again, as he had lost count of the number of sessions during the night, but he had to admit, with Mary it was very exciting. As the sun got hotter, they slowly drifted back into the house, some to bedrooms and some to the big (still well stocked) bar.

The Roadie followed Ned to the bathroom looking a bit concerned. 'What's up with you, are you not enjoying yourself?' Ned asked.

'I don't know what to do,' was the reply. 'I'm supposed to be in Buffalo since yesterday, now Amanda will fuckin kill me for sure.'

'Don't worry,' said Ned. 'I was supposed to ring Jayne and I didn't get around to it yet, you can't have your cake and eat it you know.'

'Were you supposed to go to buffalo as well?' Asked the Roadie.

'No,' Ned answered. 'I promised to ring Jayne just to keep in touch, but I was supposed to be in Philadelphia though to re-visit my aunts, then go to Boston on Thursday, that I hope to do.'

'There's no point in me trying to make it to Buffalo now, anyway, my new girlfriend has asked me to stay for a couple of days with her in Oakland. I'll make some excuse to Amanda and promise to come and see her during my next holidays, hopefully I'll get away with that.' Suddenly, the Roadie seemed to have a new lease of life and was smiling again, having given himself complete absolution.

Mike called a meeting of the band, to inform them that they would move out that evening. Some of the lads were not too happy with that, but he pointed out. 'If we hang out here any longer it'll get messy, those girls need to get back home and our friend here must be kept on side, OK!'

The girls were disappointed also, but that couldn't be helped. A few phone calls later and everything was ship shape including a ticket for the Roadie to Boston at 8am on Friday, also one for Ned later that evening to Philli. The bus filled up again for the trip to the Hotel to get their belongings and on the journey Ned said to Mary.

'I wonder how did your brother get on with Jenny, I'd say he's a great hammer man.'

'What does that mean?' She asked naively.

'Well, it's fairly obvious, making love is really an endless attempt at driving home a nail, just picture it.'

'Oh, your horrible,' she laughed, making a playful swipe at him, which ended in a very involved kiss.

Goodbyes were said outside the Hotel and the bus full of girls headed off, the Roadie sitting in the middle of them, having a great time.

'Out of sight out of mind,' thought Ned, as he remembered Amanda waiting in New York State, not forgetting Brenda of course, waiting for him in New York City. His aunts were thrilled to hear that he was paying them another visit and seemed OK with the fact that he had had a few glasses of wine since he'd seen them last.

'It'll give them a chance to get some in, Yummy.'

Chapter Eight

They all got their flights between six and seven that evening, Ned to Philadelphia, Mike and the other band members to Boston. The Singer was moaning about not getting to Nashville but the lads just laughed and said.

'At least you'll be on time at Friday's gig, you might not be as lucky the next time.'

Ned had a great snooze on the plane, getting into Arrivals at midnight where his two aunts and a young lady he had not seen before, greeted him. She also seemed pleased to see him which made him wonder, but he didn't have to wonder too long as she took her turn to hug him.

'Who is this lovely lady?' He asked his happy relatives.

'Oh, that's our neighbour Lizzie, she's off work for the next couple of days and she has volunteered to show you a good time, you young-uns would have more fun without us,' one aunt volunteered.

Now Lizzie is probably a very nice girl, but Jaysus she's ugly, Ned concluded as he smiled at his aunts for being so 'considerate' while at the same time, desperately thinking of a way out of this situation without hurting anyone's feelings.

'I'm not too sure about the next couple of days, I didn't sleep a wink on the flight from San Francisco and I feel I'm coming down with some bug or other,' he lied.

Lizzie looked very sad at this news, which added to the sad way she looked already. She had glasses that must have started out as Coke bottles, she had awful curly hair and he would swear he could see a moustache. Underneath it came her teeth, they were pointing in all directions and needed a good brushing, so he began to cough and cough, getting louder until he was bent over spluttering.

'Are you alright son?' Enquired one aunt. 'Let's go back to the house and get some hot whiskey into you.'

The mention of whiskey gave him an idea. 'I'll get as many hot whiskeys as I can without getting pissed, then make out I'm pissed, that might solve the problem.' These thoughts were flying around his head as his aunts bundled him from the building to their car as quickly as they could, with Lizzie trotting behind carrying his bag.

'Where is she staying tonight?' He asked, almost afraid of the answer.

'Oh, she staying with us,' was the reply. 'She has been talking about you non-stop since we showed her your photo, isn't it just lovely to be young.'

He could see by the way his aunts were beaming at each other that they were attempting some match making here, so when they were all in the car and heading back he decided to pull one out of the bag.

'Is it all right with you ladies if I call my fiancée in New York when we get back, she knows I'm not well and she'll be worried about me.'

There was complete silence for about thirty seconds then one aunt spoke. 'You never said you were engaged, does your mother and father know?'

'Not yet,' he replied, 'so if you're talking to them don't breathe a word, OK!'

Ned, who was in the front passenger seat, took a look in the mirror where he could see Lizzie biting her nails and she looked on the verge of crying.

'Not a pretty sight,' he thought, 'but I must do what I'm doing as this proposed romance must end here.'

'All right, you can ring her, so where is this one from?' the reply to his request and the question, came in the same breath.

He had to do some fast thinking. 'She's from New York, but her grandparents came from somewhere in the auld sod,' he lied.

'Is she nice?' Came a squeaky, shaky voice from the back seat.

He took another quick look in the mirror. His admirer was trying to hold back the tears but wasn't doing a good job of it and he really felt sorry for her, but he had to answer.

'Yeah, she's beautiful, five foot eight and a fashion model.'

That did the trick, Lizzie began to sob loudly and he could remember feeling bad about things before, but now (as the country song says) he felt he was 'The number one heel in the country.'

'Could you drop me home first tonight Miss Brady?' Lizzie asked. 'I'm not feeling too good myself.'

There was complete silence until they reached her house and they had hardly stopped until she was out of the car, running up the drive.

'You've really broken that little girl's heart,' moaned the older aunt, 'and her family are worth a fortune.'

'It's your fault auntie,' he said. 'You should never have tried getting us together, match-making is a thing of the past in this day and age, or don't you know?'

'Well I told her not to do it,' claimed the younger Aunt, 'but she wouldn't listen, come on in and ring your lovely model in New York, don't mind her.'

There was a phone in the bedroom, which he could use, but firstly, he would have some hot tea and scones followed by a hot whiskey for his ailment, which seemed to have subsided since they got back. He just remembered and began coughing loudly again, until the younger Aunt said with a grin.

'You can drop that charade now, I hope you're a better musician than you are an actor and I suppose the fashion model is a myth as well.'

'Honestly, I really want to ring my girlfriend in New York, who (you're right) is not a model, but a restaurant manager and I'm mad about her.' Then looking around furtively to make sure the other aunt had left the room he added. 'Can I have a few hot whiskeys tomorrow also to convince your sister, I don't want her to cop-on?'

She smiled and handed him the hot glass. 'Enjoy that,' she laughed 'and don't keep that poor girl up all night.'

He began to wonder how many phone extensions were in this house and what rooms might they be in, this could be a problem. After not talking to Brenda for over a week, she's liable to say anything, so what if the older aunt picks up the phone. Brenda will want to talk about what they got up to in her apartment and the old dear could have a heart attack. These thoughts were uppermost in his mind as he sat on the bed sipping the hot whiskey and staring at the phone.

'Jaysus', he moaned. 'I must ring her now that I've told them, so here goes and I'll take the chance.' With that resolve he dug out his little black book.

Brenda sounded sleepy for a few seconds, but she came to at once when she recognised his voice.

'Where are you darling? I've missed you in me.' Was her opening statement, and then before he could say a word she was away, telling him in detail how much she had missed him and how she had taken care of the situation on her own. 'Oh come on darling, say something,' she pleaded.

'I can't get a word in edgeways Brenda,' he began.

'If you were here now you could get more than a word in,' she was sounding real sexy now. 'My legs are wide apart for you.'

He knew he had to stop her so he shouted. 'Brenda, Brenda, hold your horses.'

She cut in again. 'Oh Ned, I want to be your horse and you to be my jockey.'

'I'm in my aunt's house in Philadelphia,' he roared, 'she's probably listening on the extension.'

Brenda was silent for a moment.

'Are you alright?' He asked.

He could hear a faint moan and realised she was becoming excited, so he decided to throw caution to the wind saying.

'If anyone is listening on the extension would they please hang up, because what is about to happen may not please you?' He heard a faint, but positive click and wondered which one had got the earful. 'Aw fuck,' he thought, 'how am I going to face them in the morning?'

Just then he realised how bad an idea it had been re-visiting his aunts, he should have spent the time with Brenda, instead of having phone sex with an audience from downstairs, but he realised another week with her without a rest would probably have killed him. All he could hear were low moans coming down the line.

'Guess what I'm doing?' The question gushed from the phone.

'I can, but I'd prefer to hear it from you,' he said.

'Are those old bags still listening?' She asked.

'Jaysus, I hope not,' he answered in a shaky voice. 'If they are, I'll be destroyed altogether, anyway, they're not old bags, they're lovely.' He decided to add that little piece, just to make things easier in the morning and try to erode any fall-out caused by Brenda's comment.

She told him of her love for him and he agreed he had missed her desperately, leaving out (of course) all that had happened in between. If the aunts had remained on the line they would have called in a priest to exorcise the house the next morning, but there was no sign of panic when he sat down to a big breakfast which they had both prepared. He did notice something though. The younger one of the two had a smug little grin playing around her mouth and he couldn't help regretting having asked her to hang up, as she would have had a great time. Lizzie's parents rang to find out what had happened on the previous evening, because their daughter was crying loudly and refusing to get out of bed, she also said she would never eat again. Luckily the younger aunt took the call and softened the situation for Ned, by saying that the young lady was disappointed when she heard of his engagement.

The mother's answer was. 'I'll talk some sense into her, she can't expect guys to fall for her on a first meeting, no matter how beautiful she thinks she is.'

Ned's aunt had replied. 'I think that's sound advice, anyway, there's nicer men out there for her than my nephew.'

The couple of days flew in Philadelphia and he met all his other relations in that town. Then on Friday morning the younger aunt whose name was Sarah, volunteered to drive him to the Airport and this was the first time they had been alone during his stay. At the first set of traffic lights he glanced at her and could plainly see her grinning from ear to ear, so he knew it was a matter of minutes until she said something, so he kept quiet until she could hold it no longer.

'Your Brenda is a very sexy lady and I'm glad you pointed out to her that we're not old bags,' she stated.

He thought for a moment, and then replied. 'I'm sorry she said that and she is a sexy lady, but it's a pity you didn't hang on until the end.'

'Ah, but I did, I knew I would fool you when I hung up and picked up real quick, it's a great trick.' She was openly laughing now. 'You must think because I'm fifty-five and single that I'm an old fool. I've had more sexy men than you've had hot dinners and my current beau is forty going on twenty, so I'm OK thank you.'

Thinking of her current lover made her glow and brought softness to her face, which made her look years younger. Then he remembered.

'My mom told me that you used to be a beauty queen.'

'Yeah,' she replied wistfully. 'I won all the Carnival Queen competitions for years and a few Dairy Queen things as well. Actually it made me very unpopular with all the local girls and they had a big going away party for me when I left Mullymore, a sort of a good riddance do.' She glowed as she told Ned about her lover, plus what they got up to and it made him feel a lot better about his naughty phone call.

'Actually,' she boasted, 'when your call ended the other night, you missed a better one, I was pretty steamed up so I phoned John and we got up to all kinds of shenanigans for over and hour, you would have picked up a few tips.'

As they eased through the traffic, they seemed to be getting more comfortable with each other and he learned a lot from his frisky aunt that he had never been told before. He also found out, that his sainted mother had been pregnant with him on her wedding day, that his oldest aunt (the one they had just left) had slipped away to England to have her unwanted baby, which she immediately gave up for adoption. She herself had been madly in love with a young policeman but her brother, (his dad) made her stop seeing him because he was supposed to be a heavy drinker. She also informed him that Conn (the bands Sax man) was adopted from a lady who was in town with a travelling show. A young priest who was moved shortly afterwards, was credited with being his father. In a way, he was glad that the journey ended, as he began to fear what he might hear next.

They hugged each other and Sarah promised she would make it back to Mullymore soon, even if it were only to show off her new lover.

'I'd put the wind up a few of those old hussies who were glad to see the back of me years ago, because they know I've got the low down on them,' she said with a grin.

She was still waving as the Departures door closed behind him and he felt glad now, for paying the visit. He had lots to mull over on the short flight to Boston, but the one piece of news uppermost in his mind, was the revelation about his premature arrival.

'Jaysus, I was nearly being born a bastard,' he mused, 'and poor fuckin' Conn wasn't so lucky!' He had a nasty thought which he cancelled at once. 'That would be a great way of shutting Conn up the next time he's acting the Bollix, because the smart-arse always looks down on people like that.'

His other cousins were waving at him through the glass when he entered the Arrivals Hall.

'I'll have to talk another load of shite now,' he groaned, as the hugging began. Relations came out of the woodwork that day. There were about fifteen at the Airport and on the way back to town, they called at another four houses, choc-a-block with first, second, third cousins and he was really miffed by the fact that one of them was black.

'Aunt Sarah mustn't know about this lad,' he mused.

Later on, another cousin explained that his brother Joe had been adopted. 'I could see the look of dismay on your face,' he said.

His extended family in Boston knew how to eat. He was given food in every house, but he was really impressed by the feast, which was laid before them that evening. There was stuffed turkey; a gigantic roast with all the trimmings and that was just the food inside the house. The very neat back garden had a barbecue piled high with grub and the huge crowd was tucking in like it was going out of style. He walked around sticking out his hand introducing himself, as he tried in vain to log all the names being fired at him, then he saw this real pretty girl walking towards him, hand outstretched.

'And which cousin might you be now?' He asked.

She blushed profusely and her eyelashes did a dance. 'I'm not your cousin I'm afraid,' she gushed.

'No need being afraid, looking like you do,' he said. 'I'm Ned and I'm pleased to meet you.'

'I'm pleased if you're pleased, but I hope you don't turn out to be a chancer, like most other guys,' she added.

'Me a chancer,' he laughed, 'I wouldn't know the meaning of the word.'

They both laughed heartily and clicked their glasses in a toast.

'Here's to me taking you home after the dance tonight, that is if you plan to go,' his enquiring almost begging tone did the trick.

'OK,' she answered. 'I live next door, so pick me up later and we'll take it from there.'

Then he got a brainwave, so he asked. 'Would you like to bring me around and introduce me to my relations, while you're doing that we can get to know each other better?'

'That's a great idea,' she said, 'as they're not all cousins, I'll keep you from wandering.'

Her comment gave him a great boost, causing a rush of adrenaline as he did a mental 'Yummy-Yummy' and he had to fight the urge to rub his hands in glee. This lovely auburn haired lady introduced herself as Margie, a name that immediately clicked in his mind as the ideal subject for a special request during the dance. Special requests usually worked wonders later in the night. The band's Lead Singer sings a song at every gig called (Margie's at the Lincoln Park Inn) where the subject in the song is a sort of loose woman. Dancers seldom listen to words and hearing her name will make Margie feel special, or so he hoped, but not this dancer though. Later at the gig, as he watched her move gracefully around, he could see the look of displeasure taking over her lovely face.

'I've blown it,' he thought, as the set ended and she made a beeline for the stage.

'So that's the kind of girl you think I am!' She stated.

'What do you mean?' He countered, in the din of the crowd.

'Don't give me that,' she said crossly, 'you must know that song is about a prostitute.'

'I'm sorry,' he answered, almost managing a tear, 'but I thought it was just about an unhappy marriage and I pass no remarks on the words when I'm not singing it,' he lied.

Ned was the complete opposite at rehearsals. If he heard even one word that didn't make sense in a song, he would be on it like a flash, now he hoped this bluff would work. He could see she was mellowing, but he could also hear the members of the band losing the rag.

'For fucks sake,' roared Conn. 'Would you announce the next number and leave the birds until it's over.'

She could see he was under pressure, so she gave him a weak smile and said. 'I'll see you later.'

Ned turned around like a bull and thrust the microphone into Conn's hand saying.

'You should announce the fucking thing yourself.'

'No I won't, it's your fuckin' job,' he replied, ramming the mike back into Ned's hand.

'Well if it is, maybe it's about time I got paid extra for it,' he thundered in return.

He had wanted to say that for ages, as he was pissed off with the lads always saying, Ned do this, Ned do that, treating him like a door mat. A second later he was standing facing the patrons again, a big cheesy grin on his face, like he had been told the funniest joke instead of a string of fucks.

'And now ladies and gentlemen, boys and girls, everyone on the floor for a Quickstep.' 'Such a stupid intro,' he thought as he grabbed the trombone, realising he always made a boob like that when under pressure. It sounded as if there were four kinds of people at the gig. 'Ladies and gentlemen, boys and girls, my arse!'

He was in bad humour for the remainder of the night, apart from smiling at Margie every time she boogied past the bandstand and he could see she was aware of his demeanour. His cousin Tom had brought them both to the gig and he was taking them home as well, now after signing a few autographs while talking to none of the band, he made a quick exit. Before leaving, he gave his number to Mike with instructions to give it to nobody unless in a crisis.

Later, as they joined Tom and his girlfriend back at the car, Margie asked. 'Was the row about me?'

'Not you in particular, they were jealous I was talking to such a lovely girl, so they had to show their displeasure in some way.' He knew that had scored points.

'Imagine how small minded they are,' she said, her voice drifting away as she thought about it.

Ned was wondering how he would make a move on this good looking stranger, when his problem was solved by Tom who swerved to miss a cab, causing Margie to hurtle across the seat into his arms and he was glad when he noticed she was happy to stay there. That first kiss told him all he wanted to know, then their hands were everywhere, grabbing, rubbing, kneading and still her tongue remained halfway down his throat. He pulled his mouth away and whispered in her ear.

'Not now Margie, lets hold on until later.'

'But I can't bring you to my house, can you take me to your room instead?' She was almost pleading.

Tom had been tuned in.

'You had better stay in the car for a while,' he said, giving him a knowing look. 'If you make any noise inside the house my mother will investigate, so I'll put the car in garage and give you a key for the side door.'

It was a good call to stay in the car. This gorgeous young woman went to town on him and after the late night visit from the L.A. blonde; he never thought he would get such a working over again. This lady did the lot and insisted on going all the way as well, then at 7am, even-though he was in bits, she asked if he would take her to his room.

'We would make too much noise and Tom's mum would not be pleased,' he insisted.

'OK,' she said. 'Let's do it one more time,' and once again her auburn curls were all over his lap.

This session finished reluctantly for her at 8am and then she informed him that her mother would be up, so she would have to come out the front door of the house instead of the garage door.

'Anyway, I need to go to the bathroom,' she said and then with a promiscuous smile she continued. 'You're hot stuff Ned.'

'Jaysus, I'm not as hot stuff as you are and I've got to be on a plane for Chicago at 3 o'clock, I'm bollixed.'

'Don't be rude Ned, I want to remember you as a nice boy, just come to the bathroom with me.'

He looked at her in shock, she was serious, but he ushered her inside and ran to the downstairs loo. Looking in the mirror, he saw this completely broken man looking back at him and then he heard her on the stairs. She descended one step at a time, just like Liz Taylor in a blockbuster movie, while he stared up at her in awe.

'Jaysus,' he repeated, 'you're looking better now, than you were going to the dance last night.'

'Oh thank you Ned, a couple of kisses and hugs can work wonders for me.'

She timed it perfectly, just as Tom's mum was coming from the living room.

'Hello young lovers,' she cooed, 'it's lovely to know that a couple of kisses and hugs can please young people today and thanks for washing up.'

'Who the fuck washed up?' He wondered, 'it must have been Tom and his bird.'

He walked Margie down the path and kissed her on the cheek in the full gaze of Tom's mom. The older lady hadn't a clue what came from the younger woman's lips as she smiled and said.

'I'd love to screw you again sometime, OK!'

'I can hardly wait,' he said, but instead he should have said. 'I can hardly walk,' that would have been more like it.

Tom got him up at one; they had a quick snack and headed for the Airport. Margie was waving like mad from her front door, now dressed in a white Marilyn Monroe frock and high heels to match. All that was missing was the wind, the grating and the blonde hair. She looked stunning.

'How did you get on, or in other words, how many times did you get on?' Tom quietly enquired.

'So you know the story,' said Ned.

'Yeah I taught her all she knows I don't think,' he replied, 'that's why I had to leave you both in the car in the garage.'

'I never met anyone so insatiable,' said Ned, in what was the equivalent of shock. 'She nearly fuckin' killed me, how often do you travel?'

'Well, I used to get to her at least once a day before I met my girlfriend, but now it's once a week, did she mention me?' He asked.

'No, there was no time for talking,' was the true answer.

When Ned told him what she had said about the song he played for her at the dance, he concluded that she was paranoid.

'She thinks everyone knows her secret,' he said.

'What happens if you get her pregnant?' Ned asked.

'I insist on Condoms,' said Tom, 'tell me, did you use one?'

Ned had a bad moment when he realised that he had tried to get one on but failed, because of the speed by which she had made the connection.

'No,' he replied, 'but I was careful, anyway, she seemed to sense what was going on and as she said, took care of it.'

'Well I hope she's OK, because she might come looking for me if she's in the family way,' mused Tom. 'Despite the fact that she fancied you more than me.'

He worried about that all the way to the hotel in Chicago and hardly got a wink of sleep on the plane.

'No women for me tonight,' he swore.

The lads behaved like nothing had happened and he was glad, because he just wasn't in the mood for any agro today. Ned was like a zombie during the Chicago gig and told the lads a little fib about a flu that seemed to be hovering. (Mr. Ivory) the Piano player, having gone back into his shell since the beach-party, was heard to almost whisper.

'Maybe it's a dose he's got!'

Ned heard him and laughed. 'You're the dose,' he said.

They all remembered what Mike had said about going to bed early tonight, so apart from a few hugs in the hall there was no lovin' done in Chicago, as the double gig in New York was uppermost in everyone's mind. They would be flying to Kennedy Airport at ten in the morning, then more sleep and as Mike said.

'That's the time to start thinking about Carnegie Hall.'

Ned started thinking about Brenda the moment he got to the hotel, so he gave her a ring, but there was no reply and when he realised she was working he was glad. Now she would have to talk about the weather instead of loving and she said that she would be making her own way to both gigs. He breathed a sigh of relief at this news and told her he was looking forward to seeing her later, after a big snooze. Mike was like something wound up as he guided them from their rooms to the diner. From there he shepherded them to the stretch limo, which took them to the famous Carnegie Hall, only this time they were taken to the stage door.

'WOW.' 'I think I'll shit myself,' volunteered the Bass man.

'Me too,' was the Drummer's comment.

Mr. Ivory jibed to the Drummer. 'You won't be able to shit, you'll be sitting down.'

'Listen lads, less of the crap if you'll pardon the pun,' said Mike sternly.

'They'll be OK Mike, I think we're all wound up a bit,' said Ned, 'we'll never find the time coming around.'

Their gig was scheduled from 9.30 until 10 o'clock and that half-hour to them, would be the toughest thirty minutes of their professional lives. Anyway, that was they're thinking as they walked about backstage, waiting their turn to sound check. In the big stately dressing room that they had been given, they were speaking in awesome whispers to each other, quite unlike the usual boisterous fashion adopted by The Nova's Showband. Not a swearword, dirty joke or attempts at piss-takes of any kind and Mike could hardly believe it, so he decided to check it out.

'Why the whispers, is it the old story of the Hallowed Halls?' He enquired.

'What do you mean by Hallowed Halls Mike?' The Roadie asked.

Before the Manager could answer, the Piano man replied and he wasn't whispering, he roared at the top of his voice.

'My God, it's always the same, every time you hear something new you ask for an explanation at once, could you just let it go and ask some other time?'

The Roadie's bottom lip began to tremble and he ran from the room in tears.

'That was a bit insensitive,' said Mike, and he was joined by everyone in the room in full agreement.

'I think you'd better go and apologise to the chap,' said Ned, 'all of us may not be as well educated as you, then after your apology maybe you could answer his query.'

The little bit of a fracas did one good turn at least; it put an end to the whispering. In about five minutes, the two semi banished members came back smiling, albeit thinly and the Roadie spoke up.

'I'm sorry too and in future when I hear something new, I'll check the dictionary.'

Ned found out afterwards how the Piano man answered the question. The Roadie had been outside the dressing room door when he saw Mr. Ivory come out, walk over to a stagehand and talk to him for a minute. Then he gave the man a playful slap on the shoulder and went in search of the offended one who had purposely disappeared. When he was eventually found, yer-man apologised and immediately told him the meaning of Hallowed Halls.

Just to get his own back, the Roadie asked. 'Did you write it down?'

'What do you mean?' Came the question.

'I saw you asking the stage hand, at least I make myself look foolish among friends,' he said.

He told Ned afterwards. 'That's why I was smiling from ear to ear when I got back to the dressing room.' 'His nibs was really pissed off and begged me to say nothing to the lads, a promise which I kept until now of course.'

Ned would not be on the controls tonight and they would be depending on a sound engineer who seemed to know his stuff, as he took them through the sound check flawlessly. He had asked for a running order of their show and a break down of the instruments used, plus taking note of lead and harmony vocals during the set. They would go through numbers one and five, as they covered the full band plus vocals.

'So when you're ready please,' he requested.

The sound in the hall was mind blowing and they could hear everything crystal clear. He could hardly believe it when the man told him how low the P.A. wattage was.

'It's all about the acoustics of the room, it's the best in town,' he claimed proudly.

After the rehearsal, a feeling of awe was once more prevailing, until the Roadie made a comment that made everyone crack up. They were talking about the view from the stage and how high up some of the seats were on the balcony. They wondered if they would they be able to see anyone up there later on?

'Up there is called [The Gods],' said the Roadie calmly, 'and before the dimmer of you ask what that means, plus how I happen to know, well I asked the stagehand while you were sound checking. I discovered earlier how to get information like that.'

Everybody in the room went into convulsions at the story and the smugness of its delivery, that is, all except the Piano player who ducked into the toilet. The Roadie was obviously pissed off at the Piano man and this proved it. He was only too keen to divulge the secret, which was supposed to be kept forever, or so Mr. Ivory thought.

There were four fifteen-minute acts on before The Nova's Showband and their thirty minutes, would bring the first half of the show to a close. For openers, a well-known Guitar playing singer, who sat on a high stool and held the capacity crowd in the palm of his hand. Next, a fabulous Irish Traditional Band currently making a name for themselves around the world, then when act number three went on, everyone was in the wings watching spellbound and the dressing rooms were empty. A young man with black curly hair and an equally young auburn haired girl, were tapping out the rhythm of the reel with steel tipped shoes, flanked by five more fellows and five gorgeous girls, each one as competent as the other.

'Who are they?' Ned's question was pitched to the nearest stagehand, which seemed to know all the answers.

'They're from Boston,' he answered. 'The lead guy is called Michael Roundley and the girl is called Brigin, the group is collectively known as 'Sir Reel.'

'Jaysus, they're fantastic,' enthused Ned, that outfit is really gonna go places, but tell me about this Roundley fellow, he can't be Irish with a name like that.'

'I don't know where his dad is from, but I'm sure his mother is Irish, she was a well known step dancer herself,' came the well-informed reply.

Ned felt a real thick when he went back to the dressing room. There, plastered on the wall was a huge poster naming all the acts plus where they were from and smiling boldly at him from one of the photos was the one and only Michael Roundley, with his dancing partner Brigin Maguire.

'I was so busy looking at the photo of us that I saw no one else, Pathetic!'

The fourth act was a well-known Irish Comedian called Hal Fox and our heroes had to make do by leaving the dressing room door open, so they could hear the jokes. The last fifteen minutes was psyche up time and they were walking around the room rubbing their hands while generally boosting each other's morale with comments like.

'We'll be huge here, it's going so well, and all we have to do is play and look happy.'

Then Mr. Ivory put his big foot in again. 'I think we'll fuckin' die,' he moaned, 'we've no hope after that Roundley fellow and his gang.'

They all glowered at him and the pensive atmosphere that prevailed, was finally shattered by a torrent of fucks being showered upon him. The burst of expletives also included Moron, Wanker, and Spoilsport and strangely enough it was Conn, who called the poor unfortunate 'A Bastard.'

Deadly silence settled on the room.

'If Conn only knew the score he wouldn't use that word,' Ned was thinking.

'I'm no bastard,' the Piano man roared at Conn and then Mike intervened.

'If I'm not mistaken, the comedian is on his last joke and the way some of you are behaving is also a joke, in fact, you should be out there now trying your material.'

Then there was a bang on the now closed door. 'You're on in two,' a voice shouted.

'Jaysus,' exclaimed Ned, 'we must have missed the five minute call, I hope no one heard us.'

By now, they were all on their feet heading for the stage, just in time to hear the M.C. who was also the comedian saying.

'And now, could we have a big Carnegie Hall welcome, for a band which is the biggest thing since Showbands began, in

Ireland, the U.S and England, let's hear it for 'The Nova's Showband.'

The applause was so loud that they missed the Drummer's first count causing the Piano man to start on his own, which pissed him off again, but the Drummer immediately counted into his mike and the 1,2,3,4 leaped at them from the monitors. To look at the happy faces you'd think they were best buddies. Even Mr. Ivory was smiling. As Mike and the Roadie watched and listened from the side aisle, the manager said.

'Those guys are definitely pro's.' Quickly he noticed the blank look on the Roadie's face and countered. 'I mean, they're professionals.'

'Oh yeah Mike, I knew what you meant,' he fibbed.

Every number got a rapturous applause and twenty minutes into their show they began to get loud requests for their latest single, which really chuffed them. The Singer was particularly pleased and promised the audience that they would be closing with that number.

Ned had a strange thought. 'I wonder will he be calling himself Steve or Barry tonight,' and there was a grin on his face as he began singing The Haunted House.

Mike had arranged that the resident band in the City Plaza Ballroom would play the full opening two hours tonight and the lads would do from 11 until 1 o'clock. That gave them ample time to sign autographs, talk to people during the break and still be in lots of time for a cuppa before their second gig. As he was signing a picture for a young woman later on, Ned could feel a pair of arms slipping around him from behind, so he decided to play it safe and turned slowly to find himself looking into the smiling face of Helen, not Brenda. She demanded a big hug and began whispering into his ear.

'Standing right behind me is my fella and I think he suspects something, are we doing it tonight?'

'Well I've got news for you, standing right behind your fella is my girlfriend, so I'm afraid we won't be doing it tonight, now let's get out of this clench.'

As he spoke he tried to push her back gently, but alas, this lady had other ideas. She removed her arms from around him and then suddenly took his face in both her hands, giving him a big sloppy sexy kiss. He could feel her being dragged away from him, by the feminine looking guy she had said was her boyfriend and suddenly this person was trying to hit him.

'Who the fuck are you and would you ever go away and leave me alone?' Ned asked, giving the impression that he didn't know his assailant, as this person tried in vain to slap him.

The attacker decided that he might have more success verbally, so for openers he exclaimed.

'Your band is crap!'

'And you would know would you, genius?' Said Ned grinning.

'I know you don't want to hear this, but you're a crap Trombone player as well,' enthused yer-man.

'Well', said Ned. 'I don't know you from Eve, sorry I mean Adam and you're probably right, but I'm from a different school of Trombone players, I'm a successful one, so have a nice day loser.'

That really got the pansy's dander up and his voice went up a couple of tones, while all through this Brenda was watching quietly, wondering what was going to happen next. Is this guy going to kill her man with words or is she going to lose him to this very sexy lady who was kissing him earlier, she decided to stay out of it. Then Ned turned and addressed Helen.

'Maybe you should take him home now, before I give him a box and before you and I become bad friends.'

'So you don't want to screw me in The Woodlawn Hotel tonight then, where is this other bitch you'll be doing instead?'

She was screaming at the top of her voice and looking around desperately for the object of Ned's affections. Thankfully there were girls all over the place making their way back to their seats for the second half of the show and she didn't know Brenda, which was a bonus. Just then Mike arrived with a bouncer. He had been watching the spectacle and decided it was bad publicity for the band, so with his help the bouncer gave the angry couple a choice of leaving or going back to their seats.

'The remainder of the show will be good now the shit is over.' Helen said, so they picked the latter.

'Jaysus, what is it they say about a woman scorned?' he was thinking, as he made his way over to Brenda who had melted into the crowd.

'Is it true, what that crazy woman was saying?' she asked.

'Partly,' he answered. 'I went out with her back home and she thinks she owns me.'

'But how did she know the name of the Hotel?' was her next question.

'Loads of people know where we're staying, they keep asking, so will I see you later?' He enquired.

'I'm here with a couple of friends and they're dropping me off at the Plaza, see you,' she said, giving him a dubious peck on the cheek.

'Give your name at the box office, I'll organise for you to get in free,' he said, giving her a return peck on the way out the door.

'That horn of yours will get you killed yet,' opined Mickey Joe.

'I won't be the first man to die for his instrument,' Ned laughed, as they sped towards gig number two.

There were people everywhere and they had to push their way into the venue via the main entrance.

'No stage door here,' someone commented.

'Lads, don't get carried away, just wait until we get back home to the Patrician Hall Carrickbay, or some tent in a wet field.' Came the rejoinder.

They were entering the comfortable band room in The City Plaza Ballroom at that precise moment and they were brought back to reality with a bang as the downward spiral continued. It was the Drummer and he sounded as if he was begging.

'Don't mention Carrickbay or any of the Carnival tents, I want to savour this a little longer.'

'The inevitability of time, oh no, you can't fight it,' the Piano man had never sounded so sombre, almost scary.

'Can you imagine the kind of gig we'll have tonight, if everyone is feeling like those two,' said Ned. 'Personally, I'm gonna have a ball, so I want you all to get a grip of yourselves, or failing that, be like me, get a grip of a woman.'

Slowly the get a grip comment seeped through and there were a few late laughs around the room.

'You all have two hours to click and anyway, most of you have dates for later on, so lets bring them all back to the hotel or their apartments and do the biz.'

It was Mike, who was now trying to drum up some interest in his men and it seemed to be working.

'Just one more thing,' he added. 'The Promoter is putting on a spread after the gig and you are all invited, including any friends in tow, so that's something to look forward to.'

The gig was really buzzing when they went on stage and Ned gave them all the thumbs up and shouted. 'Sock it to them lads!' Around midnight, he started looking for Brenda, but still no sign. 'Maybe she was annoyed and went home,' he thought.

At least in The City Plaza Ballroom you could see most of the people on the balcony, unlike Carnegie Hall where they were just like blobs. At 12.30 he breathed a sigh of relief, there she was waving down at him and he felt a surge of affection for this lovely woman, who was once again complete with bun together with a cute little black number. Earlier at the concert he thought she was wearing a black suit, but she had obviously shed the jacket in the cloakroom to reveal this lovely low cut black dress. His loins began to stir as he thought. 'She's gorgeous.' Ned was doing his job very well, but he was on autopilot from the moment he decided he couldn't wait to get Brenda home. Immediately after the gig he was going to ask the Promoter for the loan of his office, where his love and himself would have a knee-trembler, it was the only way.

'I love you,' he said, over the heads of the massive crowd.

'I love you,' she replied, blowing a kiss for good measure.

'That does it,' he thought, 'the manager's office it is.'

The Roadie started giving out the band pictures early. He had guessed there would be a mad rush at he end, so he took up his position at the right hand side of the huge stage and a large queue formed immediately, much to his delight. Ned was of the opinion that the Roadie felt he was an equal member of the band, because in his own way, he was on the same stage performing, but tonight there was another agenda, he was hoping to score and score he did. Before the gig ended he had taken a young lady to the bar for a drink, chatted her up and was back in position in lots of time to resume his P.R. duties.

'You know, that chap is worth his weight in gold,' the Bandleader was thinking. He was busy telling the punters.

'We'll be back soon, sorry 'we' can't stay another month, 'we're' very busy when 'we' get home, but 'we' can't wait to pay another visit,' and he could hear him saying to everyone. 'Have a nice day.'

Ned was savouring every minute of the last gig and he knew by the looks on the lad's faces, that they felt the same. They were 'giving it the lash' yet a state of melancholy was battling to take over and that had to be staved off at any cost. He was torn between the love of what he was doing now and his feelings for the lady he would love later. Just then he saw Mike walking past the stage so he gave him a prod with his trusty trombone and beckoned him over, this had to be quick.

'Would you ask the Promoter if I can borrow his office for a while after the gig, I need to talk to Brenda, he'll understand.'

Mike grinned at the request, giving him the thumbs up, and then he blew a quick kiss to the lady in the black dress and felt a surge of emotion as he wondered where the zipper was. The bright lights in the hall flashed four of five times as a signal to end the gig, but the crowd was roaring for more so they struck up their latest record for the third and final time. After finishing the vocal the band cut volume and the Singer said his farewells to the crowd, then he said.

'And now, I'll hand you over to Ned Brady our Band Leader, a big hand for him everybody.'

Ned took the mike, smiled lavishly at the Chanter and began to introduce the band. He gave them all glowing references and when he got to the Singer he gave him a huge build up.

'Show your appreciation for the voice of The Nova's Showband, Steve, take a bow, this man thrilled audiences in Nashville recently, appearing at the Grand Ole Opry of all places.'

The punters went mad. The Singer bowed and scraped even more vigorously than he had in the past, Mike looked up at Ned, a look of disbelief on his smiling face. The members of the band looked on, mouths wide open.

'What's that fuckin' eejit gonna say next?' Mouthed Mickey Joe, still using the side of his gob.

Ned just kept bullshitting away, not really sure of what he might say next, so when the bright house lights flashed again, he knew it was time to pull the plug. People got up on the stage to pose for photos with members of the orchestra; others invited them down to floor level to stand into group shots. It was just a marvellous, unforgettable, euphoric experience, which would be talked about often, with everyone asking the Singer about Nashville and the Opry. He felt lucky that him and Ned had had the altercation some days ago as lots of people (having being there) were all complaining about the live commercials and their favourite singers only getting one song in most instances. When he heard Ned announce it he felt like hitting him, but after the reaction it got, he felt ten feet tall and the old ego was cooking. Ned got a tug on his sleeve and turned around not knowing what to expect, but he was glad to see a smiling Brenda, towing a photographer.

'Can I have a picture with the leader of the band?' She asked coyly.

'Yes of course, but the conditions are, you must kiss him first.'

'Say no more,' she said, as her arms slid around his neck.

There was no sign of it ending, so the photographer kept moving around them, taking a picture from every angle until his roll of film ran out.

'Did you get one?' She asked.

'I think so, and after someone pays me, maybe I could have an address to send the photos to,' he replied.

Still in Ned's arms, Brenda took care of the snapper's request and then he told her of the plan which he had cooked.

'I love your cooking,' she said, going for another kiss.

The Promoter vacated his office and before he left he handed our hero a key, advising him to lock the door while he was 'having his meeting.' Brenda had been too shy to walk boldly in, deciding instead to mingle with some people about twenty feet away and wait for Ned's all clear. As the Promoter disappeared up the stairs she got the signal, then quickly sped into the office and into his arms. They kissed as he locked the door, very gently at first, until all the pent up desire of their time apart, began to manifest itself. As they moved backward to the big mahogany and leather desk, only six words were uttered.

'I love the dress, it stays,' he said.

By now, the little black number was willingly around her waist, as he sat her on the desk with both her legs firmly locked around him. Ned's theory is, you can't have love without lust and their bodies agreed that this was a perfect example of both. If they each lived forever, this high would never be repeated as they neared the zenith of their sexual existence. Later, they locked the door and slowly headed up the stairs to the party, which by now was obviously in full swing, judging from the noise. It was a slow process, having stopped on every second step to kiss and pledge their undying love for each other, but as they got to the second last step he almost fell back in shock. She was holding him very tightly now, whispering in his ear.

'Don't panic honey,' she began, 'but I think I'm pregnant.'

He tightened his grip on her to save falling, stifling his usual 'Jaysus' as his mind exploded. 'How did we let this happen?' He thought. 'Simple, you wouldn't wear rubbers you Bollix!'

'Are you all right honey?' He could hear her enquire.

'Yeah,' he lied, drawing his head back and smiling into her beautiful but worried face. 'You gave me a shock,' he continued, 'but we love each other, we make love very well and we'll both love the baby when it arrives, we've still got the key to the office you know.'

'If we go back down there, I'll screw you to death,' she threatened, giving him a big happy kiss.

While they still held each other, he couldn't stop thinking if his mum, who had told his dad the same story years ago, a story that could have changed their future. What would have happened, if his dad had not taken responsibility to marry his mother?

'Jaysus, I would have been put up for adoption, maybe spend years with the nuns or the Christian brothers, that would have been a bummer, but again my mother would not have allowed that to happen, not to her 'Edward.' Then he remembered something Brenda had said to him, on the day she introduced him to her boss. 'I'm safe,' she had promised. They joined the party amid a barrage of jibes.

'You must have the job done by now Ned,' it was Conn sticking his oar in.

'I'd love to shut that fellow up,' he thought, 'but I can't say anything to him because of my own situations, past and present.'

Then Brenda spoke up. 'Twins on the way lads,' she bragged, rubbing her still lovely flat stomach, draped beautifully in the now slightly rumpled dress, which was once more reunited with the stylish black jacket.

'I thought Ned was firing blanks,' roared a quite drunk Mr. Ivory, much to the pleasure of the others. 'He should have had those results years ago.'

Ned and Brenda laughed at everything as they downed drink after drink, getting really into the spirit of things. The Promoter thanked the band plus it's manager, Mike thanked the Promoter who broke open a huge bottle of champagne and they all laughed as the bubbles went up their noses. It was the first time for the Mullymore lads to have bubbly, but Brenda was very disappointed when it all ran out. Their flight wasn't until 6.30 the next evening leaving no one in a hurry, but Ned didn't want to get too drunk so he asked the Promoter to call a cab. He had something to ask Brenda later. They kissed and groped all the way back to her apartment, where she reluctantly realised that her second hand was needed to get the key from her handbag.

'It won't jump out on it's own you know,' he said.

Inside, she led him to the dimly lit bedroom with the huge bed against the far wall.

'My home is your home,' she said, with a hiccup or two, as she slid out of the black dress.

Full of mixed emotions, she didn't notice he wanted to ask her something. She was tipsy, madly in love, pregnant and very aware of the fact that the person she shared all these things with, would be getting on a plane at 6.30 this very evening, to fly three thousand miles away from her. Suddenly she collapsed on the bed in floods of tears and realising what was wrong, he lifted her long stocking clad legs, complete with beautiful black high-heeled patent leather shoes, on to the covers, then climbed on to hold her almost naked body closely. She cried herself to sleep that night while being held firmly in his strong arms, his question would have to wait.

Brenda had taken the Monday off to spend with Ned and later, see him off at Kennedy Airport, so it was almost

11 o'clock when they both woke up. He opened his eyes to her gentle kisses and as he sat up in the bed, he couldn't stop admiring this gorgeous, now completely naked woman, smiling back at him.

'Is it any wonder she's in the family way,' he thought. 'One would have to be a eunuch not to make her pregnant, or maybe wear at least two Condoms, as the Irish man says, to be sure, to be sure.'

Brenda wasn't the only one with emotions that day. How was he going to handle flying three thousand miles away from her and not be able to see or touch this lovely creature, now carrying his child? It wouldn't be easy, so they talked for ages, mostly about the still invisible being, which would tie their futures together in such a permanent fashion.

'I don't hold you responsible Ned, I thought I was safe, especially that first weekend, it's my fault entirely,' she stated.

'Shush pet,' he said, 'neither one can blame the other for being in love and doing what lovers do. I've been crazy about you for years and often back then, I swore I would do just that to you sometime, I'm serious.'

That did it; she pushed him back on the bed and jumped on him saying. 'This will be our last session for some time, let's remember it.'

'I remember it every time,' he moaned, as she had her wicked way.

They were both exhausted, yet aware of having to be at the hotel at four to catch the stretch for the Airport. The Roadie had promised to get Ned's things together including the trombone, but he would need to shave back at The Woodlawn. She led him to the shower reminding him that the last session was over, but she would spoil him by sponging his body from head to toe. It was as good as making love and he had to count more than sheep to keep from taking her again, then it was back in their clothes and out. He watched with pleasure, as she brushed and combed her hair, before donning a very elegant wine coloured trouser suit, which she said, was to stop him getting ideas.

'I don't know where you got that idea from Brenda, you're sex on legs no matter what you wear,' he said, giving her a playful slap on the behind as they left the apartment for the waiting taxi. Then he asked. 'Why are you sitting across from me?'

'Well, if I sit beside you, we'll start kissing, one or both of us will drop the hand and that will be that,' she explained.

'I suppose your right,' he agreed.

Brenda had many lovely traits but probably her nicest one was, she would never blame the man for anything she could not take the blame for herself, like in this case. Back at the hotel, the lads were scurrying around getting their bits together and Ned could hear the Roadie on the phone making his excuses to Amanda in Buffalo, about his no show situation.

'As God's my judge Amanda, the manager was to blame, every time I had planned to go and see you, Mike came up with something new for me to do. He even messed Ned about as well, he intended coming with me to meet Jayne but all the plans were changed, we couldn't help it I swear.'

'Thank God Brenda went to the loo,' said Ned. 'You could be heard in Mullymore shouting out Jayne's name, did she mention me?'

'Yes,' he answered, 'out of sight out of mind was her comment and she expected a phone call from you at least, as you promised.'

'OK,' said Ned, 'not another word about Buffalo until we go through emigration, then I'll give Jayne a ring and like you, I'll blame Mike.'

'Who'll blame me for what?' Mike questioned. He had been passing by just then and heard, so Ned explained and he laughed. 'If that's all I'm blamed for I won't worry, let's move it.'

Just then, Brenda came striding back clutching a sealed white envelope that she placed in Ned's pocket.

'Is that money?' he asked.

'No,' she replied. 'Remember that sexy thing you asked me to do with a razor, well, I've just been busy with a scissors instead and I want you to have the contents for underneath your pillow.'

That really got him going again but there was no place to go. They had given back all the keys so he would have to use his imagination, as for underneath his pillow, can you imagine what his mother would say after her curiosity forced her into opening the envelope. He told Brenda, that an older woman back in Ireland had given him a shock one night with her Shaven Haven; he didn't say that it only happened one week ago and going back to the pillow, he hadn't said he was still living at home, no way! They both sat in the back seat of the limo on the way to the Airport, beside the Singer who was listening to country music full blast on his transistor radio, which he had 'bought in Nashville,' as he told everybody.

They spoke mostly in whispers about their present situation and she repeated that it wasn't his fault, so if he didn't want to take it any further she would understand.

'I'll still love you both always,' she said.

'I'll tell you something no one knows Brenda, my parents want me to take over the pub so we could live there, what do you think?' He asked.

'I don't mind where I live as long as you're there,' she said, 'but give yourself more time before you decide, it can only be for one reason, 'LOVE.'

Ned hadn't cried for a long time, but as they held on to each other at the Departure gate, the tears flowed freely. All the lads said goodbye to Brenda and she waved in return as the last kiss continued.

Then they heard Mike say. 'Come on Ned, they're closing the gate.'

The tears were tripping them both as he gently held her at arms length; slowly he removed a gold band from his little finger and placed it on the wedding finger of her left hand.

'It was my grandmother's wedding ring,' he said, 'my mum gave it to me.' 'I'll say I mislaid it if she passes any remarks and you can give it back when we get the real one.'

Still at arms length she whispered. 'It's beautiful and as far as I'm concerned it's the real one, I love you, so you had better go now or you'll be left behind.'

They both smiled, knowing what that would mean, as they kissed each other's hands with an extra kiss for the ring from him. They promised to talk in the next twenty-four hours and then he turned and ran through the gate.

Chapter Nine

He was in another world as he searched for his seat and was thrilled when he discovered it to be in the centre, between two lovely elderly ladies. He had hoped it wouldn't be an isle seat, because he didn't want to be tempted by the hostess's legs as they made their way up and down the plane, no woman or part of same, was going to upset this euphoric feeling which was sweeping him along.

'God is good,' he thought, as he closed his eyes and whispered. 'I love you Brenda and our baby too.'

But sleep was not to come yet, its postponement came in the shape of the Roadie who was full of beans after being invited to buffalo on his holidays.

'What did Jayne say when you rang her?' He asked.

Ned stifled his usual 'Jaysus' because of his two travelling companies and tried to find an answer.

'Oh, her number was continuously engaged, so I'll have to drop her a line when I get back, but for now it's sleep and more sleep, see you later.'

After the recent revelations and his real love for Brenda, was it any wonder he forgot to ring the beautiful Jayne and beautiful she was, then reality struck him in all directions. He could no longer dream of getting to know Jayne any better and he would never discover what really lay above those gorgeous knees he had lusted after. The same would be the case with smooth Mary in San Francisco.

'What have I gone and done?' He whined.

'Pardon,' said the lady in the window seat.

'Oh, it's nothing really, nothing a brain transplant won't cure,' he answered, failing to quote the type of transplant he really needed and he couldn't be rude. Just before he dozed off, he made a pact with the man above, that his womanising was at an end and an old adage, which he hoped would help him, came to mind. It went like this. (Blessed is he who knows where it is and passes it by). Some time later he heard a soft feminine voice asking.

'Would you like some food Sir?' and in his semiconscious state he mumbled.

'No thanks Brenda just give me a kiss instead and let me sleep.'

The two older ladies, who were letting their little tables down burst out laughing, as did the stewardess. Ned was leaning forward sound asleep, his lips pursed, as he waited for his love to kiss him.

'One of us should kiss him,' laughed the lady in the isle seat. 'He won't settle until someone does.'

'Well I can't,' said the staff member, it's well outside my duties to kiss passengers, you have a go.'

'Oh no,' they chorused. 'If he woke up and found an older woman kissing him he would be offended, lets shake him instead.' The two ladies shook him gently saying. 'Wake up young man, this lovely girl has got food for you and she will have to take it away if you don't eat it.'

When he awoke he had a silly smile on his face.

'I don't know where you were in your dream, but I can guarantee, you were enjoying every minute of it,' one of his new neighbours said, as the stewardess placed his food on the table, which one of the women had lowered.

'Yes, I was miles away, back in New York with my girlfriend who's,' he stopped short amid sentence.

'Are you all right, is her name Brenda?' it was a double-barrelled question.

That put him in a real tizzy, he was about to tell three strangers that his girlfriend was in the family way and to make things worse they knew her name, what next?

They realised what he was thinking by the look on his face. 'Oh, you told us her name earlier, when you were asking her to kiss you, do you miss her?' They asked.

He was now, a bright shade of red and for a man who maintained he hadn't blushed in years it was embarrassing.

The three women decided to lay it on thick. 'We nearly drew straws to see which one of us would fill the breach, seeing that Brenda wasn't around, you were sitting like this for ages.' The stewardess struck the pose he had been in, just to explain what she meant.

Ned, now fully awake, saw the funny side of it and had to remember his new motto, so he wouldn't ask the pretty staff member to follow through. 'Eyes off,' he thought, as he thanked her for the food and began to tuck in. After exchanging a few pleasantries with the two ladies during the meal, he settled down for more sleep and didn't hear a thing until the announcement to fasten their seat belts, on the final approach to Dublin Airport. The Roadie's friend was there with the Bandwagon and the members gasped when they observed the old machine.

'The auld bus looks crap,' said the Drummer and the lads all agreed, no stretch cars here yet.

Mike's brother picked him up as he had to meet the Record Company about their new single and he took his leave after some arrangements were made for the immediate future.

Ned was glad to see his parents in the Arrivals Hall, but even though his mother seemed happy, his dad looked a bit worried and drawn.

'What's the matter with you dad?' He asked as they hugged each other.

As usual his mum answered. 'Your dad has had a mild stroke but he's not too bad.'

He looked at his father for confirmation of this fact. 'That's true son,' he answered. 'I got a bit of a wallop the week after you left, but I'll be OK.'

This tall elegant man he loved and admired had changed, the spring had gone from his step and his big broad shoulders were stooped. He wondered if his going away had anything to do with the stroke and they both put him at rest at once, blaming it on the staff that was robbing him in the pub.

'We hope you'll take that place over son, or it will be the end of your dad,' said his mum sadly.

On hearing that, he almost told them about Brenda and himself, but for some unknown reason he held on. The time is not right yet, a shock like that could kill his father, and as the car sped for home, he felt really strange behind the wheel for the first time in almost a month. They wanted to hear all about the two aunts in Philly, who had been on the phone telling them how fine a son they had and they pointed out in answer to his obvious question, that they had kept their brother's health a secret from them, for now.

'They were great craic altogether, they couldn't believe that I was a non-drinker,' he lied. 'Before I knew it, there was a bottle of wine in front of me and bang went the auld pledge.'

Strangely enough, his mother's answer was non-judgemental to a degree, especially dealing with a subject of such magnitude, concerning her only son.

'Not to worry, you're a grown man now and a glass or two of wine will do you no harm, as long as you stay away from (the hard stuff).'

She was so glad to have her pride and joy home and being their only child, added to her pleasure. What would have happened, he wondered, if his parents had panicked years ago when they discovered his mum was prematurely pregnant? She could have ran away and had him adopted and now they would be childless, but as the thought entered his brain he cancelled it immediately, because even till this day, the love and devotion between his parents was palpable. For the remainder of the journey Ned was like a gramophone. He told them all about the tour, albeit the censored version and they enjoyed it immensely. He watched his father's face in the mirror when he mentioned playing Carnegie Hall and the pride was obvious. He wasn't thinking.

'Why not me lord.'

Ned was wondering if he would ever play the accordion again after the stroke, but now was not the time to ask, as his mum kept the questions flying.

'Tell me this and tell me that now Edward.' That brought him back in a flash to some of the intimate situations he had experienced in the U.S, but especially to Brenda and the way she used to say Edward, as she neared her summit. Suddenly, it was back to reality as the car rounded the bend and the sign said Welcome to Mullymore.

'It's a far cry from where you've been,' said his dad, echoing his own thoughts.

'Do you want to call?' Ned asked, as they drove past The Central Bar.

'No,' he answered, in a voice without expression. 'Just bring us home, I'll see enough of them for the remainder of the week.'

As they drove up the steep hill to the big White House that he also called home, it hit him.

'I think I know why your staff is robbing you dad,' he said, 'it's mainly because, every day from anywhere in the town, they can see this big White House and they say, fuck him, why should we graft while he lives in that mansion on the hill.'

Ned's mother was in shock at her son swearing, a glass of wine maybe, but that four-letter word.

'Edward, stop swearing,' she demanded.

'What you're saying is probably true,' his Dad agreed, 'but none of them built this house for me, I worked hard to get what I have and I didn't rob a penny, just being honest did it.' On that note, his dad climbed proudly out of the car and looked admiringly at his castle saying. 'My answer to that is, fuck them.'

'Oh my God Edmond, you and your son are going to the dogs altogether, get into the house before the neighbours hear you,' she looked around furtively, as she turned the key and ran inside.

Edmond looked around saying. 'As you know son, the nearest neighbour is half a mile away, your mum must think I've got a very powerful voice.' While they both emptied the car, he was glad to see that his dad was still able to lift and carry things. His father noticed the concern saying. 'I still have to do it in the pub.'

Ned got the presents from his case and handed them out and as well as his own offering, he had a few trinkets plus the inevitable up to date pictures from his dad's two sisters, which were viewed with interest, especially one particular shot.

'Who's that young man with Aunt Sarah?' asked his mother.

'Cradle snatching, by the looks of things,' came the smiling answer from the subject's brother.

'Oh Edmond, I wasn't asking you, I was asking our son,' she was putting on a fake huff now.

'I'm afraid dad's right,' Ned said with a laugh. 'Sarah's a great character, I'd say she was a demon in her day.'

'She had them coming from far and near,' said her proud brother, not realising what his statement had inferred. 'There was one chap who used to write to her every time she won a Beauty pageant or Carnival Queen competition, begging her to go out with him.'

'What happened?' Asked Ned with interest.

'Well, she agreed to meet him once and she said he was really good looking, but an egotistical fool, he told her he intended to marry a beauty queen and nothing else would do, how shallow can you get'.

Ned was fascinated by yer-man and asked. 'Well dad, what ever became of the fellow?'

'Well, Sarah wrote and told me that after she emigrated, the chap took up with and married a beauty queen from the next parish, but it only lasted a couple of years until he started chasing his dream again, now she's on her own with a child.'

'Jaysus,' Ned thought, 'he must have been a screwed up individual.'

The band had two nights and days off, but on Wednesday a meeting was scheduled for Mike's office at 2pm, to plan tactics. The good news was, the airplay on their new single would be starting in two weeks and that should set them up for the remainder of the year. Ned had written a few good songs (or at least that's what he thought) in the last while, but it was impossible to get his own band to even listen, let alone record any of them. They were a crowd of jealous arseholes and wouldn't give him a chance, even though Mike had shown interest and the biggest problem was the Lead Singer. If he couldn't write them himself, which he couldn't, then no one else especially Ned, would get the break, but he was prepared to wait and save hassle. They were lucky to have a very popular person in radio on their payroll, which meant the airplay was guaranteed so to speak and they weren't pissing in the wind when they released a record, but he always remembered how hard it was in the beginning. They got no exposure on their first single which was equally as good and only their second one had appeal across the water, becoming a hit over there, the same fate would have befallen it at home as well.

Mike had set up a launch for the new single and they all had their input into the guest list.

'Will you be bringing Susan, or is it one of the locals who will be getting the night out?' He asked Ned.

That gave him a jolt, he hadn't thought about Susan for ages, nor had he phoned her since before England. Then he remembered her prediction. She had suggested that he would probably forget all about her anyway, but was there any point in staying in contact now, because it looked like what she said had come true. Susan's forecast had been a lot simpler, as it had not included Brenda and the baby. He went very pale at that thought, which caused Mike to enquire about his health.

'I'm OK,' he answered. 'I'm just worried about my dad, lets leave it closer to the date and I'll probably ask someone,' he promised.

Only himself and the Roadie were reluctant to pick partners for the do.

'Thinking of Amanda?' He asked the seemingly lost soul.

'Yeah,' came the wistful answer. 'I think I'm in love.'

He decided it wouldn't be wise to ring Susan for some time, because he knew he would blurt out the truth and in doing so he would just offend a very lovely lady. From filling up his diary at the meeting, he knew he would be back in her area four days before the function and then he might try the, (I lost your number) routine. They kicked off in Galway on Thursday to a rapturous welcome and the fans asked all the questions about the tour, but only some of them were answered. Cynthia Rose was tagging along with Conn, who seemed to be happy with his lot; she would be asking a few questions herself and maybe answering a few as well. She, with The Blue Dots Showband, would have been threading the boards on many occasions since they had seen Conn and it was well known, she had her share of studs strategically placed around the country. There were a few girls there that Ned had chatted up on occasions, but tonight he couldn't care less. He had phoned Brenda twice since he got back, but because of the cost, they had only spoken for a few moments altogether, just enough to confirm their love for each other and the void they both felt.

'We'll meet soon,' was their promise.

As usual, they all drove to Galway separately, so on the home trip, Ned sifted through his life and the one thing, which was becoming clearer was. Don't tie yourself down.

He was almost at panic stations when he got back to Mullymore, so he parked the car outside the pub for a while, trying to decide whether or not he could make a future there. It won't be as plush as the big house on the hill and he would miss a lot of home comforts, but then if he and Brenda were happy, that would replace the other less important things in life, plus when the baby comes along, everything will be complete. The word baby brought him to high doh.

'Jaysus,' he groaned. 'I'm not ready for this at all.' It would be bad enough trying to stop the bottles of vodka from walking out of the pub, without having an instant family to rear. 'You were told to wear rubbers you Bollix, but like most men, your head was controlled by your tackle and now see where it's got you.'

In a mental haze he started the big car and headed up the hill, tomorrow night was looming fast. It took him a while that morning to fall asleep, tossing and turning mumbling names, mostly of women he would have to stay away from in the future, then suddenly he sat bolt upright in the bed. He had just seen Susan standing in front of him wearing a very short skirt, her arms outstretched and she seemed to be pleading with him.

'Well Ned, what about our baby, the one we both know we want, or did we not fall in love that night after all?'

'How am I going to tell her?' He mused, trying to hold panic at bay, as the feelings he had or thought he had for Susan, welled up inside him again. 'She'll never forgive me after all my bullshit, so I'd better steer clear of her from now on.'

The weekend flew and the gigs were good, with the same reaction from the fans everywhere. 'Oh me sister Mary was talking to you's in Boston.' Ned wondered if talking was all she did and with whom, then on the Sunday night, three tough looking guys sidled up to him after the dance, they had this to say.

'We were at both your dances in San Francisco and thanks for doing the second one for us.' They continued with some more small talk, slapped Ned on the back, laughed and walked away.

Then a very glamorous young woman walked over and asked. 'Do you know those fellows well?'

'Never saw them in my life before,' he answered, as he found himself admiring this lovely smile and beautiful pearly white teeth. 'Could I borrow those teeth?' He asked. 'They would last a lifetime blowing that auld trombone of mine.'

She laughed at his honesty, but got back at once to her original question in the form of some information for him. 'They're suspected of committing Bank robberies around here in the last few years and they've just been to some fund raiser in the States.' Then she leaned over and whispered into his ear. He soon forgot the lovely whiff of her perfume when she said. 'We think they're in the RA.'

'What's the RA?' He inquired, knowing the answer already.

'Where have you been?' She asked, 'it's the IRA silly, we are trying to find out the name of the big band that travelled over from Ireland, specially to play at their gig.'

'Who, is we?' This time it was Ned with the question.

'Sorry, I should have introduced myself.' 'I'm Sandra Boyle and I'm a Reporter with the local paper, but I also send stuff to The Nationals.' 'Now to answer your question, the 'We' I mentioned are all the papers, who are looking for information on the big gig in America, so if you know anything about it, or if you ever have any hot news about your own band, give me a ring.' As she ended her sentence, she produced a card from a very cute little handbag and thrust it into his hand.

He excused himself for a moment, asking her to hold on until he would speak to the Roadie, who met him with.

'I see you've forgotten New York already.'

'Shut up, listen and don't look,' Ned ordered. 'You've already seen the bird I'm talking to, OK!' 'Slowly go around all the lads and tell them she's asking questions about the fundraiser in San Francisco, tell them to say they know nothing about it.'

'All right, I won't make it obvious,' he replied.

Ned went back to the young woman who luckily, had not gone to talk to anyone else in the interim, so he changed the direction of the conversation with.

'We're having a record launch on Monday week in Dublin, if I get our manager to ring with the details, maybe you would come along.'

'What's wrong with you ringing me?' She enquired.

'Well,' he began, not knowing what would come out. 'I'm sort of involved and I wouldn't lie to a lovely lady like you, I'm sure you understand.'

He or his ego, thought they noticed a little bit of disappointment sweep across her pretty face before she answered.

'That's OK and it's nice to hear a Showband member owning up to a serious relationship for a change.' 'The one's I've met have all claimed to be single, but going back to your launch, you'll still have to ring me yourself, see you,' and like a shot she was gone, thankfully without talking to anyone else.

His thoughts went back to Belfast and failure, then he picked up the trombone to put it in its case and he addressed the instrument.

'What is it, when you're around I can't go wrong, even when I tell the truth, it's weird?'

On his way home he rang Brenda to see how she was coping and found her in floods of tears, lying on that big bed in that dimly lit room, where it had all began.

'Please calm down and tell me what's wrong?' He asked, while she howled down the line.

'I'm sorry Ned,' she sobbed. 'I'm not pregnant after all.'

He was stunned, but he felt a weight being lifted off his shoulders and he heard himself mumble. 'Good, now our liaison will get a proper chance without the pressure.'

'What was that Ned?' She asked.

'Oh, I'm talking to myself trying to get enough coins, how do you know?' He asked.

'Because my period came today, you silly man,' she answered.

That was the second time in twenty-four hours he was deemed silly, by two different women.

'Oh I'm sorry,' he replied, slapping his hip with joy, 'but it's not the end of the world eh!'

She was laughing through her tears now, saying how much she missed him and hoping they could try again soon. 'Can I keep the ring?' She asked.

'Of course,' he answered. He still loved Brenda, but now he was glad they weren't getting together just because she was pregnant and next time around he would take Mike's advice, (Condoms). He drove home full of the joys of life and slept like a top, to be awakened by his mum, who brought him a huge breakfast at noon on the dot.

'It's nice to have you back, so I can spoil you rotten,' she said proudly.

They talked more about the American tour and all the relations (close and far out) he had met and then he asked her about his dad's health.

'Well at the moment it's not too bad, but he's got to ease off with the work, if not, he's liable to get another stroke or worse,' she was looking at him now in an expectant way.

'It would be impossible for me to quit the band and go running a pub,' he said. 'I'd lose a fortune in the band while trying to run the pub and I'd lose a fortune in the pub while on the road with the band.'

She knew he was sincere, but she wasn't giving up yet.

'There are ways and means these days of stock control, where it would be impossible for them to fiddle you and you could always get a good manager.'

She was really trying to soft soap him, but he knew now was the time to put his cards on the table for good.

'Look mum, I've got a couple of friends in the music business who had pubs, but lost all they made in the band plus all they made in the pub and they thought they had good managers, is there any point in that?'

'Sure you know Edmond, he hoards things and he would hate to see the pub move out of the family,' she said.

'Now's the time for him to flog it while it's still a going concern,' he answered. 'My two friends held on until their pubs were run into the ground, then they could get very little for them.' 'They even tried leasing, but in both cases the leaseholders wouldn't pay the rent and had to be evicted.' 'In one of the scenarios, there was a small restaurant involved and it had been leased to an ex member of staff.' 'When the owner went to inspect the place after the tenant had gone, he found that all the kitchen equipment, place settings, even the cutlery had been stolen and that part of the story is etched on my mind.' 'When she was working for the owner as the cook, she had been filling a bath pan full of fresh steak and chickens, covering them with tin-foil, then a layer of kitchen scraps, before handing that over the wall every night to her husband.' 'Ironically, she was cheating on him with almost every other man in town at the same time.'

'My God that's bad,' she said. 'If that's the situation, maybe we should both talk to your Dad tonight or tomorrow and get him to see sense.' She sounded convinced.

Ned agreed to this, telling his mother that he probably wouldn't be around tomorrow evening, but tonight or all day tomorrow would do for the meeting. Now that he had the latest news from Brenda, he decided it would be safe to give Susan a ring. He hadn't spoken to her since the night he managed to find the only phone working in Carrickbay, before that awful gig, so at seven that evening the phone rang out on the other end for about thirty seconds, then a man's voice answered.

'Hello, can I help you?' He asked.

'This is Ned Brady here, could I speak to Susan please?'

'Hold on a minute Ned,' the friendly voice answered.

When she said 'Hello, who is it,' his heart began to thump, because she sounded so curt and business-like.

'It's Ned, Ned Brady,' he answered, his mouth totally dry.

'Oh, it's you, so you got around to ringing,' she didn't sound pleased.

'Well remember, I told you on the phone the night after we met, that we were heading for England and almost immediately afterwards to America, so things were very busy since I saw you, tonight is my first real night off since we got back, now here I am.'

'I understand the phones in Carrickbay may not be working too well, but what about the phones in London and New York, or you could have sent me a card.'

'You didn't give me your address darling,' he reminded her.

'I don't think I'm your darling,' she reminded him.

'Oh, don't be like that Susan, I saw lots of real funny cards in London and the States, so I brought some home to you because I didn't have your address, now I can send them to you from other places.' He then reminded her that he was not from Carrickbay, but from Mullymore, another town were the phones don't always work either.

As the conversation continued she began to mellow, then she asked. 'Are you ringing me just because you're playing down this way on Friday night?'

His next sentence broke the ice. 'Not at all, I know we're playing there on Friday, but I'm ringing to see if I could take you out for a meal tomorrow night, what do you think?' the spoof was on. There was a pause and he thought. 'How hard am I gonna try here?'

Then she spoke. 'All right, I'll go out for a meal with you tomorrow night and we'll take it from there.'

'That's grand,' he answered, 'see you at eight.'

There was some more small talk, including a wry comment in the shape of a question from Susan. 'Are you sure you'll remember how to find me?'

'Not to worry,' he laughed, 'there's only one Fiddler's Lane.'

The meeting with his parents went well the following day and give his dad his due, he saw the folly in Ned giving up the band, or trying to run a pub while on the road.

'It doesn't work,' they agreed.

'We'll sell it so,' said his dad, a little ruefully.

His mother gave her husband a big hug saying. 'I'm so glad Edmond, at last we can see the world and our first stop will be with your sisters in Philadelphia.'

The following morning, feeling a lot more relaxed now that the pub was sorted out and his love life was going a bit more smoothly, he headed out on the seventy mile journey to see Susan. As usual there was a load of crap on the radio, so he put on the demos of his songs that he had done in a friends studio, before going to America.

'Better the crap you know than the ultra crap you don't know,' he thought.

A lot of stuff went through his mind as he drove leisurely along, waving at everyone he saw. Slowly his mind drifted back, until the music was replaced by thoughts from his distant past and how at the age of ten, Edward Seamus Gabriel Brady decided there were two things he was destined to do in life. Number one, he would become the worlds greatest lover and number two, he would rid himself of his awful third Christian name.

'Why in the name of God had his parents called him Gabriel after an Angel?' He would think, as he walked across the fields to his friend's house, not realising of course, that everyone was supposedly named after an angel or a saint. The Brady family were well off farmers living in the countryside, prior to moving to town and the unknown pub trade, but he had vivid memories of the day he had questioned the unnecessary appendage.

'But sure you are a little angel Edward,' his mother proclaimed, ignoring his pained comments.

His dad quietly agreed with his son and on these occasions he always wished he was playing his accordion in the local pub in Ballypratt, a couple of miles along the road.

'Only for me son, she was going to call you Mary instead of Gabriel, but I convinced her that it might cause you problems later on in life and as I have explained to you many times, Gabriel is mostly a male name.'

'Now dad, Gabriel is bad enough, but why call me Mary after a woman and why do I need three Christian names anyway,' he had asked in horror.

'Your mother is very religious son,' his dad said 'and calling you after The Blessed Virgin Mary, meant to her that you would be closer to God.'

His mum often said. 'When you become a priest Edward, you can pray for all of us sinners, especially your poor father.'

That was his first inkling of the plan his mother had for him, so he vowed then, that it would never come to pass if he had any control over the situation. She obviously hoped to have more children and as was the norm for most big farmers, at least one son would be a priest, whether he wanted to or not. As the years went by, Ned always joined in helping his dad on the farm and sometimes they would help with the crops on the other farms. This type of gathering was called a Meithil and it was at one of these said affairs, he first got the feeling that there was more to life than picking potatoes. Now aged eighteen, Edward knew he was going to be a big man. He had really stretched over the past few years and one day, just before he headed off to the potato picking, he admired himself in front of the bathroom mirror.

'There's more growing here than my frame,' he mused as he perused his well-developed equipment.

Some of the young lads in the Seminary, where his mum had enrolled him against his will for phase two of her plan, were very confused about their sexuality and on a few occasions had invited him to join in, while they tried out a few visionary tactics. He had laughingly told them that they were a hole short to get him interested, but the way the 'Rev Ron' (one of the teachers) was looking at all of them, no one would have any problem getting a partner. Ron chatted up Edward one day and was told to give him a shout again if he sprouted tits. This pissed off the overly effeminate Ron, but there was nothing he could do about it. Now his thoughts drifted back to the job in hand today, which held more in store than just picking spuds.

His mum had introduced him to young Emily Shearer, who was now a well rounded 18 year old, whom he hadn't seen for years since they played around the haystacks in her dad's farmyard and he immediately noticed a spark of interest in Emily's eyes that day. He had given her hand an extra little squeeze and she returned it immediately. Today Emily would be helping her mum in the kitchen and the pangs of excitement grew, as lunchtime loomed ever closer. Home from teacher training college and looking gorgeous in a low cut blouse, short skirt with a little frilly apron, Emily blushed when she saw him come through the front door. Emily's mum who was also (a fine thing) was busy seating everyone for lunch, taking special care with Edward's Uncle Tom, who was as everyone said, more like his big brother. The story about his Uncle Tom was, that he was a bit of a lad with the ladies and had been an old beau of Emily's mum

'Marie' before she had been married. It was suggested, that he still chased her the odd time. As Marie leaned over to serve the bacon and cabbage, his mind flashed back to the first hard-on he ever had and he could still see her face as clearly as he did in his fantasy, on the night he discovered the joy of sex during his first DIY.

The lunch was great as were the stories and jokes and then came the sweet served by Emily. As she stood too close to him placing the dish on the table, he could feel her hip pressing against his arm and he knew that today, he would find out if he stood a chance with her, then a sinking feeling swept over him as he saw his Uncle Tom talking to Marie at the end of the table.

The reason their romance came to an end was. Uncle Tom had become a priest and Marie had joined the Nuns probably on the rebound, but she had left the order after a few years, then met and married Emily's dad after a short courtship. To her dismay, Tom left the priesthood two years later and came back to buy the village Post Office, about a mile from her front door. He noticed his Uncle Tom and Marie taking the odd strange looks in his direction, next they would switch their glances to Emily, who unaware of this was putting some of the used dishes in the sink. Everyone got up from the table, thanking their hosts as they headed back to the potato field, but just as they reached the gate, he felt a gentle yet firm hand on his shoulder and for some reason he was not surprised.

'Could you meet me later in the pub for a drink?' Tom asked.

'Why Tom?' He answered, with a question. 'You know I'm not supposed to drink.'

'It doesn't matter, I must talk to you and it can't wait,' said his uncle.

'I was hoping to ask Emily out tonight,' replied the nephew, 'and anyway, I can't be seen in the local pub drinking, my mum would kill me.'

'You won't get in any trouble,' said Tom. 'I'll pick you up at the house at 8 o'clock and you can tell your mother some cock and bull story, we'll go into town instead and remember, don't ask Emily yet, it's far too soon.'

'Maybe you're right,' was the reply. 'I can wait another day.'

The potato picking went very well and Edward discovered that he had a very good aim, with a few rotten spuds, which he had thrown over the evening. He scored a bull's eye on the arse of his uncle's trousers while he was bent over working, then he had a direct hit on the butt of Tommy Gilpin's ear, which brought everything to a halt while the disgruntled young neighbour held court, to find out who his assailant was.

'If I catch him I'll fuckin' kill him,' roared Tommy, while everyone laughed loudly.

Edward straightened up later on for a breather, just as a very big rotten spud, flung by Tommy Gilpin, hit him straight on the nose. It spread out all over his face going up his nostrils, into his mouth, his ears and mangling his hair.

'I caught you doing that you wanker!' He roared at a stunned Tommy and the war was on.

Tommy fought back. 'I know it was you who hit me earlier and if you hadn't stood up at the wrong time, I would have missed you, by the way, I'm not as big a wanker as you, for that's all you fellows do at them boarding schools.'

The war was on again. The other workers had to hold the two lads for a few minutes until they calmed down and throwing spuds was outlawed for the remainder of the day. Our hero kept an eye on Tommy Gilpin from then on and he started thinking of what a good idea it would be to ride Tommy's sister Madge, just to get even. At that precise moment, Fr. Ron's face flashed in front of him and he grunted.

'And fuck you too.'

'What did you say?' Asked Uncle Tom, who was now picking spuds beside him to keep him out of mischief?

'Oh nothing Tom,' he replied, going very red.

He spent the rest of the day thinking of his chances with the lovely Emily and he couldn't help wondering what his uncle had to tell him.

'Maybe he wants to tell me, not to make the same mistake as he did with Emily's mum, seeing that I'm headed for the priesthood also.'

They spoke very little on the short trip to town, but it was obvious that Tom was in deep thought. 'Two pints,' he said to the bar man and then he remembered, he hadn't asked his nephew what he wanted to drink, or whether he would even take a drink.

'I might as well have a pint,' he said to his uncle, after the latter checked. 'It's in keeping with my sharp shooting today.' 'Jaysus, I can still see Tommy Gilpin's face when I hit him and then when I caught him hitting me.'

His uncle smiled also at this thought and when they had about three gulps each from their drinks he could wait no longer.

'What do you have to tell me uncle, do you not want me to break her heart like you did with her mother?' 'I may not become a priest at all you know, no matter what mum wants and anyway, maybe she won't go out with me at all,' he continued.

'I wish I could be sure of that,' said Uncle Tom wistfully. 'I wish I could be sure.'

'What the fuck's the problem?' Asked the nephew tensely, 'are you her father or something?'

The air was charged for about two seconds or so, then Tom quietly told him what he didn't want to hear.

'Yeah, I'm her father, but she doesn't know it yet and we were hoping we would never have to tell her, but now I guess we will.'

Edward didn't make a sound; he just listened as his uncle told the story. Tom and Marie had not met for many years and he couldn't believe it when she showed up at his Parochial house in Hammersmith one cold evening, to tell him that she had left the order. He had asked her why and she simply said that her love for him was still greater than her love for God, so there was no point in her remaining a nun. Then he took her into his house as his housekeeper, where they spent every available second together in bed. No one knew that she had left and she stayed for about a year, but try as he might, he couldn't turn his back on the church, so she decided she would go home and break the news to her family.

'We kept in touch by phone over a period, but then she informed me that she had met Jack Shearer and he wanted to marry her real soon.' 'I was distraught, but I hadn't the guts to break free and when I asked her not to rush into anything, she just asked who's rushing? Then hung up.' 'About six months later, I met a neighbour from home who lived in South London and he told me there was going to be a big wedding in the old parish in a week or so.' 'Marie would be marrying Jack Shearer, the biggest, richest farmer in the neighbourhood and my heart almost stopped.' 'Just one day later at 6pm, my door bell rang and there, crying her eyes out, was Marie.'

'I couldn't go through with it without seeing you one more time,' she blurted out, through her tears.

'We hugged openly on the footpath for what seemed ages, then I asked her in.' 'She told me that her excuse for getting to London, was to pick up some final bits for her Trousseau and then she informed me that her future husband plus all her family, wanted me to perform the marriage ceremony.' 'I couldn't believe by ears, but she put me at ease when she told me, she had said no to this idea.' 'I told her I was glad and jokingly said that a [Loose Cleric] like me, couldn't do the job right anyway.' 'Now I know, that was the night I should have ceased being a priest and that was the night I became a [Father] in real terms.'

Anger, shock, dismay and every other possible emotion flashed through Edward's mind, as he stared into his pint, still remaining totally silent.

'Fuck this,' he thought, 'the one good reason I may have had for not becoming a priest, turns out to be my first cousin.' For a split second the now leering face of Fr. Ron made an appearance, reminding him of the horror of returning to the Seminary and carrying out his mother's wishes.

Just then his Uncle Tom's voice jolted him back to reality.

'Marie is telling Emily tonight,' he said. 'In the circumstances it's for the best, anyway, only for Marie and I, there would be no Emily for you to lust after.'

He was glad to hear his uncle say this, because he was ready to blame Tom and Marie for even existing, let alone creating Emily.

'Let's both drink to the last statement you made uncle,' he said and then laughingly he asked. 'Is Madge Gilpin related to me in any way?'

His uncle burst out laughing, pointing out that as far as he was concerned, the answer to that was no, but it was possible that a few of the men in the village could be wondering. He felt like getting plastered drunk, but Uncle Tom reminded him of the consequences of that when he got home. He advised him that his mother would kill them both, if he went down that road.

'When will you hear the outcome of Emily finding out and do you think Marie's husband Jack knows the score?' Queried the nephew.

'The first part I'll know tomorrow and I'll inform you, as for the second part, I think Jack knows all the time, because they haven't had any more children, plus he looks at me strangely from time to time.' With that, Tom who had finished his third pint to Edward's one, got up to leave.

Life's cruel, he was thinking, as he followed his uncle out to the car. Four people have lost out here. Tom and Marie have missed out what could have been a life of love together with their daughter and possibly more kids. Emily hasn't had the love of her real dad while poor Jack must be devastated by the doubt or knowledge that his wife loves another man and his daughter belongs to someone else, even though he has loved her unconditionally.

'Thank God Uncle Tom told me in time,' he mused, as he went in his front door and headed for bed. Tonight his equipment would not be checked out.

He heard the phone ringing at 9am and stretching himself he thought. 'No potato picking today, it's Saturday.'

His mum knocked on the door to inform him that he was wanted on the phone and his first thought was that it was his uncle, to tell him the outcome of Marie's revelation to Emily, but a shock lay in store.

An agitated female voice said. 'This is Emily, I would like to meet you today.' 'I've got my mothers car and can I pick you up in about an hour?'

'That's OK,' he blurted out, 'where?'

'At the graveyard, see you,' she said and she was gone.

He was sitting on the graveyard wall from 9.55, marvelling at how peaceful all the graves and their inhabitants were, while thinking. 'Is this the only place a person can have some real peace?'

Just then, a lovely but sad Emily brought the car to a halt a couple of feet away, then she leaned over to unlock the passenger door as her invitation to him to get in and without a word, they drove off down a narrow road leading to the lake, where Tom and he had often gone fishing. When they reached the lake the area was deserted, so Emily parked the car and you could see her white knuckles as she held on to the steering wheel for dear life. For once he was at a loss for something to say, but he didn't have to stay that way for too long, as Emily let go her death hold on the steering and in an immediate flood of tears, flung her arms around her very receptive cousin. One of his first impulses was to kiss this gorgeous girl, but he wisely put this thought out of his mind and joined her crying loudly instead. Slowly, he took her arms from around his shoulders and with his fingertips under her chin, he dried her tears on a hankie, which he happened to have in his pocket, then looking straight into her lovely blue tearstained eyes he said.

'I'm going to kiss you now cousin Emily, even if it's the last kiss we ever have.'

Without a word their lips met, gently at first and then with a wild abandon, as if they were trying to catch up on lost years, or maybe trying to make up for years that would have to be lost. A beautiful but sinful kiss was the only way he could explain it and it went on for ages. Then they remained cheek to cheek, both running their fingers through each other's hair, as if prolonging the time before they would have to look at each other. Emily got the courage first and drew back to look deeply into her cousin's eyes.

'We've had a narrow escape,' she said.

'I don't think I've escaped,' he replied, 'this moment will haunt me forever, but it has made me decide what I must do and that is, forget about becoming a priest, the time has come to stop living a lie.'

'Last night I told my mum that I would be a nun, but she soon talked me out of that, reminding me that two wrongs don't make a right.' Emily replied and then she added. 'There's something I've got to tell you, but you must remain sitting where you are.'

'What is that,' he enquired, yet guessing what it might be.

'I loved you from the moment we were introduced the other day and my mum said she noticed it too.' 'I presume you saw the way I looked at you, because you squeezed my hand and I nearly passed out,' she said.

'I loved you from the same second and I will love you all my life, even though it will have to be as cousins,' he replied, 'but I do realise what we must do from this moment on.'

They both shook hands on their life friendship and continued to talk for hours about the past. Like the time they played around the haystacks and he was pleasantly surprised when she remembered with such detail.

'There's something else I remember from back then,' she said smiling.

'What's that?' He enquired.

'I always called you Ned in those days and you seemed to answer to it all right, so why is everyone calling you Edward now?' She asked.

'My mum hates that name and when she enrolled me in the college years ago, she put down my three Christian names, so I went spare, threatening to run away if she used the third one.' 'Imagine how Fr. Ron would have reacted, if he had known I was also christened Gabriel.'

Emily had burst out laughing at this and during the giggles she asked. 'Who in the name of God, is Fr. Ron?'

When he explained, she went into more fits of laughing and he remembered that as his weakest moment. He was thinking.

'I'll run away with her, cousin or not, now that I'm quitting the priesthood no one will ever find us.' He was brought back to reality by the sound of her voice.

She had raised her right hand and seemed to be giving him her blessing. 'From this moment on Edward Seamus Gabriel Brady, you shall be known to all as Ned and by the powers vested in me by my father, who was once a priest, I have spoken.'

'You sound more like Sitting Bull than a priest,' he said, as they laughed loudly.

She also talked fondly about Jack, the man who had been her father for the past eighteen years and how he had been hitting the booze recently.

'I think he knows,' she said.

She also tried to explain her feelings for the man she knew as Uncle Tom, who had been catapulted into her life as her real dad. She had always liked him, but now she would have to see if she could learn to love him. Then she said.

'But I hate him now for what he has done to us.'

Ned jumped in quickly telling her what Tom had said, that only for him, there would be no Emily.

'I suppose that makes sense alright,' she mused and starting up the car she continued with. 'I'd better drive us home.'

He went looking for Tom soon after Emily had dropped him off and as he knocked loudly on the Post Office door, he looked furtively up and down the street, as if he was afraid to be seen visiting his uncle.

'Are you going to see her?' Tom asked. 'Her mum told her last night, so I think you should give her a shout.'

'Oh, she's been to see me bright and early this morning and we're just about getting our heads around the situation,' he answered, 'that's why I called to let you know.' 'I also pointed out to her what you said, that only for you she wouldn't exist and it helped her to understand.'

He said goodbye to his uncle and as he turned away from the door a car drove up, the driver honked at Ned and slammed on the brakes. It was none other than Madge Gilpin, looking very sexy and smiling from ear to ear.

'I've borrowed my dad's car to go for a drive, would you care to come along?' She asked with an expectant look on her face as he hopped on board and the car sped off along the same narrow road he had gone earlier that day with Emily. During some small talk, he viewed the driver out of the corner of his eye. She had grown into one heck of a lady had Madge, a totally different ball of wax to her brother Tommy, thank God. She informed him that she was studying to be a nurse and loved it; also, she had found out all about the birds and the bees.

'Such as?' He enquired.

'Well you know,' she said.

'No I don't,' he answered.

'Oh, you must know, how and when to and how and when not to,' her voice tailed off and she was now a very healthy shade of red.

'I'm sorry to be so backward,' said our hero, 'but at long last, it seems I've met someone who can teach me a thing or two.'

She stopped the car at the very spot he had visited earlier but the engine was still running, then he panicked, perhaps she was thinking of turning back because of his comments.

'Sorry Madge,' he said. 'I'm afraid I don't know a lot about the birds and the bees, as I don't get much opportunity, but it would be nice to find out from a lovely young lady like you.'

He relaxed when she reached for the ignition, switching off the engine, yet his mind was in turmoil. How was he going to approach this situation? His only experience with girls was the odd quick grope with members of the domestic staff in the college, if he happened to meet an agreeable one in a dimly lit corridor, a sort of, you scratch my back and I'll scratch yours situation. Just then Madge put her head on his shoulder and whispered.

'Let's take our time pet, it's a long while until morning, just hold me.'

He hadn't been called a pet before but it sounded very nice, now he had his right arm around her, running the fingers of his left hand through her lovely long hair when another panic struck him, which made his body go rigid.

'What's wrong pet,' she asked in the sexiest voice he had ever heard.

'I love you calling me pet,' he said, 'but I've got a problem.'

She smiled at him in a questioning fashion and waited.

'I'm on the wrong side of you, I'm right handed and absolutely no good at all with my left hand.'

'That's not a problem,' she roared laughing and with one bound she was on top of him. 'I hope that's not the gear stick,' she murmured, as the ecstasy began.

They both awoke to an awful scratching sound and burst out laughing at what they saw and heard. A cow was busy licking the window and the side of the car, surrounded by all her family.

'It's a good job they can't talk,' she said. 'You could imagine the gossip in the village, student nurse and clerical student, found naked and screwing by the lakeside at 7am.'

Suddenly, he stopped laughing.

'Did you just say 7am?' he asked, too scared to look at his watch, which by the way, was the only thing he was wearing at that moment. 'Jaysus,' he said, his voice now a high pitched screech, 'if I go home at this hour I'm dead, I think my mum has been looking for an excuse like this for years to kill me and now she's got it.'

Madge just smiled calmly at him, her hair cascading over her ivory shoulders, then in a flash, her head disappeared from view and a flood of pleasure immediately replaced the flood of panic.

'Ah well', he thought, 'if I must die, it will have been well worth the pain.'

It was 8am when they got to the phone box on the edge of the village and nobody saw him as he made a quick call to his Uncle Tom.

'Don't ask me any questions now,' he said, 'but can you cover for me, I've been out all night with a young woman and there's no way I can face my mother at this hour, can I say I stayed with you?'

'Where are you now?' Tom asked with a giggle in his voice.

'I'm in the phone box and I can see your front door from here, is it open?'

'It'll be open in a minute, just run in and I'll sort you out.'

Ned jumped back into the car for the one hundred-yard dash to the post office and in those few seconds Madge and himself made another date for that night. This time she would call to his uncle's house and they would take it from there.

'Don't worry,' he shouted in to her. 'I'll fix it.'

She sped off as he burst through the door, to be greeted by Tom, wearing loud pyjamas. 'I suppose you'd like a couple of hours kip?' Asked his host.

'Can I stay for a while please uncle and is it OK if Madge comes here to see me tonight?'

'I suppose that can be organised, as long as you don't keep her this late.' 'I'm going to play cards in a house up the road, so I'll be away till 2 or 3am if that suits you,' said Tom.

'You're an angel,' shouted our hero as he jumped into bed, to fall asleep with the thoughts of the past twenty-four hours milling around in his mind.

When he awoke, he knew he had something important to do before his next big date with his new lover and it entailed talking to his mother. He walked back to his home on the big farm just outside the village of Ballypratt, which had been owned at one time by a very wealthy English Protestant family called The Pratt's. It had taken many years to buy out all the ground rents for the village plus some of the surrounding land, from the remaining members of that family and one of the last farms sorted out was Ned's home, one hundred acres of lush ground running down to the river. These thoughts were coursing through his mind, as he strode through the front door and met his mother on the bottom step of the stairs.

'Well now young man,' she began, 'where have you been for the past twenty-four hours?' 'The sooner that college opens the better.'

That was it, the cue for his announcement.

'I'm glad you brought that up mum,' he said calmly. 'I'm not going back to college and please don't try to make me.'

Whatever she heard in his voice struck her dumb, she stood there, her mouth wide open as he sidestepped her and continued up the stairs. When he came out of his room later on the way to the bathroom, he could hear her sobbing downstairs.

'I must not relent now that I've told her,' he thought, knowing in his heart, the decision was made.

It took a long time for her to forgive him, but his dad was glad from day one, because he had gone through the trauma with his own brother after going all the way and that was worse. Ned and Madge had many repeat sessions before she went back to nursing in England and even though the love feeling he had had for Emily never raised it's head everything else did, but he knew she had been a great help in getting over his cousin. Strangely, she and Emily both chose Australia as their future home and he often thought, if he hadn't got involved in music, he probably would have gone to check out the land of his hero Ned Kelly, plus both girls of course.

About Madge who he cared for deeply, his Uncle Tom always said.

'She made a man of you, you know.' That wouldn't be the last time a similar comment would be made about the bold Ned.

He had been so engrossed in his past on the way to meet Susan, that he had driven through villages and towns on autopilot, still stupidly waving at people even though he was miles away. He snapped back to reality as he rounded a bad bend, almost smashing into a big herd of cows, being driven by two happy ladies in aprons and Wellington boots.

'They would make some noise if they all started licking my car,' he thought, going back for a second to the past that had been with him for the last seventy miles.

As he looked at the two women in the wellies, he tried to imagine how hard their lives had been, compared to that of his own mother, who enjoyed the best of everything and took life for granted almost all of the time. They were probably two maiden aunts, who unlike his own relations had not discovered what life could be like if they had (taken the bull by the horns) and emigrated. Looking at them and their big herd of cattle (which probably included a bull) in the rear view mirror, he attempted to transplant them, minus the animals of course, to some big city in the States, where they would both have lovers of the same calibre as the one his Aunt Sarah has. While the ladies and the cows became smaller in the mirror, so also did his imagined scenario for them and he came to the only intelligent solution. They never got the opportunity.

He remembered that he had been listening to his original songs earlier, but now as he drove through Glenrone, he decided they would have to wait until a later date. Particularly, because of their failure to hold his attention, he had switched them off sixty miles back.

'Yes,' they (probably) need some work alright.' That thought made him smile, so he decided to get Susan's opinion on them later. 'The more the merrier.'

Chapter Ten

He decided to wing it with Susan, because he knew if he tried to script the evening, he would be sure to blow it and she hated spoofers. Around the next bend he saw the sign, (Welcome to Glenrone) with the little village stretching out in the distance and he smiled as he remembered the last time the band had played here. He couldn't help wondering, if the two lads with the open necked shirts had managed to score yet.

'Ah well, we'll find out on Friday night hopefully,' he thought, as he drove slowly through the village, comparing the Dance Hall, which hadn't been painted for years, to Carnegie Hall and The City Plaza. 'Jaysus,' he uttered under his breath, afraid someone might hear him. '*Thegat's Segome Megess, Weg've Begeen Reguegined Fegor Egeveger, Feguck.*' He had slipped into the Ben-Lang for a moment, not even trusting the empty car with his thoughts; of how they had been ruined by the classy venues they had seen since being here. A mile further on the left was the Fiddler's Lane and as he swung the big car into the narrow space, he immediately noticed a difference. The potholes were gone and the hedges had been trimmed, suddenly a smile spread over his face, he had found his introduction to Susan, who moments later opened her front door looking gorgeous, but cross.

'Hello Susan, I see you have had the Fiddler's Lane done up for my arrival,' he said and laughed.

'Maybe in your wildest dreams,' was the dry reply, as she offered him her fingertips in an attempt at a handshake?

'Jaysus, I hate limp fingers like that,' he thought, immediately deciding that he would have to take this situation easy and back-pedal totally on the bullshit, or she would blow him out of the water. Nevertheless, he held on to her almost lifeless digits and bravely attempted a compliment.

'You look lovely as usual this evening Susan,' was his cautious, opening remark.

'Seeing this is only the second time you've seen me, how can you use the words, as usual?' She asked scathingly.

Divine intervention is the only way he can account for his reply, which jumped uncontrollably from his almost paralysed lips.

'But this is my third time to see you, my first time at the dance where you were looking absolutely gorgeous in your little black number and high heels, the second time was at lunch the following day, when you looked ravishing in your tight blue jeans, white blouse and yellow boots, not forgetting the fetching little frilly apron.'

That did it; a little smile began to creep across her pretty face, causing her to renew her grip on his hand. Drawing him closer, she said with a grin. 'What a load of bullshit.'

In front of the open door, their arms slid around each other and they kissed gently.

'I've missed you, you bold man Ned Brady,' she said, 'and for the life of me, I don't know why.'

'Well that makes two of us missing each other, but I know why,' he replied, and then still holding her closely he asked. 'Where is the nicest restaurant in this neck of the woods?'

'Without a doubt, the best food served around here is by my mother in this very house,' she said, 'but if you want to beat that, you'll have to drive another thirty miles to the city.'

As her sentence came to an end, he heard a voice inside the house asking. 'Is someone taking my name in vain?' It was Susan's mother, who now stood framed in the doorway.

'Oh mum, this is Ned Brady, you may remember him as my guest for Sunday lunch some time ago, but it's a long time so you've probably forgotten,' Susan said, while looking knowingly at her mother.

'Now let me see,' came the reply, 'out of all the young men you've brought home to Sunday lunch, I can't place this one, but don't worry, you're welcome anyway Ned.'

He knew they were ganging up on him and his mind flashed back to his feelings that evening, when Susan had walked him to the car. Now his exact thoughts were. 'If I'd done what I wanted to do, when we were crossing the garden, her mother would have had no problem recognising me today.' Yet he knew if he had tried anything then, he wouldn't be here now, so easing out of the embrace, he stuck out his hand and pumped the nice soft grip of the lady of the house.

'Bring the young man in for a cup of tea,' the older woman advised her daughter with a nice friendly lilt in her voice, making Ned feel really welcome and relaxed.

'I suppose you may as well come in while I'm powdering my nose,' she agreed, taking his hand.

'Of all the noses I've ever seen, I don't think this one needs powdering,' said Ned loudly, making sure her mother heard him as he took Susan's face in his hands, kissing her on the end of her pert nose.

'Well maybe it didn't, but now it does after you slobbering all over it,' she said, laughing loudly, as she ran up the stairs.

'Your daughter is gorgeous,' he said, as he sat down for the tea.

'Yeah,' her mum agreed, 'she makes out she's a real tough cookie, but she's the complete opposite.' 'You really hurt her by the fact that you lost contact for such a long time and she hasn't been outside the door for ages, so be nice to her please.'

'I promise you I will Mrs. Prunty, we were out of the country for most of the time and the pace was hectic.' Putting his hand in the inside pocket of his jacket he pulled out a load of funny cards with messages to Susan, from all over England and the U.S, not an address on any of them. 'She forgot to give me her address which was a pity,' he said. Ned knew those cards would come in handy one day and now was the time.

'Give them to her when she comes down and if you stay over, I'll see you tomorrow, I'm off next door, so take care,' she added.

Ned mulled over what Mrs. Prunty said about him staying over and was busy trying to work out if it was a good or bad idea, when Susan walked back into the room in a totally different creation.

'I thought you were dressed already,' was his initial compliment.

'Oh not at all, I had that outfit on all day, I'm in the Solicitors office in the village now and he likes me to dress well for work.'

He pushed aside a jealous pang, wondering if she fancied anyone in the lawyer's office, as he held out his hands to this beautiful creature that was walking towards him. He remembered giving points of one to ten to the girls he had met in America and here in the village of Glenrone, he was holding hands with a twelve.

'I'm stuck for words to explain what I see and feel,' he stuttered.

'You could try,' she said, smiling fondly at him.

'Well, I covered a lot of ground on the tours which took in Hollywood California and saw no one as beautiful or elegant as you, could I have a twirl please?' He asked.

She stepped back a few feet, spun to the left then to the right, ending with a cute curtsey. 'Let's go before you get bold,' she said. 'I can see it in your eyes.'

The lady was so right, she must have seen the positive bulge in his pants instead of a look in his eyes and had taken the initiative, knowing what might happen. About a mile down the road, he handed her the postcards full of funny messages and pictures, but no addresses, then as he heard her laughing loudly he felt a real cad, but he must not let this lovely lady know the truth, him being so lucky to be with her again. That morning, he had taken the postcards from his suitcase, pouring over them for hours, trying to think of funny but caring messages that would suit the pictures and hopefully please her as well. From her chuckles, giggles and sometimes loud laughs, he knew he had got it as close as could be, then he realised how worthwhile those hours had been.

She took him to a real swish restaurant in the city and the young waiter led them to a nice table by the window. As he handed them their menus he kept looking at Susan in awe, but Ned didn't blame him because he couldn't take his eyes off her either. The menu was one of the most comprehensive he had seen on his travels and they poured over it for ages, giving them a chance to get to know each other better while doing so.

'Would you like to see the wine list?' the waiter asked, hovering.

'The lady will choose,' Ned said, gallantly.

Susan blushed, took the wine list and holding it up so the waiter couldn't see her face, she whispered across the table to her beau. 'I don't drink, sorry,' she said.

Then he addressed the waiter. 'We'll order the food first and make up our minds about what to drink later.'

'That's quite alright,' he answered, standing with his pen at the ready.

They both passed on the starters, Susan ordering a chicken dish and our by now hungry hero asking for a T-bone steak with all the trimmings. He knew he had to deal with the fact of her not having a drink, in a way which would not make her feel bad, so he began.

'Don't worry Susan, I hardly touch it myself and it's only over the past few months that I've had wine at all, before that, it was the odd pint.'

She relaxed now grinning from ear to ear, as he told her about his aunts in Philadelphia giving him the huge meal and no wine, because his mother had told them in a recent letter that he was a teetotaller. The food arrived and he ordered a glass of wine, with a coke for Susan, while she kept plying him for more stories from the English and U.S tours. 'Well Ned, a good looking fellow like you must have been beating the girls off you, come on don't be shy.'

'First of all, thanks for the compliment and secondly, I suppose we all could have clicked, but because of the fact that we played in a different city every night, it left it impossible to take anyone out.' His voice had that sound, hoping he would be believed.

His latest girlfriend wasn't letting go that easy though. 'I wasn't suggesting that you took ladies out,' she answered, 'but you could have taken girls home on the night, like you took me home after the dance, remember.'

'Do I remember, will I ever forget,' he began, 'there's a big difference in taking a girl home and taking her back to a hotel.' 'There wouldn't have been a hope of getting a girl into any of the hotels and our manager warned us all not to try, your family home is so different, plus you had a house full of chaperones to boot.'

He told her many stories including the visit to Niagara Falls, leaving out the lovely Jayne of course, the girl he had given eleven to. The steak was marvellous and he had another glass of wine. Susan loved her meal too and then as they talked away the waiter brought the sweet trolley and her eyes popped out of her head as she quizzed him on its contents, before settling on lemon cheesecake.

'Desserts are my only weakness,' she said.

'You'll have to watch that beautiful figure!' he jibed.

'As long as I know you're watching it, I won't bother,' she countered.

'No need to worry then,' he said. 'I can't keep my eyes off it.'

As if they both got a signal, their hands entwined across the table, a similar look of affection on their happy faces. After their fingers reluctantly slipped apart, Susan picked up her spoon and slowly began eating her cheesecake, while Ned slipped an After Eight into his mouth. A beautiful, highly charged silence prevailed until the coffee arrived, then they held their cups aloft, clicked them together and toasted each other.

'Here's to the future,' he offered.

'Amen,' she answered, in a biblical tone.

'Well Susan,' he began. 'I'm sure you'll agree there's something special going on between us and because we're both so young it frightens me.'

She reached across the table again, taking both his hands in hers and he was glad to see a happy smile on her lovely face. 'My thoughts exactly,' she answered. 'Firstly, I know there's something very special happening with us and the fact that I'm not even twenty-one yet, has me panicking, thank God you understand.' Before he could answer, she put a long sexy finger across his lips and continued to speak. 'The truth is, I'm still a virgin and I intend to remain one until I get married, I'm not sure how that fits in with your idea of going steady, but that's the way it must be.'

He squeezed her hands tightly, thinking back to his experience with Brenda in New York. 'I'm so happy to hear everything you're saying,' he said. 'I'm not much older than you and having kids at our age would not be a good plan, plus I've always wanted to marry a virgin.'

She was absolutely glowing and they both agreed it was a good job they were in a crowded restaurant with a big table between them, otherwise they would have kissed on the spot.

Why had he given this girl so little thought over the past couple of months, she deserved better and now he was wondering how they were going to manage, feeling this way?

'We'll not always have a big table between us when temptation comes along.' He said.

'Every time things get steamy, we'll ask God for strength and he'll look after us,' was her answer.

'In other words, he'll become the big table,' he said, as they both broke into laughter.

'It's no laughing matter Ned Brady,' she said, wagging that gorgeous digit at him again.

He thought for a moment, realising how good God had been to him over the years, even though he had walked out on the Church? It wasn't to be, anyway, he didn't walk out on God, just religion, because he didn't like the way the man above was being represented by those appointed to do so.

'You've been miles away for the last few minutes,' she said, looking concerned.

He decided to tell her a little bit about his time in the Seminary, which she hammed up by saying how fine a Priest he would have made, then took it all back when she realised his becoming a man of the cloth, would have meant that herself and himself would never have become acquainted. Ned continued to tell her about his mum and dad who he was sure, would be glad to meet her, also about his father not being well and having decided to dispose of the pub, which was draining him in every way, every day.

'I'd like to meet them sometime,' she said wistfully, 'meanwhile, let's make a plan on how I can remain a virgin, OK!'

He noticed she hadn't mentioned his status in that area during her statement, so he decided to let sleeping dogs lie.

'Your mother suggested I might stay over, what do you think love?' He asked.

'I've got the phone number of a nice guesthouse in the village and my plan is to ring my aunt Mrs. North and book you in, it might be the best way to stop tongues wagging, do you mind?' She was looking expectantly at him, hoping he would not be offended.

'That's a great idea pet, you go and do that, I'll sort out the bill and then we can be on our way,'

He kept an eye out for a sign he had seen on the way down which said, 'Doon Lake' and sure enough, there it was large as life stating it was but one-mile. He thought, this would be a good romantic setting for himself and his lady to practice self-control or fail to do so, it had to be tried. Gently slowing the car he asked.

'Is it OK if we drive down to the lakeside, it will be a nice place to talk?'

'Well haven't you great eyesight,' she chuckled. 'Imagine I never saw that sign, but seeing you have it's alright with me, remember I trust you.'

The big car rolled quietly to a halt at the edge of a very lovely clean lake, which was sporting a killer moonbeam.

For a moment, his thoughts went back to another lake and his forbidden love for his lovely young cousin, not forgetting chapter two on that occasion, his nights of lust with the extremely passionate Madge Gilpin. He looked around for cows, but there was no sign of any as yet.

'You seem a bit edgy,' she said, looking directly at him.

'Sorry love,' he began. 'I was looking to see if we had company even though it doesn't matter, anyway, to be on the safe side, lock your door.'

She did as he asked while he found some nice romantic music on the radio, then he reached into the back seat for a cushion, which he jammed between the two front seats, before moving towards her, arms outstretched. Without a sound, she wrapped her arms around his neck as they began kissing gently and it was some time before he introduced his tongue, which she accepted gladly. They must have stayed for two hours talking and exchanging kisses, as her perfect body relaxed, reassured by the fact that there would be no roving hands or roaming fingers. During their time there other lovers had arrived, parking their cars strategically, each couple having no interest apart from their own situation.

'We must come here again,' enthused Susan, 'especially if there's a moon, isn't it lovely on the water.' Then turning to him once more she added. 'You're an angel.'

'It's little wonder my mother gave me that third Christian name, Gabriel,' he said with a laugh, as he eased the car back on to the exit road from the lake.

On the remainder of the journey, it was her turn to move over on to the cushion and he could feel the touch of Susan's beautiful long black hair rubbing against his cheek and that wonderful perfume. Was this what heaven was going to be like, well if so, it would have one very agreeable Angel Gabriel. As they approached Glenrone, she suggested they should pick up the key and introduce Ned to Mrs. North, she also warned him to stay away from her two gorgeous twin cousins Mrs. North's daughters, who were good friends as well as relatives.

'If they're good friends of yours, then I'm perfectly safe,' he countered. 'Would you take one of their fellows?'

'Stop messing,' she said, giving him a box. 'Just let them see how nice a guy you are and this is the house on the left.'

It was exactly midnight and they each agreed that the past five hours had been heavenly bliss. He passed on his version of heaven and hell once more, by maintaining they were both here on earth, not up there or down there but all around.

'They are just a state of mind and during my life I've been swapping them around, tonight I'm certain that we've been languishing in heaven, tomorrow who knows?' He claimed.

'You're a heathen Ned Brady and don't let my mother hear you talking like that, but when you think about it, it makes sense, there's not much support in a fluffy cloud.'

She seemed to be drifting through those clouds looking for heaven as she finished her statement, so he brought her back to earth with a big wet kiss on her full lips. Over the evening, he had gazed quite often at those sexy red lips and had found himself associating them hopefully in the future, with deeds from his past. Like for instance, Patricia on the aeroplane to America, Helen in The Woodlawn Hotel, Brenda in the big bed in that lovely dark bedroom in Queens and Mary the sexy twin on the beach in San Francisco.

She brought him back to the present. 'It's ten past midnight so we'd better get the key honey.'

He wondered if he had been musing out loud, as he walked around the car to open the door for his lady, with two things in mind, to be the nonchalant gentleman and to get another glimpse of Susan's lovely legs. Mrs. North was a nice lady and shook hands with them both, insisting they join her for a cup of tea which Ned suspected was a ruse, so she could get a chance to check her niece's fellow out. All went well, with the usual amount of scrutiny, but as he got into the car he was glad to hear Mrs. North say to Susan in a loud whisper.

'You've got a nice chap here girl, take care of him now.' As Susan laughingly assured her on that score, the landlady said loudly to him. 'Be in no hurry back young man, you know where your room is and breakfast is served all day, good night now.'

As the car approached the Fiddler's Lane, she kissed him on the cheek cooing proudly. 'You were a big hit there young man,' she was using Mrs. North's terminology now.

He decided to brag and get even by saying. 'I'm always a big hit with the ladies regardless of age,' then glancing in the rear view mirror, he asked his usual spoof question. 'Who's that hunk looking back at me?'

As they parked at her house, his girlfriend was battering him black and blue for fun, saying, 'That will teach you not to blow your own trumpet in my presence,' then she smothered him with kisses and suddenly they were reliving their time at the lake. The timely arrival of the outside light could be considered good or maybe bad, but who knows. Were they really falling in love so soon?

Susan's mother was waiting at the door to welcome the young couple home and he could have sworn, that he saw her take an extra glance at the big car as he thought. 'I wonder if she's glad to see me, or does she consider me as a fine catch for her daughter?' One way or the other it didn't matter, but full marks to her for creating such a lovely being as Susan, who was now slipping out of the jacket of her cute bright blue suit. There was more tea brewing and he noticed only two places set at the table. She wasn't going to play gooseberry and he had to restrain himself from kissing this lovely lady as he shamefully flashed back to his earlier, silly thoughts about her.

'Mum's a bit disappointed that you're not staying, but she understands.' Susan was addressing them both now. 'Thanks mum for getting the room ready and also for the tea.' They both said goodnight and she gave her mother a big hug. 'I'll be up in a few moments,' she promised.

As they sipped the tea, Susan put Ned in the picture. 'Mother will be waiting in my room to hear all the news, she's very happy for me, but she's still a little worried about my going out with someone in the music business, you guys have a bad name.'

'Well darling, you and the remainder of your family are musicians and you are all nice people, it all depends on the person,' he stated, standing up for his peers.

'I agree,' she said, 'and we've been talking lately about recording the family, how do you think 'The Prunty's' would look on an album cover?'

'Great', he answered, 'you have four good-looking brothers for the back line of the picture, but just make sure that you and Mary sit in front, showing a bit of leg, that will do the trick.'

'You're an awful man Ned Brady and you're leg mad,' she howled, then suddenly she became serious. 'Maybe you would introduce us to your record company boss, or do they do Traditional Irish music?'

'Yeah, they do all kinds of stuff, but I'm not sure if it would be a good idea for me especially,' he sounded cagey.

'Why?' Came the inevitable one word question.

'Because the guy who owns the Record Company is a very randy man, who would tip a cat going through a skylight, or get up on a cracked cup as they say.'

'My God, what do you mean by that?' She asked, all agog.

'They're a couple of old saying describing sexually active men, but he's just a chap who likes chasing women really.'

Ned smiled to himself at some of the stories the Record Company man had told them and they had to agree, that it was no wonder his surname was O'Toole.

'Are you one of those chaps Ned, who does funny things with cats in strange places?' She asked, really concerned.

'Not at all,' he laughed, 'how would I get up to a skylight, I hate heights anyway.'

The smile came back to her face when she realised it was all a joke of sorts, so she said. 'Only for this big table I'd give you a thump.'

'There you go Susan, a big table has saved one of us already.' All she could do was laugh.

Before they parted, he suggested that he would come to her house on Friday evening after his band rehearsal and hear the family play some tunes, then talk to them about an introduction to the bands record company.

Susan agreed to this and as they had their last hug of the night in the hallway she mused out loud. 'That cracked cup idea would really put me off, see you later.'

He could still hear her subdued laughter as the door quietly clicked shut and he hoped she wouldn't mention any old sayings to her mother, as she reported on their date. Ned had a contented smile on his face as he drove slowly to the guesthouse, reluctant to put more space between them and he found himself really looking forward to seeing her later that day, after her work. They might even find a nice lake a bit closer to Glenrone and he decided he would ask Mrs. North about that later on. He would tell her some cock and bull story about wanting to fish or go boating, making sure she would not get a look into his car boot, because there was no fishing equipment to be seen. As he climbed into the comfortable bed his mind was focused again on Susan's attributes. He laid quietly, eyes closed as his thoughts ran riot, comparing Susan's looks to some of his screen idols.

'Yeah, Lana Turner with black hair, Ava Gardner's lips, Susan Hayward's smouldering eyes, Betty Grable's legs and a body to equal any one of them. He could feel the emotion build to fever pitch, so with a clear picture of his new love's face in his mind, he made a conscious decision.

'Tonight, the chicken would be choked.'

Subsequently, having made sure there was no evidence to be seen of his bold deed, he slipped into a deep contented sleep and later while having a large tasty breakfast at noon, he found out more about The Prunty family in one hour, than Susan could have told him in a week. Basically, they had been very big farmers for years, but seeing that all their sons were in college, Mr. Prunty was now in dairy farming only and the new house that Ned had been in stands about one mile away from the farmyard. Mrs. North (encyclopaedia) continued.

'The eldest son will soon be a Doctor, the next two are the twins, they're doing Law, the youngest lad is doing Agriculture and Mary is a Nurse, I suppose you know all about Susan yourself,' she paused, waiting for any excuse to continue.

'Yeah, she works full-time in the local Solicitors office I believe,' he answered.

'But I'm sure she told you about doing Law as well and being the baby of the family, she has only one year done in college.' Mrs. North was smiling and it was obvious by her demeanour that she was pro The Prunty's.

Not revealing what he already knew, he asked. 'Are you related to Susan in any way Mrs. North?'

'How did you guess?' She began. 'Yes I'm her aunt, I'm a sister of her mother's, could you tell?' She did a little pose for him, hoping he would notice.

'You're both very fine ladies and Susan tells me you have two lovely daughters of your own, she has already told me

I can look, but not touch.' He offered. On hearing that, the landlady disappeared into another room and came back with a picture of two gorgeous girls.

'Little wonder Susan warned me off,' he began, as he looked at two almost carbon copies of the new love in his life. Smothering a 'Jaysus' as he stared, he asked. 'Are they twins?'

'Yes they are and do they remind you of anyone?' she asked proudly.

'My God, it's uncanny, they're like extensions of Susan and she of them,' he answered.

'It's all in the genes,' she said, as she looked lovingly at her beautiful girls.

That reference to genes, made him wonder how they would look in 'blue jeans? He was thinking frivolously now, seconds before remembering Susan's warning.

She produced another picture, this time of two fine looking young men. 'My two sons are also twins and they are both Airline Pilots.' She was glowing with pride as she said that and he was half expecting her to lead him to the window, where she would point to a couple of aircraft sitting on the back street.

A sobering thought hit him, making him weigh up the pros and cons of eventually having a family with Susan. First of all, the fact she is so gorgeous would guarantee that he would want to make love to her at every possible opportunity. Secondly, if that were the case, the chances of her becoming pregnant would multiply and thirdly, seeing that twins run in her family he would end up with a houseful of children. Then he saw the bright side of that possibility which brought a big silly grin to his face. 'If they're all as good looking as Susan, won't it be well worth it?'

He could hear Mrs. North's voice somewhere in the distance. 'Are you alright young man?' She asked.

'Never better,' he answered, following with a question. 'Are there any lakes around this area?' 'I think I'd like to do some fishing.'

'Oh yes, there's a few, but the nicest one is a mile out, take a left at the village sign on your road home and it's half a mile from there, you can borrow fishing gear if you want as my sons do lots of fishing,' she said, keen to help.

He gladly accepted, saying he would drive out first and take a look. It was called the Deep Lough and was just as beautiful as the last one, but there were fewer parking spaces, so they would have to be there early. There were a few signs warning visitors of the fact that the water was deep, which explained the name. Deciding to while away the evening at the lake, he put on the tape of his original songs again, then producing a pen and the lyrics from his gig-bag containing something for every situation, he set about making changes to one of the songs.

Mike had promised. 'If you get it right, I'll ask the record company to pick it for our next single, no one will know it's your song until it's on record.' Ned was looking forward to seeing the band member's faces if that happened, but Mike would say the record company boss picked it from the bunch and he had the last say. None of them had ever shown any interest in the songs, so they wouldn't know it was his until they read the credits on the record label and in the back of his mind he was thinking of using a pseudonym, but he still had to settle on one. 'Too late then lads,' he thought as he changed a few lines and before finishing, he'd even changed the title to, 'Every Memory Of You.' This wasn't a happy love song as it featured a total marriage break down, but he had written it before he met Susan, so she didn't feature as the inspiration for the song or the changes. Like before, he would get his friend in Dublin to do the demo, therefore it would never leak out. Would he tell his girlfriend? No, not a soul must know, just in case.

Susan smiled when she saw him sitting in the big car parked across the road. It was 5.30 on a fabulous evening in this nice country village and she really loved her life at the moment. After a tough first year at college she was lucky to get a place with one of the biggest Law practices in the country, which just happened to have a branch in her home village. Everyone in the office was nice and she concluded this was the profession for her. On top of that, she had a loving attentive boyfriend, who seemed to think the world of her and above all, understood about her top priority, to remain a virgin. She very much wanted to hold on to Ned, but she must also become a good Lawyer and having an early family would stop that from happening. He jumped from the car and walked around to open the door for his lady, who quickly kissed him full on the mouth before easing herself into the passenger seat.

'There goes those knees again. 'Gods good,' he was thinking as he circled the car. 'He'll give me the strength to keep my promises.'

Susan asked him to drive her home so she could change, even though she looked a million dollars in yet another lovely outfit. He understood and had a cup of tea with her mother while the transition occurred, half an hour later she strolled into the kitchen, this time in a tight blue skirt, pale blue blouse open quite low with wine coloured high heeled boots just below the knee.

'Your daughter's a knockout,' he said, addressing her mother, much to Susan's pleasure. 'I'm just lost for words, lost for words.'

'It's the first time that's happened since I met you,' replied the object of his praise.

'We're eating locally tonight Mrs. Prunty, would you and your husband care to join us?' His request brought a pleasant smile to the lady's face, with an equal reaction from his girlfriend.

'No thank you Ned, you young folk go and enjoy yourselves, I remember when we were your age we didn't want our parents tagging along.' As she spoke it was plain to see from the glow on her face, that she was back in time, reliving some of her past happiness.

Susan decided to show her fellow off to the locals tonight, so she booked a table for 7 o'clock in the village pub-cum restaurant.

'Do you think it's a good idea?' He asked, 'I would safely say, my two friends with the fly-away collars will be there for openers.'

This was the first time he witnessed his lady angry, a bright colour invaded her pretty cheeks and she blurted out. 'I'm sure of what those two and others will say, do you see that Prunty hussy, playing the virgin with the local lads while she's being ridden senseless by that Showband fellow.' 'Oh my God Ned, I'm sorry for being so rude,' she continued, her voice fading.

He was parking the car when she hit high doh, so he switched it off and reached for her. She was shaking in his arms whispering her apologies, but all he could do was laugh.

'I couldn't have said it better myself,' he stated, 'and in the future don't apologise for speaking the truth, do you hear me now!' She began laughing along with him as he held her closer, then nuzzling her ear he made a plan. 'You sit where you are, the spoof starts here, I'll go around and open your door, take you by the hand and assist your exit from the car, then we'll walk hand in hand into the pub, OK!' 'Anyway I want to get another glimpse of your lovely knees.'

'You lovely devious man,' she purred, as she placed a well groomed hand in his and with the other one, she boldly hiked up her skirt showing a lot more than usual, as she swung her long legs on to the street.

Both knew they were being watched but didn't really care, anyway, his eyes were riveted on those gorgeous limbs he was longing for. She spoke to lots of people in the bar as Ned ordered the drinks and they decided to have a laugh there before going into the dining area. They would catch up on the scandal in Glenrone, which was being passed on by a very excited Susan, who kept gesturing alluringly, touching him as often as possible either by accident or on purpose. They didn't care how long it took for the food as a good time was being had and then the two yokels came in, both wearing grey polo necked sweaters. They waved and smiled at Susan in an ogling fashion, she returned the wave followed by a big sunny smile, then they both turned a vacant stare in Ned's direction to be greeted in similar fashion by him.

'Let's not bother with them,' she said. 'We're having too much fun to let anyone spoil it.'

'I agree,' he answered, 'but I'm having another problem, which I suppose should not be a problem.'

'What's that honey?' She asked with concern.

He reached across the table, took both her hands in his and answered her question. 'I love you Susan,' then as his grip tightened he continued. 'Is it too soon?'

'It's hard to know when something that important is too soon or not,' she answered, 'but then I've got a problem also, I'm in love with you, which makes for good timing really.'

'Thank God there's a table between us again love,' he said. 'I think we had better buy a fold up one to carry around, either that or a set of handcuffs for me.'

She burst out laughing at the handcuff idea. 'Are you sure you don't want them for some other reason?' she inquired.

'No, only your safety in mind, in case I can't control myself,' he replied.

'Don't worry,' she assured him. 'I'll make sure you control yourself and if we had those yokes, I'd probably handcuff you to the metal rail outside or to the door handle of your car, how would you like that?'

She was trying hard to be tough and he knew it, so he would have to stop being frivolous, as they would both need to work on making sure she remained a virgin.

Susan was having the very same thoughts and was glad when the waiter called them for their meal, as it would be much easier getting used to these revelations, out of the view of the locals. The restaurant area was quite large with only one couple dining as yet in the far corner and credit to the young waiter for setting their table at the opposite end. He had taken his pint and she her mineral from the bar, so both declined when the waiter brought the wine list, they just sat at the table smiling at each other.

'What are you thinking?' He asked.

'I'm glad we told each other,' she answered, reaching across to hold his hands.

'I've felt like this since the first night I met you at the dance,' he declared softly, not divulging of course, the similar feelings he felt for other girls he had met since that memorable night. Really ashamed of himself now, he waited for her reply.

'Ditto here,' she answered, as a sad look crept over her lovely face. 'I went through a few bad months wondering about you, if you cared at all, even if you were alive or dead, I just hadn't a clue.'

'That will never happen again, I promise,' he insisted. 'If you don't hear from me for a month, it will mean I'm dead.'

The food was great, just as good as the big city, so they spent about an hour and a half eating, talking and scoffing another pint plus a cola, then Susan asked a searching question.

'What is your plan for the next three hours or so, are we going home to mother?'

'Well darling,' he began. 'I'm glad we have another three hours together and even though your mother is a lovely lady, I'm not taking you home to her.' 'We are going to drive out to a place called The Deep Lough which you probably know, there we will kiss and talk the entire time away, if it's OK with you.'

She burst out laughing and said. 'You silly man, of course it's OK with me, come on, I can hardly wait.'

'Another woman calling me silly,' he thought, as they got up from the table, 'not to worry, it's just a term of endearment, in this case anyway.

There were a couple of whistles, plus a laugh or two, as the young couple walked past the yokels holding hands and Ned was tempted to say. 'See you all tomorrow night,' but that comment would probably have stopped them attending the dance and he had no problem taking their money. They went through the same ritual getting into the car and the faces just inside the pub window were plain to see.

When he started the engine, he drove out the other road in the direction of the Fiddler's Lane and Susan asked. 'I thought you weren't taking me home pet, what changed your mind?'

He slowed the car and at a wide spot in the road he did a U-turn. She could hear him laughing before he explained the plan. 'We were being watched leaving town, if we had gone the other direction they would probably guess our destination and follow us, I didn't want to be annoyed by those eejits in the middle of a passionate kiss, would you agree?' He obviously thought that everybody behaved like the members of his own band, now they both waved at the pub as they drove past and he couldn't help asking about the terrible twins, who once more were dressed almost identically.

'Oh, they're harmless really, the reason they always look the same is that they do everything together, including shopping for clothes, resulting in their buying two of everything, they think it's a great idea.' She was laughing heartily as she told the story.

Ned had a different thought, which was prompted by his experiences in the seminary, but he wasn't sure if now was the right time to mention it, as he hadn't told Susan the nitty-gritty about his time there yet.

She noticed he was miles away and that prompted her question. 'A penny for them?'

'Oh, I was thinking, they may be a little mixed up about their sexuality and have a deeper interest in each other than clothes, you never can tell these days.' He answered.

'God, I never thought of that,' she said, aghast, 'but didn't you hear them bragging about what they would do to me and others?'

'Yeah,' he replied, 'but have you ever seen either of them out with a woman?'

Susan admitted that she hadn't and they both concluded, that it didn't really matter anyway.

Chapter Eleven

There were two other cars in the little car park when they got there, one at each end.

'Reminds me of the restaurant tonight,' said Susan. 'Where are you going to put it honey?' 'My God, that sounded rude.'

'We've only got one choice,' he answered. 'Slap bang in the middle and I don't think you were a bit rude.'

They could be heard laughing back in the village as he parked the car, carefully locking the door with his elbow, he didn't want to panic her so he would lock the other door quietly, after he took her in his arms. The cushion had been put in place between the front seats earlier in the day and now everything was in train for some serious courting. The Lough was awash with moonlight and there was barely a ripple on the water, as they sat back surveying each other. She had her lovely legs crossed elegantly, with one long wine boot placed carefully alongside the other and the tight blue skirt about six inches above those knees, that were glistening in the moonlight. Slowly he reached over and wrote something with his fingertip.

'What did you write on my leg?' 'Please do it again only slower, I missed it,' she declared.

Slowly and in real cheeky fashion, he put his index finger on her knee just at her hemline, then instead of starting to write immediately, he moved in the other direction, boldly baring another couple of inches of those lovely limbs, while she looked at him in fake surprise.

'I didn't have enough room last time,' he managed to say in a sexually charged whisper and then he slowly wrote in large invisible letters. 'I love you Susan!' ending with an exclamation mark on her kneecap.

That did the trick, they both launched themselves into each other's arms, feverishly searching for and finding eager lips, which remained engaged for half an hour at least, before they came up for air, then without a word they became more comfortable, continuing to kiss. The radio had been playing soft music in the background but now it was playing something different, it was the time signal for midnight, which took them both by surprise. Ned looked around the car park and he counted four more cars that had arrived during their kissing marathon and one of them was parked about three feet away. By the look of things, this couple had a different moral code to that adopted by him and Susan and he had about ten seconds to scan the scene. A young man was astride a young blonde lady in a fully reclined passenger seat and she was smiling at Ned, while in receipt of some fast, final strokes from her lover. He smothered a curse word as he tore his gaze from the action and back to his lovely girlfriend, who was taking a tissue from her handbag and applying it just below her eyes. She wasn't aware of the goings on and in his distraction he hadn't noticed her crying, so he took her gently in his arms and asked her what the problem was.

'Those were the most beautiful hours of my life so far,' she began, 'and a little while ago something sensational happened to me as we kissed, do you understand what I mean?'

'Yes I do,' he answered. 'I could feel it happening but I didn't want to mention it to you, that was why I almost picked you up in my arms to make you feel safe during it and your kisses became so intense.'

She looked at him really concerned and asked. 'Are you annoyed pet?' 'I couldn't help it.'

'To answer your question first, no I'm not annoyed at you, I'm thrilled for you instead and I sincerely hope the same happens every time we have a kissing session.'

She put her head on his shoulder and swore her undying love for him, as he promised her the feeling was mutual and then while they were whispering sweet nothings he said. 'In a moment, take a look at the car on our left and let me know if you're familiar with the occupants?'

They moved apart, she took her hairbrush from her bag and slowly began brushing her hair. Simultaneously, she glanced at the people in the front seat of the other car, now boldly illuminated by the interior light and she gave a little gasp as she waved her brush.

'My God Ned, have they been watching us kissing all this time and how did they get there without us knowing?'

'I think I can answer both you questions,' he said. 'We were so happy kissing that we never heard them arrive and they were so busy making love, they had no time to watch us, actually, I was privy to the final throes of their union, do you know them?'

'Yes, they were both at my school, only a couple of years older, she's Mandy the town bike and he's a fierce man for the women, he asks me out at every dance but I just laugh at him Thank God.' She slipped into a thoughtful mood for a moment then asked. 'Will they think we were making love also, I wonder?'

'No chance,' he answered. 'We were sitting beside each other while we kissed and a couple couldn't make love in that position unless they were double-jointed magicians, those two, they were on top of each other instead.'

Susan was smiling again, happy in the thought that her sex-life wouldn't be the topic of conversation in the village over the weekend.

Then he remembered something he had forgotten to ask her. 'Can you come to the launch of our new single in Dublin on Monday night honey?'

'Oh Ned, I'd love to, but I'm so busy in work it would be impossible, there's a big case on at the moment and I'm in charge of all the searches, so I've got to work every hour just to stay ahead, I'm sorry pet.'

The way she called him pet made him want to start kissing all over again, but he knew it was time to take her home and as he reversed the car out, they both took a quick look into the neighbouring vehicle, where the inside light was still on. The other couple had resumed operations, only this time the lady was on top and seemed to be giving as good as she got earlier.

'Good for you Mandy,' Ned shouted as they drove away.

'I don't know how she survives.' Susan said with real disbelief in her voice. 'She's been with every man in the village and a couple of the women as well, as far as I know.'

'Are you kidding me?' he asked, 'does that go on in a small place like Glenrone, the women I mean?'

'Yeah, there are whispers about herself and two sisters, who keep visiting each other, plus going on holiday together, no one is sure,' she said.

He changed his usual exclamation to 'My God I'm shocked!' 'When you say two sisters, I presume they're someone else's sisters, not hers?'

'That's right,' came the answer, 'but it gets worse, the story is that the sisters sleep together all the time, even if they don't have a stranger in the house, what do you think of that?'

'I believe that happened a lot in England years ago, especially among the members of one well known literary family,' he continued, 'but tell me, how could you be sure it's going on in Glenrone?'

'Well, it seems to be the opinion around here and how do you know about it happening in England?'

'Oh, I read it somewhere and I often wondered how they managed with all the petticoats.' 'It would be difficult enough for a man and a woman, but two women?'

They were laughing at that as he helped her from the car and they kissed their way to the front door. She had asked him in for a quick cuppa, more as an excuse for spending the extra time together than the actual tea, then while the kettle boiled, she excused herself and went to the bathroom. He was bursting to go, so he picked the small toilet under the stairs and as he came out from there she was swishing past in a beautiful pink negligee, matching dressing gown, with pink high-heeled slippers. He did a double take to confirm if it was Susan, or Brenda, whose night attire was identical. 'Thank God for sharp dressers,' he thought.

They stood in the middle of the kitchen floor, their arms loosely around each other as she explained her reasons for changing.

'I went in to say goodnight to mum and dad, then I wanted to get out of that tight skirt, so I hope you don't think I'm trying to lead you on.' 'By the way, my parents said to remind you that you're coming to hear us play tomorrow evening, is that still on?'

'You bet,' he said, 'as for leading me on, I don't think you do that at all, because if you were, you'd be doing it with everything you wear you gorgeous thing.'

He felt very happy and contented, as he drove the mile and a half to the guesthouse, feeling much better for not making love to Susan. He knew she was different, this was real love and he would have no problem waiting for her, then for a second, he wondered if Mandy had had it for the third time yet, tonight. Jaysus, how would a fella keep up with her and there was always the danger of what you might get from her.

He swore again as he looked in the mirror later while putting toothpaste on his brush. All he could see was a set of beautiful sparkling teeth surrounded by a face, which was not Susan's. The imaginary face he could see was that of Sandra Boyle, the newspaper reporter who he had to invite to the record launch, then he remembered he must ring her in the morning. Mike, who could be a fairly comprehensive brownnoser when he wanted to, had told him to make sure she attends.

'How am I going to do this?' He asked himself as the face of Sandra faded, to be replaced by his face of panic. 'I must be cracking up, I'm crazy about Susan, but I've got to ask another good looking woman to the do, who I'm sure, wants to fuck me and anyway, how can I have a real relationship in this way?'

He was thoughtful as he brushed his teeth slowly, then he remembered something Susan had said as part of her chastity pact.

'I understand the pressure you will be under', she said, 'so if there's a situation whereby you cannot get out of taking some girl home for business of other reasons, then go ahead, as long as you don't tell me anything about it, OK!'

It was the 'OK' on the end, which made him feel he wasn't hallucinating, as he tried to remember the full content and the meaning of the opt-out clause she had given him, in case of a problem. 'Well God bless your cotton socks,' he said, half hoping her face would appear in the mirror, but no such luck. 'And I'll bet you'd look lovely in cotton socks as well.'

As he became drowsy, he couldn't stop thinking of his session with Susan earlier and another sight that he failed to shift from his brain, was the smile on Mandy's face knowing he was watching her being humped? Mrs. North had another wonderful meal ready for him at noon and he managed to read the local paper during and after that. He had seen lots of big posters around the village and on poles along the road for their big dance in Glenrone, now he discovered a huge advertisement on the music pages for it also.

'They're giving you lots of publicity anyway,' said the landlady, looking over his shoulder.

'That's good,' he said, 'it's better than keeping it a secret like some venues do.'

As he flicked over to the next page, there she was plain as day, a big picture showing the pearly teeth, with a banner headline saying. Music and dancing round up, by Sandra Boyle and as he drank his tea it leaped out at him. The Nova's Showband, going from strength to strength play in Glenrone tonight. If you want a great night out be there and catch this entertaining outfit play and sing anything from country to the latest pop songs. Band leader Ned Brady informs me, they will be launching their new single in Dublin next Monday evening, just like myself, every journalist and D.J in the country will be there, so watch this space next week, for all the news from that function.

'Jaysus,' he hissed. 'I haven't phoned her yet, so I'd better do it before 1 o'clock.'

'Oh hello Ned,' she began. 'I was hoping to hear from you sooner, but I presume all's OK for Monday, did you see the bit on Glenrone yet?'

'No, not yet,' he lied. 'I see a paper here and I'll have a look now, are you making your own way on Monday?'

'Yeah, no problem, I've got the old Jam-Jar to carry all my junk, so looking forward to it.'

'Well that wasn't too bad after all,' he heard himself saying. 'She may act tough, but she's probably very nice really.'

Ned was also staying tonight, so he went up to the room, got his song words and proceeded to the car parked out front, to practice. For the next while he would listen to the old Hank William's song 'Lovesick Blues' and watch for any action in the village, which might include Susan walking across the street.

'You've got it bad,' he was thinking, just as she came out from her office and strolled to the newsagents. 'Wow, she's wearing the blue jeans and those high heeled yellow boots, I hope she sees me,' his voice faded as she emerged once more, waving at him immediately, then as if she was a magnet, he started up the car to drive the one hundred yards to her. 'I was hoping you'd see me,' he said.

'Same here,' she replied, 'in fact I was looking out for you earlier and I saw you getting into the car, the paper was just an excuse.' She blushed brightly as she ended.

'That's nice, because I still love you today and I'm looking forward to doing so tomorrow as well.' He told her this without taking his eyes off her lovely face.

'I told mum about us, she's thrilled, so I told her about the pact we made, she says it's very mature of us and both mum and dad are looking forward to you becoming their son in law, how about that?' As she completed the sentence, they were both wishing it were dark and not the middle of the day on a quite busy village street.

'In some cases that could be scary, but not with you, I'm actually looking forward to it immensely,' as he said that, he took her hand, kissed it and confirmed that he would see her at home at seven, after their rehearsal.

She put on an outrageous wiggle for the twenty yards back to her office and he shouted after her. 'Make sure you put lots of Rosin on you bow later, but if you keep walking like that, the pact is off,' that cracked her up altogether and as she turned around to wave she looked a picture.

Starting up the car he thought. 'Jaysus, I have to look and listen to these ugly fuckers for the next four hours, well that's my little bit of hell for today.' 'It's not too bad I suppose, after being in heaven for the past two days, not forgetting, heaven begins again at 7 o'clock.' He was looking forward to hearing The Prunty family play as a unit later. The night he stayed in their house they were only messing and that really sounded well, but he as yet had not seen his love with a fiddle under her pretty chin, he could hardly wait for that. His band members were all there when he arrived and they seemed glad to see him.

'You look a happy bunch Thank God, why?' he asked.

'We're looking forward to taking Belfast by storm tomorrow night,' said Mickey Joe, 'after what you said, it seems to be the place for the birds.'

'It's for the birds alright,' said Mr Ivory the Piano man. 'The only storm might be a bomb in the hall, to blow us all sky high.'

'Negative thoughts like that are not allowed,' Conn offered, as he assembled his beloved saxophone, giving it a rub with a piece of chamois leather for good luck.

'The shine from that thing is blinding me,' said the Bass man.

Then Ned saw the Guitar man going into the gent's toilet, complete with instrument and tape recorder. 'Where is he off to?' He asked.

'It's that fuckin' song you're learning,' said the Piano man. 'It's full of chords he can't work out but he won't ask me, he just keeps wondering why anyone should want to sing a song, written by a stupid fucker who brought on his own premature demise, with a feeds of drink and prescribed drugs?'

'What Bollix did that?' the Roadie enquired.

'Stop extracting the urine about a country legend,' requested the Singer. 'I sing loads of songs written and recorded by Hank Williams and I'm proud to do so.'

'I wonder would he be proud?' The Drummer asked, 'as for your new version of taking the piss, I think you heard that first in Nashville, when you introduced yourself as a singer.'

'Here we go again,' Ned thought, as he headed for the jacks to retrieve the Guitar picker.

They were ready to go at 2.15 which was great for them and to hopefully put a smile on the Guitar man's face, he asked them a funny question he had read in a music magazine.

'Guess what they call a Guitar player instead of a Guitar player?'

Some of the immediate flurry of answers was not nice, so the guitar man asked.

'Come on, tell us will ya?'

'They're called plank spankers,' said Ned.

'They mostly look like spankers alright,' said the Drummer. 'And some of them look like wankers too,' he added.

The Guitar man smiled wickedly and answered. 'You also fit the bill, the plank bit that is, because you're as thick as two short planks and sometimes those sticks sound like they never left the tree.'

Ned began to think the bomb would go off long before Belfast, so he put his foot down. 'OK lads, no more crap, there's a job to be done and we're going to do it starting now, ready, a one, two, three, four.'

The Sax and Trumpet players had worked out an intro in the wagon on the way down and everyone came in on cue, it sounded great. As usual there were a few hiccups that were ironed out and they moved on to the next number, this time featuring the Singer. Ned had decided to bring an old guitar which he strummed in the Seminary years ago, then later on in The Slugs group and he asked John the Bass man, if he could plug it into his amp. It was the Lead Singer's idea to have as many rhythm instruments going as possible, while he was singing.

'That's how they do it in Nashville,' he said.

He checked the tuning, ran over the few chords and away they went. The smiles of approval from the Chanter said it all and you could almost hear. 'Fuck me, that's the business.'

'I want more money.' Ned said jokingly and the swear words came thick and fast.

'It's about time you did a bit of work, in between blowing the odd note on that auld slip horn, you do feck all except chat up birds, it's no wonder you score so often,' it was Mr. Ivory and he meant it.

'Auld jealousy will get you nowhere,' Ned said, taunting the aggressor.

It was like water off a duck's back to him, so that situation went away, but wouldn't be forgotten. The third song for today was the current number one in the pop chart, making it a must for Belfast on Saturday and Dublin on Sunday. The Guitar man was looking forward to singing this and playing the very visually exciting solo, which he had off to a tee after hours of listening and swearing. The whole band would be featured and he was watching Mr. Ivory closely, hoping he might make a mistake, but no such luck. With one hour to go, they decided to run the three songs again to check retention, which passed quite smoothly Thank God, then Ned told the lads about the good food in the pub and promised he would see them later.

'Oh, I suppose you're dining with the in-laws,' was the correct opinion from the band.

'Yes lads and the hall will be full of her family and relations tonight, so behave yourselves please,' with that comment, he got into his car.

Before he drove off, the Roadie got into the passenger seat saying. 'I've been on to Amanda in Buffalo, it seems Jayne has been asking for you, what will I tell her at the weekend?'

'Tell her there's a lot of trauma in my family at the moment, with my dad not well and the up-coming sale of the pub.' 'I'll ring her soon and I hope to see her during the holidays in May, mums the word about the pub to anyone.'

'Don't worry, you can trust me,' the Roadie answered, then as he got out of the car the very excited young man gushed with enthusiasm. 'That's fuckin' great news about the holidays, I'll tell Amanda to expect me, but I'll have to save every penny from now on.' 'Whoopee, are the burgers nice here?'

'What are you Whoopeeing about?' asked the Singer.

'Oh Ned's after telling me the place will be full of birds tonight and it's about time I had a court, would you agree?'

'But I thought you were mad about that American chick, you're always promising us that you're going to her.' The Singer sounded like he might want that to be true, anyway the Roadie wasn't crazy about him either.

Ned drove leisurely to the Prunty house, by now they would all be there so he wondered how he would be greeted. They were pleasant the last time, but would some of the brother's think that he was (as they say in the States) giving their sister one, or would they all be happy to see him. He quoted his mum. 'God is good,' but there was no need to worry. When she heard the car, Susan came to the door dressed completely in a black cat suit looking stunning and he hardly had his feet on the ground before she flung her arms around his neck, kissing him full on the mouth while he kissed her back giving her a big bear hug, then he held her at arms length to admire her.

'You're the cutest lady I know and your wardrobe must be as big as a football field,' he said.

Just then, a female voice cut across the performance. 'Unhand that man and let him come into the house,' the voice belonged to Mary who was standing in the doorway dressed identically.

She met him with outstretched hand and a welcoming smile, giving him a kiss on the cheek, with a hug for good measure. She felt and smelled good too. Now each girl took him by an arm marching him into the huge dining room, which he had not been in before and there seated at a very large table were the members of Susan's family, with the four brothers also dressed in black.

'This is the nicest escort I've ever had,' quipped our hero, as much to put himself at ease as everyone else and he stood back to present the girls with a flourish.

Mr Prunty was also seated at the table not dressed in black, with his lovely wife standing behind him, one hand on her husband's shoulder.

'Now Susan, introduce us to your young man,' requested her proud mum.

She began with. 'Well, mother you've met, this is my dad John, my brother John, this is Hugh, this is Phillip and this is my brother Michael who is six foot two.' Then she continued with. 'You have met and been hugged by Mary but you still have to hug my lovely mother.'

This he did and she felt like a young one, actually, she was quite flushed afterwards while rubbing the creases from her grey dress.

Now John junior spoke up. 'Before we play any music we're going to eat and I'm sure you're wondering why we're all dressed in black, it's so you can get the visual effect as well as the sound.'

'I was thinking that,' he answered. 'The band must look well, or you're on a loser.'

They were all seated at the table except Mary and her mother, who began by serving the soup. Susan was seated next to Ned, just across the table from her father who was a very jolly man and he joined in talking about the line-up of the band. Over the years he had played almost every Traditional instrument out there, including Uilleann Pipes and he was the only man other than himself, who owned an Ocarina, or a Sweet Potato, as they were known.

Now John Junior took up the conversation again. 'As you know, we all play fiddle and during one set the six of us play, two of the lads play accordions, Mary plays concert flute, both wood and silver plus keyboards, Hugh plays almost everything but mostly pipes, bass, banjo, guitar, mandolin, bouzouki and when we use drums, guess who plays those?'

Slowly Ned turned around to a blushing Susan. 'She does I'll bet,' he smothered his usual 'Jaysus' replacing it with. 'My God, I'm looking forward to seeing and hearing that performance,' he howled.

She stood up and gave a bow, saying. 'That's why I wear the cat suit, it gives me more freedom getting in and out from behind the kit.'

Michael continued with. 'Brother John plays a few things himself including piano accordion, harmonica, fiddle of course, keyboards, all the whistles, saxophone, clarinet and swaps the drumming with Susan, as well as that, we all harmonise and everyone dances, so I hope I've covered the remainder of what we do.

They had finished the soup by now and the two ladies were busy serving the main course, so Ned knew he had to ask. 'Where have you been hiding yourselves?'

'We were all in college,' John began, 'as you know we have quite a way to go with that yet, at least the youngest two.' As he glanced at Michael and Susan he continued. 'We've decided we would like to record and that is why we're requesting an introduction to your record company, if possible.'

'With what you've got to offer that should be no problem, I've never witnessed so many instruments being played by the members of any one family and by the way, do you write?' Ned asked.

'Yeah, songs and tunes and guess who's our best writer?'

Again Ned turned his gaze on the once more blushing Susan. 'That's not you as well is it?' He asked in a jibing sort of way.

'Oh, I do a little bit, you and I must write a song together sometime, a love song perhaps,' she was crimson, as she glanced around the room.

'I'd like that,' he said, 'maybe next time I'm here.'

The conversation died a little, while they busied themselves eating and Ned asked if they had any photos of the group.

'That's another reason why we dressed up tonight, dad is going to take a few pictures later in the studio and maybe you'll stand into one, it would be nice to have someone famous in the picture,' John added.

'You'll embarrass me if you say things like that, but did you mention a studio?' Ned enquired.

'Yeah,' said John. 'We've got a little place out the back for rehearsals, it also saves packing instruments and equipment all the time, we write out there as well.'

Ned found he was looking forward to seeing the studio and could hardly wait to see his love behind the drums. 'Wow.' There was a choice of sweet and he could see why Susan liked cheesecake. Along with fresh fruit salad there were varied puddings and an enormous strawberry cheesecake. He waited and sure enough Susan stuck up a pretty finger and asked her mum if she could have the large piece of cheesecake please. Ned was thinking about the future for a few seconds, wondering if she would continue to have a sweet tooth later in life, but he couldn't picture the love of his life as a roly-poly, anyway her mother's figure was perfect at fifty. After the coffee, the family members drifted one by one towards the back of the house, until he was alone with Susan.

'That was a fabulous spread honey,' he began, 'I hope Mary and yourself didn't mind that I chose your mother for the praise?'

'Not at all,' she answered. 'Mary was involved all the way through, but she would want mum to get the acclaim.'

As he leaned over to kiss her, he was brought back from the heaven of her lips, by the sound of music coming from the rear of the house.

'That's my cue to take you through, come along maestro,' she stopped speaking, slipped her arms around his waist and in between planting velvet kisses on his eager lips she stated. 'You know I wrote a song about us after we met and you disappeared,' then still holding him she asked, 'would you like to hear the chorus?'

The look on his face was enough, so she began to sing softly.

'I'm just a broken hearted lady,
A broken hearted lady,
And I know my man is up to something shady,
When he drove away that evening,
Was it to Africa or Perth?
But the way he keeps his silence,
I think he must have left this earth,
I was hoping he was gonna be my baby,
Now all that's left's a broken hearted lady.'

As she finished, the tears flowed from both their eyes and they held each other very close.

'I'm really sorry for disappearing that time love, it won't happen again, I promise.'

If Ned has a heart, that's where that undertaking came from and she knew it, so her smile returned. Stepping back, she took him by the hand, guiding him through an open triple glazed French window, into a soundproofed room thirty feet by twenty, with all the instruments and amplifiers either miked-up or hard-wired, to a twenty four channel mixer including all the latest effects.

'My mother intended this space as her patio,' Susan proffered, 'but she's thrilled really, now don't be laughing at me behind my little drum kit.'

The little drum kit in question was bigger than the one in The Nova's Showband and in better condition, but of course it didn't have the mileage up yet.

'What would you like to hear first Ned?' John asked.

'It's totally up to you, but maybe you would start with the six fiddles.' he suggested.

In a couple of minutes it was like the light orchestra, there were fiddles everywhere and at last he saw it. There she was smiling at him, the fiddle under her chin and he was definitely in heaven at that moment. The eldest brother, who was obviously the leader, gave a verbal count and they struck up a selection of reels. He had never heard the like. That lasted about six minutes and immediately they went into a set of jigs. Next they made a few changes, piano accordion, button accordion, mandolin and banjo with Mary on the silver flute and his little honey Susan, still on the fiddle. It was the best set of polkas he had ever heard and the fabulous thing about it was, they were playing quite intricate arrangements in all the pieces, something that he hadn't heard this type of band play before. The run of the mill Traditional outfit would have all the instruments playing in unison, which was OK, but this was different, completely new to him. Mr and Mrs. Prunty were looking proudly at their offspring and no wonder, as the instrumentation changed once more. Hugh put his mandolin down picking up an electric guitar and while checking the tuning; he played a few killer rock-n-roll riffs.

'Jaysus,' Ned hissed to himself, 'imagine what guys like that think, when they come to hear bands like ours.'

Now he was brought back to reality by some very nifty drumming. He had taken his eyes off Susan for a moment while speaking to her parents and he had missed the thrill of her climbing behind the kit, but as he watched she was giving it socks, checking out all the skins with a pattern or tattoo. What they were about to play was a Celtic rock version of an Old Irish song and it was brilliant. As he listened in awe to this family of amateur musicians, he realised how screwed up the world of professional music was. His own band members were passable musicians and I suppose you could say their vocal line-up was strong, but there were some combo's out there who had players sucking their instruments instead of blowing. He could remember one young lad from Ballypratt, who bought a guitar and started his first group the same day. He had allowed his mind to drift for a moment, but it came back to reality when a certain lady took a drum solo. Her siblings stood to the sides and looked on admiringly as their cute sister went to town on the kit. Nothing escaped, snare, toms, high-hat, crash cymbals, a little novelty cymbal on a high stand, a cow-bell, one bar of total silence, then back with the full kit.

'Jaysus,' Ned said again in a whisper, while clapping wildly along with everyone else in the room and he just kept applauding as the full band struck up once more to end the piece. He watched as she shyly yet elegantly climbed from behind the drums, quietly slipping into her black high heels on the way and as she reached the front of the stage he was there hand outstretched.

'And you play barefoot!' He exclaimed.

'No,' she replied, I've got a little pair of flat shoes back there that no one ever sees.'

'What can I say?' He began. 'Apart from the fact that I've just heard the best drum solo I have ever witnessed, you deserve a big kiss for it.' She gladly accepted the kiss, as the other musicians put their instruments on stands.

'We're going to do some A-Cappella vocals now,' said John, 'featuring four, five and six parts, see if you recognise The Mountains of Mourne.'

Luckily Ned had heard the term A-Cappella before and was able to comment.

'That's a very difficult thing to pull off, I've heard a few poor attempts and I'm looking forward to this, I think you're all fabulous.'

'Thank you Ned,' they chorused in perfect harmony.

Following a hearty laugh from everybody, John gave them the key using his perfect pitch and they hit the introductory chord. During the song, John, Phillip and Susan, took solo lines, it was a knockout. When the piece came to an end and the compliments were issued, Mrs. Prunty ushered them back to the dining table where they all had tea and cake, plus a chat about the plan which the musical family had.

'We would like to record without touring,' said John, 'and I think our market is in the United States, would you agree?'

Ned was glad to hear of their lack of interest in touring (for totally selfish reasons), as he had to admit. If this band went on tour looking and sounding like they do, every hot-blooded male in his right mind would want to bed his darling and that would not do. He heard John's comment and question and he had to drag himself back from his dream world to reply.

'I would agree,' he answered, a happy smile on his face. 'With the right distribution, plus air-play in the States, you would sell million's, it's a big place with a lot of Irish and they would lap you up, especially the girls.'

'You wouldn't like me traipsing all over the world, with people lapping me up, would you Ned?' Susan asked.

'If it was what you wanted to do and lucrative, then I would be right behind you, I think I'd ask for the job as your Roadie.' he lied.

'Thank you honey,' she said, kissing him on the cheek. 'But there's no need to worry, I just want to be a good Lawyer and a good wife.'

That gave him a colossal adrenaline rush, tempting him to grab her and drag her outside to the car, but he knew that wouldn't go down too well. Instead he paid back her little peck on the cheek and took a quick look at his watch, which almost caused a heart attack. His band was due on stage in twenty minutes, but he still had to shave and change. Time would be tight tonight, so he excused himself, once more congratulating the musicians and of course the chefs. He kissed Susan, said he'd see her later and shook hands with Mr and Mrs. Prunty as he headed for the door. Thank God the potholes were gone and as he raced down the Fiddler's Lane at full speed, his thoughts drifted to another band of amateurs he had heard in Buffalo N.Y. not forgetting The Loaf, probably the best piano player he had ever heard (for a baker). The band members all looked at their watches, as he rushed through the door of the grubby dressing room, almost knocking Conn over as he walked about, lovingly massaging notes from his darling saxophone. Ned concluded, that Conn thought in reality he was feeling Cynthia Rose up, every time he played his instrument, bless him.

'For fuck's sake, would you hurry up,' the Trumpet player hissed out of the corner of his mouth.

A couple of members seconded that by shouting Mickey Joe's new word (Bollixolutely), while informing him that the place was full, not for a moment taking into account, the fact that he had just struggled up the floor through the said throng, but he decided not to take up the cudgel, even though he still had five minutes to go. Patience might be considered a virtue, but it's also a miracle he concluded, as he ignored the undercurrents.

The relief band put their best foot forward in their last set, with a medley of Elvis hits and they had the crowd jumping when they announced the main attraction. 'And now, from their sell-out tours of England and The United States, would you put your hands together for the fabulous, Nova's Showband. The huge crowd tried to rush the bandstand, but because of the fact they were already packed like sardines in the hall, all they could do was roar and scream, clapping loudly. As usual, they kicked off with their signature tune called 'Travel on' which Ned sang with ease, using the time to check out who was in and who was not. He looked at the sea of faces and standing in the centre of the mass roaring their heads off were his two buddies, beige shirt collars out over the jackets once more, only this time they were smiling and waving directly at him.

'They have decided to give their blessing instead of agro, seeing I'm courting a local,' he decided. Now, if that were the case he would reciprocate, so he smiled and waved back at them, much to their joy. Tonight, they would not rip up the band photos he presumed.

The lads loved to have a good band on before them as usual, because it was much easier to whip a happy crowd into a frenzy than the opposite and as the night progressed they couldn't put a foot wrong. It was about an hour later that he saw the complete Prunty family plus their cousins The North's, make their way slowly along the right side of the crowded floor. Susan and her sister Mary had identical silk dresses, the only difference being, Susan's was black while Mary's was red. The twin North sisters, were also dressed beautifully and it was easy to see the resemblance between them and their relations, they were also a pair of corkers. Three of Susan's brothers had the same cute girlfriends as before, but young six-foot plus Michael had a new lady on his arm. She was tall and willowy like a fashion model and it looked like it wasn't their first date. Both sets of parents were glowing and no one more so than Mrs. Prunty, as she smiled up at Ned on the rostrum.

'Jaysus, I'll have to behave tonight,' he thought, as he viewed the line of young ones sitting on the stage, zips glistening, just daring him to check them out with his trusty trombone. 'She'll make a lovely mother-in-law in a few years,' he was thinking as he announced the Guitar man to sing the current pop chart topper, making sure he wouldn't put his thoughts into the bulletin.

Next was Ned, yodelling his way through 'Lovesick blues' much to the amusement of Susan and the girls as they gyrated each time he yodelled. The next set started off with the Lead Singer warbling their latest single and Ned laid it on thick, as he told the people about the big launch on the coming Monday in Dublin. The song went well enough to warrant a repeat performance later in the show, much to the bliss of The Chanter, who kept bowing for ages after the song ended. Ned's future brother's-in-law smooched to everything with their partners, it didn't matter whether the tempo was fast or slow and they were having a good old lie-up. Susan picked her mother for her first jive of the night and she roped her obviously shy dad into the scenario while putting them both through their paces. The wiggle of Susan's hips (anytime he got a glimpse of them through the huge crowd) began to hypnotise our hero, so instead of singing harmony to the Guitar man and Mr. Ivory he was almost standing still, his mouth hanging open with his brain on the short strokes. It was obvious she was doing it on purpose.

The Drummer, who realised what was happening, played a few very loud rim shots, screaming at him simultaneously. 'Come back to us you Bollix.'

That did the trick, like the consummate professional that he is, Ned fell back into step at once like nothing had happened, yet knowing full well that he must take his eyes off his girlfriends rhythmic, hypnotic buttocks, at once. There were loads of requests, so he got stuck into reading them out to the joy of some of the audience and the displeasure of others, then to butter up the Drummer, he read out one request from the blank rear of one of the legitimate messages, it said.

'And now, the next song is specially for the best drummer in the hall tonight.' It worked on the double; the band drummer did a mini solo roaring loudly. 'Good man Ned, Good man Ned.'

'Unknown to anyone else in the hall, apart from two that is, the request was meant for someone else and the confirmation of that came via a big promising wink, which passed between the two lovebirds. The Drummer was the happiest man in the room for the remainder of the gig and Ned could have fallen asleep as far as he cared. One hour after the dance ended, the band members were still on stage signing autographs and telling the stories of their lives since they had been in Glenrone before, even the Roadie was telling everyone about his trip to Niagara Falls, but he was keeping quiet about Amanda.

Susan had approached the stage earlier, to compliment the band on its performance and pass on a couple of important messages.

'Number one,' she began. 'I still love you, number two, The Prunty's and North's all enjoyed themselves and you're invited back to our house for tea, they'll all be there, Oh, I almost forgot, thanks for the request.' With that she gave him a big wet kiss full on the mouth, promising more as tomorrow was Saturday. 'I don't have to get up early Thank God.' She added.

Before she rejoined her family, he begged her not to change out of what she was wearing. 'I've been fantasising all night about how you will feel in that dress and I can't grab you here, but I'll be home soon,' he promised. As he watched her walk across the dance floor, he had to fight the urge to follow and hug her forever, but the vision of her trusting, smiling mother, cancelled that out. Then he remembered what he'd just said to her and it brought a goofy smile to his face. 'I'll be home soon,' had a great ring to it.

He was chatting away to some fans when he felt a tug on his sleeve, so he excused himself for a moment and turned towards this (as yet) unknown solicitation. There, smiling mischievously at him, was none other than Mandy the town bike, who he had witnessed getting her 'pound of flesh' the previous night, in that car out at the lake.

She took him by the hand saying. 'So we meet face to face at last, my name is Mandy, how are you?'

'I'm well,' he began, 'but we have met face to face already, a little over a day ago out at the Deep Lough, you were enjoying yourself in a car a few feet away from me, remember.'

She didn't blush, but decided not to try a bluff either, so she said. 'You've got a good memory for faces, especially when you were busy yourself.'

'It was the look on your face I remember most, you're a very pretty girl but lady, were you happy?' Then he concluded with. 'I may have been busy, but you were busier.'

That made her laugh out loud and she asked. 'Can I have a very special autograph promising that you will keep our secret, I know I'm a little late with you, as you're stepping out with our local solicitor, who by the way is lovely and not as bold as poor me, you're lucky.'

For a second, he thought he caught a note of sadness in her lilting voice and she looked a little sombre en-sync, but she brightened up again when he handed her a picture, which read. To a beautiful, happy, satisfied face in the night, which will not be forgotten by the onlooker, Take care, signed, Ned Brady. He was tempted to sign his name as 'Ned the Bed' but refrained, thinking that Susan or some of her friends might see it, he couldn't have that.

'OK Ned Brady,' she said, 'who in this bunch is available?' 'I'm on the loose tonight and I could use a hug.'

She was viewing the other band members as she spoke and he thought. 'They got her nickname accurate all right, but I can't have her screwing one or more of the band, because the word would to around like wildfire.' 'Hold on,' he suggested. 'I'll check if any of them are in hugging mood tonight, back in a minute.'

He mooched around the stage, putting her case to three of the members who were not as yet involved and give them their due, the first thing they did against his wishes was to look directly at Mandy, grinning in an inane fashion.

'Fuck me', said the Piano man, 'she looks a bit of alright to me, has anyone got rubbers?'

'That's what she'll do to you alright,' Ned promised, 'but you might need galoshes instead of ordinary rubbers.'

'What the fuck are galoshes?' inquired the Roadie, 'and who's the cute blonde you were talking to Ned, you're not going to try and fit her in before that nice girlfriend of yours, are you?'

The four fellows gave him a dirty look, so he shrugged and went back to his packing.

'I thought that eejit promised to check the dictionary in future, instead of asking around,' said Mr. Ivory, who was still showing signs of interest in Mandy, much to Ned's annoyance.

'You'll probably get a half-gross if you go near her, but come over and say hello anyway.' The introductions over, Ned headed for the dressing room.

On the way he met the Roadie. 'Galoshes are waterproof overshoes,' he began, 'a little bit like Wellington boots.' 'So what are they made from? I hear you ask, 'Rubber,' he answered himself at the top of his voice and then went back to his packing.

'He must have bought a dictionary and carries it in his bag, what other way could he have got the answer so soon?' Ned thought. 'Jaysus, he can be dumb or crafty at the drop of a hat.'

The deliriously happy Drummer noticed Ned was talking to himself as he entered the band room and began with a question that was killing him for hours. 'When you finish that conversation you're having, could you tell me who handed up that request for me tonight?'

'I'm afraid I don't know,' came the calm answer, 'it was part of a bunch of requests, but someone's just told me of a joke, do you want to hear it?'

'OK,' the Skinner answered, disappointed at not being able to trace his fan.

'This young nun ran into the Convent looking all dishevelled and the Reverend Mother asked, what's the matter child?' 'Then the postulant said, Reverend Mother, I've been graped, the older lady corrected her by saying, I'm sure you mean you were raped.' 'No,' said the young nun, 'there was a bunch of them.'

The Drummer gave a half-hearted laugh and Ned knew his tale had died. 'You can't win them all,' he mused as his thoughts went back to his love and the fact that she didn't have to work in the morning.

Before he had finished changing, a disgruntled Mr. Ivory came into the dressing room. 'That fucking blonde is just a prick-teaser,' he fumed. 'She was running her hand up and down my leg really getting me going, then when I asked her out straight if she wanted to fuck, she called me all the names under the sun and fucked off instead.'

Ned was shocked by this outburst from the usually non-swearing wizard of the keys, so he suggested. 'Maybe you were a little forward in the way you asked her, don't you think?'

'Not at all', he answered, 'when we were in L.A. I asked quite a few birds that way and it worked, anyway, what did she expect, she was holding my crotch when I said it to her.'

The Drummer and Trumpet man cracked up when they heard that. They just rolled around the room splitting their sides laughing.

'It's no laughing matter,' came the vexed reply, 'the bitch got me in the mood, then ran she away.'

'Look,' said the Drummer, 'this is Glenrone in the arsehole of the Irish countryside, it's not fucking L.A., would you cop yourself on for fuck's sake.'

Ned agreed, adding to the displeasure of the other man and as they left the room he was still fuming.

They homed in on Mike who was talking to the Committee Secretary about future dates, he saw them coming, said goodnight to the man and met them in the middle of the dance floor his pockets bulging, plus a big smile on his face.

'I must get a briefcase one of these days,' he said, 'we did well tonight, this sixty-forty lark is great.' As he finished speaking they were entering the band room so he began pulling bundles of money from every pocket, doling it out to the musicians who were standing in a ring around him. 'This is a bit like the Indians attacking the stage coach, in the big Western's,' he added.

'Yeah, you big paleface with huge stash, we hard working braves and want-um split to get more wampum for our tribes.' This came from the now smiling Piano man who had joined them at the sight of money, having forgotten all else.

'Now I know for sure why he's in the Band,' Ned concluded, as they headed for the door, suit covers slung over their arms, small suitcase in one hand consisting of sweaty underwear, shirt, plus other unmentionables, not forgetting the token canister or stick of deodorant which was a must and sometimes applied outside the shirts.

Without a thought for the long journey home, they joyfully shouted to the Bandleader. 'See you in Belfast tomorrow night and don't be late.' It was the money talking he deduced, they couldn't wait to make more tonight.

He felt like reminding them that it was later today they were playing, but he realised it would be tomorrow before they got paid so he left it alone. Anyway, he would just be called a 'Smart Bollix', which in itself would be a contradiction in terms, so he asked himself. 'How can I be smart and a bollix at the same time?' After giving that a moments thought, he realised it was indeed possible and it was happening every day.

As he climbed into the big car, happy thoughts of Susan flooded back and he couldn't wipe the smile off his face, wondering how the black dress would feel to the touch. There were quite a few cars at The Prunty house when he arrived, but before he could ring the bell the door swung open and there she stood in all her splendour. For a moment he just looked, also taking in the black patent shoes, which he hadn't had time or space to scrutinize earlier.

'I'm back in heaven again,' he began, as they met half way in a loving clinch and he got his first feel of the silk dress.

'I was keeping an eye out for you,' she said, 'come on in and meet everybody.'

'I've got a joke I must tell you about keeping an eye out, but it's very dirty,' he said.

'You can tell me the next time we're sitting at the lake,' she answered.

He knew he wouldn't as it's content was gross, so he carried on with. 'Guess what?' 'Mandy the town bike put a proposition to me tonight, in a roundabout way and in doing so she paid you a compliment, saying that you are a lovely lady, plus I'm a lucky guy, what do you think of that?' he asked.

'Isn't she a bold bitch, did you tell her what we saw?' she asked.

'That was the first thing I said, but she didn't seem to care, just like water off a ducks back, she immediately asked if I could fix her up with any of the other lads so I went through the motions.'

He continued to tell her about the Piano player's interest and ultimate failure. This she enjoyed, laughing heartily as she led him into the crowded room and introduced him to those he had not met before. The place looked like a fashion show. He met the beautiful North twins who were gorgeous of course and they really were the image of Susan. Next were their slightly older twin brothers who were very like young Michael Prunty and just as tall, complete with glamour puss girlfriends. Then Susan introduced him to her younger brother's new girlfriend, who indeed, was a model and on her way to the big time. Next he shook hands with the three girlfriends he had met before and last but not least he met Mr. North who had been away on business. The lady of the house was in the kitchen as usual, looking elegant but flushed by the heat and again tonight, she was being helped by a very lovely Mary who had her frilly apron on over her red dress. There was also a third person in the kitchen that Mary introduced as her boyfriend, a chef from the city and he was giving a hand.

'Jaysus, how will I remember all these names?' He asked himself, as he stood beside his love with a sensitive hand on her right hip. Still smiling and joining into the conversation, he was weighing up how far he could move his hand without being chastised by Susan, or being blamed for groping her daughter by Mrs. Prunty, so he was curtailed to one inch up, one inch down and boy, did it feel good. Susan took him by the hand saying she wanted him to meet someone else, but instead, led him out to the back porch where she faced him and slowly wrapping her arms around his waist, she gave him a very wet, sexy kiss. Her lips always reminded him of velvet and his thoughts ran wild. 'Just imagine what it will be like when she really gets naughty, God give me the strength to wait and I know it'll be worthwhile.'

This was the hungriest kiss they had so far and each one wanted it to go on for a lifetime, knowing that the close proximity to the others was an added turn on. Another of Susan's attributes was, even though she must remain a virgin and not at any time touch Ned's private parts or he hers, she had no problem with the most intimate kissing or verbal fantasy. Last night at the lake, she had laughingly threatened him.

'Just wait Ned Brady, until we are married, I'll eat you up and from that day on you'll never look sexually at another woman, I promise.'

He didn't doubt her either, because standing here, their arms clenched around each other, their tongues playing find the tonsil, he knew it was more satisfying than a dozen quickies with Mandy, or any other woman. Reluctantly their lips parted and while they got their breath back he decided to say.

'I know what you meant last night, when you promised I would never look at another woman after we're married and I'm looking forward to you eating me up very much.'

That led to another intimate kiss, but realising they would be missed, they called it a night for now and went back to the others, knowing they would have a session later in the car, an idea which appealed to them both. By now a beautiful buffet was set up with wine a plenty as the guests covered all the topical conversational tit-bits of the day. About an hour went by and people began to check watches, tomorrow may be Saturday but they all had beds to go to, so the crowd slowly dwindled. With heartfelt compliments to the chefs, Ned said his goodbyes and Susan stated she was walking him to his car, which would need to be moved from the front door.

'You and I can't court directly underneath my parents bedroom window, so just drive down the lane a little bit.' she stated.

And court they did. Ned hadn't yet seen as much of Susan's lovely legs as he did that night, because during the session, the silk dress had ridden up to reveal two shapely thighs, leaving little to the imagination.

'Don't worry', she said, 'it doesn't crease.' He didn't.

Before parting, they both promised not to fall in love with anyone else until they would meet again, then he walked her back to the front door where he took her lovely face in his hands kissing it all over, finishing with a gentle touch on her magic mouth.

'When I get back to your aunt's house, there's something I must do to stop me going crazy,' he said.

'Is it what I think it is?' She asked knowingly.

'Yes,' he answered, 'just think of me for the next half hour or so, that should cover it.'

He got into the car and drove away, looking forward already, to seeing her fleetingly at lunchtime tomorrow. Later in the comfortable bed, after the lust had been dealt with, he fell into a deep sleep, knowing he had to surface around noon so he would be ready to meet his love at one o'clock.

'Well, did you enjoy it without me?' She asked, laughing. By now she was sitting across the table in her aunt's guesthouse, sharing the late breakfast he usually had as she waited for his reply.

'It was great,' he answered, 'even though my arms were empty my hand was full and I whispered your name all the time, well I hope I was whispering.'

'You're a very bold man Ned Brady, but I love your honesty, anyway I've got something to tell you,' she was blushing brightly as she spoke.

'You didn't, Jaysus, you didn't, did you?' He asked.

'I did,' came the red-faced reply. 'I hope you don't dislike me for it, do you?'

'I'll never dislike you as long as I live,' he said and then he continued with a question. 'Did you like it?'

'Yes,' she replied enthusiastically. 'I put my head under the covers to make sure I wouldn't be heard calling out your name, it's not the first time I've done it thinking of you and I did it many times after you went missing, I loved you from day one.'

'The table comes in handy once more,' he stated with a grin, 'if I had you up in that nice comfortable bed you'd have no chance.'

'That's why we must not allow ourselves to get into that position,' she mused, 'but as you say Ned, God is good.'

She washed the food down with some tea, thanked her adoring aunt, gave him a big kiss, and then hurried back to work, knowing they would talk soon on the phone and if the sexual pressure built up before they met again, they would solve it thinking of each other. There would be no secrets about that.

Belfast was a long way away and he knew it would take all the available time he had to make it without speeding. That was another promise he had made to Susan, not to drive fast.

She had said to him. 'I don't want to read about you being in a crash, I couldn't handle that.'

As he drove out of the village, he saw the sign for the Deep Lough and gave it a wave. 'See you soon,' he said, as he planned another visit there with his beloved Susan.

Chapter Twelve

On the long journey North he had lots of time to think. First of all about Susan, then about her talented family band, which he would mention to their record company man at the launch of their single on Monday and next he switched to the impending auction of his dad's pub, coming up in a couple of weeks. He knew his mother would be pleased but his father would miss the camaraderie and the traditional music played there to rapturous applause at the weekends, which (before the stroke) he always took part in. Now as he pitted the plus against the minus, extracted from some of the stories about staffing he had heard his parents speak about, then selling it was the only solution. Two of the shocking tales he had heard from his father's premises, were the catalyst for his decision not to take the business over. One story went as follows.

Over the past two years and especially since he had been ill, his father was told that two of his young barmen would arrive at the surrounding dance halls or parties, with bottles of spirits which they would mete out to their cronies outside for free, then, when they were full of booze they would go in and join in the fun. It was commonly known that this liquor belonged to The Central Bar in Mullymore.

Another classic was, on Christmas Eve the previous year; the Boss had been talking to his two bar men about the weather and things in general as they cleaned up prior to going to Church to Midnight Mass. The younger one forgot that the owner was present, prompting him to nick a pack of cigarettes, but after opening them up the penny dropped, so he closed the box and put it back on the shelf at once. Later when they were ready to leave Ned's dad said to the young man.

'Don't forget your cigarettes.'

The bemused barman said. 'Oh, they're not mine.'

'I know that,' the Boss answered, 'but seeing that you have opened them, you may as well take them.'

The young guy, who had gone beetroot red, grabbed the cigarettes offering his boss one in his panic, even though he knew the older man didn't smoke. At a later date, the other staff member denied seeing anything, despite the fact that he was just a few feet away. The young fellow was let go soon afterwards, but he now moved to the other side of the counter to become a non-paying customer when the owner wasn't there, which was worse. He would sit there all day drinking and the senior staff member couldn't refuse even if he wanted to, because of what they knew about each other. After catching him there a few times, Ned's dad got him a job miles away, driving a van for a supplier he knew, just to get rid of him, otherwise he would have still cost him a fortune.

'Ah, God is definitely good,' Ned thought, shaking his head. 'Imagine that happening to me while I'm on the road, roll on the auction.'

Luckily he had given himself enough time for the journey, because while driving along north of the border he encountered quite a few roadblocks and noticed that each group operating the barricades was dressed differently to the other, which scared him a bit. He recognised members of the British Army by their uniform, likewise with the Police, then another faction dressed in everyday clothes stopped him and these guys were not a bit nice. They also seemed to have had few drinks earlier, which unnerved him, but he had two worse frights to come. As he sped around an acute bend the torches were flashing on and off, then drawing near he saw the balaclavas, this put the shit crossways in him.

'Can I help you gentlemen,' he enquired, after turning down the window.

'When you get out and open up your boot we'll tell you,' a sarcastic voice answered.

He couldn't make out who or what they were in the dark, all he was sure of from their accents was that they were Irish like himself and being a peaceful chap normally, he couldn't understand the sound of hatred in this stranger's voice, especially seeing that they had never met before. After going through the interior of the car with a fine toothcomb, they checked the boot thoroughly before reluctantly sending him on his way. About five miles further on, another torch, more balaclavas, only this time they were friendlier, joking about the gig. He wished he had left a couple of hours earlier, because he believed these people only came out after dark, most of them under the illusion that they were protecting the Irish from the Irish. All these thoughts were running through his brain for the remainder of the journey and he couldn't help thinking. 'What a mess.' When he got to the venue, the first question he asked the Roadie was.

'Any roadblocks sham?'

'Not a sign, were you stopped?' Came the statement and question.

'Yeah, five fucking times, that's never happened to me before,' said Ned. 'You'd think there was a war on.'

'There is, the only difference being, in Northern Ireland they call it, 'The Troubles.'' Then the Roadie asked. 'Do you know what the letters W.A.R. stand for, apart from war?'

'No, but I'm sure you're gonna tell me,' Ned bantered.

By now, the storyteller was in convulsions at the content of the up and coming joke.

'Yeah,' he screeched. 'It means, Wankers Acting Rough, ha, ha, ha.'

Ned hadn't the heart to tell him his joke was crap, because everybody was always putting him down and he had probably made up this masterpiece himself on the spur of the moment. Instead, he joined in laughing much to the joker's pleasure, resulting in his trombone getting a wipe with a cloth for good measure. The other lads came in with the news, that a good Chinese restaurant existed next door but one to the hall and when they had finished with the old Chinese custom of tune-een, they were all going there for a feed. That sounded good to all. Before they left for the food, the members of the resident band started filtering in and Ned couldn't believe his eyes when the great trombone player he had seen and heard on his last visit to this town, walked up the floor.

'Jaysus, I hope he doesn't recognise me as the guy who couldn't get a dancing partner on that infamous night, I'll introduce myself and find out,' so with that in mind, Ned walked over, hand outstretched.

'Hello, how are you, I'm the bone player in the other band,' he prompted. 'I'm pleased to meet you.'

The other man smiled and for a moment our hero thought the worst, but in a northern drawl he said.

'I'm pleased too sir, how about ye.'

They talked small talk for a couple of minutes; long enough for him to find out that his new friend had just joined this band. 'I got fed up with the other boys you know, they wouldn't practice, too fond of the gargle.' He sounded a little disappointed and seemed to be a man who took his music seriously.

'No harm in that,' Ned was thinking on his way to the restaurant and before seeing the menu he said. 'I'll have the sweet and sour chicken please.'

They talked about a variety of subjects including the impending gig and the roadblocks got a mention, but they had to keep it down and clean, as the room was full of stylish people.

'*Segome Negice Begirds Hegere Tegonegite Shegams.*' Ned was letting the band know, that that he had seen some nice birds here tonight, using his best lingo.

'*Yeg,*' said the Drummer, as he scanned the room, not even bothering to finish the Ben-Lang version of yes, which is *Yeges* of course.

The lingo came in very handy that night and they spoke it to the Chinese waiters, who thought they were from Mars or somewhere as exotic. Back at the gig things were hotting up and even though they had not played this city before, the Promoter was expecting a full house.

'Ah, you's has got lots of plays on the wireless, in the last few weeks,' he said. 'Yous'll do well the night, don't worry.'

The only thing Ned was worried about was, if the girls who shot him down the last night were here and recognised him, he'd be sunk if the true story got out. The Bone player who was sounding great gave him a wink and Ned waved in return just before they went to change. Later as they were nervously standing in the wings, the band's MC/Singer gave them a mighty build-up and he nearly told the crowd where they had eaten last while all the girls rushed to the stage. The change over was slick and in a matter of seconds they were giving it all they had, but as they moved into the second and third number the crowd stayed put. At the end of the first set he got a big hand for the resident band, then they went straight into another selection of lively numbers and he was glad to see that the big swaying, but as yet not dancing crowd of girls were looking admiringly at them.

'You were right about the Belfast birds Ned.' Conn shouted. 'I think we'll have no bother scoring here.'

Moving to the tempo with the others while viewing the nearby faces, he saw her.

'Jaysus,' he gushed, 'there's the big bird who asked me for the ladies choice the last night, I hope to fuck she doesn't sus me.' As his wish ended their eyes met and even though he looked away at once, he knew the harm was done. A couple of minutes later he felt a tug on his trouser leg and there sure enough was his past admirer, now very much in the present, but still admiring him.

'I know you,' she bellowed up at him, in her best Belfast accent.

'I don't think so,' he shouted back rather timidly, trying to keep up with the tune.

The lads noticed what was happening and the Drummer did his usual few loud beats for attention, then he roared.

'Negad Hegas Scegored, Bege Wegide Tego Thege Begig Fegat Regitchegard Egon Thege Regight Hegameger.'

He had just told all the band members to be wide to the big Richard the Third, 'Bird' on the right hammer and now everyone was watching this lady pulling on Ned's trousers. The more they looked, the more she pulled. Se knew he was rattled and he said to her in the Ben-Lang.

'Feguck Egoff Egand Legeave Mege Egalegone.' She was really pissing him off now big-time and he was thinking. 'If she doesn't leave me alone, I'll explain what I'm saying in English.'

Every time she tugged she would say. 'I know you,' and then she would ask him. 'What's that you're saying, are you speaking Gaelic?'

He could have done without this. By now the band members would have concluded, that this large lady had been his date on his last visit north and nothing was going to change their minds. She managed to tell the Lead Singer that she had met him before, naming the date and the venue, so his goose was cooked, but during the break in one of the songs, his thoughts flashed back to Susan and a big happy smile spread over his face.

'You look like you had an orgasm,' shouted the Trumpet man, again using the side of his mouth.

All Ned could do was laugh, realising the crowd of mad bastards he was working and travelling with, but the thought of his loved one spread through him, bringing a massive calm to his turmoiled brain.

'Who cares what that big bird says or thinks, I'll just ignore her from now on and tell the lads that she tried to chat me up on my last visit, but was pissed off when I picked another lovely girl instead, so fuck her.'

He had been on autopilot again for the past ten minutes, but now the grin was permanent and nothing was going to knock his concentration. Anyway, he wouldn't be asking any of the women here tonight big or small, because he had Susan and that's the only girl he wanted. The band was going down great and most of the adoring girls stayed in front of the stage, then during their last hit single, a few of them grabbed the Lead Singer, pulling him off the stage into their midst. He was really enjoying it and didn't miss a word of the song, even though they were touching him in strange places. At this juncture Ned noticed two men laughing their heads off over at the side of the hall. 'Guess who?' It was Mike the manager and the Promoter, who were getting a great kick out of the spectacle.

'Jaysus.' Ned hissed loudly to no one in particular. 'I'll bet those two Wankers set this up and the Singer will think it happened because they couldn't resist him.'

He decided (using hand signals) to check this possibility out, so he stopped strumming the three chords on his seldom used guitar, pointed to the Chanter who hadn't noticed the drop in rhythm as yet and wasn't in a position to do so anyway, then pointed knowingly at the two mentors. They got it all right, frantically nodding and pointing in return, obviously happy with the outcome.

'If only the poor fucker knew,' Ned thought, as the Singer tried to climb back on stage being hindered now by the members of his own band. 'Some day or night when he pisses somebody off he'll be told alright, it'll probably end up in another row.'

After that bit of excitement died down, Ned knew something was up when the Drummer began hitting his snare drum loudly once more.

'*Cheginks Egon Thege Regight Hegameger,*' he roared, pointing to most of the staff from the Chinese restaurant that they had been in earlier. These small China men were beaming up at the band and their mouths were going through the motions, singing along word for word, or at least that's what it looked like.

'That's mighty,' roared the Singer over the noise. 'They know all my songs.'

The side of the Trumpet players mouth seemed to be busy again, but it luckily was impossible to decipher most of what he was attempting to say, but his new word 'Bollixolutely' was definitely in there somewhere. A thought struck our hero as he swapped the guitar for the trombone. The Roadie's right, it's sticking out a mile, money has to be the reason for this band staying together, they all fuckin' hate each other.

He decided he would learn the old song called, 'Money is the root of all evil' and that would be a good laugh every night, the punters could dance to it as well. Suddenly, another familiar female face had joined the throng, which was by now getting a bit boisterous having been infiltrated by a couple of burly bouncers to supposedly calm them down. The new arrival was a cute little blonde and Ned nearly passed out when he saw her. This was one of the nastiest ones he had asked out to dance on his last visit to Belfast and now she was a few feet away, her gaze moving from one to the other band member. She panned the stage from left to right then back again and he was glad when he saw no sign of recognition on her face, as she now slowly looked them up and down.

'Two can play that game,' he decided, his gaze moving coldly over the bits he could see of her in this huge crush and while they just stared at each other, the Trumpet player, who's mouth was almost around at his ear asked.

'What the fuck does she want?'

It wasn't easy having this conversation, as both musicians were otherwise engaged playing the backing for a pop song being sung by the Guitar player, but lots of practice in the art meant it could be done without compromising the whole outfit. Then all hell broke loose. The big lady (who hadn't given up on Ned yet), noticed the stand off, so giving the blonde a nasty push, she entered into a tirade of what looked like swear words and pushed her again. In seconds they were both on the floor and you couldn't believe how quickly a circle was created, but before the two on hand bouncers threw them out, he could swear that the little blonde was winning, she was a tough cookie. That gave him a great idea, now that the good looking blonde had been ejected she would certainly go home, so it would be safe for him to say that she was the one he took home on his last visit and it would also explain why the big lady was jealous, causing the attack. He introduced the next song and apologised for the ruckus, then as he stepped away from the mike he heard Conn saying.

'I think you were the cause of that, what the fuck were you up to the last time you were in this town, are you wide?'

He was wide all right, the lads had been trying to tie him into something on a few occasions during the gig, but now that both ladies had been ejected it would hopefully remain a mystery, or at least until their next visit. The row was soon forgotten and the dancers got back to what they came for, joined by some of the people who had been standing so far. The buzz was palpable. About ten minutes before the end, the Roadie was in situ with the handouts and making no bones about the fact that he was a big cog, in this seemingly well-oiled wheel. Those remaining minutes would be used wisely, now that certain girls had noticed his association with this pulsating music machine, one of them would later succumb to his charms, or at least that's what he was hoping. They got two encores before bringing proceedings to a close with their sig tune, during which Ned gave the usual spiel and tonight for obvious reasons he gave a huge build up to the Roadie who boldly stood up and gave a bow.

'The cheeky fucker,' said the Trumpet man, who was laughing so much his mouth remained in front for a change.

Then Ned noticed a look of apprehension on the face of the Singer. It looked like he wasn't too happy with all the attention and applause going the Roadie's way; so realising just in time he decided to pull out all the stops to make up. He knew if he didn't, he would moan for days and piss them all off.

So turning around to the bands rhythm section, while gently waving down the volume simultaneously, he roared at the top of his voice. 'For fucks sake lads, give me a break; I'm going to spoof. Now what can I say about this man?' He began. Then ignoring the multiple lewd suggestions from the orchestra he continued, while pointing at the smiling Lead Singer. 'We almost lost him to Nashville Tennessee while in The States,' he said, frantically wondering how he would follow that.

'It's a fucking pity we didn't,' the Piano man had no need for a mike as he shouted at the top of his voice, having forgotten the bands drop in decibels.

Most people heard him and laughed, not knowing that it was a heart felt wish, so our hero dug deep to pick up the threads. 'Yes folks, to those of you who are familiar with the Grand Ole Opry, Steve, our Lead Singer performed there recently and they wouldn't let him off the stage, so I can tell you now we were glad when he turned up the following night in Philadelphia to rejoin The Nova's Showband. He was late, but a more experienced singer for his having sung in such a famous venue, so let's hear it for the man with the velvet voice.'

It worked, the punters went spare, the Singer bowed so low he almost hit his head on the stage and all the while on the rostrum, insult after insult was flying. Then the emotional singer took the mike and got a big round of applause for Ned.

'For one of the nicest guys in the business, give a big clap for our Band Leader and my best friend, Ned Brady.'

That triggered a fresh torrent of put-downs. First one from Mr. Ivory went.

'He doesn't need a clap; he's got it already. Best friend my arse. It's a good job they're not travelling together tonight,' and 'I didn't know how much you cared.' While the comments were bandied about and as the volume built up once more, every man had on his happiest smile. 'That's showbiz.'

Belfast was conquered musically that night and new fans were brought on board to hopefully remain. They told everyone how excited they all were about their new single out next week and Ned got a special kick from telling the girls about Susan, his one and only love.

'She's a lucky wee girl,' said one fan and he had a feeling she was one of the ladies who had shot him down, that night he had gone to Belfast without his trombone. They would be travelling to Dublin after all the courting was done and it seemed that everyone scored except Mike and Ned, who would accompany each other so they could make some last minute plans for the do on Monday night.

'This next one could be the one,' enthused Mike. 'The people at the record company think so anyway and our radioman on the inside is getting great vibes also. If that reporter bird turns up I hope you look after her Ned,' he continued, 'we've got to get every inch we can.'

'Do you mean column inches or are you speaking about penetration?' Ned enquired.

'Publicity/Sex, no matter what way you look at both, you end up with penetration don't you.'

Mike's answer brought a smile to his face for a second, then he realised he must tell him about his feelings for Susan and the fact that he can't cheat on her, especially in front of the other band members.

'I'll let you into a little secret,' said Mike. 'I spoke to Sandra, the lady in question the other day to invite her along and she told me you had already made it known to her that (as she put it) you were spoken for, but she says that doesn't pose a problem, because she's not looking for a relationship.'

'What is she looking for then?' Ned enquired.

'The aforementioned penetration I think.' said Mike. 'She also said to mention, if you're interested you can stay with her at her flat after the gig in Dublin tonight, she said something like, tell him he won't regret it.'

'From the way that sounds, I'm beginning to think I'll not forget it either. I keep seeing those beautiful white teeth every time I think of her, one slip and I could loose a couple of inches.'

'Stop bragging Ned,' said Mike, 'from what I've heard, you only have a couple of inches.'

'Fuck off,' said the offended one, giving him a box, 'we're not all as badly equipped as you, you know.'

'Did you ever hear that theory?' Mike wanted to know. 'The story goes, big man small prick, small man all prick.'

There were no disruptions on the roads and dawn was breaking when they reached their Hotel. Ned was a bit disappointed when the half-asleep night porter informed them that there were no pints of draught, because the bar was locked and he concluded that they were probably having the same problems as his father. Both men decided on a small Brandy each after Mike advised. 'It'll help you sleep.'

'Jaysus,' said Ned. 'It'll take a train to wake me, the minute my head touches that pillow.'

While they waited, he was wondering why night men in hotels were called porters, especially in a situation like this when there was no porter. That reminded him of Australia and the Slim Dusty song, 'The pub with no beer' and his longing for down under came flooding back. When he was younger, he always wondered why the people didn't fall off, seeing they must be walking upside-down and ever since he had read about Ned Kelly the BushRanger, he had wanted to visit. 'Sometime please God,' he said out loud.

'Ah come on, give the old guy a chance,' said Mike.

'Oh, I wasn't thinking of him, I was fantasising about going to see some Kangaroo's and Wallaby's down under, wouldn't it be fantastic to get a tour there one day.'

'Anything is possible,' Mike answered, 'but for now, just remember what we must do.'

'Yeah,' said Ned, lots of penetration.'

He couldn't say if the Brandy had anything to do with it, but as he predicted he was out cold from minute one and didn't surface until mid-day, to partake of the late breakfast, which

Mike had organised with the receptionist, who it was known, was being interfered with by their hard-necked manager. The other band members showed at the same time and were still going on about their success in Belfast the previous night. The conversation covered the gig; also what happened afterwards and all it seemed had a good night.

Mike looked across the table at Ned during this exuberant exchange of stories and said one word. 'Penetration.'

Tonight's gig in Dublin was in a new venue for them and even though they had a good following in this city, they were leaving nothing to chance. The gear had to be assembled around 5 o'clock and they would have a run through a few numbers to get used to the hall. Ned's first post lunch chore was to phone Susan and tell her how he felt, but the one thing he omitted was the lady with the pearly teeth. That would have to be 'Top Secret'. The Diamond Ballroom was a big flashy place, getting its name from the glitzy lobby, which was in the shape of a diamond, and in case the clientele didn't notice this, the owner was taking no chances. The black and white floor was a collection of diamond shaped tiles working their way to the centre, where, if you still hadn't got it, you would find one big white diamond shaped tile with (wait for it) the word Diamond emblazoned thereon, in black. If you happened to be totally thick and just chanced to look up, you would see hanging from a diamond shaped ceiling, a large diamond shaped crystal chandelier complete with glass baubles, (you got it) shaped like diamonds. Mike had primed the band members about this phenomenon and warned them that if they couldn't look at it in awe complimenting the classy finish, then they should ignore it altogether, just in case one of them might make a nasty comment, which would culminate in the band being cast forth, i.e. sacked. As they stood outside the gigantic doors of the venue Ned checked the story with everyone.

'OK! If you don't want to say something nice about the place, say fuck all, got it.'

Mr. Ivory had one comment to make. 'You'd think we were about to enter Buckingham Fuckin' Palace, the way you arse lickers are going on, spare me this crap.'

'Hold on a minute,' said Conn. 'I understand why the owner has such pride in his hall; it's like my saxophone and me. I'm forever polishing the ivory inlays on my keys, until I can see myself in them.'

'You'd get some fuckin' shock, if Boots Randolph looked back at you some night,' said the Lead Singer. 'Ah, good old Nashville,' he continued.

'Fuck you and Nashville and the horse you rode in on,' said Conn, ready for war. 'If you had listened to some of the singer's out there, maybe it would have helped you sing in tune, you leave the sax playing to me in future and I'll leave the singing to you, alright.'

At that second, they all heard the bolt being drawn back on the inside of the door and thank god the timing was perfect, one moment later the fat wealthy looking gentleman who opened it, would have found at least two members of the orchestra in mortal combat on his doorstep.

'Sorry it took so long,' the large gentleman said. 'You're all welcome to The Diamond Ballroom, come on in until I show you around, I've had a great chat with your nice young Roadie and he was knocked out with the place.'

'Hello Mr. Kelly, I'm the Bandleader Ned Brady, let me introduce you to the lads and by the way, we have heard great things about your fantastic venue.'

Introductions over, the now happy or otherwise bunch were ushered into the Foyer by the Boss, who seemed to be smiling far beyond his ears. Ned noticed at once that the cuff links in his prominent white shirt cuffs were also diamond shaped, with a little sparkler in the centre and it didn't stop there. He also had a diamond shaped tiepin to match and Ned found himself wondering if his Y-fronts were diamond shaped as well.

'What do you think of my hall?' he kept repeating, seemingly unable to hear the accolades being poured on the place, by the subdued members of the band. It sounded like he got such a kick out of admiring it himself, that the requested opinion of others didn't really matter.

'The Roadie was cute,' Ned was thinking, 'he'd buy and sell all these other arseholes you know, all they want to do is squabble and try to be smart, but the Roadie used common sense in this case.' To make conversation, Ned mentioned the launch on Monday and was glad to hear that this diamond clad guy and his wife would be there.

'Oh, your manager and record company both invited us to the do. I've been playing the record and I think it's very good, in fact my wife loves It.' he said.

Our hero couldn't help wondering what this wife might look like. She could be big and fat like her husband or the opposite, so he decided to have a bet with himself.

'I'll wager she's a big fat dog,' and as he walked beside his employer for the night, he almost went, 'Bow Wow.'

They switched on and ran through a few numbers to get the feel of the venue, agreeing for a change, that this was the closest they had been to The City Plaza in New York, or the big venues on the English tour. After returning to the hotel for their evening meal they found Mike talking to the head receptionist and this fact caused a few smart comments to be made, but the loudest came from the usually grumpy Piano man.

'You'll be to the makers name in her tonight.' he hissed.

Both Mike and his woman heard it and she blushed profusely.

'Don't mind him,' said Ned, trying to make the girl feel better. 'He's only jealous.' They had just sat down in the bar when he was called to the phone.

'It's Sandra,' the sexy female voice said. 'I hope you don't mind my calling you, I wanted to check if your manager mentioned anything about me.'

'Yes he did Sandra, how are you? He said that I could stay with you tonight, but I've got a room here so I'll have to come back with the band first, as they must not know what I'm up to. I can't trust them you know, but if you give me your address I'll drive around to you later, is that OK?'

'That will be fine,' she agreed, 'have you got a pen?'

'Just a moment,' he requested. 'OK, shoot.'

'That's very sexy,' she said, 'do you always say that to strange girls.'

He was laughing when he replied. 'I don't think you'll be a stranger for too long, would you go along with that?'

'You'll find I'll go along with most things, but you must know I'm very choosy,' she said. 'You may think I'm up for anything, but it's my decision in the end.'

He was about to make a joke, saying his plans centred very much on the end, her end, but he decided against it, remembering what Mike had said. 'Penetration,'

The venue filled up quickly that night; the word was out as Mike said, spreading like wildfire and advance orders for the single are colossal. They could feel the buzz and this was it. They had fans from all over the country that night and during their second number Ned almost had a heart attack. Standing about twenty feet down the hall being held closely by her boyfriend The Chef who was smiling over her shoulder, was none other than Susan's sister Mary and they both waved. Ten feet away stood Sandra, pearly white teeth flashing, a knowing grin on her face.

'Jaysus, what will I do,' he whined to himself, so after the next song he called the Roadie to the stage. 'Remember the bird who was asking the questions about the second San Francisco gig?'

'Yeah,' said the Roadie, 'she's over there on the right hammer, why?'

'In about ten minutes, find her and tell her that my girlfriend's sister is here and she must not come near me, do you understand?'

'Yes,' said the Roadie, somewhat bemused. 'I'll tell her word for word and don't worry, I won't tell those other eejits anything.'

He was feeling a bit better now that his pigeon had taken wing, but he was getting the usual stick from the other guys like. Get on with the fuckin' show, do you want to send a telegram to someone and other stuff which he ignored. About ten minutes later as planned, he saw his message being delivered and without looking stage-ward, Sandra melted into the throng.

'What the fuck does she want?' he wondered and he realised it would be a few hours yet, before he got an answer to that question. Ned was thrilled when someone actually requested the new single, which as far as he knew was still a secret. 'How do you know about the song?' He asked the keen punter.

'Oh, it was on the new releases on the wireless yesterday,' answered yer-man.

'So it was on the wireless eh,' he thought, the Plugger is on the ball all right, he's hoping to buy a new car out of this one and he promised to pull out all the stops.

'There won't be a stone left unturned,' was his comment one evening recently, while admiring Ned's new purchase. 'She's a beauty and where did you buy her boss?' Was his question, as he circled the Bandleaders car with approval?

'Would you believe?' Ned began. 'I stopped for petrol at 'Tractamotors' in Cavan on my way to a gig and from the moment I saw it, I knew it was meant for me even though I had no intentions of buying a car at the time.'

'That's a good one,' the Plugger answered, 'but Cavan is a bit too far away for me.'

'No problem,' said Ned. 'Tractamotors' have a branch in Dublin and I'll drive you over there any day, I promised the man in Cavan that I'd mention them to all my friend's, you'll get a great deal.'

'OK then,' said the potential customer. 'I want to look real 'snazzy' going around promoting The Nova's Showband, so I'll give you a shout when I get my finances sorted out.'

Ned saw a couple of girls that night that he had pointed it at in the past, but Thank God he had no interest in them anymore, yet he couldn't make out this Sandra bird. Maybe she just wants to talk and even if she wants to talk dirty, well he could handle that OK. Then during his millionth rendition of The Haunted House, he had a scary thought. 'What if she's a vampire?' He had read about vampires in Bram Stoker's Dracula books and this being Dublin the home of the famous writer; maybe he had sent his cousin Sandra to suck his blood. 'She can suck whatever she likes, but not my blood,' he was thinking, as he sang the words about the ghostly monster, which was sitting on the hot cooker in the song and then the significance of the teeth really hit him. 'I can't remember if her eye teeth are longer than the others, Jaysus.' He never was as glad to reach the end of a song, as he was that night, so he quickly introduced the next number.

The Lead Singer asked him. 'Have you seen a ghost or something?' 'You're very pale sham,' but he ignored him and picked up his guitar.

He was amazed later at the number of fans, who came up and said in varying ways.

'I notice you're playing the guitar now Ned, it sounds great. By fuck, it didn't take you long mastering that auld guitar, good on you,' etc.

He in turn tried to explain that he was only chancing his arm, but they didn't want to know, especially when he told them that a fourth chord to him was like a trip into the unknown. The fact that he had been strumming guitar now for about ten years, remained a well-kept secret. During the last set, he looked over to the left where he saw the owner of The Diamond Ballroom minus the jacket and every time he lifted his hands to brush the sweat from his fat face, the cuff links flashed like the shields from the movie Ben-Hur. Standing beside him, a satisfied smile on his face was Mike, looking very much the manager as he chatted away to a gorgeous tall curvy woman in her early forties, with blonde hair.

'So Mike has found his fantasy at last,' he thought.

Their manager was always on about finding a good looking woman of forty or fifty, that he could go on a Caribbean Cruise with, preferably as her guest and it looked like it had panned out at last, then his theory fell apart. The fat guy rubbed the sweat from his brow once more, then decided to dance, so whom did he ask? The good-looking blonde standing the other side of Mike of course, who fell into his arms immediately?

'She's no dog,' the bandleader thought, tumbling to the situation enfolding before his eyes. This lovely woman was the Boss man's wife and when he saw the diamonds on her left hand as they passed by the stage, he knew Mike's search wasn't over yet.

'More fuckin' diamonds, between them they're wearing a fortune.' Ned's sixty forty smile was back with a vengeance that night and from looking at the crowd, having had lots of practice lately judging bulk figures, he had their takings sussed to the last pound. 'Was there sixteen hundred in her?' he asked Mike.

'You're close, stick another eleven people on that and you've got it, I wouldn't want to be on the fiddle would I?' The manager ended with the question.

Both men usually played a game trying to guess attendances, so Mike knew there was no problem, but Ned's theory was. Sure it'll keep him on his toes in the long run. The vibe was mighty after the gig; firstly he talked to Mary and her boyfriend then drifted around signing autographs and chatting.

'Can it get any bigger than this?' He asked himself.

It was fortunate that Mary's boyfriend had an early interview in the morning, so he wouldn't be seen talking to Sandra, just in case she came up to the stage, but when she didn't appear in the following fifteen minutes, he presumed she had gone home to wait as planned. He wasn't happy at all about the arrangement and after seeing Susan's sister who looked so much like his lover, he was tempted to find to phone and ring Sandra. When he mentioned this, the manager wouldn't hear of it, so the plan had to go ahead. After their takings were split up, most of the band headed back to the Hotel, some with girlfriends others alone, then Mike told Ned there was someone he wanted him to meet. He knocked on the office door and it was opened by the elegant good-looking blonde, who extended her diamond clad, well-groomed hand to Ned on introduction. He nearly collapsed with shock when this gorgeous woman squeezed his hand boldly, twice, then calmly held on to it as she continued the conversation. Her eyes were twinkling, so he decided she was daring him, slowly he tightened his grip on her and she took up the cudgel. It was at that precise moment, that he promised himself he would break all celibacy rules and ride this woman, sooner rather than later.

Mike noticed that something was going on, so he excused himself saying. 'I'm off to say goodnight to the Boss, so I'll see you back at the Hotel Ned, goodnight to you both.' He reversed from the office gently closing the door, knowing that three was a crowd.

'Will you give me your phone number?' Ned asked as the door closed.

'If you promise to tell nobody you have it,' she answered.

'I promise,' he said, 'could you get away for a few days when we're touring, I'd like to get to know you, you're beautiful.'

'Why would you want me to travel with you?' She asked.

He decided not to beat around the bush so he told her straight up. 'I'd like to make mad passionate love to you in every possible way and in every position,' he said, chancing his arm, but he could see this raunchy approach was working.

'You've got a roving eye,' she countered.

'That means, between us we've got three roving eyes,' he said laughing and if your husband doesn't come back soon, I'll start now.' He was looking desperately around the bare office as he said this, in a fake bid to find somewhere they could hide.

'I can travel any time it suits you,' she offered, picking up on his previous request, 'but we could always go to our villa in Spain for a week, if you can get away from the young ones.'

'Twenty-four hours with you would be better than a year with a young one,' he told her, not taking Susan into that scenario of course. 'Jaysus, poor Susan.' 'God help her stuck with a horny fucker like me,' he thought.

The door began to open so their hands parted and only just in time, because in seconds the fat one had descended upon them, still minus the jacket but boldly sporting the diamonds.

'Wasn't that a marvellous gig Ned,' he began. 'I see you've met my wife Kate, isn't she a lovely creature.'

Ned could feel the blood rush to his cheeks, aware of the broad grin on the blonde's face, while her two roving eyes twinkled at him. 'Yeah, Mike introduced us and we were talking about holidays in Spain,' he stuttered.

'Now Ned, never be short of somewhere to take your young woman (I'm sure you have one) because, we've got a place on the Costa-Del-Sol and you're welcome to it anytime. That is of course as long as we are not using it, Kate goes down there often on her own as well.'

He nearly broke out laughing when Mr Kelly said that. 'Goes down, how are you.' 'I wouldn't mind going down there sometime,' he answered, 'but it wouldn't be much fun on my own.'

He decided the older lady might be put off if he said he had a young woman, so guilt ridden, he made the last statement to impress her, because the idea of her going down on him had become of great sexual interest and her answer convinced him it had worked.

When she extended her hand to say goodnight she said. 'Perhaps we might bump into each other while I'm down there sometime,' then she squeezed his hand again very firmly.

He noticed her emphasis on the word 'Down' and his imagination ran away with him, just as guilt kicked in again. 'I've got to finish with this business before I marry Susan,' he was thinking, as he headed for the car, 'it has to be that fuckin' trombone.'

He paid a quick visit to the hotel bar where it was like the middle of the day, instead of the middle of the night and he let it be known that he had a headache, so he would be hitting the hay at once.

Mike gave him a wink and said, 'goodnight, see you tomorrow.'

Back in the car, he dug out Sandra Boyle's address and it was then he noticed he had used the same piece of paper to write down Kate Kelly's phone number. Luckily, the latter had not asked him for the note so she could put her number on it, because she would know Sandra and the cat would be out of the bag in yet another way.

'Jaysus, I'm an awful *Ben-Gal Lancer,*' he hissed.

Ned had conducted many sorties into Dublin's flat land in the past, so finding Sandra was easy, but it was with much trepidation that he rang her bell.

'I shouldn't be here, I shouldn't be here,' he kept singing to himself and then he heard the key turn in the lock and the door swung open. He checked out her sparkling teeth at once and was glad to notice that they were all completely even, then she ushered him into her nice cosy flat, which he noticed contained a big bed. 'Yeah, that'll do,' he was thinking.

She had shaken hands with him on arrival and he was still holding on to her hand, so he drew her close planning to plant a kiss on that nice mouth, containing the teeth, but she had other ideas. At the last second she moved her head to one side.

'I don't kiss on the first night, in fact I don't like kissing on the mouth at all, there are other parts of the male anatomy which I much prefer kissing and I know you'll love it too.'

His equipment woke up when he heard that. There was only one problem, Ned the Bed kissed every lover on the mouth and that region being (for now) out of bounds, pissed him off, so he tried again. This time she just ducked the other way and he missed by a mile, her head now landing on his right shoulder. To save this happening again she took his hand and led him over to a large sofa, where she sat him down and offered him a drink.

'What will you have?' she asked.

He decided not to be smart and say a kiss, so he settled for a beer, which she poured while standing just in front of him, her long legs apart. Before sitting down, she poured herself a stiff vodka and Ned felt like saying that he had something stiff for her as well, but again he decided to wait and let her make the next move. That she did, after some light conversation and a few large gulps from her drink, she reached across and put her hand on his now obvious hard-on, then she moved from the sofa to kneel on the floor just between his legs, gently easing the zipper down. After that everything was easy. Ned's now rampant tackle just popped out in all it's glory, to be devoured by the large sexy mouth of this lovely looking woman, who was behaving as if possessed. He lay back and listened to her moans, thinking of the big fat girl in Belfast, hoping that would make this magic thrill last longer. The Gangsters moll in Los Angeles had been on the same kick, calling herself the Queen of Fellatio, but from the experience he was now having, it looked like she could have some serious opposition for that crown. She moaned, he groaned, until he could take it no longer, then his brain exploded. There was no point telling this woman that the end was nigh, as it was patently obvious this was her Modus Operandi and finishing the job was the cherry on the cake for her. He thought she might stop after his second climax but no, she kept going for a hat trick, which left him as weak as water and with legs of jelly.

Eventually she raised her head and smiled. 'Did you enjoy that?' she asked wistfully.

'Yeah,' he answered, 'but I'm bollixed now.'

She took another slug from her pint glass which must have contained half a bottle of Vodka and said with a grin. 'You're bollixed now, just wait until morning.'

'No,' he began. 'I'll only stay on one condition which is, that we both get into that bed and if I'm able, we screw madly for the rest of the night, OK!'

'It's not OK,' she replied. 'I get my rocks off doing what I do and I'm not going to let any guy put me in the family way, so there. You can leave if you want, or you can have the bed while I sleep on the sofa.'

He was doing his best to understand what was going on and his L.A. experience helped. 'OK,' he said. 'I'll stay for a while and you can tell me more about yourself, maybe then, I'll understand what makes you tick.'

They talked for hours after she poured the remaining half of the bottle into the pint glass and topped it up with coke, as she explained her reasons to him. Seemingly, a man she trusted had taken advantage of her some years ago, now she won't have sex anymore. 'I get a better kick from what I do, without the risks,' she said. It was 5am when she let him out the door, after extracting a solemn promise that what happened tonight would remain a secret. If the story got back from any quarter, they would chop the lot off him and he knew she meant it. She also planned going to the Hotel later that day, to interview the band members for her showbiz columns.

'I don't want to lose good drinking time at the do, talking to you lot about gigs,' she said. 'Anyway, you and I may come back here afterwards and repeat the performance, what do you think?'

'We've got a phrase in the Ben-Lang which covers what you did to me tonight, it names the deed in the lingo, do you want to hear it?' he asked.

'Yeah, go ahead, I hope it's not vulgar,' she said.

'Well, you gave me a Speed-Wobble which makes you a Speed-Wobbler and the abridged version of the act is a Speedo, get it?'

'Oh, I got it alright and it was beautiful,' she said grinning. 'By the way, you can kiss me on the cheek, because I know you're about to ask me.' With that she presented her cheek and he did what he was told, then she added. 'I know most of the Ben-Lang and I've caught lots of guys out talking about me, so be warned.'

As he got into his car, he was wondering if she was one of those control freaks and he found himself pondering for a moment, whether or not he should quiz her on it sometime, maybe best left alone he concluded. The night porter was on the ball, letting him in at once. He informed him that everyone had gone to bed and Ned would almost lay a bet on it, that there were at least four non-paying guests upstairs. He couldn't help wondering who had scored and if any of the ladies were specialists, like his newfound friend. 'Jaysus, she wants to do the same again tonight,' he was thinking as he fell asleep.

They got up for lunch as usual; most looking the worse for wear yet in high spirits, because of the exciting evening and (hopefully) the night ahead. Mike had asked them all to attend in the function room afterwards for a meeting and to help put all the promotional material in place for the launch, which was kicking off at 6 o'clock. When they got in there the people from the Record Company were working flat out, hanging a big banner over the stage and other colour posters around the room. Frank O'Toole the M.D. was deep in conversation with a ravishing brunette who had gorgeous legs, which caused Ned's antenna to propel him in their direction.

'Oh, hello Ned, let me introduce you to Samantha from the model agency of the same name, herself and five of her best will be gracing us with their presence this evening, so don't forget to have your photo taken with the most beautiful girls in town.'

'There's no chance of me missing an opportunity like that Frank,' said Ned, as he shook this lovely lady's hand. 'Pleased to meet you Samantha.'

'And likewise,' she replied. 'I haven't heard your band yet, but I believe it's very good, Frank has promised to give me a copy of your latest record, so then I'll be able to judge for myself.'

He felt like saying. 'That's what you think,' but changed his mind, knowing that least said was easy mended, about the session musicians who played most of the backing on their records. The lads had been pissed off; when the record company boss suggested how much money he would save in studio time, by using session heads, as he called them.

'They'll come in with the dots written out and fly through the tracks in no time, it'll save hours of rehearsal for the band and nobody will know the difference,' he said.

Anyway, the lads would sing the harmonies and of course the Lead Singer would be on vocal, much to his joy. After a string of fucks, the band members backed down, accepting the idea and it all went like a dream.

'That's the way they do it in Nashville,' said Steve, and the disgruntled Piano and Guitar men had chorused. 'Fuck you and Nashville, you can stick it where the monkey stuck the nut.'

'I think I lost you there for a moment,' Ned heard the lovely Samantha say.

'Oh I'm sorry,' he answered. 'Meeting a glamorous lady like you, reminds me of my girlfriend Susan, who can't be here tonight.' 'She's studying Law at the moment and she's working every hour God sends in a Law firm in her hometown, I just realise how much I miss her.'

'Susan's a lucky girl,' she answered. 'Most men I know would be chatting me up instead of talking about their girlfriend, do you have a picture of her?'

Ned dug out the wallet and proudly handed over a recent picture of his loved one.

'She's very beautiful,' said Samantha sincerely. 'A sharp dresser as well I notice, maybe you'd bring her to town to meet me some day you're both off and she can try on a few outfits.'

'I'll do that,' he answered with enthusiasm, 'she'd love to I'm sure, because she's always dressed in something different every time I see her.'

He really enjoyed meeting a gorgeous woman with class who he could talk to, admire, but not chat up. It was refreshing for a change, but then he remembered Sandra Boyle who was a horse of a different colour. He decided there and then, that he would pass on Sandra's planned session for later tonight, using the true story that he was wasted. Some other time maybe, just to make sure they got the news coverage, but not tonight Josephine. Just before 6 o'clock the media people began to arrive and it looked like a large cross-section from Radio, TV and the Newspaper world was turning up.

The Trumpet player sidled over to Ned and again out of the side of his mouth he hissed. 'Some of those wankers won't be playing The Nova's Showband, the latest by Bach would be more in their line me thinks.'

'I agree,' said Ned, but you know the story, we have to be nice to them no matter what they're like, all the stops are out on this one.'

'Fuck them,' continued the Trumpet man, not having heard a word Ned said. 'Look, they're eating and drinking already, the fuckers will scoff the lot before the others get here and look at them, you'd think they've never had a square meal in their lives.'

'Don't worry,' Ned was trying again. 'It's not costing us anything and by the way, there will be six lovely fashion models here later to pose in photos with us, so tell the lads to be nice to them. Make sure we get as many pictures as possible.'

Just as he mentioned the models, they walked into the room dressed in the latest fashions, each one sporting a white sash with a promo for The Nova's Showband. A few of the band members had gathered around and as the girls entered they all went 'Wow.' Ned left it to the Trumpet player to explain who they were and he really enjoyed the task, while the only anti-remark came from Mr. Ivory.

'Who the fuck is paying for them birds?' He asked.

'The Record Company is,' said Ned, 'so you can relax again, but as I said earlier, treat them nice and get lots of pictures with them, just don't chat them up.'

'Why, do you want to keep them for yourself?' 'The Ned the Bed image seems to be slipping lately.' He ignored the Piano mans open sarcasm and moved away to talk to Sandra Boyle who had just entered the room.

After publicly failing to kiss her, he took her by the hand and brought her over to the free bar, where he poured a large Vodka and mixer for the journalist. She raised her glass, smiled at him and said.

'I told you I don't kiss people on the mouth, but you tried again tonight didn't you? Thinking I would have to comply in public.'

'But Sandra, you kissed me in a more complicated fashion last night, are you afraid of catching something from my mouth, or have I got bad breath?' She just laughed at his whining question and took a big slug from her glass, nodding to other members of her profession who were arriving steadily and heading straight to the bar, trancelike.

'Are we having another session tonight?' she asked.

'What type of session do you mean?' he parried.

'Don't be a smart arse,' she said grinning. 'Same as last night of course, I enjoyed that, did you?'

'Yes I did, but I wouldn't be able for it again tonight, especially after this gig, which I'm sure will go on until the wee small hours.'

She laughed out loud at his comment and said. 'So you won't be able for it, all you had to do last night was sit there while I did all the work, you like your bread buttered on both sides, don't you? Well if you can't manage it tonight, how about tomorrow in the park, I've always wanted to do it in the park in broad daylight, to see how the deer would react.'

'I wouldn't worry about the deer,' he said. 'I'd be more worried about the park keeper or whatever he's called, catching us at it.'

'They wouldn't bother us, because they'd only see one person in the car and they would think you were there for fresh air, or the good of your health,' she answered, laughing loudly.

He began to smile at the idea and he could feel a stirring down south, as he found himself considering it for a moment.

'I'll guarantee it'll blow your mind,' she stated.

'That's not all it might blow, so I'll think about it for a while and tell you later,' he answered.

'By then, I may have found someone else to take to the park,' she said, 'you should count yourself lucky I picked you, you know.'

'OK,' he answered, 'you've convinced me, so I hope I don't live to regret it, we'll fix a time later, alright.'

'Let's meet for lunch, I'll do my stories in the morning and get them off to the papers, then after lunch I'll get you off,' she was laughing loudly as she spoke and he was afraid that half the people in the room would hear her. Then she held up her glass as if in a toast and had another few large gulps of her drink.

'What happened you earlier today?' He asked. 'I thought you were coming in to interview the lads in the band.'

'Well to be honest, I didn't feel the Mae West after all the Vodka I had last night, so I decided I'd talk to them tonight instead, anyway, I could do a story on your band with my eyes closed don't forget.'

They both decided to mingle and as he watched her walk away, he couldn't help wondering if there was some kind of message for him, in what she had just said.

'She's strange', he was thinking, 'such a good looking girl, yet totally fucked up because of a bad relationship.' 'I hope I don't regret my knowing her.'

Their new song called 'The look in your eyes' was playing away in the background and lots of media people seemed to have good things to say about it, all of them of course having got a copy about a week ago from the record company. Frank O'Toole knew the record business inside out and believed in going the whole hog with a project, once he agreed to take it on board. He was also a bit of a lad with the girls and Mike used to tease him, saying it was all down to his surname. He made no secret of the fact that his interest in women came from being unhappily married to a battle-axe called Maude, who watched him like a hawk and as he said, drove him into the beds of others. Mike also told Ned, that Frank was a regular visitor to Sandra Boyle and the only comment he would make was. 'She's thorough.' It was obvious that he had also been warned not to comment in case he too, would get the chop and he wondered how many men were living in fear of her at the moment, so he decided to tell her it wasn't going to work with him. 'So there.'

The six beautiful models worked the room talking to everyone, while posing for pictures with anyone who asked and Ned was thrilled when two of them mentioned Susan to him.

'Samantha tells us you're girlfriend is gorgeous,' they said. 'We believe you're bringing her in to the agency soon and we're really looking forward to meeting her.'

'Oh, thank you both very much, yes she's a lovely lady and I'll mention it to her on the phone later,' was his appreciative answer.

As the girls walked away after having their photo taken with him, he began having pangs of guilt about Susan and his involvement with Sandra. 'This has got to stop,' he thought as he headed for the phone in the hotel lobby and when he heard her voice on the other end his heart skipped a beat. After exchanging words of love he told her about the launch, then he repeated what Samantha had said after seeing her photograph.

'She says you're beautiful,' he said, almost sobbing.

'I'd be far too shy to model clothes,' she said, 'but thanks for showing them my photograph.'

'Susan darlin', you're doing it every day of the week,' he reminded her. 'You're always dressed like a model.'

'Thanks honey, do you miss me?'

'I miss you all the time, so I'd like to see you on Wednesday night, we're not playing until Thursday and the gig is only fifty miles from your house.'

'That would be lovely, I'll look forward to it and don't forget to mention us to the record company, see you on Wednesday, I love you.'

She sounded really sincere on the phone and it strengthened his resolve to bring to an end his 'thing' with Sandra, tomorrow in the park would be the last. As planned, the band was going to play for an hour or so, in case anybody wanted to dance and they also wanted to perform their new single, which they had honed to the same quality as the record.

'We'll let these so and so's see that we can play,' said Mr. Ivory, 'just in case they might think we use tapes or something.'

'No one gives a shit,' Mike said, 'but playing a few tunes is a good idea anyway, it'll give a lift to the proceedings, so to speak.'

During the first song, Ned noticed Frank out dancing with Sandra and they seemed to be having a ball. 'I wonder does she let him kiss her?' he thought.

Having the six beautiful models at the party was proving to be a good idea, all the photographers were lining them up for special photos for their individual papers and the radio jocks were scrambling to be in them all. Tomorrow would be a good day for The Nova's Showband in print and it looked good for the airplay too, but towards the end of the proceedings, Sandra Boyle was beginning to look the worse for wear. Her teeth were still flashing but that wasn't all that was flashing. Being a firm breasted lady she didn't wear a bra and by 1.45am almost all the buttons on her white blouse were open, leaving nothing to the imagination. Ned saw Mike coming towards him and he heard the manager say.

'For God's sake Ned, could you bring that bird home or something,' and he sounded like it was Ned's fault.

'The or something, could be a problem,' said the bandleader, 'so I'll get her a taxi instead.'

'OK,' said the Manager. 'She's getting messy.'

He was glad when Sandra accepted the offer of a taxi and as he escorted her to the Hotel door, she mumbled in a pie eyed way.

'Don't forget lunch tomorrow and our visit to the park afterwards, I'll be starving after writing all those stories in the morning, 1 o'clock then.'

He waved to her as the taxi drove away and he couldn't help wondering what she meant exactly by saying, she'd be starving tomorrow. 'She probably means, that it will take more than lunch to whet her appetite,' he thought.

The six models departed at 2.30, having been asked out on many occasions and in many different ways. One of the disc jockeys even tried the old, his shoes under her bed routine and he died a death, then at the very end Samantha came over to Ned, reminding him to bring Susan in to the agency some time soon.

'I mentioned it to her on the phone tonight and she's looking forward to it, even though she says she'll be no good at it.'

'Rubbish,' she answered. 'I'm a good judge and she's got it alright, see you both soon.'

He was very impressed by Samantha and couldn't help wondering what his chances would have been with her, if there were no Susan on the scene. Enough of that, lots of sleep had to be acquired before his lunch date and the afters, so he said goodnight to the stragglers and went to bed. There he kept getting pleasant flashes of Susan's face, sometimes in the same frame as the face of Samantha, then suddenly it would be the flashing teeth and the firm breasts of Sandra. As he slipped off to sleep, he wondered if she might let him kiss her tomorrow and he also gave some thought to the fact that the three girls names began with the letter S. His mind did a recap of all the women in his life while he tossed and turned that night and his subconscious ran it's own ratings contest, which he tried unsuccessfully to alter any time he didn't agree. Brenda from New York kept getting ten, with Susan only an eight.

'Jaysus, I haven't contacted Brenda for ages,' he heard himself say, as he sat upright in the bed.

It took a few minutes to settle afterwards and before he went back to sleep he made a promise, that he would tell her of his plan during the holidays next May. Over the past month, it had become obvious he would have to settle on one woman and the best way to do that, would be to have a week long fling with each one, during the four week holiday they were planning in the New Year. The first week would hopefully be with Susan, next one with Brenda in New York. He would try and go to Buffalo to see Jayne for the third week if she was interested, if not, it would be Mary of the Shaven Haven in San Francisco, then back to Susan for the fourth week. Deep down he knew the woman for him was Susan, but he wanted to be sure if that's possible. There was a knock on his door at eleven the next morning and in walked Mike with Frank, the record company boss.

'Where are those pictures of your girlfriend's family band?' the latter asked.

Ned was trying to find an answer to that question, as he rubbed the sleep from his eyes and then he remembered. 'Oh sorry Frank, I'm jacked,' he said, while heading for the wardrobe. 'They're here in my jacket pocket, I'll have them in a minute,' he added.

'Which of the two is yours?' Frank asked, 'they're nice, are they twins?'

'No, they're not twins,' said Ned, pointing proudly to Susan, who was holding her fiddle in one photo and grinning cheerily from behind the big drum kit in another. He could hear Frank counting so he decided to give him some help by saying. 'There are six in the band Frank.'

Luckily the record boss wasn't annoyed by his comment and he answered in dismay. 'I know there are six members in the band, I was trying to count the musical instruments, do they really play all those?'

'Yeah they do, Hugh plays at least fifteen instruments including the Ocarina, or Sweet Potato as it's known.'

'The only Sweet Potato I've heard of, you can eat,' said Mike.

'Yeah,' Ned answered. 'It's shaped the same as one of those, hence the name I suppose.'

'How do I hear this band?' Frank asked.

'If it's OK, I'll take you and Mike to their home, they'll play for you in the studio where those pictures were taken, just give them a weeks notice because of college so they can all be there,' said Ned.

By now Mike was looking intently at the pictures and then he made a comment. 'If they play as well as they look, then they must be some outfit and an ideal line-up for the U.S, I would say,' he was sounding like a manager now. Then he looked at Ned and asked. 'Well, what have you got planned for today?'

For some reason the latter went a bright shade of red before he answered. 'I'm meeting Sandra Boyle for lunch and after I drop her home, I'm off to the pictures, theres a couple of good ones on.'

'Be nice to her,' was the advice from both men, as they left the room, then the manager added. 'Why don't you take her to the Movies with you and keep her sweet?'

Sandra arrived at the Hotel on the dot of one and flounced up to reception, asking for Ned. The receptionist pointed across the lobby saying.

'He's over there behind that newspaper.'

He may have been behind the paper, but he had been looking across or around it most of the time and had seen her getting out of the taxi just outside the window. He couldn't believe his eyes when her two lovely long legs swung out of the cab, almost wearing a micro skirt, which revealed dark stockings with suspenders and sporting very nice sexy high heeled shoes.

'Jaysus, what kick is she on today?' He asked himself. 'I haven't seen her that scantly dressed before, maybe she intends to go that extra mile in the park later.'

She walked over and hooked a well-groomed finger in the top of his paper revealing his face, then posing cutely she asked.

'Well what do you think, maybe I could get a job with Samantha's agency as well?'

'No better woman,' said Ned. 'So you must have heard, they asked Susan to call into them.'

'Yeah,' she sounded a little scathing, 'it seems Susan gets all the breaks, don't you think.'

'What I think is, that we leave Susan out of this scenario,' he said.' 'I told you about her the first time we met so you can't complain.'

She apologised profusely, knowing she had overstepped the mark and after a couple of exchanges mostly about the weather, they both proceeded to the dining room, where she told him about her mornings work which was now wending it's way, to the music columns of the nation.

'Thanks for looking after me last night,' she said.

'Oh, it was no bother at all, you seemed to enjoy yourself anyway and you had loads of admirers including me.' He decided to boost her morale pre the visit to the park and it worked.

'How come you can be a musician and a nice guy at the same time?' she asked. 'I was hoping you would be a real bastard like the others.'

'You've obviously been hurt very badly and he must have been a musician, but could it be possible that you left yourself open to be hurt?' He waited for a reply but it wasn't forthcoming so he continued with. 'Have you ever given any thought to the fact, that there are other men around who are not in bands and would love to ask a good looking woman like you out.'

She was looking out the window when she answered.

'Yeah, I've tried them as well but they're all morons, at least the band men as you call them, will ask before they try to hump you, but the moron, he just throws the leg over hoping for the best and if you're not strong you get screwed, they don't care at all.'

'So it's a no win situation,' he suggested.

'Sort of,' she answered. 'But you're different Ned Brady and I'm really beginning to like you, but I keep thinking about your girlfriend all the time and that's the main reason why I won't go all the way with you, what we do is just for thrills.'

'Then why are you wearing that belt for a skirt and stockings with suspenders?' he asked.

'Well, haven't you great eyesight,' she said, sounding a bit surprised. 'How do you know that?'

'I saw you getting out of the taxi earlier and when I saw the giggling gap I thought, girlfriend or no girlfriend I've got to make love to that woman.' He almost said. 'I've got to have some of that,' but stopped in time, as it probably would have offended her.

She gave him a playful slap and asked.

'What in the name of God is the giggling gap?'

'It's the piece of skin at the top of a woman's stocking and when you get past that your laughing,' he said coyly.

Not having heard it before she laughed heartily leaned over until her face was only inches from his and while licking her lips in tantalising fashion she whispered.

'I can't wait any longer to get this mouth around you, so please, can we go?'

He could feel a stirring in his nether regions when he heard that and was severely tempted to kiss her lovely mouth while it was only inches away, but refrained in case it would put her off. That could wait and as he opened the car door for her with his eyes glued on her hemline, he wasn't disappointed by her display. Only for very scanty panties, he would have seen the lot and she had caught his reaction so she said.

'If it was Summer I wouldn't be wearing any, but I promise I'll remove them when we park, anyway, I'm wearing this outfit totally for your benefit, so there will be lots to see.'

Ned was ready long before they found a spot and as he drove the big car on to the grass at the roadside, she kept her promise and slipped out of the tiny briefs. He was about to ask if he could have full sex with her when she went into action, within seconds she had opened his zipper and was devouring his enlarged tackle much to his enjoyment. The roadway, while not a main road was quite busy and there were lots of people out walking or running in all directions, which made our hero quite nervous. She was making a little humming noise, which he discovered was a continuous moan of enjoyment and she seemed to be in another world, but he was very much in this world. The more cars and people he saw, the more worried he became, regardless of the thrills that were racing through him, then when he looked in the rear view mirror, he saw a man walking two greyhounds about five hundred yards away, but they were heading directly for his parked car. Keeping his eyes glued to the mirror while trying to focus on what was happening to himself, he could feel that Sandra was on the home straight, but when he looked in the mirror again, so was the man and his two dogs, then he took one more look at her almost naked body and that did the trick. As the man and his canine pals walked past the car he had to try very hard to look normal, even though he was having one of the greatest orgasms of his life. With all visible spectators out of the way, he was once more concentrating on his sex life and his lover who was now thrashing about, as she also went over the top. But the danger wasn't over, he had taken his eye off the ball so to speak, not having seen the park warden approach from the right on his bike and now that gentleman was knocking on his window. Luckily, Ned felt a little chilly earlier and had donned a big floppy sweater that a fan had knitted for him last year, this he pulled down to cover his wilting, bare kit.

'What are you doing here?' The man asked, trying to look beyond Ned's pullover. 'And I didn't know you had company,' he added.

Sandra was by now sitting up in the car, having pulled down the short skirt as best she could to cover her bare bottom and she boldly flashed a big smile at the man.

'I was just resting on my boyfriend's lap after a hard night at a great party.' 'Is there anything wrong with that Officer?' she asked.

'The problem is madam, you are not supposed to park on the grass and that is why I became interested in this car, but I must say, I'm a bit suspicious as to what you two have been up to.'

He was sounding real technical now and she took over, saying.

'My name is Sandra Boyle and I was at a big Record launch for my boyfriends band in town last night. I'm a journalist and during the festivities I had a few too many, now what could we be up to seeing I've got a sore head.'

Ned was still in shock and half naked under the big jumper as he listened.

'Sandra Boyle,' said yer-man. 'I know you I think, you're from down my way and I read all your showbiz columns, you're giving this Nova's Showband great coverage these days, would the boyfriend here be one of them?'

'You're on the ball,' she said, 'this is their Bandleader, Ned Brady, say hello Ned.'

He nearly had heart failure but managed a hello and then he almost died altogether at her next statement.

'Have you any records in the boot Ned? Go and get one for the man before he leaves.'

He tried to imagine how he would manage that, without putting his underpants and trousers back on, so he gave her a dirty look while he told the fellow he had no records until next week, but if he gave Sandra a ring she would send him one by post. He seemed happy with that and before he mounted his bike he told Ned not to park on the grass the next time he's here.

'There'll be no fucking next time,' he growled, as he watched the warden ride away. 'I don't think I'll ever drive through here again as long as I live. Just imagine the folks in Mullymore talking about me being caught screwing in the park and what would Susan and her family say? Jaysus, let's get to fuck out of here,' he continued.

'But Ned it was marvellous,' she said, 'we both came at the same time.'

'You'd better include the fucking park keeper in that as well, he also came at the same time, to fucking arrest us,' he answered.

'But he wasn't going to arrest us,' she said.

'It's a good job he knew you or we'd both be heading for the cop shop now.' 'But tell me, has he caught you up here before?' he wanted to know.

'What do you think I am?' she asked, sounding very offended.

'I think you're a risk taker for extra kicks and I've had my fill of it,' was his answer.

'Come on now, calm down and we can do it again,' she said, laughing.

'You're definitely taking the piss now,' he said, as he started up the big car and drove it off the grass towards town. He wouldn't be the better of that for a while and he was feeling very uncomfortable, because he had done a hurried job on his underwear and pants, so he didn't speak a word until he got back to Sandra's flat.

'You're angry at me aren't you?' she asked.

'I'm more angry at myself,' he answered with a sigh. 'I had a bad feeling about it all the time you know, sex is for indoors, not the park.'

'Well,' she began, 'seeing that you got a fright and seeing that I like you, I've decided to give you a treat if you're interested.'

He looked at her suspiciously, thinking she was offering more of the same, but the coy look on her face intrigued him so he decided to check it out and asked. 'What exactly have you got in mind?'

'Many times since we met, you have suggested having full sex with me and I wouldn't let you, well I've changed my mind, so consider yourself having got past the giggling-gap.'

He was about to say no and she knew it, so she gave a couple of little wriggles and the tiny skirt slipped up revealing all. That did the trick and he was rampant again.

'There's only one condition,' she said.

'Are you still not going to kiss me?' He asked.

'No it's not that,' she replied. 'It's almost impossible to make love without kissing, you must wear a rubber, that's the deal.'

He panicked for a second and then he remembered that he had one in his wallet, which Brenda had given to him in New York.

'That's not a problem,' he began, 'but what is this making love bit you're talking about, I thought we were just going to have a screw.'

'You call it what you like,' she said, 'come on, let's go in before I change my mind.'

It was marvellous, just as she said in the park. He had never been with such a thorough lover and they got into positions he had only ever heard about, while all the time she kept checking. 'Are you ok, are you enjoying it, what do you like?' By now she was kissing him with real fervour and he heard her say 'I love you' more than once, but he cruelly let it go unnoticed. During the session, the few bits and pieces she had been wearing totally disappeared, apart from the shoes, stockings and suspenders which she kept on (as she said) to add to the thrill. Now she was sitting on the bed, sipping a large measure of vodka that she had prepared along with a Scotch for him and he had to admire how beautiful she looked, after putting so much energy into the proceedings.

'That wasn't too bad was it?' she asked.

'No, it was wonderful and maybe in a while, you'll let go that hurt which has been destroying you,' he really meant it too.

'Does that mean you wish to repeat the performance?' she enquired, kissing him on the cheek.

He had been thinking about that in a mercenary fashion along the lines of, seeing that Susan won't make love to him and she had intimated that he could see girls as long as he kept it to himself, then why not the lovely Sandra Boyle, who wanted him even though he had a girlfriend. It didn't make him feel too good, but now he answered her question.

'Yes Sandra,' he said, 'but none of this I love you stuff, you know I love Susan, so on those conditions, I would like many repeats and now that you're kissing me, it makes it complete.'

'Did you not like what I did in the park?' She asked, looking inquiringly at him.

'Yes I did, it blew my mind as well as other things, but it must be kept for indoors, especially during the day.'

'OK spoilsport,' she said and jumped on him again. 'We're indoors now aren't we?'

She wouldn't hear of it, when he suggested going home, insisting he get a good nights sleep before going to see Susan the next day. She also invited him out to dine that evening in a good restaurant in town and he panicked for a moment, wondering if it might be the place Mary's boyfriend was starting as Chef. Putting his mind at rest on that score, she informed him that she knew the Chef, and she said.

'That's why I'm taking you there, he's marvellous.'

'There's that word marvellous again, that's how you described our session in the park, is he marvellous at that as well?'

She gave him a thump saying. 'I've only experienced his culinary skills, so there.'

Then he had a thought, which he voiced. 'I don't have any more rubbers, so how will we manage?'

'Oh, I'll have to trust you I suppose, but there's always the other way unless it puts you off.'

Her voice was no more than a sexy whisper, when she said that. This time it was him who jumped on her and the sparks flew.

Luckily the food was nearby because he was hardly able to walk, so he suggested spending the night on the couch. 'What will I say to my girlfriend tomorrow night, if I'm unable to put one foot past the other, she'll cop on and dump me, then I'll never forgive you,' she knew he meant it too.

'Alright then, let's sleep together but without any hanky-panky,' she answered. 'I'm wrecked as well and I really don't want to get you into any trouble with Susan.'

The meal was great as was the wine and the staff treated Sandra like a celebrity.

'I get good value here by giving them a mention in my column the odd time and it works wonders,' she informed him

The Chef came out from the kitchen for a chat later and they both complimented him on his handiwork, which culminated in Irish Coffees. After all that happened in the last twenty-four hours, they were both ready for sleep the moment they got into bed, but when he saw her magnificent body as she walked naked from the bathroom, he knew if he even touched off her under the covers, he would be a goner. Full marks to Sandra, she kept her word by staying on her side of the bed and in a few moments they were both in the land of nod. Sleep for him that night was not as smooth as usual and before morning he had sat up three times, to escape from a recurring dream which kept haunting him. In it he was in Court, sitting between two burly Policemen and the person in the witness box whom he recognised as the park warden, was sitting on a bicycle and pointing at him, while everyone was staring coldly. His first thought was. How did they manage to get the bike into the witness box? Then he noticed that Sandra Boyle was sitting across the Court Room heavily pregnant and if that wasn't bad enough he also recognised the lady judge, who was now asking the defendant to please rise for sentence. The shock of the judge donning the black cap, coupled with the fact that she was his loved one Susan, made him jump up in a cold sweat and each time the dream was identical. Seeing Sandra sleeping calmly beside him was helping and on each occasion he would drift back into a deep sleep, then back into the same bloody courtroom. Was this the way it was going to be in the future? He thought. Luckily, after the third repeat the dream went away and he awoke refreshed at noon, to the aroma of a lovely breakfast cooked by the Journalist, who was floating about in blue jeans, boots and frilly apron.

'Where have I seen this before?' he was thinking. 'She could be the third Prunty sister, the blonde version.'

They talked at length about the new single during breakfast, also the publicity she would be doing on it and the band over the next few weeks. She informed him that she had been hired by the Record Company, to get as much publicity as possible in as short time as possible, keeping the momentum going and hopefully, ensuring a hit.

'I hope you'll give me a ring for a chat one of the days, she said. 'I'll put no pressure on you to do so, but I can let you and the band know how things are shaping up.'

'I'll definitely keep in touch and apart from the shock I got in the park, plus my new bad dream, I really enjoyed your company, but I can't lose Susan, I'm mad about her,' he answered.

'I understand,' she said. 'I'm OK with that and as you know, I'm not looking for a relationship, but I would like to meet you again when you have some time off.'

As she walked with him to his car he promised that he would keep in touch and when he drove away, he couldn't take his eyes of her beautiful frame in the rear view mirror. He wondered if she would ever marry and settle down? Just imagine some quiet, shy country fellow taking her on in holy matrimony and later discovering her sexual prowess. He would either be delighted by the revelation, resulting in a life of happiness and a house full of kids, or the alternative, total disgust and immediate suicide. But if he went for the first option, Ned was sure he would enjoy it. The greatest possibility was, that she would never take anyone on full time, because of the old hurt in her life.

'What a pity,' he mused.

Chapter Thirteen

Heading out of the city in the direction of Glenrone and Susan, he kept analysing the dream he had last night. His mother would say it was a message from above, to put the fear of God into him and he cringed, knowing what her opinion would be about the carry on of the last couple of days. Next, his thoughts drifted to his dad and the big day in his life on the coming Monday. The Central Bar was up for sale by public auction and he promised he would be there, to stop the human vultures from stealing everything not nailed down. That damned venue hadn't been the luckiest place on earth for his father, but it had been much worse for it's past owner and his lovely wife.

The pub's landlady and her head barman had just closed shop one night, when someone got in and shot them both dead. The landlord was arrested for the crime but he had an airtight alibi, having been at a card game with three of the biggest business men in town when it happened and a young friend of Ned's from Ballypratt, had a very unusual story to tell during the court case, which failed to convict anybody. One day, this young lad who he used to play guitar with, was walking along the street in Mullymore, when he bumped into the owner of what was then known as The Bridge Bar and the publican offered him a job.

'Ah, the man I'm looking for,' said the businessman. 'I've got a job for you that is really up your street. How would you like to sit and look at Television all night and get paid for it?'

'It would all depend on what's on,' the young man answered.

'Well this is T.V. with a difference,' said the landlord. 'It's surveillance equipment, the very latest sent to me by my brother in The States, to help me find out who's robbing me in the pub.'

'But I wouldn't know anything about that kind of stuff,' said the young fellow, 'and it would interfere with my guitar lessons.'

'I'll pay you well,' said the Publican, 'but you must keep it top secret from everyone, even my wife, for when she gets a few scoops in her she talks a bit too much,'

They spoke about it for a while, then the older man brought the young chap to the pub, where he plied him with tea and sandwiches and in the end, Ned's friend agreed to give it a try, the secrecy being an added bonus of course. He began to think he was a detective or something in that line, so he accompanied the Boss up a rickety flight of stairs to an old wine cellar, which just happened to be directly above the bar and it's two cash registers.

The young lad whose name was Jimmy, once said to Ned. 'Who ever heard of a fucking wine cellar upstairs? It could only happen in Mullymore.'

He had been arrested on the morning after the double killing, about two hours after the Pub Landlord was picked up for questioning. The Publican gave evidence that Jimmy was on the premises taping the goings on downstairs, when the fatal shooting occurred, so naturally the Police saw him as a key witness. Everyone kept asking about what went on and Jimmy was quite the celebrity for a couple of months, even though he would have preferred being popular for playing his fender guitar in his band The Slugs. The same group which later spawned two present members of The Nova's Showband as well as Ned and that was where he honed his three or four guitar chords, recently back in practice. When the cops saw the film footage, they came to the conclusion that the perpetrator had to be the landlord, because of what was happening behind the counter minutes before the shooting.

In full view of the camera, the bar manager and the landlady spoke lovingly about a love tryst they had had the previous Wednesday night, in a Hotel not a million miles away and how much in love they were. Then it happened. They made passionate love to each other as young Jimmy zoomed in and out ecstatically, almost losing it while the spectacle enfolded before his innocent eyes. He told Ned, he was still as high as a kite wondering what to do about his condition, (which would have enabled him to play golf without bringing any gear) while he watched them dress. He had zoomed close up to the Landlady as she prepared to put her lacy bra back on her magnificent breasts, then suddenly, she let out a high pitched scream and began pleading with somebody. 'Please don't, please don't,' but the plea didn't work and Jimmy Jones will never forget what happened next. He heard two gunshots in rapid succession and on camera he saw the results of the first shot take its toll. The woman had tried to cover her breasts with her two beautiful hands, that had given much pleasure to her lover just minutes earlier, but as he looked into the black and white monitor, all the beauty before him turned into a mess of black carnage, as the buckshot tore into the hands and chest of the victim. In a daze, he switched over to position two and focused on the results of the second shot. The bar manager was lying on his back behind the counter with a similar gory wound in his chest and by the look on his face, there was no doubt that he was dead. Still in a daze, Jimmy sat there unable to move. His first impulse was to run down the narrow stairs and get away from this mess that he found himself in, but his legs wouldn't work, then he was brought back to reality by a loud scream.

Seemingly, the killer had ran from the building leaving the front door open and four or five young people had wandered in, wondering why the pub was open so late, now they had stumbled on the tragedy. Their next move was to run to the Police station two hundred yards away and report their findings, then within minutes, Jimmy saw two cops on the monitor standing behind the bar. This was his cue to vacate the pub, so he switched everything off and tiptoed down the stairs. Letting himself out the door quietly, he ran the two miles to his home where he got into bed immediately, to lie awake for the remainder of the night with the bedclothes over his head.

The court case had been a gruelling experience for young Jimmy and five days a week for almost a month, he had to attend the Town Court House to give his side of the story. He was questioned many times about the Landlord and why he thought he had been employed. On each occasion he just repeated what the Publican had said to him, but he really got a shock one afternoon when the Lawyer for the prosecution suggested that maybe he, Jimmy Jones, pulled the trigger on that fateful night.

What the Lawyer was putting to him was, that maybe while in a sexual trance, he had taken the gun and keys supplied by the Landlord, gone down the narrow stairs to the pub, then shot the victims as instructed by his Boss, who knew the condition he would be in after witnessing explicit sexual behaviour. The young man denied this wild accusation, but wasn't the better of it for days and by the way the locals looked at him subsequently, they seemed to have their doubts about him too.

After questioning up to one hundred people including the bar manager's wife, the case ground to an unsatisfactory conclusion. She also had an airtight alibi from her brother and his wife, who swore she was tucked up in bed in their house ten miles away, when the killing took place. Now with the prime suspect the husband, being found not guilty, he was set free to continue running his pub. This he did for a couple of months but without much success and even though his clientele mostly believed he didn't do it, they were reluctant to try and enjoy themselves in a venue where such an atrocity had occurred, so nobody was surprised when the For Sale By Public Auction board went up outside the premises.

It was in the local paper that Ned's dad had seen the sale notice and to this farmer who had been thinking for years of becoming a Publican, the advertisement flashed like a beacon, as if to say. This is the opportunity you have been waiting for, to get away from the drudgery of farming, so act now and act now he did. Edmond Brady contacted a man who had shown interest in his big farm by the river in Ballypratt and by the auction date he was the first man there, with more than enough money to buy his dream, which he immediately christened, The Central Bar. His wife was also keen on the move, because number one, she wanted to live in town and had recently received a piece of information that the lovely big white house at the top of the hill overlooking Mullymore would soon be on the market, so she would not be forced to live upstairs in the pub for too long.

At this time, Ned was playing rhythm guitar in Jimmy Jones's group The Slugs and they had been doing quite well, having recorded some of Jimmy's songs for a single release, which had received quite a lot of airplay plus favourable comments from the music critics. Then came the murder and that blew all their hopes and plans out of the water, but as they say, it's an ill wind that blows nobody good, so out of the demise of the group came Ned's, Nova's Showband.

Jimmy Jones used to tell a funny story, about the time he phoned a promoter down south regarding a date for The Slugs and the man said.

'My God, dat's a funny name for a band.'

Jimmy had a standard reply to this comment, as it wasn't the first time he'd heard it.

'I'm sure you've heard of The Beatles.'

'Oh yes I have, dey are very big aren't dey,' he replied.

'Yeah, they're huge,' said Jimmy. 'Once upon a time promoters thought their name was silly as well, but lived to regret that conclusion.'

After a long silence the man said. 'Hold on a minute until I get my diary, I wouldn't like to miss out, just in case De Slugs get as big as De Beatles.'

Ned remembered asking Jimmy. 'What happens, if the fab-four find out you're using their name to get work?'

'Fuck them,' he replied, 'all's fair in love and war, this is war, showbiz style.'

It was some time later that Ned came face to face with his first trombone. Because The Nova's Showband had a trumpet and sax, he decided to get a bone and forget about the guitar. It never crossed his mind, if he would be able to play it until after he bought it, but luckily he mastered it fairly well without any lessons and the fact that he was by then living in the big white house at the top of a hill was a plus. Because nobody could hear some of the weird noises coming from the bell, that is except his long suffering mother who kept telling him it sounded fine and their dog Shep, who whined loudly before running from the house every time he blew into it.

Deep in thought about Monday's auction and the fact that his father wasn't well, Ned missed most of the journey to meet his girlfriend. Some of the six or seven years in The Central Bar had been good, but another reason for selling now, was a new phenomenon which Edmond Brady wanted to keep under wraps until after the auction. He firmly believed he saw the ghost of the murdered landlady flitting around the bar after closing time one night and she seemed to be looking up to where she had once noticed the missing ceiling tiles, which allowed the camera to spy on her and her lover.

'It's time to move on alright,' he informed his family recently. 'If the word gets out, I'll never be able to sell the place.'

For the last few miles of the journey, his thoughts focused totally on Susan and whether he would be able to cover up his infidelity since their last meeting. All he could do was hope that she wouldn't ask too many questions about how he spent his time, as to how he felt about her, there was no doubt he loved her more every day and his time with Sandra Boyle had not effected this in any way. He timed his arrival nicely, as the receptionist informed him she had gone to powder her nose and would be out shortly, so he walked back out the door, not wanting to hug or kiss her in front of her friend, then while he stood outside rubbing his hands with excitement, he heard the office door opening. Turning around quickly he saw her framed in the doorway, wearing another designer suit, this time in white with shoes to match of course and he couldn't believe how short the skirt was.

His first thoughts, had he voiced them, would have brought his romance tumbling down, but in the nick of time he changed direction. What almost came out would have been. My God, your skirt is almost as short as Sandra Boyle's and by the way, do you have any panties on? Whoops that was close. What burst forth instead was.

'As usual Susan you look stunning and I love the skirt, you've certainly got the legs for it, come here,' and just like the movies, they floated into each other's arms for an overdue hug that went on for ages.

'I'm starving,' she volunteered.

'We can't have that now can we,' he replied.

He was just about to ask her if she had somewhere in mind when she solved the problem.

'My brother John and his girlfriend went to a wonderful restaurant last week, it's up in the hills about five miles from here and they said the food was marvellous, how about it?'

'My God,' he thought. Susan is using the word marvellous also. 'That sounds great,' he answered and the drive will be nice as well.'

All the locals passing by were saying hello to Susan and she in turn was trying to speak to them while attempting to kiss Ned at the same time, so they both knew they had to get out of there.

'It's too early for the restaurant, so let's drive out to the Deep Lough for a while.'

Susan was kissing his ear as she gave him this advice and talking him into it was easy. Soon the big car swung into the narrow road and in a few minutes they were parked, literally yards away from the water, so without a word their arms went around each other as the kissing began. When their lips parted, her mouth found his ear again and what she said drove him crazy.

'I'm going to need your help with a problem.'

At first his heart sank because he kept imagining all kinds of things, but it raced immediately when she finished her request.

'I want us to make love tonight,' she said. 'It's been driving me mad lately, especially when I'm in my room, I've been going to bed with your photograph and all kinds of things have been happening, please help me.'

He sat back from this beautiful young woman and he could easily see what she was going through.

'Susan darling,' he began. 'I feel the same as you and I can understand the bedroom situation as I do the same, but if we start making love now it will spoil things for us afterwards, even though it would be lovely just remember your wish.'

'But I think it's a bigger sin doing it to ourselves than if we did it together,' she said. 'I know I've been harping on about remaining a virgin but I can't fight it any more.'

'Susan pet,' he said, lovingly stroking her cheek. 'I'm not worried about it being a sin; I saw the other side of that when I was in the Seminary. People like us who love each other could not be committing sin, it's the people who preach one thing and practice another, they are the sinners.'

'Oh Ned, you must tell me all about that part of your life soon and as I've said before, you would have been a lovely priest,' she said, amid fits of laughter, then her previous worries came back and she became sad again. She looked so bothered, that he reached out once more and took her in his arms and what he suggested to her next would go a long way in solving the problem.

'I'll tell you what we'll do,' he said softly. 'Starting tonight, you touch me, I touch you and that will mean we're not doing it to ourselves, but we must not go all the way. I intend to keep my promise to you and anyway, the way I feel you'd probably get pregnant the first time we would make love.'

She clung to him and he felt a little sob shake her lovely body.

'Are you OK with that?' he asked.

'Yes Ned,' she whispered, 'but you'll have to show me how it's done honey.'

He loved it when she called him honey and he kissed her real intimately in return, then he told her his plan for the evening.

'I think we should find this restaurant, have a lovely meal, tell each other as often as we can how much in love we are, then come back here and I'll make you feel on top of the world.'

He could tell that she didn't know whether to laugh of cry, but she was nodding in agreement to his suggestion and that made him happy, then slowly she began to smile which led to loud laughter, as they drove away from the lake. Several times during the fabulous meal, she reminded him of her lack of experience with men, each time he put her at ease by telling her that he would lead her through it and everything would be great. Never once asking how he was seemingly such an expert, had proved to him that she meant what she said when suggesting, if he took girl's home, he was to keep it to himself. The thought of touching her at last, kept him high all through the meal and Susan confided in him that she felt the same. No matter how this evening panned out, they both agreed they would not forget this quaint country house restaurant with it's menu written on a scrap of paper and the old gentleman who flitted around silently serving the exotic food, which was being cooked by his elderly wife in their tiny, yet well equipped kitchen. There were no pints on the menu tonight, so they both chose a nice red wine and a very nervous Susan gulped down her first ever glass, ages before the food arrived. He reached across the table taking her soft hand in his and he couldn't help thinking of the pleasure those long beautiful digits would mete out to him later.

'I'm having very sexy thoughts,' he informed her.

'Me too,' she gushed. 'I hope I don't make a mess of it and my parents will kill me for drinking.'

'Don't worry pet,' he assured her, 'you'll be wonderful and anyway, we've got the rest of our lives to get it right.'

He was now holding both her hands telling her how much he loved her and he could see a smile of confidence envelope her lovely face, then they talked about every subject under the sun, apart from what lay ahead that night. Susan had had a call from the model agency and she was going to see them a week from now, so Ned informed her that he would drive her to the city, killing two birds with one stone by bringing her to meet his parents on the way home.

'I was hoping I'd get to meet them soon,' she said. 'Will they like me, do you think?'

'They're going to love you as much as I do,' he answered, taking both her hands again. 'Look at the time!' He exclaimed, glancing at his watch. 'I feel a cuddle coming on, so we'd need to head back soon, how about you?'

'Yeah, me too, I'm really looking forward to it now, lets go honey.'

He paid the bill, sent their compliments to the chef promising they would be back soon, but before they left the restaurant, the owner suggested ringing in their booking next time and he would make sure the menu carried different dishes for their pleasure.

'We keep a note of what our customers have on each visit and give them a varied choice the next time they come, that way, it remains interesting for out patrons.'

On the five-mile journey back to the lake, Susan sat so close to him she was almost on his knee, while she showered him with kisses and words of undying love all the way. Luckily they were the only lovers parked at the Deep Lough that night, because, within seconds of switching off the engine, they were kissing and touching each other everywhere, completely aware of how far they could go, while the feelings of tenderness and emotion were palpable.

Later, as they drove the short distance through Glenrone and along The Fiddler's Lane to Susan's home, she still had her arms wrapped around his body, with her pretty head on his shoulder.

'I could eat you,' she purred into his ear.

While silently wondering if her meaning and his were similar, he answered. 'One day I'll let you.'

'I hope so,' she said. 'I look forward to it.'

The house was in darkness so they decided to call it a day, knowing that tomorrow she would come to her aunt's guesthouse at lunchtime and wake him up pleasantly. Ned lay awake for at least an hour that night, going over and over in his mind, the absolute pleasure he had personally derived from getting physically close to Susan at last. He compared the experience to other love trysts he had had, such as his nights with Brenda in New York and his sessions of the past few days and night with Sandra Boyle, then his mind flashed to the sex mad girl he had met in his cousins house in Boston. None of them came close to the loving pleasure he got from Susan.

'My God, I can't even remember the girls name in Boston, that's bad.' He mused.

Other faces flitted past, like Helen in the Woodlawn Hotel and the extra smooth Mary on the beach in San Francisco, the collage was endless. If there ever was a time to give ratings to girls this was it and in a one to ten situation Susan kept getting twelve. Before he drifted off to sleep, he knew the time was fast approaching when he would have to call a halt to his womanising, in case he'd lose her. Roll on the bands holidays in May next, that's when the final decision would be made, for better or for worse. Then he thought.

'What if they all dump me?' 'That would simplify things and I could hardly blame them.'

He slept like a log all through the morning, awaking only to the velvet touch of Susan's soft hand being bold.

'You should lock your door,' she said, 'anybody could have come in and had their wicked way with you.'

'I left it open on purpose,' he said grinning, 'because I hoped you would do just that and it worked.' As his sentence tailed off he grabbed her, pulling her luscious body on top of him in the bed. 'Let's finish what we started last night,' he said, as he began tickling her, much to her enjoyment.

'No way,' was her reply, trying to be stern. 'You got the chance last night but you were chicken, now you'll have to wait until our wedding night, so there.'

The mention of their wedding had the same effect on them both and without saying a word they held each other very tightly.

'I'd better go back downstairs or my aunt will be thinking all kinds of things, you hurry down honey, lunch is ready.'

He gave his face a 'cat's lick' as his mother called a quick wash, jumped into his pants, donned an unevenly buttoned shirt and still barefoot he skipped down the stairs to his love, who was by now comfortably seated at the dining table.

'I love your outfit as usual,' he began. 'You'd never think you had been to bed in it, would you?'

She rubbed down a couple of little creases in the jacket trying to make a big deal out of it, but she couldn't hide the happy laugh, which kept bursting from her pretty mouth.

'I hope you didn't mind my reference to our wedding day, I think of it quite a lot lately and it makes me very happy.' She seemed in another world as she softly spoke about her dream and he smiled.

'I think about it also and I was thrilled when you said it, but we're too young yet so we must show restraint, what we did last night is the answer, then we will have everything else to look forward to.' He sounded so sincere that she nodded in agreement.

They spoke about the auction on the following Monday and she wished them well, then they talked about his gigs for the weekend which were all over the place, so at 2 o'clock after a lovely meal, she kissed him passionately before going back to work. A shower was on the cards and at 3 o'clock on the dot he was ready for the off, not giving a second thought to the journey in front of him. Again he would use the drive to think about his future and how he hoped it would take shape.

When he got to the venue, the Promoter informed him that there was a meal for the band in a local posh restaurant and the lads were already there.

'That makes a pleasant change from the ham sandwiches and cold tea in the band room the last time they were there,' he was thinking, as he got back into the car.

Lots of airplay on the wireless and the huge write-ups in all the papers from the pen of Sandra Boyle, surely makes a difference. He had read most of the bumph before it was printed, in fact he had dreamed up some of it at times when a pen wasn't always handy, but it proved that Miss Boyle has a good memory even when she's distracted and she had left nothing out.

The other band members had been getting a great vibe around the town and were in a buoyant, cheerful mood when Ned arrived. Loud hello's and did you enjoy the spin? Was the order of the day instead of the usual? What the fuck kept you and are we not good enough to share the meal with. Etc.

The Roadie was in exceptionally good fettle, for which he had two reasons. Number one, the new full colour handouts of the band had arrived that day and he was looking forward to dishing them out, but even a greater joy had befallen him earlier. He had received a letter from Amanda in the U.S. inviting him to spend the following month of May with her and her family. Fame had also transformed the Lead Singer into an on going pleasant fellow and he kept singing part of an old song to the Roadie called, 'Buffalo girl won't you come out tonight' which brought smiles to his phizog. To annoy him, but only for fun (this time) Mickey Joe, Conn and the Drummer were loudly planning his replacement, but when they mentioned The Blue Dots Roadie they got his dander up for some reason which he didn't share.

'I'll tell you what Conn,' he declared. 'Maybe you could hire Cynthia Rose instead and then you'd know what she was up to all the time, or who she was up on all the time.'

You could cut the silence with a knife, until the Piano man who was playing poker with the guitar player, intervened.

'For fuck's sake lads, less of the shite, were having a hit record and more success than we deserve, so take it easy,' the Piano man was deadly serious.

'Let the fucker's apologise to each other now, we've got a job to do, OK!' This voice belonged to the usually quiet Guitar player.

Ned couldn't help noticing the change that success was bringing to the band members. Before this he would be left to sort out a problem like the last one, but now, it seemed the outfit was sprouting a bunch of (would be) bandleaders, the next move will be, they'll all want to be managers.

'I must monitor this development,' he mused.

The antagonists said they were sorry and calm spread across the room once more.

'It's a good job no one else was around,' Ned was thinking.

The gig was huge and at two in the morning the punters were shouting for more.

'Jaysus, we'll never get home,' he shouted to Mickey Joe.

The latter grinned and looked like he was chewing tobacco, as he roared his reply once more out of the side of his mouth.

'Bollixolutely, and if music be the excuse for making money, then play on sham.'

He had just fitted that nugget of wisdom including his new lingo word in between riffs on his trumpet, so he went back to doing what he does best, kicking his right leg out to the tempo of the song along with the front line. Choreography at it's finest no doubt. After a couple of encores they pulled the plug as they call it and wound up proceedings.

A good-looking leggy blonde had been giving Ned the eye all night and she made a beeline for the stage, as the last note was fading. 'He's got the pictures,' was his answer to her first request for an autograph and he duly pointed to the busy Roadie.

'No, you get the picture for me and I want you to sign it,' she was turning on the charm and the sex appeal which included a pout.

As requested, he got the promo photo and scribbled his name on the back, then handed it to her.

'Oh come on now, put something nice on it,' she said. 'Lot's of love and kisses would do for a start.'

'But we've only just met,' he countered.

Then she laughed and said. 'Next you'll be telling me that you're spoken for.'

He would have enjoyed telling her about Susan, but at a meeting the previous week, it had been agreed that the band members should keep all involvement's under wraps, in the interest of success and they had all given a flat no to Mike's suggestion that they should go with girls they didn't fancy, just to boost ratings. He took the picture back and put loads of kisses on it and then at the bottom right corner he drew a matchstick woman. Placing three kisses strategically on the figure, he asked the girl for her name and added this to the caricature before handing it back.

As she was trying to decide whether she liked what she saw or not, the Roadie tapped him on the shoulder and whispered into his ear.

'I'm chatting up your one's friend, they have a flat down the town and I think it's on if you're game ball.'

Ned looked at him and then turning to the blonde he said. 'Could you excuse me for a moment, I need to speak to my friend.' He guided him to the back of the stage saying loudly. 'A couple of hours ago, you were on your way to Buffalo and now you're on your way to a bed down the street with a total stranger, who probably transmogrified last weeks Roadie in the same bed, while a member of the orchestra saw to the blonde who's been chatting me up, it's not a good idea.'

'OK Boss, sorry, I'll blow her out so,' he blurted.

'Just make sure you do it nicely, remember the meeting.' Ned could hardly keep from laughing as he turned in the direction in which the interested one had stood, but he now noticed she had joined her friend to await decision time. He was within earshot about a minute into the Roadie's excuse and his conclusion was, that this man should be writing fictional novels.

'Don't tell the lads, but I have just been diagnosed with a rare blood virus and by the time I get the wagon packed, I'll hardly be able to stand up, let alone court a girl.'

'Oh you poor beggar,' said his potential date, 'tell me, is it contagious, I mean can I get it?' She looked worried now and had noticed that her potential date was having problems with the meaning of the word, contagious.

'Not if I'm standing beside someone,' he said, taking a guess at what the word meant and getting it right for a change. 'But if I was to kiss anybody, it could be dangerous and if I made love, then my lover would almost be sure to get it.'

'Have you got the clap?' the blonde asked.

'Oh Jaysus no,' answered yer-man. 'That's a hoor of a yoke altogether, my problem can be treated, no sweat.'

Ned had stopped to talk to someone as a bluff, so he could hear the Roadie's story but not interrupt it and now he moved in.

'Did I hear somebody mention the word sweat?' he enquired, not daring to repeat the unmentionable clap word.

'Yeah,' the blonde answered, 'it was one of the words alright, but we've got a hard day ahead of us tomorrow, so we'll probably see you gents again, goodnight.'

As he watched them almost run to the door Ned said to the Roadie. 'I think that story might do us more harm than having girlfriends, would you agree?'

'It was the only fuckin' thing I could think of at such short notice, but you must admit, it was effective,' he was trying a feeble smile.

'There's no girl dumb enough to go near a bloke with those symptoms, just keep it between the two of us.' Ned advised. 'The others guys might not understand, but you can be sure of one thing, you'll never get your hole in this area again.'

Just then, Mike walked up the floor pockets bulging and like the pied piper; the lads followed him into the band room.

'It was mighty tonight, our biggest take yet, the auld record and the spoof is doing the business and lads, don't forget the chicks, there's a few nice ones still around out there.' Mike was keeping the pressure on and was glad to hear that at least four of the band had (clicked).

'What happened you and the Roadie?' The Singer asked Ned. 'I thought you both had it sussed with those two, did he say something to offend them cause they seemed to run for the door?'

'No, the only problem was that his one couldn't wait until he packed the van and I was only spoofing to the other one, they have to be at work early in the morning so they left.'

He couldn't believe his ears, even though the Singer was turning on the charm himself, he was also watching what they were up to. Jaysus, that beats Banagher.

The Friday, Saturday and Sunday gigs were just as good as the Thursday and Monday morning saw a very tired, yet fulfilled Ned Brady drive slowly by his dad's pub in Mullymore. In just a few hours, he would be inside keeping an eye on the time wasters, who would turn up just to see how well his father would do and lift anything they could in the interim. Also finding out who bought The Central Bar would be of great interest to some of them, so they could talk about it later. He parked the car quietly and let himself into the big White House, but as he prepared for bed, a disquieting thought struck him. If Brenda had been pregnant he would now be going to bed upstairs in the pub and he wouldn't be getting up later for an auction. A feeling of shock passed through him, as he realised the close shave he had had with a very different life. Brenda is a lovely lady but the time wasn't right and before sleep took him, he realised he would have to visit her in May to bring their situation to a satisfactory conclusion, one way or another.

His mother called him at noon with news of an early lunch so they could be on site for 2 o'clock and she also had a little nugget of information that brought a smile to his face.

'There will be an American man there today who you've heard of, but you must treat him as a stranger, he's your Aunt Sarah's fellow from Philadelphia and your dad has brought him over to bid for the pub as a sweetener, he's staying at the Hotel so no one will tie him to us, understand.'

'What happens if the word gets out?' he asked.

'No one will be the wiser, the only other person who knows is your Uncle Tom and as he says, if someone finds out after the auction, it won't matter a hoot.'

He stifled the usual 'Jaysus' realising this was his mother he was talking to, so he said instead. 'Isn't dad the crafty codger coming up with that idea, its no wonder he uses so much butter on his bread at the speed he melts it.' Within seconds his mother's face had gone very red and then the penny dropped so this time he went the whole hog. 'Jaysus' mother, look at the face on you and the price of beetroot, it was your idea so, wasn't it?'

She was so embarrassed that she didn't even hear him taking the Lord's name in vain (as she called it) and was very relieved when he began to laugh. Then she said.

'This is our nest egg Edward, I don't want your dad to work after the auction, so we must get the largest possible price for the pub, that's my reason for coming up with the idea.'

She sounded justified and her flush went away, but there was still one question he had to ask. 'What happens if the auctioneer sells the pub to the wealthy American?'

'That's been taken care of, your father told the Auctioneer that he heard a member of the Philadelphia Mafia was in town and wanted to buy the pub as a base for some racket or other, so he must be kept out at all costs, later if necessary, Edmond will say that someone set him up by lying to him.'

'That's going to backfire big-time next year, when Aunt Sarah comes home on holiday with a member of the Mafia, she's got a lot to say as she is, but I'm sure she'll be using some choice language when she hears this.' He was shaking his head in disbelief as he spoke, even though he agreed with the idea of his dad retiring, he had worked long enough.

'Don't worry,' Mrs. Brady said. 'Sarah knows and can't stop laughing at the thought, it will fit in very well with the local memory of her when she was a beautiful young wild girl, they'll expect it from her.'

For a few seconds, Ned had a mental picture of the dangerous Mafia guys back in L.A. when they were on tour and he couldn't help wondering if they had shot each other yet, he also conjured up a picture of the gangster's moll who had seen to him so thoroughly at four in the morning in what became known as the almost forgotten Faron Young affair. It all seemed so long ago.

'Was it worth it?' 'Yeah, of course it was.'

He was about to leave for the auction when the phone rang and luckily he picked it up.

'This is Kate,' said a mature, sexy female voice.

'Kate who?' He asked, thinking he'd probably regret it at a later stage.

'Don't tell me you've forgotten me already, it's Kate Kelly from The Diamond Ballroom, we spoke about spending some time together in my villa in Spain.'

'Oh yes Kate, of course I remember. I'm not likely to forget such a beautiful, elegant lady like you in a hurry, it's just that I'm rushing out the door to attend the sale of my father's pub in town and it starts in a few minutes, please forgive me.'

'OK, I could call you later if you tell me which number you will be at, it's a pity I didn't know about the auction, as I could have driven down and bid for the place as a sweetener, it works wonders for the price you know.' She was giving a sexy giggle as she spoke and it sent a dangerous thrill through his body.

'Thanks for the offer,' he heard himself say, 'but my dad wouldn't hear of an idea like that, it would be against his religion.'

Then he gave her the pub phone number and said he would wait there for her call. He didn't want a strange woman calling his home twice in the one day, in case his mother became suspicious and the thought hadn't left his mind when he heard his mum's voice.

'Who was that lady on the phone Edward?'

'Oh just a young fan enquiring about the new single and some souvenir pictures,' he lied.

'From the way you described her she can't be that young, does Susan know about her?' His mother wasn't usually so nosy, but since he had told her about Susan and her impending visit, she had suddenly become protective of this young, yet to her unknown girl who had stolen her son's heart. 'I'm going to like Susan,' she had said as she gazed at the lovely picture. 'She's a beautiful girl and you're a lucky boy.'

Ned's mum had mellowed over the years and was now secretly glad that he had left the Priesthood, having slowly realised after failing to have more children, that it would have meant the demise of the Brady family had he stayed on.

'Some boy,' he was thinking, going back to his mother's last remark as he rushed out the door to avoid any more questions.

Mike had said to him on a few occasions. 'Make sure you keep that Kate Kelly sweet, we want as many dates as possible in The Diamond Ballroom next year.'

Ned had suggested that they wouldn't get many dates if her husband found out, so Mike obviously gave her the phone number and suggested she mention Spain again, as that would be relatively safe. He had to admit that the idea of Spain with the gorgeous Mrs. Kelly appealed to him, especially since he would probably be betrothed to his lovely Susan by the end of the following year. He would try and fit the trip in next May during the hols, roll on May.

He had never been to an auction before and he was very disappointed when the Auctioneer didn't sound anything like Leroy Van-Dyke, the singer who had the big hit with the song of the same name some years ago. This guy was saying in little more than a whisper. 'Any advance on blah-blah-blah,' none of the jargon the country singer used on the record.

But there was no problem hearing the bids from the well-dressed American, who took up the running every time there was a lull. After each bid, the man Ned knew as John would have a sip from his large Brandy and wait, while the other interested parties went into separate huddles, obviously to work out if their finances would stretch much further. The sign for the visitor to stop bidding would be, the first time Mr. Brady, his wife and their son formed a similar cluster to discuss the last offer, which to them could clinch the deal and if or when that happened, it would be up to the real customers to carry on raising the stakes or not. The owner of another pub in town was really keen and after he bumped it up quite considerably, a smile came to Edmond Brady's kind face and he looked in the direction of his wife and son, signalling that it was time for their confab under the guise of coffee for three, which as if by magic appeared from behind the bar on cue.

'I'm happy enough now,' the Publican informed his folks. 'I think Mr. Cosgrave has it with that last bid, he probably wants it for his son.'

Then they heard a sound, which caused all three to splutter into their coffee cups. It was the voice of the silver haired visitor again, adding another thousand to the tally. Silence descended on the people present and if looks could kill, then Mr. Cosgrave glaring at the stranger would have proven fatal.

The interested party had another chat with his family and The Brady's gave a joint sigh of relief when he spoke. 'I'll raise it another thousand and that's my final offer, take it or leave it.'

Edmond Brady rose from his chair and went up to the quiet Auctioneer, instructing him to accept the tender, while Ned looked around for the man who he now considered, could really be a member of the Mafia. The object of his interest was standing at the bar, a broad grin on his face and a fresh, large brandy in his hand, he had just made an extra two thousand pounds for his girlfriends brother and he was proud.

Now his next move was his boldest yet, brandy aloft, he approached Mrs. Brady and holding out his hand he said loudly.

'I'm sorry I failed to buy your nice little bar.' 'I was hoping to turn it into the first in a chain of gambling joints I've got planned for your country, I was tempted by your tax situation, which is much more lenient than ours in The States at the moment.'

The local wags heard every word and the gossip for the immediate future was in train. The man who Ned had heard so much about from his aunt in Philadelphia, gave him a sly wink, downed what remained of his drink and loudly took his leave with.

'I loved your town, perhaps I'll include it in my itinerary next time I'm passing through, se y'all.'

Everybody looked at him as if he had three heads, then he walked out the door to await a thank you phone call that was planned for his hotel later, before his departure for the Airport. Ned advised his parents to go back home and relax after the excitement, so when Mr. Cosgrave paid the deposit to the Auctioneer, they did just that. He didn't want them around when the phone rang, because discretion was important at all times, so he sat on his own sipping a coffee, fantasising about the possible outcome of the call. If she's in the mood tonight, he could be there in two hours, or better still, meet her halfway, find a lover's lane and have a knee-trembler, something he hadn't had in a while, plus, there was always the big back seat of the car if needed.

'Ned, you're wanted on the phone,' the bar man's voice brought him back to reality.

She was very gushy and called him 'Ned darling' in her opening sentence, which did wonders for our horny hero. So he decided to go for the jugular just like the big stars do and was about to ask. 'Do you want to fuck me,' but changed it at the last second to. 'Would you like me to make love to you tonight Kate, we could meet somewhere, anywhere, I feel rampant and I hope you do to.'

There was a pregnant pause and he thought he had blown it until she spoke.

'I didn't think I had that effect on you darling, of course we can meet tonight.' 'Do you know that big pub at Castlecross, they've got a nice guest house where we can get up to all sorts of things, we can't leave you in that condition, can we?'

Still giving all the credit for his success with women to the trombone, he headed home to shower and shave. Tonight he would add some sexy aftershave Sandra Boyle had given him that she simply called Leg-Opener and a mint or two wouldn't go wrong for the journey. He remembered that her husband sweated a lot and maybe that had put her off him, so he was making sure that wouldn't happen tonight.

'What would you like for your tea?' His mother asked, 'the three of us will celebrate.'

'Sorry mum,' he replied. 'Mike phoned and asked me to meet him at his house, it's something to do with Radio interviews, but I'll take you both to a nice restaurant tomorrow night instead, to make up for it.'

He heard his dad's voice from the living room and he was glad to hear what his father had to say. 'That's alright son, you go ahead, your mother and I will be well rested and raring to go by tomorrow evening, take it easy now.'

That last part of the sentence made him wonder if his dad knew what he was up to. Ned's Uncle Tom told him his dad was a bit of a lad when he was young and the girls used to queue, to chat him up. 'Like father like son,' is what his uncle said.

His mother stood at the door watching for a glimpse and a hug from her boy and as he approached, she began fanning the air with her hand.

'My God, you must have poured half a chemist on yourself, it's a lot of aftershave for a meeting.'

'It just spurted out,' he said, as he wondered at his choice of words and then he continued with something even more suggestive, had his mother been on that wavelength. 'It's a new one and it has a huge hole in the top, I'll know better next time, cheerio mum.'

He had judged the Kate Kelly situation correctly and as he gave her a friendly but firm hug, he tried to work out how much money it would take to buy what she was wearing, not counting the top of the range two seater she had stepped out of. There must be a few pounds in the dance game and immediately that thought gave him a brilliant idea. To get the great deal that he had got while buying his car from Tractamotors, he had promised to keep an eye out for potential customers for their Cavan and Dublin outlets.

'Jaysus, where better to look than Kate or Paul Kelly and they might be changing both their expensive cars anytime soon,' he mused, 'but now is not the time.' 'I'll wait until the next gig the band is playing in The Diamond Ballroom and then I'll strike, but first things first.'

The big village pub was quiet and they had no problem finding their own nook, while a young lad brought a menu and wine list. It would be much better to take this situation slowly even though his adrenaline was pumping, so they both browsed through the bill of fare, chatting away as they did so.

It was Kate who mentioned their reason for being there first, by asking him. 'Are you excited?'

'I am,' he answered as he quickly lied to her. 'I've never met a married woman on a date before, I hope I don't disappoint you.'

He didn't mention his romp on the plane to New York with Patricia and all the subsequent sessions with her in The Woodlawn Hotel. Patricia had taught him a lot and between that experience plus the few tips he had picked up since, he felt fairly confident about pleasing this elegant creature.

'You won't disappoint me darling,' she purred, putting her beautiful bejewelled hand on his knee. 'I don't want to be talking about my husband behind his back, but you may have noticed he's a little older than me. Now between that and his drinking, I've got to do without, it's been that way for years I'm afraid.' The feel of her hand squeezing his knee rhythmically had him as high as a kite, until her soft voice brought him back to reality. 'Would you like to freshen up before we eat, when we finish our drink we could go into the house for half and hour. I'd like to change into something more comfortable as I've had this suit on all day and don't worry, the room is booked.'

He immediately agreed to her suggestion, but couldn't help wondering if they would make it back for the food and that was worth a thought because he was starving.

'Would you carry my case for me darling?' She asked. 'I packed in a hurry and I'm not sure what's in there, I just grabbed something short and light.'

Ned was enjoying being called darling and as he dug his gigging bag out of it's second home in the boot of his car, he couldn't help wondering what was going to happen in the next half hour. The landlady checked them in and didn't show any interest in whether they were married or not much to his relief, but you couldn't miss the rings so they probably did the trick, anyway, she looked the greedy type, the money being her only interest it seemed.

In the safety of the room he put the bags down, turned to his companion and at that second they both knew there was no time to lose. Their hands were everywhere, the first thing he did was to manoeuvre her tight skirt up around her waist and then he found something he had not experienced before. She was wearing crotch-less tights and as he perused this new phenomenon he heard her giggle, while she busied herself with his zipper.

'They are my Mary Poppin's stockings,' she informed him between kisses. 'I bought a load of them in Spain on my last visit.'

He refused to dwell on the idea of what a load of Mary Poppin's stockings might look like, as her hand closed around his equipment. That would have to wait.

'Your Member of Parliament is in fine fettle,' she gushed, as the pleasure of her capable hand took its toll.

'Why do you call it my Member of Parliament?' he managed to ask. 'You must have known it was looking for your vote.'

'No, it's because I think most Politicians are pricks,' was her whispered answer.

She knew he was going to crack up after hearing that, so with perfect timing she guided him inside her hot body and laughing became the furthest thing from their minds. This would be the best knee-trembler of all time.

They began pummelling, gyrating and grinding, continuously striving to give maximum pleasure to each other, both feeling the intensity of the inevitable, yet trying to stave it off as long as possible. Kate let out a high pitched screech and dug her long, strong fingernails into Ned's back, but as it happened, he was feeling no pain at that precise moment. They stood as one for another few minutes before slowly collapsing on the bed, then this lady with the unusual political sense of humour whispered.

'You're like the failed Politician, you have just lost your deposit.'

That really cracked him up, so he spent the next few minutes kissing her all over which she really enjoyed, then with a chuckle he said. 'Let's have a look at those sexy stockings you've got on.'

This woman wasn't shy, then she didn't have to be looking as good as she did. Quick visits to the bathroom, something very seductive for her to wear and now forty-five minutes later they were sitting down to wine, dine and have a laugh. It would be logged as the best three quarter hour experience of his life, unless the remainder of the night brought something more exciting, if that was possible. He knew his mum and dad would wonder why he didn't come home, so he decided to ring and tell them he was staying with Mike, that over, he relaxed to enjoy this woman. She told him her life story to date and he listened spellbound, only speaking the odd time to ask her for more details.

Born into a large farming family in the Southeast, just a stones throw from a magnificent beach, she had had a lovely childhood with her brothers and sisters until tragedy struck when she was fourteen, with the death of her beloved dad from Cancer. Her mother and two older brothers tried their best to run the farm, but it was too great a burden, causing them to sell out for what they could get. Sadly it wasn't enough to support them all, so the family had to be broken up, with Kate going to Quincy Massachusetts to her aunt. She had pined for her siblings for years, dreaming that oneday they would all be reunited and walk once more on the white sands of their local beach. Winters were cold outside Boston, but her spinster aunt was a kind lady, making sure her life was as comfortable and fulfilling as could be, while she studied hard to become a hairdresser, a career which she excelled in.

It was shortly after qualifying that she went to one of the biggest hair emporiums in the city for an interview and there she met it's suave, good looking, rich owner by the name of Paul Kelly, who was besotted by her from day one. He had been the dandy of the wealthy set in town for years, but from the minute he set eyes on Kate Molloney he never looked at another woman, that is apart from their hair.

'Tresses' was the name of the salon and as the business grew, his love for Kate Molloney did likewise and then Paul Kelly decided he would branch out and start 'Tresses No.2' with the capable Kate at the helm. It was a huge success also, but it had it's price, because of the long hours the couple were seeing very little of each other and strangely it was effecting her even more than him, proving to Kate what she desperately wanted to know. Ned could see how she was living that time all over again and her lovely face glowed with happiness as the story enfolded, making him wonder how a lady who was once so much in love with one man, could now be seeking the attentions of another.

Back then, this strong, non-drinking six footer became the centre of her world and the big age difference wasn't a problem, but what became their first problem though, was his revelation to her over dinner in a posh restaurant one night, that he hoped to open a chain of 'Tresses' all over Massachusetts. This she knew would be the end of them and she told him so, as it was, they hardly ever saw each other, now if he intended marrying her he would have to 'hold his horses' so to speak. He couldn't handle losing her, so before they left the restaurant, three very big decisions were made. One, the Tresses shops would be sold. Two, when that was done they would get married and Three; they would go back to Ireland and get into a business where they could be together all the time.

Two very positive things came from those decisions. A couple of hours later, they went back to his house where they made love for the first time which was wonderful, then two months later, they were married back in Ireland with their families around them. Because of their wealth, the wedding reception was held in a marquee on her beloved sandy beach beside her old homestead and she got to walk once more on the white sand that she had missed so much. Little did she think the last time she was there, that she would return and be the happiest woman in the whole south east as she walked hand in hand with her lovely husband. Within a year of coming home, a city dance hall came on the market, which they bought, renovated and christened The Diamond Ballroom. They were now in business together as planned, but all was not well.

Paul missed Boston and the life there. He also missed the hairdressing and the compliments for his creativity, plus the chain of 'Tresses' that he had planned. Then real bad news came. He was told he couldn't have children and this was the biggest blow of all. He had wanted children so badly with this lovely young woman and now that was not going to happen, so he turned to the only alternative he could think of. 'Drink.'

Paul hadn't been a boozer in the past, having only shared a good bottle of wine with a meal, or a glass of Sherry at home after a hard day, but now he was different. She often got calls in the middle of the night from some worried Hotelier, to say how drunk he was after a day on the binge and could she come to take him home, as he would be in no state to drive. What she usually did was, phone a taxi and while she waited she would dress in something comfortable because she knew he would be too pissed to notice, then with someone's help, load him into his car and drive him home. Some nights if he was very drunk, she would make sure he was safely belted up and then she would leave him to sleep it off in the garage.

'I blame myself for taking him away from his dream in The States,' she said. 'He gets no kick from running dances no matter how successful, he says any moron could do it.'

The food arrived and they both tucked in, Ned perhaps a little more ravenously than his comrade and naturally the conversation died down. As he munched away an extraordinary thought struck him like a bolt of lightening, causing him to choke on a mouthful.

'Are you alright darling?' She enquired, handing him her topped up wineglass.

'Yes pet,' he answered, realising he had used one of the fond terms he often used to Susan.

They both continued eating, but his mind was busy with the thought, which had made him choke. He had just made mad, passionate, unprotected love to this lady within the last hour and she had just informed him, that the reason she had no children rested with her husband. There was no mention as to whether she could, or could not conceive, but he was now very aware that a fine specimen of womanhood like her, who looked not a day over thirty-five, could have an army of babies. For about ten frivolous seconds, he closed his eyes and all he could see were little tots running around in army uniforms, with diamonds all over them.

'Jaysus,' he groaned silently. 'What happens if I've left a bun in the oven, the husband will know he didn't do it and he'll be asking questions, but maybe there's another side to this scenario. What if it's a set up, where she wants some young man to do the deed so the husband can take the credit and bring up the child as his own.' The tackle had ruled the head again.

She noticed he was preoccupied and asked. 'Hello, I'm over here, a penny for them?'

She took him by surprise, so he blurted out the first thing he could think of, which he knew as he listened should only be for Susan's ears.

'If I was married to a beautiful girl like you, I don't think I'd be going out drinking every night. I'd stay at home and make love all the time.'

'Oh, you're such a nice young man,' she said, in little more than a whisper and as she said it he could feel her sexy stockinged foot, press down on his equipment underneath the table.

'Let's finish now and go back to our room, I want to take you up on your suggestion.' The promise in her voice had him ready to throw caution to the winds once more and he realised he was a lost cause. She signed for the food and wine, plus another bottle for the room and then after giving the waitress a tip she took him by the hand. 'The sky's the limit tonight,' she said, handing him the bedroom key.

They had lunch the following day and he had to go easy on the food because he was taking his parents out later. His mother would have an inquiry if he didn't do justice to the meal and Kate thought this was very sweet, complimenting him for being so good to his parents.

'You're so lucky to have them and them you,' she said sincerely, remembering her own situation.

Later, as he carried her bag to the car, she asked him not to forget Spain. 'It will be like the past twenty-four hours,' she said, 'with sunshine.'

He promised he would try and meet her soon, but as the band was very busy, Spain would probably have to wait until their holidays next May, the first week, preferably.

'That will be fine,' she enthused, 'but lets try and meet here again in the near future.'

'She has it all, yet she has nothing,' he thought, as he drove away. 'If I'm not careful, I'll end up the same way.'

Chapter Fourteen

His parents met him at the door in happy mood and they had a question plus some information for him. It was a two-pronged question, regarding what time and where they were dining, also some man had phoned earlier looking for him.

'I told him you were in the manager's house,' said Mrs. Brady. 'I even thought he sounded like Mike, but he told me he would call back at seven.'

Ned lay on the bed for an hour and caught forty winks, wishing he could just pass out for the night, yet looking forward to treating his parents who were always there for him in the past. At seven on the dot the phone rang, so he grabbed it seconds before his mother, who was still curious as to the identity of the previous caller and rightly so.

'You're a right Bollix,' was Mike's opening statement.

'Why?' he asked.

'I rang and luckily before I got around to dropping you in it, your mother informed me that you were in my house, so I was able to do a U-turn telling her I was from the Record Company, next time you intend to pull that stroke please let me know.'

Ned ignored the complete statement because he knew his mother would be listening, so his answer was. 'Well tell me Frank, where is the record in the chart this week?'

'They're listening to you,' he stated.

Ned waited for an answer to his last question.

'Seeing that you mention it, I've been told it will be number one on Friday and I hope you don't mind my suggesting that it's about time you got a place of your own, so we don't need to have these cryptic calls.'

'Yippee,' Ned shouted, 'that's great and I do agree with your suggestion, it's long overdue.'

They talked away for a while with Mike doing most of the speaking in the form of questions. 'Well how did you and Kate get on?'

'Often,' was the short answer.

'Good, I'll ring about those other dates tomorrow and by the way, don't forget to ring Sandra Boyle, she has played a big part in our impending number one.'

Ned really wished he was living on his own when he heard the direction Mike's conversation was going, but instead of roaring into the phone, he had to make do with a whisper. 'I'm not a fucking gigolo Mike, this is the last fucking time I'm going to do anything like this, just remember.'

'Sorry mate,' said Mike. 'It's a pity they seem to want to charver you and not the Singer, but as you know, his ego gets in the way and pisses them off. But they're two good looking ladies and I wish it was me they wanted to shag.'

Both men brought the call to an end, with Ned almost calling him Mike in front of his parents who were now standing a few feet away checking their watches.

He was thinking it was time for a move, as they headed for the car and in his absent-minded state he almost did it again.

'Mi**, I mean Frank called to tell me, we will be number one at the weekend.'

They were really happy for him and he got a hug from his mother, while his proud relaxed father looked on, then his dad said.

'Do you know, I think all our problems are over, I feel such a weight off my shoulders even though I've got the loose ends to sort out yet, but I'm really looking forward to spending Christmas with your mother and my sisters in Philadelphia.'

During the meal they extracted a promise from him, that even though he would be away a lot, he would look after the house while they were on holiday and he agreed. In it's own way, that chore would put any move on the back burner and he had an exciting thought about the asset of living on his own in the big while house on the hill, even for a while. He would get Susan to spend some time with him in their absence, the only snag being, could Susan and he keep their hands off each other in an unsupervised location like that.

His mother was reading his mind, prompting her to say. 'Seeing we will have met Susan before we go away, you could have her join you over Christmas.'

'Yeah, that reminds me,' he said. 'I hope you have nothing on next Tuesday and Wednesday nights, because I'm bringing Susan to Mullymore. I'm driving to Glenrone after Sunday nights gig, then early on Tuesday morning, we're going to meet the people in the model agency and afterwards we will be heading here, would you believe she's more excited at meeting you both than she is about the modelling thing.'

'Oh, I'm really looking forward to meeting her, aren't you Edmond?' she beamed.

'Indeed we are son, it reminds me of the first time I brought your mother home to meet my folks, I was nervous as could be, but I needn't have worried because they loved her from the minute they saw her, just like we will love your Susan.'

The words 'your Susan' filled him with pride. 'Yeah,' he thought. 'She is my Susan.'

Ned was very tired after his sex session of the previous night, which he blamed on having stayed up talking to Mike until dawn, about the success and the future of The Nova's Showband. What he was really up to the night before would remain a secret, because if his mother found out, he would be banished forever.

'You young fellows have no sense of time,' was his mum's summing up of the situation, as she got into the car. 'You all burn the candle at both ends, never thinking of tomorrow.'

He smiled to himself remembering last night, knowing there wasn't a candle in sight and Kate told him she had made another purchase in London which made candles redundant unless in a black-out, but she wouldn't be introducing it while he was around. When they got home, his mother insisted on coffee and they talked about the auction while they drank it, including how useful John from Philly had been as a sweetener. It was almost impossible to quantify the gains accrued by his intervention. Along with his masterstroke at the end, which netted an extra two thousand pounds while giving the entire family heart failure, there were the other times he had kept the proceedings going when interest waned and all seemed lost.

'Let's have a toast to John,' said Mrs. Brady, raising her coffee cup high.

Mr. Brady laughed as he described his phone call to John, just before he left for the Airport. 'I promised that himself and Sarah won't have to put their hand in their pocket or handbag all over Christmas, which gave him an idea of a possible new profession for them both and he's considering starting (Sweetener's Incorporated) hiring themselves out to the highest bidder, pardon the pun.'

'He'd need to be careful in America,' said Ned. 'Did you see the looks he was getting from Mr. Cosgrave, who ended up paying over the top for the place and that was only Mullymore, you could get shot for gazumping, or whatever it's called in The States.'

'Maybe he's in the Mafia over there, he didn't seem too put out at what he was doing,' said Mrs. Brady. 'All I can say is, Thank God for him and may God forgive me.'

Ned got to bed early that night, but before he went to sleep he did some thinking and decision-making. Now the pub was sold, he could no longer use the address for his mail and that would be a big problem. Until the day came when he got engaged to Susan, he could envisage the possibility of needing an address that was not his home, then like a bolt from the blue came the answer.

'The flat over the pub,' he almost shouted. 'That's the problem solved, after all I was planning to live there with Brenda and if I can rent it from the new landlord (who will need all he can get) then I won't have to change my address at all.'

He wondered what would be the best way to approach the situation. The new owner might be pissed off after paying so much to his father for the pub and may tell him to fuck off, or if he rents it to him, the word would get to his parents the same day, now he couldn't have that happen to spoil their holiday.

Then the second nugget of brilliance hit him. He would get the Roadie to rent it for the moment using his money, he can live there until after Christmas, then tell the landlord he can no longer afford the rent, but he knows somebody who is interested in taking it off his hands.

After hopefully having a good Christmas in the pub, the landlord will go along with the idea, but until then the Roadie can take in his letters. A good night's sleep under his belt (or wherever it goes) he was fit as a fiddle and the thought of a fiddle made him picture his Susan.

'Ah,' his Susan. He loved those words together and he loved the way she held and played the fiddle, not leaving out the fabulous rhythm she could rock up on that big drum kit.

He wondered if they would ever play music together in the future, but one thing he was sure of (God willing) was that they would share many rhythmic days and nights together in each other's arms.

He decided to leave early on Thursday for the gig, so after a late breakfast he said goodbye to his parents and headed off. He would not see them again until the following Tuesday evening, when he would be taking Susan home to meet them and he was really looking forward to that. The weekend gigs produced nothing new, apart from the fact that all were good and there was a great interest shown in their first number one record. It was played on the chart programme on national radio and was listed in bold black capitals, in the official music mag, 'Dance Time.' Of course the same magazine carried a large article on The Nova's Showband, penned by guess-who? Sandra Boyle of course and the main thrust of the story was an in-depth interview with one Ned Brady, the talented bandleader of this very successful bunch. He couldn't remember saying any of it to her and she came dangerously close to telling the fans what he had for breakfast, especially on the morning she had cooked it for him. Perhaps he talked in his sleep while she jumped nude behind her typewriter and banged away, but the only banging away she did while he was there, was in bed.

Thank God Mike had sent her the official press release, which covered the Singer and the other band members in depth, or he would have had a mutiny on his hands. He couldn't help wondering what Susan would think if she read it, but she knew the score about all that stuff being hype, nevertheless, the description of him and his habits was very graphic indeed.

Mike had booked them into some nice Hotels and they all enjoyed the fruits of their hard work, even the Roadie was going around full of his own importance as happy as a pig in shit. Ned used up every spare moment writing to his harem, whose names and addresses he had been collecting for years. Some of these girls he had only ever spoken to, but he felt now was the time to make contact, informing them of the bands current success and hopefully keep them on board as fans. The Manager had asked all the members to get their pens out, but he had a feeling the other members of the orchestra weren't pushed and he felt a bit of a Judas each evening as he hunted for a phone to ring his love. Then after speaking to her and hearing her words of affection, he felt like going back into his room to tear up all the letters, but on each occasion he talked himself out of going down that road.

'Some of them won't even reply,' he told himself, 'but I've got to contact Brenda in New York, Mary in San Francisco and Jayne in Buffalo to plan my holiday in May, or the whole thing will be a mess.' Of course he never gave a thought to the fact, that contacting and going to see them could cause it's own mess.

Jayne told Amanda, the Roadie's girlfriend in Buffalo, that she would reply if Ned wrote to her first, otherwise forget it and he was glad of this reprieve because he knew she was a very special girl. This relationship (if you could call it that) had to be taken one step further at least. He could still remember her singing and those legs, Jaysus; even Susan would be up against it in that department.

All members of the orchestra and management stayed on the Sunday night also, but he was the only one in the dining room for the scrumptious full breakfast, which was served by some brand new fans of the band.

'You were great last night, fabulous, fantastic and how do you stick it, all the travelling and I suppose you're off to play again tonight?'

Each one had a different comment, but it was still great to hear their interest, even at this early hour and it put him in good form for the journey to Glenrone. He was supposed to drive there after the dance but he knew he would be tired, so he asked Susan to tell her aunt that he would not be there until Monday evening. He had another good reason for staying over though. Ned didn't want to post a big bundle of letters in Glenrone Post Office, because the Postmistress is a friend of Mrs. North from the guesthouse, so she might even memorise the names and addresses on his mail. That's why he decided to send the lot before taking to the road at all, because no chances would be taken and around four he arrived at the guesthouse to be greeted by the lovely North twins who plied him with tea and cake.

'It wouldn't have to be too dark to mistake either one for Susan, but bad thoughts not allowed,' he was thinking as he got into the shower. 'They'll make a couple of lucky guys happy.'

He sat in the sitting room glancing at the paper, but paying more attention to the door of Susan's office that he could see clearly and his pulse raced when it swung open. She was dressed in black today and looking better than ever if that was possible, with her long, wavy black hair swinging every time she tossed her head.

'God give me strength,' he said, as he rushed out the door.

It was like another scene from Gone with the wind, when they came face to face. Arms outstretched they ran to each other, then he picked her up and swung her around while they kissed passionately. Words weren't needed. Every motorist passing by honked and each pedestrian made some comment to this popular young lawyer, who lately, was regularly seen kissing and being kissed in public by this young man from the music business. All the nice people in the area understood, knowing that they lived so far apart and his job made it difficult to see her often, so they took every opportunity to show their affection to each other. But there were the few nasty begrudges who went around saying bad things about them also. The happy couple didn't care though, life was too short and they intended to enjoy every minute together.

'I've been instructed to invite you home tonight, mum is cooking and dad and Mary are away, so there will only be the three of us for dinner, anyway I want your opinion on what I'm planning to wear tomorrow, is that OK?'

'That's more than OK love, I'm looking forward to seeing your lovely mother again and sampling her cuisine, lets go.' While he spoke he guided her towards the car and carefully held her hand as she climbed in gracefully.

She saw him looking at her trouser covered legs and said. 'Sorry, no legs flashing this evening, but that will be taken care of later when I'm fitting on my outfits for tomorrow, 'the sky' darling, will be the limit.'

He could feel himself blushing when he heard her say that, but he hoped she wouldn't notice, because Kate Kelly had said that to him just a week ago when she handed him the room key in the guesthouse and he wondered for a moment if Susan had the same intentions. His thoughts ran riot. A visit to the Prunty home was always pleasant, so after a lovely meal they sat down for a chat to catch up on all the news and gossip, then a little while later, Mrs. Prunty decided to retire for the night.

'I want to let you two love birds have some premium time together and there's no need to rush away son, you're both off tomorrow so relax,' as she spoke she kissed them both on the cheek and went upstairs.

Did you hear that?' Susan asked laughing. 'She called you son, you've really got your feet under the table now.'

'Yeah, that was nice, but what do you think are my chances of getting my shoes under your bed?' he enquired.

'Would you like to start tonight?' she asked and there was seriousness in her tone.

'We'd better sit on opposite sides of the table for a while until this urge passes, my resistance is at an all time low.' As he said that, they both got up from the settee and walked silently back to the dining room, where they sat holding hands across the large table.

'When we get married we won't have a dining table at all, then we'll have to make love every time we feel like it,' she said and as that piece of wisdom left her lovely mouth, she kissed both his hands which she was holding firmly.

They sat looking at each other for ages before he asked. 'So where is this fashion show tonight? You're supposed to do your thing for this one man audience and I can't wait any longer.'

'Sorry darling, that's on the way, but I think I'd better change in my bedroom while you only come to the bottom of the stairs, that way you'll get the fully dressed eyeful and a little bit of leg, if you come to my room we're doomed.' With that she jumped up and headed upstairs. 'I'll shout when I'm ready,' she promised and about twenty minutes went by until he heard. 'Hi honey, I'm all set.'

He couldn't have been in a better position than at the bottom of the stairs, as this wonderful creature came closer one step at a time, just like a professional model. She was wearing a wine coloured coatdress with a very high slit and he was lost for words when she stopped about five steps away to ask mischievously.

'Well, do I get the order?'

'If you come any closer you'll get more than an order,' he joked, 'but there's another side to the beautiful vision I'm witnessing at this moment. You look so perfect, it would be a travesty to remove anything, so come down the last five steps, let me kiss you on the cheek and then you can model for me at ground level.'

She took him at his word immediately and with outstretched hand she continued her decent. He kissed her as suggested, then gracefully she walked the full length of the hallway, did a lavish pirouette before returning and all he could manage was.

'That was nice.'

'Thank you kind sir,' she answered and side-stepping him, she began climbing the stairs once more.

'Just one question,' he asked, 'are you wearing stockings or tights? The slit doesn't go up far enough I'm sorry to say.'

She stopped, turned a little and smiled back down at him as she said. 'Before I fit on my last outfit I'll give you a little preview,' then she strode back to her bedroom.

Ned waited with bated breath for her next move, leisurely, a dark stockinged leg appeared from within, slowly joined by a heavenly image decked in beautiful black matching lingerie, then for what seemed like only seconds she walked out on the landing and back in again. He started singing, 'Here's to you Mrs. Robinson' and she laughed out loud.

Then sticking her pretty head out of the room she whispered. 'We'd better be quiet or we'll wake mum.'

It was about ten minutes until he saw her again and during that time he stayed rooted to the spot, then he gasped. 'Jaysus, that's gorgeous.'

She had stepped back on to the landing in a black evening dress, which went all the way from her smooth white throat to ground level and all he could see was the toe of a very expensive shoe, peeping from beneath the hem. The long sleeved dress was made entirely from velvet, with little black crochet gloves completing the ensemble.

He remained totally silent and she asked.

'Well, what do you think?'

'Will you marry me?' was his reply.

'You know I will,' she said, laughing out loud, 'but first things first, what do you think?'

'I think you'll be putting the Law career on hold when they see you in that,' he answered. 'I've never seen anything as nice before, honestly, where did you get a creation like that from?'

'Well, we've got a very famous ladies outfitter here in Glenrone and women come from all over to buy their fashions. Mary and I do a little bit of modelling for them at their shows, so they give us good deals on special garments like this one,' she said.

'Well that explains the never ending selection of fine clobber I've seen you in and Mary looks direct from Vogue every time I see her.' Was his heart-felt compliment?

'I must tell her that tomorrow,' she laughed.

Without asking, she went through the same ritual as before much to his pleasure. Step by step she sauntered down the long white stairs, then at the last moment he stood back giving her access to the hallway, she walked slowly to the end once more, turned and eased her way back.

'Samantha at the agency suggested you would be a natural,' he said, as he boldly made his cheek available for a soft wet kiss.

She went back up the stairs and turned her head to glance at him from the top step, then blew him a kiss before disappearing into her room. He wondered what she would have on when next he saw her and he wasn't disappointed, as she appeared in a black wrap-around skirt which didn't seem to have any visible buttons or pins for fastening purposes, a floppy grey sweater, with her now bare feet tucked into a pair of wine coloured shoes.

'I need two things now,' she stated. 'Some strong coffee and a good court.'

'I'm your man on both counts, you take it easy for a while and I'll organise the coffee, together we'll see to the latter,' he said, as he ushered her into the living room.

During the cuppa they talked about their impending trip, but for the next hour hardly a word was spoken, apart from her early confirmation that there was nothing holding the skirt together other than the belt. There were many sounds of pleasure though, and it was a very happy, yet reluctant Ned, who kissed his lady goodnight before driving his big car down The Fiddler's Lane to his second choice of a bed for the night.

'It's getting harder,' he said to her as they were cuddling earlier.

'Yes I know, I can feel it,' had been her giggling reply.'

'Oh I don't mean that, it's getting harder to leave you and drive to the guesthouse, you know what I mean,' was his almost shy answer.

Tonight he had been so close to throwing caution to the wind, but it had been his girlfriend who adhered to the parameters set by them both, while she lovingly talked him around and sleep seemed miles away as he lay totally nude in the comfortable bed. Was it the excitement of the last hours, or the anticipation of the following day that was keeping him awake? He wasn't sure, but as he lay there his mind drifted back to the Seminary and the banal quickie sessions he used to have with kitchen staff. Then the leering face of Fr. Ron flashed past much to his horror and he couldn't help wondering, if that sad individual was still groping young lad's bottoms.

'Thank God I got out of that situation,' he mused.

Just before he drifted off, he flashed back to his lovely cousin Emily Shearer who should not have been his cousin and as he wondered how she was keeping these days he realised, if they had not been related he might never have met Susan. The last vision he had was that of the flame haired Madge Gilpin and the few lustful sessions they had had by the lake, with the doe eyed cows peacefully chewing their cud as they watched. His skin crawled for a second; remembering the sound he awoke to one morning as the cow licked the side of the car, just imagine what it would have sounded like if they had all joined in. The breakfast was good and while he enjoyed some strong coffee, he had a quick read of the daily paper that Mrs. North had given him.

'I'll bet she's excited about today,' she said.

'Yeah, I think she'll be a big hit,' he answered. 'I saw some of the outfits she's bringing and they are beautiful, but of course they will want her to wear some of their own creations as well.'

'Don't forget to call on your way, I want to wish her every success,' said her proud aunt.

'Not to worry,' he replied, 'we'll see you within the hour.'

There was a nip in the air as he drove up to Susan's house, so he wasn't surprised when she greeted him wearing a heavy knit turtle neck sweater, elegant black trousers with matching boots and she had a Sherlock Holmes type cape over one arm.

'Whatever you wear you're pure sex on legs,' he said with a grin, 'maybe we should run upstairs and have a little session?'

'Not now Ned, we don't have the time,' she said, in her best bossy fashion, 'but if we had, I'd like to walk upstairs and have a big session instead.' Then she stood to one side and beckoned to the two suit covers hanging in the hallway saying. 'Use up your energy putting those in the car for me honey, you'll have to wait until tonight for your reward if that's alright.'

'Just remember where were going to be tonight and tomorrow night,' he said. 'We've got to create a good impression in front of my parents, don't forget.'

One of the many marvellous things about Ned and Susan was, their effortless ability to make conversation and after their short visit to Mrs. North for her blessing, they hardly shut up until they arrived in the city. Finding a parking space close to the Agency, Ned took the clothes and bags from the car, handing the smaller one to Susan.

'Today I'll be your roadie,' he quipped, 'anyway, I've been practising for years to be a gentleman, how am I doing?'

'Wonderful,' she replied. 'Come on you messer, let's get this show on the road.'

They were laughing as usual as they walked in the Agency door and Samantha greeted them with big hugs, then holding Susan at arms length she said.

'There's no need to ask who this is, you're even more beautiful in the flesh than you are in your pictures and that's coming from someone in the beauty business, is it any wonder he had no interest in any of us at the launch.' The last bit she said while looking at a blushing Ned.

'He told me, I came close to losing him that night.' Susan bantered, while our hero was lost for words.

They exchanged some more small talk and then Samantha said. 'Come in the back and meet the other girls, plus all the others who will be helping with the show.'

She ushered them through to a big warehouse, which doubled as a viewing area, with a big ramp stretching three quarter length of the room and as they walked in all the girls rushed over to greet Susan. Within minutes she felt totally at home. Rehearsals were in full swing and Ned was banished from backstage, but he was advised to pick the best seat in the house almost at the end of the ramp, there to feast his eyes on the style and glamour.

Girl number one flounced down the catwalk and he began at once giving marks from one to ten. This was a good-looking woman and she got an eight, hot on her heels came girl number two getting a six. Next lady caused him to take a quick deep breath and as a smiling Samantha eased her way towards him wearing a killer outfit, he could be heard saying as he exhaled. 'Ten, definitely a ten.' Then a rush of excitement shot through him as he saw walking towards him, the love of his life wearing an incredible gown, sequins flashing with every leisurely step she took and if anyone had been sitting close, they would have heard him say. 'JAYSUS, TWELVE.' She flashed him a nervous smile and just before she spun around like a real professional, he gave her the thumbs up accompanied by a big grin that said it all and then she made her way back up the ramp to vanish through the drapes.

'So far so good,' he said to himself, as he realised he was anxiously living every moment with Susan.

It was an experience he would never forget and being the complete audience was a once in a lifetime opportunity to partake in his favourite pastime of, watching girls go by. During the rehearsal, Susan modelled both outfits belonging to the Glenrone outfitter and she would stun the audience later by repeating the performance. The other models couldn't say enough nice things about her and some of them extolled her virtues later to a very proud Ned, who enjoyed every word. The fashion retailer in Susan's home town, was giving the two creations to her in exchange for the promotion they would get on the evening, while in turn, the fee promised by Samantha was waived and going to a deserving charity instead.

There was only half an hour between the dry run and the start of the show, so during that time they had a quick sandwich and some hot tea in a Café a few doors away. When they were leaving the venue, a large queue of sophisticated looking women was forming outside and as they passed through the entrance, they were donating different amounts of money that would also go to the same charity as Susan's fee.

He decided to have some fun to take her mind off what lay ahead, so he asked. 'Do you think I could stand in at the back during the show. I'm going to stick out like a sore thumb sitting among all those ladies.'

'Ned Brady, you're a fierce chancer,' she said. 'You just want to stay around the back to see all the semi naked girls, well I won't hear of it.'

'I'm only kidding,' he said. 'I just wanted to relax you, anyway, I've already been in a situation like that at the Airport.'

She gave him a playful thump and asked. 'Come on, you may as well tell me now that you have started?'

'Well, it's a long story but I'll tell you the edited version. Some time back I really fancied this lovely Air Hostess, who used to be at the dances minus her regular man, so after each gig I would talk to her and I became quite smitten to say the least.'

'Go on,' she urged.

'One night we were playing in the city and this 'Omie'/ hanger-on, asked if he could travel with me, so I foolishly said OK and we headed off. But during the dance I saw the same gorgeous girl there and this time she was showing a little bit of interest in me, so down I go again to talk and believe it or not, she's prepared to let me drive her home, but when I mentioned the gooseberry, she said no way.'

Susan just waited, eyes wide.

'I tried to get rid of my passenger by asking other members of the band to take him home but no luck, so she compromised by telling me that I could meet her at her flat the next day and drive her to the Airport for her wages, plus a fit-on for a new uniform. Very few words were spoken to my passenger on the way home that night and after a few hours sleep, I headed back to the city, but traffic was bad and I was late, so when I got to her flat a note on her door said. After being so keen I'm surprised, but if you want to follow me do so and you can drive me home.'

'Well did you?' she enquired.

'Yes, I sure did. I went to the Airport and asked everywhere, then I met someone who directed me to the building where my newest fantasy was having her fitting, so I just turned the door handle and walked in. It was like something out of Playboy magazine, partially clad girls everywhere trying to cover up, then my friend who was blushing profusely told me to wait outside.'

'That was the end of you, wasn't it?' Susan stated with conviction.

'No, we drove to a restaurant where we both had a good laugh at what happened and it was there I got the bad news.'

'Go on, go on, go on,' she begged.

'This lovely woman told me, that she had just broken up with a young Lawyer who she still loved, because she had found a French Letter in his pocket and as they were not having sex, she had asked for an explanation which hadn't come up to scratch, so she dumped him for a while, but couldn't get him out of her mind.'

'That's true love for you.' Susan said wistfully. 'What happened then?'

'She told me if they didn't get back together she would take up my offer, but a couple of weeks later, I got a call saying they had sorted out their problems and were getting married.'

'Poor Ned,' said Susan. 'Were you broken hearted?'

'I was a bit disappointed all right, but also happy for her, she was so nice with her long jet-black hair up in a bun, looking real Spanish only taller,' he said.

'Heaven's,' she said, 'we should make a move, that lovely story has calmed all my nerves, I love you Ned Brady and I'm glad she married the other fellow.'

'I love you Susan Prunty, come on and knock em dead.'

And knock them dead she did, the offers poured in but she told Samantha she could only do the odd show in the New Year, as for the moment her priorities lay elsewhere. He phoned his mother to say they wouldn't make it until around nine and there was great excitement in the big White House at the top of the hill.

'Drive slowly,' his mum advised. 'Get here safely, that's all that matters.'

Susan jammed the cushion it between the front seats again, then moved over and almost as one; they made the journey to Mullymore without incident. She asked one question which made him laugh out loud.

'Tell me honey, what's an Omie?'

'It's a word for someone who can be a nuisance, but doesn't have the cop-on to notice.' Ned replied, as he placed his hand on her stocking clad knee. 'God is really good,' he thought.

When the big car drew to a halt outside his home, he was glad to see his smiling parents walk hand in hand into the glow of the powerful outside light.

'I hope they like me,' was Susan's apprehensive comment, as Ned's mum opened the passenger door and waited with outstretched arms to hug this welcome visitor.

Edmond Brady stood back, as he had done so often before during his happy life with his wife and waited for the initial hugs to end. Then he stepped forward and took this apparition in his strong arms, savouring the memories of the times he hugged his partner who (in her prime) had all the attributes of this young woman.

'You're welcome to Mullymore and our home,' he boomed, allowing his wife back into a multiple hug, then grinning at Susan and Ned he asked a question. 'Tell me love, how did my son talk you into this?'

'It was effortless,' she replied. 'If he hadn't asked me, I would have asked him.'

Edmond looked proudly at his son saying. 'A chip off the old block, without a doubt.'

By now, Ned had come around the car and was taking part in the hugging, then four very happy people entered the big White House overlooking Mullymore, to partake in the scrumptious meal which was ready for serving. They talked and drank tea into the wee small hours and Susan giggled at the way an adoring mum called her boy, Edward.

'I'm going to call him that all the time now Mary,' she said, 'especially in company.'

Edward was wondering what his love would think, if and when his nickname of Ned the Bed first reached her ears. 'Questions will be asked,' he was thinking, as his parents excused themselves and after some more hugging they headed up the stairs to bed, no doubt to speak about their daughter-in-law to be.

'Do you think they liked me?' Susan asked.

'I'm not the only one with my feet firmly under someone else's table,' he jibed. 'You're a fixture here from now on.'

As he said that, Susan got up from the armchair she had been sitting in so primly for so long and she launched herself with wild abandon on top of the man she loved. If Edmond or Mary Brady had decided to come back down to the living room, a very different scenario would have met their eyes. This calm demure girl who had won their hearts, had now become this lusty lady who was devouring their son, much to his pleasure and in between moans she was giving him instructions like. 'Kiss me everywhere,' a command which he rose to immediately. A good hour passed in every sense of the word, before another word was spoken.

'I needed that,' she whispered, 'all the pent up emotions of the day were taking their toll.'

'Both of us needed it,' he answered. 'I love you and I hope to be around to relieve all your pent up emotions in the future. By the way, I loved your initiation, it was very exciting.'

'Thank you Edward,' she chuckled, 'and I love you too.'

Instead of chastising her for calling him Edward, he tightened his grip on her waist while giving her a big long wet kiss. Luckily they awoke before his parents, because this beautiful woman still in his arms was almost naked and boy did she look good. Now he picked her up gently and quietly carried her upstairs to her room.

'Sleep well and I'll see you later today for lunch, goodnight darling, or is it good morning I should be saying instead.'

She bade him farewell instead to cover both possibilities, then a few moments later a very weary but happy Ned climbed into bed, just inches away from this wonderful woman and his last coherent thought was. 'Some day or night in the near future, there won't be a wall keeping us apart.'

It was noon before he stirred and though only half awake he realised he was smiling. 'I'm happy, I'm happy,' he began to croon, then realising why he was happy, he sat bolt upright in the bed rubbing his eyes, wondering where the object of his euphoria was at that precise moment. Gingerly he went, tap, tap, tap on the wall, but there was no answer, then he decided to get a little bolder adding a bit of volume and a touch of rhythm to the knocking, but to his disappointment there was no reply, so with his pyjamas well buttoned he stepped out on to the landing.

The first sound he heard was like music to his ears. Susan was laughing loudly along with his mum and he could hear his dad's big voice kindling the mirth with another joke. 'And did you ever hear this one?' his father was asking his audience, as Ned opened the dining room door.

When Susan saw him in his night attire she laughed even louder. She had never seen his pyjamas with the big white flowers before, mainly because the only time she had seen him in bed he had been in the nip, so jumping up she ran to him and throwing her arms around his neck she shouted loudly.

'Poor Ned, you look like you need watering, those flowers are on their last legs.'

He threw his arms around this immaculately dressed and groomed young woman squashing her to him and then he said. 'You'd think you'd put on something nice to greet me, wouldn't you.'

'Sorry honey,' she sounded almost apologetic. 'I couldn't find a thing to wear so this will have to do, we're having great fun listening to your dad's jokes and isn't he some turn.' They held on to each other, while Mrs. Brady poured a big mug of tea for her only child.

'I don't blame you for holding on to her,' said his dad. 'Don't ever let her go son, she's beautiful.'

With a happy tear in her eye, Susan wriggled free of Ned's grip and walked over to his father. She put her arms around his neck as he sat at the end of the table and gave him a big kiss on the forehead, before holding out her hand to her future mother-in-law to join them.

'I'm looking forward to being a full-time member of this family,' she said tearfully.

As Ned drank his tea, he viewed the happy scene. 'I think I'd better change a few plans,' he was thinking. 'I'll have to stay away from Sandra Boyle from now on, no matter what promotion Mike wants and those plans for the holidays next May, looks like they have gone up in smoke also.' As his thoughts tailed off the phone rang and luckily he picked it up, because he heard a lush woman's voice saying.

'Hello sexy, do you want the good news, or the good news first?'

'Seeing that both types are good, give me the best first,' he suggested and he was glad there was a bit of distance between the hallway and the dining room, when Sandra Boyle said.

'I've been thinking about you all morning and how badly I want to screw you.'

'And the other piece if news is?' he prompted.

'So you can't talk then?' came the answer or was it a question.

'The nail has been well and truly hit on the head,' he replied.

'Well, the other piece of news is,' she said. 'Frank asked me to tell you, that your record will be number one again at the weekend, so how about that?'

His answer came in the shape of a rebel yell, which brought an interest from his family who wanted to know the cause of the outburst.

'What's the problem honey?' Susan shouted.

'Oh, there's no problem at all, our single will still be at number one this weekend, I've just got the word.'

As she realised the significance of the news Susan became jet propelled, taking off in Ned's direction with arms outstretched and throwing caution to the wind she leaped up on her man, her legs around his waist her arms around his neck.

'Oh, congratulations darling,' she screeched joyously, I'm so happy for you, let me kiss you.' She had no need to ask because at that precise moment she was showering him with kisses anyway, then remembering the phone; she gingerly climbed down from her perch and reversed in the direction of the dining room.

'Sorry honey,' she said shyly. 'I forgot you were on a call.'

'Not to worry,' he answered. 'I'll be in, in a minute, tell the folks please.'

As she disappeared into the dining room, Ned put the phone back to his ear and he knew he would be on autopilot for the remainder of this conversation, but he never expected her first comment after telling her he was back.

'She's beautiful,' she said.

'What do you mean and how would you know?' Came his double-barrelled question.

'You were speaking to nobody yesterday at the fashion show, I was sitting a couple of feet behind you but you couldn't take your eyes off the ramp and I don't blame you because as I said, she is beautiful.' Sandra Boyle waited for his answer, which was slow in coming so she asked. 'Are you there or has the cat got your tongue?'

'I'm here alright,' he assured her. 'What the fuck were you doing there?'

'Now now,' she was enjoying this. 'I was covering the show for Samantha who is a friend of mine, she also thinks Susan is wonderful and absolutely gorgeous.'

'Oh thanks,' said a quite shocked Ned, but the best was yet to come.

'I hope you don't mind,' she continued, 'but I can't get over her loveliness, when I went to bed last night all I could see for hours was her beautiful face, floating just above the bed and each time I reached out for her she floated further away. Then I decided if you were in the bed with me she would have joined us, that would have been heaven wouldn't it darling?'

There was another long pause, while he tried to work out if maybe she was taking the piss, or could she be serious? 'I hope you're pulling my leg,' he suggested.

'If you were closer it wouldn't be your leg I'd be pulling, but no, I'm serious. I think I'm in love with her, anyway, after the way men have treated me over the years, could you blame me for fantasising about a beautiful young woman like Susan.'

He could feel anger and revulsion building up in him and he wished he were somewhere where he could roar down the phone at her.

'I want you to put that idea out of your head at once, do you hear me?' He warned.

'But Ned darling, it was you who suggested having a threesome, or as you said, a menage-a-trois with some other young lady and myself and in my book, who better than the lovely Susan.'

He could sense a bit of tease in her voice and there was also a serious tinge as well, but without admitting it he did remember saying that to her during a weak moment.

'Look Sandra, I can't stay on the phone any longer, we'll sort this out some other time and thanks for the news on the record.'

He raised his voice on the last line for the benefit of anyone listening, but he was shaking, as he joined the others who had poured drinks to toast his success. Susan slipped her arm around her man as they raised their glasses and she proposed the toast.

'To Ned and The Nova's Showband, wishing them many more number one's, heavens honey, you're shaking with excitement, now I know how seriously you take your music, I love you.'

He felt a real heel when he heard her say how much she loved him, so to try and make amends, he proposed a toast to the people he loved most.

'To my mum and dad who have gone that extra mile for me, wishing them Gods speed and happiness on their fast approaching holiday. Now for my second toast and I know my parents will join me, when I welcome the girl I love into the rest of our lives, here's to my darling Susan.' As he ended the announcement, he stood back from her raising his glass and suddenly all four began to cry loudly leading to another immediate huddle.

'Sorry for crying,' he began, 'but I'm so happy, it seemed the right thing to do.'

'I'm glad you did,' said Susan, giving him a kiss on the cheek. 'It's natural to cry when you're happy and it shows your gentle side.'

'I must ring the lads in the band and give them the good news,' he announced. 'They'll be over the moon especially Steve, I hope his ego can handle it.'

'Don't be talking about the man behind his back,' warned Mrs. Brady. 'By the way Susan, you should ring home and let your parents know that you're alright.'

'Oh thank you, I will when he's finished with the good tidings, meanwhile, allow me to help you with the washing up.'

The band members were euphoric when they heard the news and the Singer shocked him by saying. 'I'll get all the lads to meet in The Central Bar in an hour, the drinks are on me and bring Susan.'

Ned's parents declined the invitation, but Susan was really excited about going to the local with her beau and even suggested changing her outfit for the visit. The other occupants of the room wouldn't hear of it, telling the young woman that you can't improve on perfection, which caused her to blush and change her mind instead. One hour later the complete band plus girlfriends, converged on the pub, even

Cynthia Rose was there with a beaming Conn, not forgetting an ecstatic Roadie who had a girl on his arm also. It was the first time Ned had seen her and probably the last.

'There's going to be some serious drinking done here this evening,' shouted Mickey Joe. 'Especially when Steve is buying,' and he was about to include his new word when one of the lads covered up his mouth, advising him that now was not the time.

'Sorry to put a damper on things,' said Ned, 'but don't forget we're gigging a hundred and twenty miles away tomorrow night, so don't overdo it, alright.'

The other girls were a bit shy with Susan at the start, but soon realised that she wasn't stuck up or snooty, so soon they were asking her all about the fashion show and what it was like to be studying Law.

'The fashion show was a hoot but the study takes up most of my time, so I hope it'll be worth it,' she said, then turning to Cynthia Rose she asked. 'What is it like to be the Lead Singer in a band?'

Cynthia Rose blushed a little because she had never been asked this question outside a dancehall before, but she regained her composure quickly and set about giving her slant on it.

'I'm afraid it's something I haven't given much thought to and seeing I'm in a fairly low profile band, nobody gets any more attention than the other. Maybe if we had a hit record like the lads it would be different, I wish.' She sounded wistful, which brought her up in Susan's estimation, no way boastful.

At that precise moment, unknown to the two ladies, Cynthia Rose had become the topic of conversation amongst some of the other band personnel, who were a little too loudly trying to ascertain whether she was pregnant or not. The Piano man, otherwise known as Mr. Ivory, was trying to stir it after a few drinks, by suggesting there was a rumour going around about her being with child and her boyfriend Conn isn't too happy, because he says he's not to blame.

Then John the Bass player put his two size nines in it by asking.

'Who babafied her so?' Which made everyone conclude that he too, was trying to launch a new word on his unsuspecting mates.

'Well it wasn't fuckin' me,' roared Mickey Joe, this time using all of his big gob and Conn, who had been 'earwigging' all the time got involved.

Luckily Ned was close at hand and intervened, bringing to an end what could have been the end of the band in their hometown.

'For fuck sake lads,' he said. 'Have some cop on, this is supposed to be a celebration not a war and anyway try to remember where we are, the locals would lap up a good break up, now that were doing so well.'

The warring band members looked furtively around the bar and sure enough they had an audience, so for commercial reasons only, calm took over. Susan was having her problems also, while talking to Cynthia Rose a partially drunk male swaggered over and began chatting her up. When she pointed to Ned, telling the man that he was her boyfriend, the guy said he wouldn't mind playing second fiddle.

'Listen,' bellowed Cynthia Rose, giving him a powerful shove. 'Play second fiddle would you, you're not even in the orchestra, Gobshite!'

Ned had noticed the incident and came over to check. 'Are you OK ladies?' he asked.

'Of course we are honey, this lady takes no prisoners, but if you don't mind I'd like to go back to the house. I'm going to invite your folks out for a meal so we'd need to go now before your mum starts making our tea.'

With that comment, Susan bade farewell to the Singer, promising to hear her band soon and after all the good-byes, the happy couple headed home.

Chapter Fifteen

Ned's parents were thrilled with the invitation to dine out, especially when the invite came from their most favourite girl in the world, their future daughter-in-law. A quick phone call to the venue they had enjoyed so much the night before and in a little while they were on their way. As the meal progressed, Susan ordered a second bottle of wine because there were numerous toasts to be made, in particular one for Edmond and Mary's trip to Philadelphia, which would take in Christmas and possibly the most of January, all going well. Edmond's sisters intended to drive the visitors around all the other relations, most of whom they had never met and everyone was really looking forward to this happening.

'I hope you will visit Edward while we are away Susan, that way he won't miss me at all.' It was Mary's way of spoiling her son even though she wouldn't be around to do it and she obviously trusted her future daughter-in-law implicitly.

'I'll spend time with him as often as I can and give him all T.L.C. he's used to,' Susan promised, realising that her innocent mother-in-law to be, hadn't given a moments thought to what they might get up to while she was away.

Later, after all the goodnight hugs, the young couple walked hand in hand into the sitting room and in the soft light they kissed gently yet passionately, listening to the strains of Mary's favourite classical record.

'Would you like to dance young lady?' he asked.

'Yes thank you, kind Sir,' she replied. 'With this nice music we don't have to worry about staying in tempo.'

As they danced and kissed, the rhythm of their hearts was sometimes louder than the music, while their hands perused each others bodies delving gently yet deeply, familiarising each other with their most intimate possessions, it was the enactment of a love that should last forever. Fleetingly, his thoughts raced back to a similar feeling of ecstasy with Brenda in New York and he realised that this was even better, without going all the way. The music stopped but no one noticed and as they pleasured each other, time stood still.

Mrs. Brady had promised everyone lunch, but when there was no sign of the young folk at noon, Mary said to Edmond.

'Would you go up and call them darling and if they happen to be in the same room, make no comment, please.'

'Don't worry, I'll be discreet,' he replied. As he headed up the stairs, he was glad to see the happy couple arm in arm descending leisurely towards him.

'Sorry dad,' they both chorused and he was thrilled to hear this beautiful young woman (who was to become the daughter he had often wished for) calling him dad.

'Grubs up you two and did you both sleep well? As for myself, I never heard a sound from my head hit the pillow thank god.'

The food was great and the coffee was endless, so it was a very happy, well looked after couple that hit the road for Glenrone a number of hours later, after they had all wished each other well until they should meet again. Before she left, Susan had extracted a promise from her future in-laws, that they would visit the Prunty family early in the New Year and she repeated her promise to look after Ned while they were away.

'No better woman,' was Ned's comment.

He knew he wouldn't have much time to spare at Susan's house, as he would need to keep on the move to get to the gig on time, but maybe it was just as well because his very excited girlfriend had loads to tell her family and she wouldn't want him there butting in. He carried her heavy belongings into the house, had a quick cup of tea, talked about the weather, kissed his love and headed back out the Fiddler's Lane. Ned would have to get as much sleep as possible between now and Monday, since he had to drive home after Sundays gig to take his parents to the Airport and later he would be meeting Frank and Mike for the trip to hear Susan's family, who were putting on a special performance for the trio's benefit, which in the long run might land them a recording contract.

He began thinking about the possible content of a bundle of letters, which the Roadie had informed him were nestling in a rubber band in the flat above the pub. The said band employee had acquired the place recently, having struck a great deal with the new owner who seemed thrilled to off-load it. The Roadie would bring all the dispatches to tonight's gig and a guilty Bandleader intended to sift through their substance, during the weekend. He was swamped with doubt, as he drove up to the Dance Hall door, but he soon put his domestic worries aside when he saw a very nervous Steve Byrne, Lead Singer, standing there waiting for him. Their Front man got into the passenger seat and Ned asked him.

'What's up Sham?' 'You look very troubled.'

'Oh I'm troubled alright, I got a very strange phone call last night from the City Band Management Agency, asking me to leave The Nova's and join their organisation. Money would be no object, especially if I took some of the lads with me,' he kept looking out the windscreen as he spoke.

'Well, what did you tell them?' Ned asked.

'At first I thought someone was pulling my leg, but he started mentioning other acts they manage and hitting me with big money, then I realised it was for real. I gave him no satisfaction which pissed him off, but he took it badly when I reminded him that we were at number one for the second week, he in turn pissed me off when he said that was only (a flash in the pan).' The Singer was calming down as he spoke and now he was looking at Ned, which helped.

'What was your answer to that?' He inquired.

'I just told him to fuck off, which made him lose the head, causing him to tell me he would get me sacked and I would never work again, then he hung up.'

'Jaysus, he's some wanker,' said our hero. 'Do the band members know about this?'

'No,' the Singer replied.

'OK,' continued the Bandleader, 'let's find Mike and tell him, but we'll keep it under wraps for now, least said easy mended.'

Mike was on the phone in the Hotel reception as the two men walked in, so covering the mouthpiece he shouted over. 'I'll join you both in the bar, mine's a pint.'

Ned thanked Steve for telling him about the offer, while they picked a table by a window with only three chairs. 'We don't want any 'Omies' joining us,' he said.

Then the Singer spoke up again. 'I would have phoned you last night, but I knew it would spoil your evening with Susan and your folks. I was on fire to get it off my chest but I wanted to wait till I met you, because it was you who gave me the job and the break in the beginning.'

Ned was saying how he appreciated that, when Mike came through the door heading for the spare chair and then grabbing the pint he asked. 'Well, any news lads?'

'There sure is,' said Ned. 'You tell him Steve.'

Mikes face grew angrier as the story enfolded. 'I know those fuckers,' he raged. 'They never create an act themselves, but go around poaching after someone else does the work. I'm gonna' ring Frank now, he'll know how to deal with this.'

They finished their pints, then all three went to the phone in the lobby and Frank wanted to know immediately, what unusual circumstance warranted such a late call.

'My wife will think it's a bird,' he proffered, but he soon forgot that problem when he heard the story, causing him to say. 'They're trying to get at me you know, I have refused to record three or four of their acts over the past year, because the Radio people don't like them. A Producer told me, if I worked with them it would cause problems for my other acts, so I backed off, they're just glorified booking agents, not managers. All they're any good at, is filling diaries for acts who have already made the big time and don't want to pay the proper percentage to the managers who made them in the first place.'

'So, what's the next move?' Inquired the manager.

'I'll make a few calls in the morning and Nanty them big time, ring me tomorrow and meanwhile, have a good weekend.' As Mike was hanging up the phone, he could hear a woman's voice shouting at Frank. 'Who was that at this hour?'

The three men were as thick as thieves, while they walked the short distance to the hall, knowing that the story for now, would go no further. Mike would keep the other two up to speed after the phone call on Friday; meanwhile all they had to do was play well and keep the punters happy as usual.

Mickey Joe and Conn looked suspiciously at the trio as they entered the band room.

'This is not a usual liaison,' the latter said.

Quick as a wink Ned came back with. 'We're trying to get some sponsorship to send Steve to Nashville for the holidays, that explains the liaison as you call it, OK!'

'I'd like to go as well,' whinged Mickey Joe, 'and my mate would like to see and hear his hero Boots Randolph in Printer's Alley, so how about it?'

'Listen lads,' it was Mike who answered. 'It's going to be hard enough to get the loot to send one guy, without blowing it by asking for more, we just want some publicity shots of Steve posing with a few famous singers to give us a boost, like Irelands number one, meets Nashville's hit makers.'

Mickey Joe kept stirring it as he struggled to button the collar of his shirt, which was at least one size too small for him.

'Posin, that's what he'll be doing alright, fuckin' posin'.

The trio refused to be ruffled by the jealous comments of the Trumpet man, especially Steve who harboured this great secret that (for a change) centred totally on him, causing both Ned and Mike to agree, that he was controlling his huge ego very well. The gig was a big success, with the new single getting an encore at the end and the smiling Roadie was dishing out the band pictures as usual while chatting up any girl who lingered, causing Ned to conclude that he was a bigger womaniser than himself. Later in the band room, the Roadie approached with a large brown envelope and slipping it into Ned's bag he said.

'That package was left at the pub for you, OK.'

'Thanks,' he replied, as a surge of guilty excitement shot through his body, knowing immediately what the envelope contained.

Saying goodnight to the other band members, he headed for his hotel with the knowledge that within the hour, the first three weeks of his holiday next May, would have taken shape. Sitting on the bed, he excitedly clawed the package open, then a pile of letters slid from captivity on to the floral quilt, but for starters he only had eyes for American stamps and airmail stickers. With his heart thumping, he fumbled until he found four envelopes fitting the bill.

'Jaysus,' he muttered, 'there's one too many.'

His hands were shaking while he laid them out on the pillow and as he sat wondering which one to open first, he decided to use a method his mother had taught him when he was a boy. He would use the other spelling of potato which went like this, pot one o, pot two o, pot three o, pot four o, pot five o, pot six o, pot seven o, pot eight o, opening the letter it ended on, which to his shock and amazement, had a New-Orleans post mark.

'Wow,' was all he could manage, as he began reading the most intimate thoughts and suggestions, of the woman who had helped to make him a man on that first flight to New York, plus later in The Woodlawn Hotel. She wrote.

'I think about you every day and I still get as high as I did on all those occasions when you made me so complete, now only having your memory to go on, it takes a little longer to reach those levels, but I manage because I love you so. I have wanted to write you every day, but I'm always afraid my letter may get you in trouble with your current girlfriend, only I could put it off no longer, so here goes. I would love you to come for a visit any time in the future as my time is my own and I have a house in Florida where we could live forever. Wouldn't that be nice?'

Even though the letter was sexually loaded it was very tastefully written, without a sign of vulgarity and the enclosed photos were wonderfully sexy without being risqué. On page four she quoted.

'I remember you telling me that you're a leg man, so I hope you like the angles, seeing that I had to use the Polaroid myself. Now I've kept my promise maybe you might send a few nice ones of you, but I do have to admit that I took a few pictures of you while asleep in The Woodlawn Hotel and your birthday suit is cute. Last but not least, she wrote. 'Before you read the remaining few lines, I want you to promise that you will write to me soon, now you can continue.' Those final lines were intimately beautiful and as he reluctantly folded the pages his head was in a spin.

'In the name of god, what am I going to do?' he groaned. 'How can I ignore such a gorgeous lady as that and live happily ever after?'

As he put Patricia Kramer's letter aside, his attention refocused on the three envelopes still on the pillow. 'Eeny meeny miney mo, catch an 'omie' by the toe.' As he uttered the word toe, his finger landed on letter number two which he picked up and scanning the San Francisco postcode, he inserted his trembling thumb in the fold.

'I might as well be hung for a sheep as a lamb,' he said to himself.

As he expected, it was a reply to his letter to Mary of the Shaven Haven in California, which went as follows.

'Dear Ned, even though I'll never forget our session on the beach that night, in your absence, I've taken up with a young man whom I love very much and although he doesn't have as much furniture in the trouser department as you, he does love the way I keep my you know what, which always makes him rampant.'

'My relations from your home town keep me up to date and their information is, you're about to wed a beautiful young Lawyer, so congratulations Ned, but make sure she gets her own little razor, it will work wonders. Anyway, I'm sure we'll meet again sometime, meanwhile be happy. Love Mary Smooth, x. x. x. x.'

He felt a little pang of disappointment in the bottom of his tummy, as he realised that the last time on that beautiful beach, was now definitely going to be the last time with that lovely vibrant young woman. As he reached for letter number three clearly stamped buffalo, he was wondering if it would be another Dear John, it read.

'Dear Ned, thank you for your letter which I must say, I was surprised to receive. Only for Amanda passing on your regards, I would have thought you were dead, seeing you have not mastered the phone yet.'

'Re: coming here for a week next May. I think you should ring me and we will talk about it first, then maybe you will be welcome. I passed on your message to Skip and Jenny, Randy and Jane and The Loaf, so if you make it, they want you to join the band again.' 'They suggested that you leave the trombone at home, just in case you lose it and they'll get one for you here. Looking forward to that phone call, I remain yours in anticipation. Jayne.'

Even though there were no kisses, he felt a stirring in his loins, as he remembered that beautiful woman with the gorgeous legs and he then began feeling bad about not phoning her. 'Was he scared?'

He picked up letter number four and the New York postage stamp beckoned at him.

'Jaysus, I hope it's not from Helen, the lady who liked drinking and making love in the shower, she doesn't have my address I hope, fingers crossed.'

There was no need for panic; it was quite a short letter from Brenda, saying.

'My dearest Ned, Re: your planned one week holiday in New York next May, I have no problem with that as the big bed in the dimly lit room is still half empty, or as you being an optimist would say, only half full. I still wear your ring so that will see me through until then, after that; it's in the lap of the Gods. Be sure to stay in touch as that will be important, Lots of love and kisses, Brenda.'

He sat looking at the letter; his hand trembling slightly and his thoughts were racing. He had forgotten the little ring he had pushed gently on to Brenda's finger thinking he was giving it to the mother of his children, but now that seemed so long ago and oh so doubtful. If she had been pregnant, their baby would be arriving soon and he would be getting used to living over the pub. He broke out in a cold sweat when the enormity of that scenario hit him. He would have hated running a pub and would he have left the band?

'It would have been too soon,' he said out loud to no one in particular and gently folding the page, he slipped it back into the confines of the envelope, which had kept its contents secret until a few moments ago. As if in a coma, he ripped open a few fan letters requesting information on the band plus a few personally autographed photos and then he came to one, which actually contained a glossy photograph of a beautiful woman.

'Jaysus, it's Kate Kelly,' he stated to the stillness of the room. 'I wonder what she wants?' Knowing full well the answer.

'Hi Ned honey,' it began.

She was stealing his fond term for Susan and that wasn't on, then he realised it was the first time his loved one's name had come to mind since he sat down on the bed, deliberately trying not to look at his guilty face in the big mirror on the dressing table just feet away. 'It's hell for me and no doubt,' he thought.

Like a magnet, the photo was compelling him to view it once more and like a small spoiled boy, he began taking quite furtive glances in its direction.

'You're a great looking woman,' he said loudly to the picture half expecting a reply and then slowly he put the photo to his mouth kissing it passionately on her full lips.

'Please say it's on,' he breathed, as another flood of shame swept over him.

Now he turned his attention back to the dispatch, it read.

'I'm going to my villa in Spain for the first week in May next year and if it suits, you would be welcome to join me and I will be on my own.' As he read her lines he glanced quickly at her picture but no, her expression had not changed. 'A good suntan would set you up for the year and have the girls falling all over you,' she continued.

'Anyway, we've got lots to talk about and even if we don't want to talk, well you know. I hope things are going well for you and the band and we are looking forward to having you for your Christmas date.'

She had underlined having you, to emphasise her real meaning of the words and just then he noticed something that had not really happened during the reading of the other letters. He was now the possessor of a fully-fledged hard-on, triggered by the subliminal, sexual connotations of the communication, so he glanced back at the picture and said.

'With the help of God I'll be there,' then as he read more, his erotic thoughts were replaced by sheer panic.

'Since that night of bliss in our love nest at Castlecross, I have missed my period and I'm hoping against hope that I'm carrying your child, don't worry honey, as I have taken the following steps.'

Worry was not the word to explain the sheer terror that swept over him causing even his palms to sweat, while he continued to read.

'As you know my husband is sterile, so prior to our tryst and knowing well what would happen, I sent him to a Doctor friend of mine in London for treatment. The Doctor has convinced him that all is now well, so he will not be surprised if my wish comes true, I'm so happy.'

Ned didn't know what to think as he took his eyes from the letter and looked at his flushed face in the mirror.

'I'm gonna' fill my case with rubbers on our March visit to England,' he swore, 'if I don't, Susan will be next to tell me she's pregnant, after a bare moment of weakness.'

The shock subsided as he read on and while she explained her ecstatic thoughts, a new feeling of arousal swept over him. Afterwards, as he lay fully clothed on the bed surrounded by all his mail, his emotions ran riot and so did his brain, until he realised he was talking to himself.

'I could be in big trouble here, maybe it's me who should be taking the steps and long ones at that.' He jumped off the bed and ran to the door, thinking he heard a noise. 'Jaysus, the lads will twig I'm talking to myself, because they know I don't have a charver with me and they'll have me committed, sure as eggs are eggs.'

He was laughing out loud now as he climbed back on the bed and removing the contents once more from one of the envelopes, he lay there for ages looking into the twinkling eyes of the lovely Kate Kelly.

'The weather in Spain will be nice the first week in May,' he was thinking as he began humming the big hit song, 'Viva Espania.' 'I must learn that song before then and maybe do it in the band for the summer, anyway, Kate would appreciate my singing it for her in the pubs of Spain, it could lead to great things.' That was when it really hit him and he sat bolt upright in the bed. 'Jaysus,' he whinged for the millionth time. 'If her story is true, she'll be halfway through the pregnancy by then and I won't be able to lay a finger on her even.'

It was a very confused Ned the Bed, who eventually slipped into a deep sleep fully clothed some time before the dawn, his thoughts for the last hour full of guilt for another young lady called Susan.

'What the fuck will I do?' he kept asking himself. 'I'll have to call it all off.'

He awoke to a knock on the door at 11.30am the next day and as he shouted 'hold on' he was busy ripping off his jacket, shirt and shoes. 'I've got to give the impression that I'm putting my clothes on instead of taking them off,' so with that bright thought in mind, he opened the door holding one sock in his left hand.

'Sorry for waking you Ned,' said a bleary-eyed Lead Singer, 'but Frank O'Toole from the Record Company is on the phone to Mike and they want to talk to you.'

'No problem,' said our half-awake hero. 'I'll be there in a minute when I put a few things on, OK.'

'I'll tell them.' Steve answered, as he ran back along the corridor.

After the initial greetings over the phone, Ned asked Frank. 'Well, what's the read?'

'The read as you call it is good Ned, I've made a few phone calls, the first one being to our man inside radio land. He says by evening, there won't be a record left in the library belonging to the artists from the City Band Management Agency.'

'That's quick,' said Ned, 'but don't the jocks have their own personal copies?'

'Yeah.' Frank was laughing now. 'For some unknown reason, they will all go missing over the next day or so as well, our man has promised a complete Nanty.'

'By the way Frank, is everything OK for Monday evening to go and hear Susan's family band?' Ned asked.

'Sure,' he answered, 'there will be lots of free slots on Radio to be filled now, the time could be right for The Prunty's.'

As he strolled back to the room he kept repeating the name over and over. 'It's got a certain ring to it, eh.' He was still thinking out loud as he gathered the letters from the bed and because of the position of Kate Kelly's photo, he must have fallen asleep with it in his hand.

'You're a good looking woman, but you're gonna' get me into fierce trouble,' he said, as he slipped the picture back into it's envelope.

He wasn't too sure how he felt about her news, but seeing that she was happy with it made him feel a bit better. Maybe it's a false alarm? Like in the Brenda situation. One thing for sure, from now on he would be more careful so in this newly found positive mood it only took a couple of minutes to make up his mind about May and the holidays.

God willing and no pregnant ladies, it's Spain for the first week, New York and Brenda the second week, Buffalo the third to see if possible what lies above Jayne's hem line and depending on the outcome of all that and the fact that he would be spending the fourth week with Susan, then he should be ready to make the right decision, or go back to the Seminary and Fr. Ron.

'God forbid, but you're a selfish bastard Ned Brady,' he said to himself.

The three remaining weekend gigs were fantastic, with Ned writing replies to the four letters over the period and making several phone calls to Susan, in an effort to stave off his guilt. He got a shock on Sunday though, just after a nice lunch, it came in the shape of a phone call from the one and only Sandra Boyle, Journalist.

'See, I tracked you down, would I be right in thinking that you're dodging me, after all the promotion I gave you this week?'

He got the distinct impression she was scolding him and realising she was speaking the truth, he decided on some light banter. Then she sent him back into shock.

'I want to set up an interview with your Susan, to cover her studying Law, her modelling career and now Frank tells me, her becoming a recording star.'

'No fucking way,' he blurted out.

He could hear her howling with laughter at his outburst and when she got herself under control again she said.

'Ned you big fool, I just want to talk to her along with her family and if you can make it all the better, because I might get a little session with you when their backs are turned, you Bollix, this is professional.'

The last word triggered some thoughts in his mind that probably wouldn't have pleased her so he kept them to himself, saying instead. 'OK, I'll set something up after Monday night and we can all meet in a hotel where I can keep an eye on you, anyway, you'll probably fancy one of her brothers instead.'

'Can I only have one of them Ned?'

'You're a bitch, Sandra Boyle,' he said.

'But you like that, don't you,' she replied, 'or are you only acting, I want to be your bitch soon again please, then I'll promise to behave when Susan's around.'

'Is that a threat?' he inquired.

'Not at all darling, I promise you'll enjoy it, Frank gave me this very sexy movie the other night and in it the guy ties up the girl, then has his wicked way with her, I want to be that girl, OK!'

'Tell me Sandra, is Frank riding you?' he asked.

'Well now, he's not called O'Toole for nothing, even though you would pip him at the post, if you follow me,' she was howling again.

Her sheer boldness gave him an idea, which suddenly made his pulse race. Mike has this amazing movie camera that he brought back from The States, which he had often offered to Ned if he ever met a willing subject, now was the time.

'OK Sandra,' he began, 'maybe tying you up and humping you, might not be such a bad idea after all, but there's one condition.'

'Consider it on,' she replied joyously. 'So I'll know what to expect, tell me the said condition?'

'The deal is, I film the proceedings,' he waited, but not for long.

'I'm all for that, there's just one snag, who will be the cameraman and won't he want to join in?' she was really excited now.

'Sorry to disappoint you dear, I'll point the camera at the bed and we stay in the frame, can we do it at your place?'

'We could, but my sister might come up from the country any time and walk in on us.' 'I'd be in trouble then because she's a prude.'

'I can't imagine you having a sister who's a prude, but she might love it and join in, that would be the perfect threesome wouldn't it.'

It was him who was laughing now, but as he laughed the perfect venue for this adventure flashed before his eyes. The big White House on the hill overlooking Mullymore would be empty from Monday, apart from him that is.

'Don't worry,' he said. 'I'll find a place.'

They had a long journey on Sunday night and after about three hours sleep his mum called him saying.

'Edward rise and shine, it's Airport time,' then stuffing pillows behind his back, she presented him with a tray laden down with a lovely big breakfast and lashings of coffee. 'Come on, get that down you, it'll do you good,' she said happily. 'We must be on the road soon or we'll miss our flight, then we will be in the way all over the festive season.'

Now Ned never considered his parents being in the way in the past, but with his plans for the immediate future, he just had to have the house to himself. With this thought uppermost in his mind he scoffed the tasty food, washed it down with piping hot coffee and ran to the bathroom.

'That didn't take you long son,' his parents chorused as he walked into the living room looking perky and his dad continued with. 'Ah it must be great to be young.'

'Make sure you've got everything now,' said Ned, as he once more with feeling, advised his parents to go through the all-important things for the trip. 'Check your cash first,' he said. 'OK, now your passports and last but not least, your tickets.'

As they produced the aforementioned pieces, Ned's dad once again thanked him for buying the tickets by saying.

'Son, you shouldn't have spent all that money, we did so well in the sale of the pub, it would only have been fair that we buy them ourselves.'

A week earlier he had gone into 'Apex Travel' in Dublin and purchased the tickets to The States, then the following day he had placed them on his parents pillow. You can imagine the reaction. There were multiple hugs, lots of tears, plus a ticking off from his folks about squandering his money, but now as they got into the car for the journey, he was thrilled with what he had done. They drove leisurely all the way, with his mum reminding him many times, to look after the house well and look after her Susan twice as well.

'But she's my Susan too mother,' he reminded her.

The usual farewells followed, then an hour later he was on his way to meet Mike and Frank for the trip to Glenrone, to audition 'The Prunty's' featuring his darling.

'Can I ask a favour Frank?' he said, as he entered Groove Records office.

'Yes of course,' came the reply.

'I have to call someone in Buffalo New York and I can't make the call from home in case my folks find out, I'll pay you for it.'

'No problem whatsoever, give me the number and I'll dial it for you, forget about money, we're all doing well.'

A couple of minutes later a very nervous Ned the Bed was asking for Jayne and he almost dropped the phone when this positive female voice came on the line.

'How can I help you?' she asked, sounding wonderful.

'Hello Jayne, it's Ned Brady here,' he almost said (Ned the Bed). 'Thanks for your letter which I have replied to; it was lovely hearing from you.

'Oh hello Ned, I see you mastered the phone alright.' She was getting in the dig.

He could hear a giggle in her voice so he knew she wasn't being sarcastic, then still shaking he asked.

'How is everybody and are you still singing lovely harmony?'

'My harmony depends on whom I'm singing it with,' she replied, and he wondered if there was a message for him in her answer.

Next he asked how her Law studies were going and because of the nature of the conversation he almost slipped up, being on the verge of calling her Susan several times. Then she asked outright.

'What's the letter about Ned, do you still want to come for a week?'

That question triggered naughty thoughts in our hero's head and he had to stop himself saying that he'd love to come for a month, if she would do the same, but common sense took over.

'Yes Jayne, I'd love to visit you on the third week in May next if that would suit, it's the first week of our two week holiday.' He lied, keeping a secret the fact that the band was taking a four-week break.

'OK,' she replied. 'My plan is to drive up to Canada and tour around, now don't be getting ideas, it will be separate rooms.'

'That would be nice and it will give us a chance to sing a few songs together,' as he was giving his answer, he was wondering if she would relent before the week was out.

'One can only hope,' he thought.

He was on a high for a few minutes after talking to Jayne, yet knowing he had lied to her about the length of his vacation as she called it, then Kate Kelly's possible pregnancy came back to haunt him and while they climbed into Frank's car it really hit home.

'You don't look the Mae-West Ned,' said Mike. 'Are you going to get sick?'

Glancing in the rear view mirror, Frank accidentally got it in one, when he said.

'You look like a man who has some woman up the stick, could that be true?'

Ned decided to come clean and told the two men his story, ending with. 'Jaysus, what am I going to do? If Susan gets wind of it I'm finished,' then eyeing Frank in the mirror he added, 'we'd also need to keep it from Sandra Boyle, Frank.'

'Don't worry Ned,' he replied. 'She won't hear it from me and anyway, it's probably a false alarm, but now, lets take this opportunity on the journey to make some New Year plans for The Nova's Showband.'

'OK,' said Mike, 'Shoot!'

'Well the way I see it is this, we should finish the album before your English tour in March, take Ned's song off it as a single along with a b-side and bobs your uncle.'

'Are you sure you should use my song?' Asked a doubtful Ned, it may not be strong enough and if the other guys find out I wrote it, they'll be pissed off big time.'

'I've got one answer for them,' Frank replied. 'Fuck them, I've got the publishing on your song, so I may as well spend the big bucks I'm going to lash out on it and not on something written by some millionaire who doesn't need it.'

'That makes sense to me,' said Mike. 'Anyway, they'll never suss it because you're using a pseudonym, aren't you?'

Ned was laughing when he answered. 'Yeah, I'm calling myself Edward Priestly, no one will have a fucking clue who I am or where I'm from.'

'How in the name of God did you come up with that handle?' Mike inquired.

'Easy,' he replied. 'My mother insists on calling me Edward and if she had her way I would have become a Priest, which would have caused me to behave in a priestly fashion.'

They all laughed loudly at that, then Mike interjected with. 'How am I going to keep a straight face when the lads start commenting on the writer of their new single.'

It was Frank who took up the chore of guessing what outrageous things would be said.

'I wonder who this Priestly Bollix is? Will be Mickey Joe's first question. Then. He's probably some big puff from L.A, Bollixolutely. The drummer is likely to suggest something similar and it will go downhill from there, but who cares. I'm going to have a head throw with the next one, we must follow a hit with a bigger hit.'

'Tell me something Ned,' it was Mike's voice sounding curious. 'How did you get the name 'The Novas' for the band?'

'It was one frosty night, a full moon and the sky was pickled with twinkling stars.' 'We were driving home from a 'Slugs' gig and it hit me during a conversation we were having about becoming pop stars so I thought, why not a Nova, the one that becomes brightest fastest, it just stuck in my mind from then.'

He sounded like he was up there with the stars, or away with the fairies, so Mike decided to let it go for now, as Ned's thoughts drifted to his song writing. He began hallucinating about people like Sinatra covering his songs, or maybe Cliff would call him and ask.

'You got something there for me?' 'Get back to reality you arsehole,' he silently advised himself. It's a good job Mike and Frank didn't know his thoughts, or they would have had him committed, then in the background he could hear his two friends in the front talking and laughing about the problems facing the City Band Management Agency.

'By now, they're wondering why they got no airplay over the weekend and they're heading into a radio free Christmas, so let's wish them well.'

Next he heard the words, up and coming Politician, so he butted in. 'Excuse me Frank, I missed the beginning of that story, would you roll it back for me.' He was using recording studio terminology now and still in a low cloud somewhere, on his way back down to reality.

'Yeah, you guys obviously don't know, but I've got this up and coming married Politician, who is also my Accountant, that I hump every chance I get and why my term for her is so relevant is, she's new to the Politics game. I've got a feeling recently, that it might not be a good idea having her do such a delicate job as the Company accounts, just in case we fall out. She could hold me to ransom.'

'Tell us more,' they begged.

'The night before The Nova's record launch, she had me up and coming all over my new suit as we drove along in the car, that really pissed me off, because I had just bought the suit for your big do and a couple of weddings that were coming up.'

'How did you hide it from your wife?' A hysterical Ned asked. 'Doesn't she smell your shirts and search your pockets for stuff.'

'Indeed, it's a good job I had a change in the office, or I'd have been in a major handling. I always buy two identical suits from my friendly tailor, so she didn't notice a thing, because I keep one of each in the office at all times, saves trouble.'

'Did she ever find French letters in your pockets?' Mike asked with a laugh.

'No thank God,' he answered. 'Things are bad enough without that, I keep them in the office and she never goes there in case I'd ask her to do a days work, the lazy bitch, that's why she doesn't know about the spare suits either.'

'Do you ever hump her at all?' Mike asked nervously.

'No fucking way, would you?' came the reply.

'Going back to the rubbers and your stash in the office,' Ned began. 'I intend ringing in the New Year with Susan in Mullymore and even though we haven't talked about it, I think we're going to do it at last, so I need some.'

'So you're going to do it eh, but that's what you want, isn't it?' Said Frank.

'You never spoke a truer word,' said Ned, 'and I don't want two women in the family way, for the New Year.'

'Don't worry,' said Frank, 'I can give you a gross.'

'The problem is, I do worry and I hope the Kate Kelly situation is a scare, because I don't want children of mine going around using someone else's name, but anyway, don't you think a gross would be a few too many, a dozen will keep me going.'

'Your either bragging, or Susan's going to be a very happy girl, come the New Year,' said Mike laughing, 'but are you not spending Monday next and Christmas Eve with her as well?'

'That's true,' he answered, 'but I'll be in her home for that and spending the nights in her aunt's guesthouse, in Glenrone.'

Frank spoke next and he sounded wistful, which was strange for him.

'You know, their parents do their best to keep us away from their daughters for as long as they can, but the day or night always comes when they're not looking and wham, the inevitable happens, which proves that the predator always gets It's prey.'

'Jaysus, Frank, you make it sound like one of those nature films where the Lion always kills it's quarry, it's much more pleasant than that.' Ned was incredulous.

Then Frank said sadly. 'I wish I'd sent a Lion after my one, but he probably would have spat her out.'

'Fuck me Frank!' said Mike, sounding American again. 'You're one screwed up guy, she can't be that bad.'

'Oh, she was lovely until a year after we got married and then the company I worked for went bust, (too much permanent borrowing on behalf of the staff) so I started Groove Records. She even designed the Logo and our catch phrase. 'Groove Records, are groovy records.'

'So what went wrong?' Mike enquired.

'Oh, the usual, I had to work all hours God made to get the project up and running, so she began suggesting that I was humping instead of working, the usual story. She was the head receptionist, in a busy hotel in the city and would deal with all the businessmen who were checking out and paying for the double rooms, after a good all night shagging session with their '<u>Floozies,</u>' as she called them. But in my case, she maintained I was doing it during the day, sometimes all day.' Frank's voice had taken on a different tone now.

'Fuck me,' said Ned, 'you can't win. Is that what I have to look forward to with Susan?' Just as he spoke her name, the car rounded the final bend and they were driving down the main street of the small town that was now playing such a big part in his life.

'So this is Glenrone,' said Frank. 'Must say I was never here before, but if the Prunty's are as good as you say Ned, we'll soon put this place on the map.'

'Look lads, there's where Susan works,' an excited Ned shouted, pointing at the Solicitors office. 'And there's Mrs. North's guesthouse where I'll be doing my snoozing over Christmas.'

'And there Frank, is the Dance Hall, where Ned and I will be hopefully taking a bag of money out of on St. Stephen's night, in between his sleeping,' said Mike happily.

'And there's the pub lads, where we're going to have a pint before we go listening to music, OK!' They agreed with Frank and as if he owned the town Ned marched in leading his gang of two, to be greeted from all quarters with.

'Welcome Ned, how are you lads and you're going to have a big one here next week.'

Within seconds, he could have had a big one, out of the shadows came a good-looking blonde and with outstretched arms she draped herself all over our hero. Now he couldn't remember her name but he never forgets a face, it was the town bike who he had seen getting her oats in the front seat of a big car, out at the Deep Lough.

'Every time I see you, you have a smile on your face,' said Ned, trying to make light of the situation.

'Yeah, I remember,' she squealed. 'I was really enjoying the fact that someone had it in for me, were you?'

He didn't like where this was going, but he couldn't back down in front of this girl, so he answered jokingly.

'Actually I hate it when someone has it in for me, so if you'll excuse me I've got to lay claim to my pint just in case one of my friends does precisely that. I'll see you at the dance on the 26th and introduce you to Susan.' He made sure to raise his voice for the last bit and he was glad to see that she got the message along with the punters.

'Just imagine the problems Tom Jones must have with fans.' Ned mused out loud. 'I'd fuckin' hate that.'

'Don't worry your head about it big fella,' said Mike, dropping into the voice and persona of one of his Showband favourites from the north of Ireland.

They sat savouring their pints, as the conversation drifted to the audition in hand. Frank didn't like being late, but he also had an aversion to being too early, so taking their time over their drinks was killing several birds with one stone. Then Ned broached a subject that was really worrying him and he pitched his next sentence to Frank, in the shape of a question.

'What are we going to do about Sandra Blooming Boyle, Journalist?' he asked.

He could see the look of surprise on the band manager's face, for in the last twenty-four hours he had asked Mike for his movie camera, to film the aforementioned lady for posterity.

Frank was real calm when replying. 'Ned my friend,' he began. 'We both know that separately we enjoy Sandra while she enjoys us, but you shouldn't let it worry you as she is a very together lady and is using us, even more than we are using her.'

Ned decided not to mention her fascination for Susan in case it would backfire on his love, who was oblivious of the whole (as she would say) tawdry scenario.

'What I'm worried about is, the whole thing might blow up on us, if one or both of us try to steer clear of her.'

'I repeat Ned, don't worry, she's a very beautiful girl who was badly hurt years ago and doesn't want it to happen again, that's why she's hanging around with us, because neither of us is available, believe me.' The record man meant every word.

'I've got this horrid vision,' the Bandleader said, that one day after I'm married, she'll arrive at our door wearing only a dress and high heels, then after flashing those gorgeous teeth, she'll peel off the dress before walking in starkers.'

'You've seen too many movies Ned, maybe the Mafia blonde you screwed in L.A. might do that but not Sandra Boyle, she's a country girl for Gods sake.'

'I hope you're right Frank,' he sighed and finished his pint.

'OK lads, it's time to roll,' the man from Groove Records said, as he checked his watch. 'You two make sure you get some good pictures, I want to show them to a few people.'

As Frank's really big car eased it's way along the Fiddler's Lane, Ned could feel the excitement building up inside, partly because he was soon to see Susan and hear the great music they perform, not forgetting the equally great songs some old and some original. He also had the feeling, that the moment he saw his love again he would know she was the only girl for him.

Chapter Sixteen

When they drove up to the large house, the outside light came on and the door opened to reveal Susan standing in the doorway in a beautiful red figure hugging cat-suit with identically coloured high heeled shoes, which she would shed while drumming later. His heart skipped a beat and both his friends in unison said what he was thinking.

'Wow,' she's cute.

'And so is she,' continued Mike, as Mary appeared in the doorway dressed almost identically and Ned had to agree.

Introductions over, the visitors passed on the tea offered, saying they would enjoy a cup after they heard some great music. Ned advised the family to begin with both girls playing the fiddles and they started off with a rousing Traditional piece with Celtic-Rock undertones, which knocked the visitors for six. As the family regrouped, some changing instruments and Susan slipping seductively behind the big drum kit to take over from her brother John, Ned asked his mates.

'Well, what do you fellows think so far?'

Frank answered as he exhaled. 'Do you want to hear my new promo line for them?'

'OK, shoot,' said Mike.

'The band that put the sex into sextet,' was the Record company man's answer.

'Wow,' said Ned. 'I love it, but don't say it in front of their parents, you know what I mean, they might think you were going to exploit their kids.'

By now they had struck up an original song, featuring a fusion of sounds, a vivacious Susan belting the drums vigorously and four of the six on vocals.

'I'd like to hear more, but I've heard enough, if you know what I mean.' Frank said to Ned. 'They're fantastic and world, here we come.'

The small audience applauded loudly as they waited with bated breath, for whatever gem the musicians had up their sleeves next and The Prunty's aimed to please. Two acoustic guitars, a mandolin and button keyed accordion mixed beautifully with six voices ranging from Bass to Contralto, it was heavenly and then without hardly a pause the same ensemble struck up silent night, it was magnificent. As the last Christmassy sound faded, the parents and their three guests applauded, while the performers walked to the centre of the room, took a bow and stood quietly hand in hand, waiting for the verbal verdict, which wasn't long coming. Ned grinned proudly, as Mike and Frank used every complimentary phrase they could think of, while the band members smiled politely. As usual after a family performance, a happy Mother ushered everyone into the dining room for the tea, which was another of her gourmet, spreads, with everything from prawns to pork laid out and her pleased husband homed in on Frank O'Toole.

'Well what future do you see for them in music, Mr. O'Toole?'

'Call me Frank,' came the reply. 'I can see a world appeal there, especially in record sales and I do believe they don't want to gig until they have all qualified in their chosen professions, which is the smart thing to do.'

Later, when they were all seated around the big table, Ned got another shock in the shape of a question from Susan's Dad. 'I believe you're parents are going to Philadelphia soon?'

The recipient of the question shot a quick glance at Susan and she grimaced, then like a shot, he told his future father-in-law his first blatant lie. 'It's on the 4th or 5th of January I think, Mr Prunty.'

Just then Mike launched his opinion on the same question, but luckily changed direction. 'I thought it was,' then came a long pause to get his mouth into gear and turning a bright red he countered. 'I thought it was the end of January, because you asked me to check flight times for you then.'

'Sorry for not getting back to you Mike, but dad got a great deal himself for early January, he knows the Apex Travel boss, so he set it up over the phone.' Lie number two without batting an eye, because he had bought the tickets.

The conversation levelled out again, with both Susan and Ned hoping nobody else noticed the close one, but they did see a marked change in Mike by his on-going silence. Mary had both strangers literally eating out of her hand, but Frank also spent a lot of time talking to her brothers about writing, publishing and recording. The eldest brother John, found out exactly, what the record label was prepared to do, in lieu of getting an exclusive on a recording / publishing deal, then later on they said their goodbyes which included Seasons Greetings. Ned and Susan walked out to the lane hand in hand, where they would enjoy the last few kisses before heading back to the city.

'Thanks for everything and weren't we lucky that my parents didn't pick up on what your manager was trying to say,' she said sincerely. 'I'm excited about recording and you and I must write a song together, maybe we'll start on New Year's Eve in Mullymore?'

Between the kisses he replied. 'That's not all we're going to start on that night and just imagine what would have happened if your parents had noticed, it would have put the kibosh on our complete plan.'

'Oh Ned, you know how much I love you and I realise now that I can't hold out any longer, but I hope you don't mean starting a family honey. Would it be possible for you to get some contraceptives, just two or three in case, the study must continue.'

He noticed she was too polite to give them anything else but their full title, then smiling at her he said.

'Two or three, if we go all the way and I hope we do, we'll need more than two or three, we'll be at it all the time.' Before the last word was fully uttered she kissed him passionately, it would be a New Year to remember.

Frank honked the horn as he drove away and said laughingly to Ned. 'I'll bet you've got one of those, eh, but seriously, you've got to be proud to be associated with that family, as well as having a fantastic talent, they're ladies and gentlemen also.'

'Thanks Frank, I am proud, very proud and that's why I'm scared of getting caught with Sandra Boyle, or some other woman,' he said.

Mike spoke up next saying. 'Sorry Ned, I almost got you kicked out with my big mouth,' then he continued with. 'Those guys know a lot about the business side of music too, they'll do well.'

The Nova's Showband had a lot of pre-Christmas gigs and even though the crowds were down a little, it was still good. Mike put them all at ease with. 'You've got all the big Christmas parties and a lot of people are saving for the festive season, but I'll bet my bottom dollar, there's no one doing better than us.'

The band members were having a great week with the girls. John the Bass man (who had not been the same since he got the knee-trembler on the English tour) scored every night. Conn was a busy beaver also, even though Cynthia Rose accompanied him on two occasions, not looking in any way pregnant. The Guitar man almost fell out with Mr. Ivory, because the latter called one of his women a dog.

'She's no fuckin' dog,' he roared.

'I didn't call her a fuckin' dog, I just think she's an ordinary dog, but when you get at her she'll be a fuckin' dog, I'm sure.'

The Guitar player thought about that for a moment, smiled and said. 'Gee, I hope so.'

Thirty minutes after the Sunday gig Ned was on the road to Glenrone, consumed by love. He had (sort of) told Sandra Boyle to fuck off, on the two occasions she had made contact during the week, but she brought him around by promising to behave, if he would go ahead with the mini Hollywood production in early January, which he knew must be done before his folks returned.

It was 5am on a cold frosty Christmas Eve morning, when Ned let himself quietly into Mrs. North's guesthouse and he could hardly wait to get between the sheets of the comfortable bed. He was due at Susan's home at 1 o'clock that afternoon, when festivities would begin and later as he drove the big car along the Fiddler's Lane, his thoughts went back to the happenings of the previous week.

True to his word, Frank turned up to the Friday night gig and slipped a pack of twenty into Ned's gig bag. 'There's the Christmas box I promised you,' he said with a big grin. 'Don't use them all at once.'

'Thanks mate,' said Ned. 'I owe you one.'

'That one you say you owe me.' Frank replied, still grinning. 'Give it to Sandra in early January, it'll keep her sweet, because all the promotion she has given us pre-Christmas has brought our single back up to number two.'

'That's fucking marvellous news Sham,' said Ned. 'I must tell the lads, but how are things with the City Band Management Agency?'

'Just get Mike and Steve Byrne in here, so I can bring you all up to date on the Nanty we've put on them.' The man from Groove Records was gloating as he told his minions the read. 'They're hurting bad and I'm told they suspect me.'

'Fuck them,' said Mike. 'Please continue.'

'Well, three of their biggest acts have singles out and they're not getting a spin or a T.V. appearance, so there's word of defections,' he said.

'Serves the wanker's right,' was the Singer's comment, as he realised how lucky he was in not accepting the offer. Just as Steve Byrne spoke, the remainder of the band members had filed in and asked as one.

'Have you come down with our Christmas presents Frank, or is there bad news?'

'Actually, it's good news that I bear, which includes your Christmas present, you're single has gone back up the chart from four to number two and as Jimmy Saville might say, how's about that then?'

'Fuck Jimmy Saville,' said Mickey Joe, 'but that's great fuckin' news Frank. Bollixolutely.'

After hearing Mickey Joe's suggestion of what to do with the sometimes multicoloured, longhaired, British disc jockey, backed up by his new and soon to become overused word, Ned had a sobering thought.

'Jaysus, Sandra Boyle probably knew our single was back up the chart on both occasions that we spoke and didn't tell me, because I told her to fuck off, even though she knew I was only messing, I must be more careful.'

His flashback ended when he realised that the driveway and street at the Prunty house was chock-a-block with fine cars, so it took him some time to find a spot that wouldn't cause having to park on the lawn. Then, just as he switched off the engine, he felt the driver's door being opened.

'Dismount kind sir,' said the ravishing Susan, who was bedecked from head to toe, in what Ned had become to know as her favourite colour, black.

'You look good enough to eat,' he said, after a big hug 'and how do you always know when I'm outside your house?'

She gave him a real knowing grin and said. 'Telepathy my man, as for eating me, I was going to talk to you about that, but there's too much to eat indoors, so it will have to wait until next week.'

He knew exactly what she meant and held her even closer. She was referring to something of a sexual nature that he had mentioned, but as yet they had not tried. She asked him to understand in case she didn't like it when the moment arrived, but knew it was time to take that extra loving step and he put her completely at ease by pointing out that she was under no pressure whatsoever.

On entering the house that was a hive of activity, it took ages to once again be introduced to everyone and there was one new completely stunning girlfriend. Susan's brother Hugh, the multi-instrumentalist, had a beautiful young blonde German girl on his arm, that he met in college and it was her first time to visit the Prunty house. All the brothers who knew her well kept insinuating that she had no home to go to in Germany, but she laughed it all off by saying she was a spy and was being paid to infiltrate their family.

'Whoever is paying you Anna, is a fool,' said Mr. Prunty, not revealing whether he believed the story or not, the only tell-tale signs were in the caring way he looked at this lovely girlfriend of his pet son.

The craic was great, even better than in the old song about the Isle of Man and over the evening everybody played music or sang and then after a guitar was thrust into his hand, Ned also joined in. Next, the young German lady was asked to sing and sing she did, it was a beautiful love ballad which she performed bilingually and you could hear a pin drop. The applause went on for ages, followed by large hugs and Ned concluded she felt good up close, (for a German).' At around 8 o'clock some more people arrived, including Mrs. North, her husband, their two lovely daughters, the Susan look-alikes, their two brothers who were at college with the Prunty lads and looked the spitting image of them also. The only thing the similar genes didn't bring to the four North siblings was the musical talent of their cousins and they always jokingly laid the blame fairly and squarely on their dad.

'Our mum can sing,' they declared. 'But dad, he can't even whistle.'

Around midnight, Ned and Susan excused themselves saying they were going for a walk, which was not entirely true, so climbing into the car they headed off towards the Deep Lough, for a long awaited court. Whilst pleasuring each other lovingly, they planned their every moment up until the not too distant New Year's Eve, which was drawing closer with every tick of the clock.

'My darling Ned,' she said. 'I want to welcome the New Year as a woman, do you mind my asking if you had any luck with the you know what's?'

'The you know what's as you call them, are in hand, or to put it precisely, in my suitcase,' he assured her, while still trying to get closer and all that could be heard for the next hour, were moans of ecstasy.

Christmas Day in the Prunty home was a grand affair, with lashings of food, drink, music and style. The girls had pushed out all the finery boats of the year and Ned felt he was back at the fashion show minus the catwalk. The buffet counter in the dining room looked quite like one, with the plus being, you could eat everything on it without raising eyebrows, if you know what I mean. Plans for later included a performance by the family band, which was supposed to be about four songs or tunes, but the crowd who had filed into the rehearsal room wouldn't let them off stage. Susan had asked Ned earlier, if he would get up and do a number with the family but he declined saying.

'I wouldn't do you guy's justice, you're in a different league.'

Susan accepted on the following conditions. 'OK, if you don't sing this evening, you'll have to sing along with me later when we're parked at the Deep Lough.

'No problem,' he answered. 'We always harmonise out there and tonight will be no different.'

Harmony was exactly what it was, they never came closer to consummating their love than that night and like a violinist tuning his or her instrument, they both knew they were ready to join the orchestra, the baton was raised and they were just waiting for the drum roll. As he drove Susan home, her head on his shoulder as usual, her arms wound tightly around his body, the first snowflakes of that Christmas began to fall and those wouldn't be the last. They both saw the first flake and as if synchronised, they began singing.

'I'm dreaming of a white Christmas,' then immediately they went into fits of laughter, because believe it or not, they were even in the same key. She kissed him on the cheek and said.

'I hope the rest of our lives together, is as co-ordinated and in tune as that was.'

'I hope so too,' he replied, with part of his brain trying to force him to think about the following May, the other part refusing to do so.

The snow was falling quite heavily as his love waved to him from the safety of her front door, after the last long, lingering, loving kiss. They needed to get to bed early, because The Nova's Showband was playing in Glenrone the following night and the lovers wanted to spend the day together away from everyone, but by the look of the weather they might not be going too far.

It was 8am on St Stephen's Day, when he took the first look out the window and the view was amazing. Even the hills around the town were shrouded in snow and his first thought was for the little old man and woman with the menu on the scrap of paper, who ran that wonderful restaurant somewhere up there.

'Their place will be quiet tonight,' he mused and then it hit him. 'Jaysus, there's not a footprint out there, if this continues we'll have nobody at the dance either.'

Halfway through his big breakfast, Mrs. North called him to the phone and it was Mike the manager. 'This is some Handlin' Sir,' he stated, again using his Northern twang. 'Mullymore is snowed in and it's still falling like mad, I don't think the lads will get out of here today.'

Ned remembered where he was and didn't swear. 'It's not as bad as that in this area, there's snow everywhere, but only a couple of inches deep at the moment, if it stays away people will travel.'

'I was really looking forward to a big one tonight,' said Mike with a sigh. 'I was expecting around two thousand or more.'

'Yeah, so was I,' came the reply, but if it gets no worse we could still have five hundred and no band, we'll have to send them home.'

'There is a solution though,' said Mike.

'Are you suggesting a band of Angels?' Ned asked. 'Because that's the only direction any band can travel from, if you know what I mean.'

'You've hit the nail on the head,' was the laughing reply. 'I'm thinking of two Angels, four Saints and the one member of The Nova's Showband who is on site, lets call you an Apostle, shall we.'

'Jaysus Mike, oh sorry Mrs. North, is it your suggesting that The Prunty's do the gig, aided and abetted by me.' Ned was aghast.

'As one of your records says in the lyrics, the Peso has dropped before your very eyes, it's the only solution, will you ask them and ring me back as soon as you can?'

'OK Mike.' 'I'll run it past them and get back to you.'

'Do you want to speak to Susan?' Her Dad asked, when he recognised his voice on the phone. 'She may still be in bed though.'

'No sir,' he answered. 'This time strangely enough, I would like to talk to your son John, it's about music.'

'Fair enough, hold on and I'll get him for you.'

There was about a two-minute pause and then John's voice came down the wire.

'What's up Ned? I never expected you on the phone so early to talk about music, has my sister anything to worry about?' He was laughing loudly now.

Ned convinced his future brother-in-law that his sibling was in no way threatened by music and then he went on to explain the situation.

'Speaking on behalf of the family,' said John, (as Ned held his breath). 'We would jump at the chance and if anybody turns up, it would give us a great boost for record sales in the future, especially around here anyway, that is of course, if the people think we're any good.'

'Oh thanks,' said Ned, 'and it's a plus that you've got all the gear in your studio.' 'I'll be over after I ring our manager, to give you a hand dismantling and transporting it, see you.'

Mrs. North, who had kept his breakfast hot in the oven, was excited by what she had overheard and could hardly control her enthusiasm. 'God works in wondrous ways,' she began. 'Just imagine, you're becoming a member of the family even before the wedding, that's nothing short of a miracle.'

He was going to say that now he was an Apostle, miracles would be easy, but he decided not to go down that road, instead he said. 'I can hardly wait.' The lady of the house decided that a hug was on the cards to celebrate the impending union, so from behind, she did just that, while he chewed a sausage and almost choked.

When he got to the Prunty household the place was a hive of activity once again. They were all in the music room putting a programme of their songs together, so John handed Ned a guitar and said. 'Put that on you and run through your songs until we get the chords, or most of them at least.'

They did this for at least two hours and he almost forgot that his girlfriend, the love of his life, was creating the pounding drum sound from behind, this would be the best band ever to play in Glenrone. Ned passed on another breakfast and spent the time dividing up the numbers into sets of three, which was the only way to do it in the Dance Halls, the concert scene being totally different of course. The dancers like to change partners after three numbers, just in case things aren't going too well with their present choice and those reasons can vary quite a lot, anything from having your toes walked on, inability to make conversation to severe BO.

A convoy of cars took the equipment to the hall later in the day and Susan's father offered the use of his tractor and trailer if needed. The Promoters understood the situation and by dance time, there was an air of excitement around the place.

As usual, a four piece local band did support to a growing crowd and at 11 o'clock, The Prunty's walked on stage, with a nervous Ned in pole position. At least a thousand people turned up as some of the outlying areas were not too bad with snow and they took to this energetic, young versatile band like a cat to cream. A few punters, including the two moron's who were not wearing their collars out tonight, (hopefully because of the snow) wanted to know what had happened to Ned's trombone.

'Oh, it's snowed in, up in Mullymore I'm afraid,' he answered, but apart from a few, he couldn't get over how little a band with a current hit record meant, to their supposed fans.

'It's true what they say,' he thought. 'You're only as good as your last performance,' and this new outfit, with a little help from him, had just given a great performance.

In the band room later, they all congratulated each other on their efforts and they applauded when Ned took a lovely but tired Susan in his arms, adding a lingering kiss to the proceedings and then he announced.

'Tonight has been the highlight of my musical career, so on behalf of myself and the marooned Nova's Showband, I want to thank you all for stepping into the breech, especially the best drummer I've ever played in front of, so three cheers for Susan, Hip, hip. Hip, hip. Hip, hip.'

That brought the tears, then more hugs, until the Promoter walked in and handed Ned a wad of money, which was the first time any one of them had thought about getting paid.

'Thanks,' he said. 'You must do this again, because you were fantastic and see the way everyone from the town, young and old, turned up when the news got out that you were on, also there's good news for you Ned, it's thawing all over the country, so Happy Christmas and a successful New Year to you all.'

As the Promoter walked out, Ned handed the money to John saying. 'You divide that up and thanks again.'

'Not at all Ned, you'll need it to pay your lads, we enjoyed playing so much we don't want to be paid.'

Just as John handed back the money, Ned turned around and handed it to a surprised Susan, who for the first time, backed away from him, not knowing what to say.

'OK,' said Ned. 'This is the way it's going to be done, there were seven of us on stage plus the P.A. system which you own, so I'm going to split the money eight ways and no arguments please.'

The little bit of authority worked, but they sent it up a bit by standing in line with one hand out to accept their share of the divvy and John had to put two hands out for the P.A. money plus his own cut. Susan was last in the line and she couldn't keep a straight face, so when Ned crossed her palm she curtseyed and said.

'Oh thank you kind sir and May I kiss the paymaster?'

'You may,' he answered solemnly, waiting with eyes closed for the touch of those wet velvet lips.

The other family members left the room, knowing they would have the gear packed before that kiss came to an end and it was around 4am when they got back to the house, where the proud parents had the usual spread ready. Mary's Chef boyfriend, who had seen his lady perform on a stage for the first time tonight, had helped with the food and he was thrilled tending to her every need, while quite obviously being appreciated for it in return. One hour later, Ned was kissing a weary Susan good morning, when she said something, which woke him up.

'When am I going to see you again darling, could you take me to the Diamond Ballroom on Saturday night if the weather holds out. I'm going to miss you and I don't want to wait until Monday.'

'I'd love to darling, but I have to get from Dublin to Carrickbay for the Sunday gig and I wouldn't be able to get you home, especially if the roads are bad.' His voice tailed off as he feverishly searched for excuses, but no more came.

'Don't worry honey,' she said gently. 'I understand, but call before you leave and promise that you will phone me every day.'

'I promise my darling,' he said, as he was flooded with guilt and relief. 'Your parents have asked me over for lunch so I'll see you then.' She stood waving at him while he turned the car and blowing her a kiss, he drove off along the Fiddler's Lane.

'You bastard Ned Brady,' he said aloud, 'but I couldn't take Susan to the Diamond Ballroom and introduce her to Kate Kelly, the woman who is probably carrying my child, that would just add insult to injury, may God forgive me.'

Mrs. North was glad she didn't have to cook for him that day, because all the members of her family were going out to dine with friends, so they wished each other a Happy New Year and headed off in separate directions. By then the roads were clear of snow with some still clinging to the hills and later, it was a well fed, but sad Ned who headed out for Cork and the bands next gig. The manager had told him earlier on the phone that he hoped they would make it to tonight's dance and even though the roads around Mullymore were still bad, they would give it their best shot by leaving early. Later, a much-relieved Bandleader saw the big red wagon roll up to the Ballroom, with a grinning Roadie at the wheel.

'I'd say, he missed last nights gig more than the band members,' he was thinking, as he watched them climb out and have a stretch.

'Let's get this stuff in,' said Conn. 'I want to check into the Hotel and have a shower.'

'Tell us about last night,' the Roadie enquired. 'Was it a good gig and were there any women asking for me?'

'Loads of them.' Ned answered. 'Even the ones who couldn't make it.' He felt bad about taking the piss out of this chap, the only one from the bunch who was man enough to ask about the previous night and knowing he still hadn't picked up on his last comment, he continued. 'Yeah there were a few asking, even the two morons.'

'I'll bet they had their shirts buttoned last night, but I believe the forecast is good for tonight.' he said

'Thank God,' said Ned, noticing that it was the second time in two days, where he had referred to God. 'I must be getting religion.'

After a big one in Cork and several phone calls to Susan, it was off to Galway in the west for another full house. Even thought he had greatly enjoyed playing with The Prunty's, he had to agree, that for this type of music, it was hard to beat the Showband sound created by the trumpet, tenor sax and trombone, being driven by a good rhythm section, which The Nova's had. After a good nights rest in Salthill Galway, they all headed across country for Dublin and the lovely Diamond Ballroom. Mike and two members of the band travelled with Ned and in between conversations, he couldn't stop thinking of what and how he would feel, when he laid eyes on Kate. Would it be noticeable that she was expecting, had she told her husband Paul yet and if so, would he be going around all proud, oblivious of the fact that later he would be shaking hands with the real father.

'Jaysus, what am I going to do?' He though. 'Paul will expect me to congratulate him, while she's there, watching and looking gorgeous. I won't be able to put two words together, but I'd better not blurt out who did it.'

He shouldn't have worried. Paul Kelly opened the big front door as usual and greeted all the lads by name, still bedecked in diamonds and gold, but not a word about impending fatherhood.

'My good wife will be along later to arrange some food for you boys, I hope you're not starving, how do you think the place is looking?'

'Oh, great as usual Paul, you must be proud of it,' the bands answer sounded rehearsed and it was, because they were expecting the question. About an hour later, when they were ready to switch on for a run through, they heard a female voice calling.

'OK lads, grubs ready.' As she spoke, Kate Kelly was striding up the floor, only looking magnificent in a black suit to the knee and patent high heels to match.

'Oh fuck, I'd love to give her one,' Conn whispered.

'And I'd like to give her two,' added Mickey Joe.

'Well you can count me in while you're at it,' muttered the Roadie, just as the mike he was holding was switched on.

'Now lads, keep it clean, only food on the menu tonight,' she said and the Roadie was glad she was laughing.

Ned had been watching her since she came out of the office and before she got to the stage he could have gone into battle, in any bed, anywhere.

'Jaysus,' he whispered, 'she has a devastating sexual effect on me and I wonder would she come around behind the big curtain right now, because I'm ready.'

He knew that could never happen, as none of the band members knew anything, only Mike and Frank and they were keeping quiet. He walked to the front of the stage, held out his hand and then nimbly stepping up on one of the chairs she grasped it, squeezing his fingers until it almost hurt.

'Happy New Year Ned, to you and all the boys, you can follow me now, there's some nice food and Christmas pudding for afters,' she said with a grin.

He couldn't take his eyes off this good-looking woman, and in particular from her tummy, which as yet was showing no signs of pregnancy. He found himself asking God to help him again for the third time in as many days. 'Please God, let it be a scare,' he was thinking as he overtook her on the glossy floor and said

'You're looking marvellous as usual and I think you've lost weight.'

'Oh, black always does that for me Ned, actually I've put on five pounds in the last few days and I can't imagine why, as I've cut back on my food intake recently.' There was a happy smile dancing around her face, as she looked him directly in the eye while she spoke.

His head was in a spin and he could hardly taste the great food, while he listened to the compliments coming from his mates and the background voices of both the Kelly's. The night was a huge success, even though some of their fans were still on holiday all over the country, but they were abundantly replaced by visitors to the city from all over Ireland and the world, some who had heard the band in London, New York and California.

His first face-to-face meeting with Kate came after the dance, in the corridor outside the toilets and for a moment they stood transfixed, then she took the initiative.

'You didn't reply to my letter,' she stated, looking very disappointed.

He looked around furtively to check how safe the area was to talk and then he answered. 'I only posted it on the Friday before Christmas, so that's why you haven't received it,' he was almost whispering now.

'Oh, thank God,' she gushed, 'is everything OK.'

Just as he was about to answer, a crowd of noisy people rushed in the door, as if they were going to miss the boat causing the intimate conversation to end abruptly, so the next time they spoke was when she and her husband wished the band A Happy New Year on their way out the big front door.

'See you all again in early March, goodnight.' They announced in unison.

'Yeah,' said Mike, 'that's our last Irish date before our next English tour, so keep well now.'

Sandra Boyle had been at the dance, but Ned told the Roadie to tell her that Mary's boyfriend was there and she would have to make herself scarce for now.

'What did she say?' Ned asked.

'That Frank was picking her up and for you not to forget the big meeting in January,' he answered.

'Thanks Frank, you're a lifesaver,' he almost sang it.

Back at the Hotel he went straight to bed, as he had to get enough sleep to sustain him the next night, because he was driving directly from the gig in Carrickbay, to Glenrone. Then, after a few hours, he was due to pick Susan up before heading for Mullymore and the big house on the hill, which only they knew to be totally empty. At breakfast the next morning, he was glad to hear that the snow was almost gone all over the country and the forecast was giving mild weather into the New Year. On the journey to Carrickbay, he tried to focus only on thoughts of Susan, but recent visions of Kate Kelly and a very ravishing Sandra Boyle kept pushing on to the scene. Both the aforementioned ladies had been by far, the best looking women at last nights dance and here he was trying to push them out of his mind.

'But it's the only way in the end,' he thought. 'I love Susan and I think that's how it will pan out, no matter what happens in May next.'

The only saving graces for a presently very cold Carrickbay were, it was on the coast and in summer it's beaches were safe, but probably its greatest asset was the big Dance Hall at the top of the only street in town. This is the place where Ned had searched for a working phone, to make his first promised call to Susan and this evening he was having the same problems. The first one had all it's bits and pieces ripped out and the second one would not accept the coins. Then, as he was turning the car at the Dance Hall, he met the caretaker who understood his plight and informed him he could make the call from his house, just across the road. He explained the problem to Susan, who said that she would say all the loving things and he could talk about the weather. The call wasn't as explicit as the one to Brenda, but he got an inkling of what to expect while ringing in the New Year, by some of the sexy things she had to say, while his answers were. 'That's suits me fine, is that possible, all night, I don't believe you and I'll try anything once.' She was laughing her head off as she told him to take care and how much she loved him.

The Caretaker's daughters got his autograph, then he had tea with Christmas cake and their dad would take no money for the phone call. By then the band members had arrived and as Ned took his gear from the car he shouted to Mike.

'Remember yer- man, the Mexican, he had a phone in the stretch car in L.A. Do you think they'll ever make their way over here?'

'All I can say is, that's the U.S of A, maybe we'll get them sometime in the next century, who knows.' Mike was sounding American again.

The crowd was huge that night and the band seemed to go down well, but Ned's thoughts were miles away and like a robot he played his trombone, strummed his few chords, sang his songs and afterwards signed autographs from habit. When they were changing in the band room later, he half expected to suffer jibes from the lads, but to his surprise, none came. They were all happy to have New Years Eve off, to rest after a hard week and before another long run, which began on January the 1st. Some of the lads would have preferred New Year's Day off, but Mike had got a great deal for it, so he decided quite rightly, to work it and as he pointed the big car in the direction of Glenrone, he mulled over two inevitabilities that were going to happen soon. The one he was most excited about was the fact that he and Susan would consummate their love at midnight on New Year's Eve. The other one that he was a little worried about was. Susan had decided to take a week off to visit Ned in Mullymore and she planned to travel to all the gigs, but that should be good news instead of a problem.

On the last two of those dates though, one Sandra Boyle, 'Journalist' would be there, so she would make it her business to seek out and interview Susan. Our hero was really worried about that, but as he drove carefully along he realised it's got to happen sometime and Frank's words were a help, when he pointed out that Sandra was a smart lady who didn't want a commitment, from any man. 'You're all horny bastards,' was her favourite phrase.

It was 6am on a frosty but clear morning when he went to bed in the guesthouse, after leaving a note for the landlady to call him at 10am. Refreshed by an invigorating shower, he had a spring in his step as he headed for Susan's and breakfast with the family. They would both need to behave normally and not give an inkling of what they had planned, but when her parents said they would phone and speak to them plus his mum and dad, he calmly told lie number three.

'Oh yeah fine, but we hope to visit all the family connections in our area to introduce Susan, so you might not get through, they are dying to meet her and mum and dad want to show her off too.'

He was careful to mention his area only, as he could imagine an invitation from the Prunty's to visit them as well and bring his parents, which could be dangerous. After loads of hugs and kisses, it was a relieved young couple that drove out the Fiddler's Lane and took the road for Mullymore.

'I'm a bit scared Ned honey,' she began. 'I'll probably mess things up when push comes to shove.'

In fits of laughter he said. 'You just leave all the pushing and shoving to me darling, that way, I can't blame you if it happens.'

She saw the funny side of it too and laughed, even though it wasn't as hearty as his guffaw. People waved as they drove through his hometown and they both beamed back proudly, each wondering if the locals knew what they had planned.

'It's nobody's business but our own,' he told her in a comforting way. 'The time has come for us to spend some time alone and do and say what we feel, but we'll need a good story for your parents when we get back, then there's my folks as well.'

She was in the middle of agreeing with him when the car stopped at his front door.

'Oh my God,' she gushed, 'we're here, hold me.'

He wrapped his arms around her and did precisely that, holding her for a full five minutes before opening the car door.

'I can't imagine being in this situation with anyone else,' she said. 'You're so calm, I love you Ned.'

That led to some more hugging and kissing until he said to her. 'We'd better go in, or I'll make love to you here long before midnight.'

He took all the baggage in and then Susan said. 'I'll put all your soiled clothes in the washing machine, while you book the restaurant, is that OK honey.'

'Oh thank you darling, but the meal is already booked for 7 o'clock, I couldn't take the chance and wait until now.'

While he spoke, he helped her to load the washing machine in between the odd kiss and cuddle as happiness reigned. They had three hours to spend before leaving for the restaurant and without speaking about it, they both knew they couldn't get involved in any kind of heavy petting, so Ned switched on the T.V. leaving it on whatever channel it was at, then Susan asked.

'Would you like some tea love? No don't get up, I know where everything is.' She made tea six times that evening, which they drank while sitting in separate armchairs, just smiling at each other, ignoring a war film on the telly.

At 6.45 Ned asked. 'Are you ready honey, we'd better head out for the meal.'

'OK, I'll just go and powder my nose, back in a minute,' she replied.

He had to try hard to control his emotions when she bounced back into the room, her nose powdered, her full velvet lips touched up and her long black wavy, freshly combed hair bouncing around her shoulders, she was a picture.

'I think we'd better leave immediately,' he said.

'I'll second that,' she agreed, standing aside, so he could open the door.

They both talked like they were wound up. Firstly about Ned's parents who had made the trip to the U.S.A. successfully, then about her folks and what they would say, if they ever found out their kids had lied to them about this week.

'We had no choice, now I'm sure mum and dad will cover for us, because they don't think for a moment that we would sleep together, but they wouldn't want to worry your parents,' he said hopefully.

'They wouldn't worry about us sleeping together, it would be us staying awake together that would cause the problem,' this piece of knowledge slipped from Susan's mouth and sent them both into convulsions.

Later at their destination, he walked around and helped her out of the car, while she knowingly made it worth his while.

'Wow, you're wearing stockings,' he gushed.

'They are especially for you honey. I want you're giggling-gap story to become a reality and I wanted to reward you for opening the car door as well.'

'And I want to have you now,' he said, pinning her against the car, knowing he couldn't, not yet.

'You've got a name for what you're planning haven't you,' she said.

'Yeah,' he replied, 'it's called a knee-trembler.'

As he held her close, he could feel the ripples of her laughter running up and down her frame and then gently slipping one arm around her they entered the restaurant. Now considered regulars in this establishment, they got preferential treatment, enjoying every moment.

'Those steaks were done to a T,' she said, as they made their way home and that red wine too, it was marvellous, you know, I'm a little bit tipsy.'

'That's a nice way to be to ring in The New Year,' he said, taking her hand and squeezing it gently. 'I'm glad you liked the wine as I've got another couple of bottles at the house.'

'Are you trying to get me drunk Ned Brady?' She asked with a happy, impish grin.

'Yes Susan Prunty,' he answered, but not too drunk. I want you to remember everything we do tonight, for the rest of your life.'

Squeezing his hand in return she replied. 'Oh, I will, I'm sure I will and so will you darling.'

Back at the house, he opened one of the bottles, filled both glasses to the brim and then they drank toasts to everyone dear to them, but most of all their loving parents, agreeing that they were very lucky to have them. Still seated in separate armchairs smiling at each other, they heard the announcer on the T.V. saying.

'And just to remind all you folks watching, there's just ten minutes of this old year remaining, so keep your glasses topped up and at the ready to welcome The New Year.'

She watched Ned nervously as he did precisely what the man had said and then she stood up holding out her hand on her lover's request, which was.

'Come with me pet, we won't need any more help from him.' As he spoke he switched off the T.V and the room light, then led his darling up the soft, carpeted stairs. The ascent to ecstasy had begun.

The central heating had been on for hours and Ned's big bedroom was cosy (to put it mildly) and as he took her into his strong arms he said.

'Susan honey, I'm going to take off all your outer clothes, then I want you to do the same for me, afterwards, we will both climb on top of the bed and let love take it's course.'

Her only answer was a loving smile, so he began the very pleasant chore, revealing the sexiest underwear he had ever seen.

'Samantha got them specially for me from Paris,' she said shyly.

He had been holding his breath in admiration, slowly he began to exhale saying.

'Viva le France.'

He just stood there while she removed his clothes, lifting an arm or a leg when necessary, then he picked her up and carried her to the bed. In those remaining moments of December, they both experienced every emotion they had ever felt for each other and as the old year slid flawlessly into the new, so also did the lovers, who had used the same medium of time to edge themselves ever closer to this, the most magnificent moment of their lives. Seconds before, she had whispered.

'Please be gentle,' and he was.

Thrilled by every loud, synchronised moan, coming from her full open lips, they both reached the summit together; their highest mountain had been scaled. Later as she slept, he lay awake looking at her beautiful, happy, contented face and his thoughts ran riot. Now they had reached this plateau, how could he keep his three promises next May, but unfortunately, the two letters to the U.S. and the third one to Kate Kelly's sister's address, (for obvious reasons) were in the post. The missiles of destiny were launched.

THE END

"The Famed, yet Unframed Picture"
"Monroe One"

I've grown very fond, of this lovely blond.
Lying quietly on my floor.
But she's past romance, as I take a glance.
Each time I enter, through the door.
She smiles back at me, but she cannot see.
The look of admiration on my face.
If alive today, she would probably say.
What am I doing in this place?
In case you don't know, her name's Monroe.
Her picture's intended for my wall.
But busy writing songs and stories,
I've got no time at all.
So, while in search of fame, I'm gonna buy a frame.
And a great big chunk of glass.
Hang her on the wall, where I can see her all.
Especially (pause) those long legs up to her ass.

"A Much Loved Tragedy"
"Monroe Two"

I just watched a movie, about Marilyn Monroe.
A lady who had everything, what a tragic way to go.
The paramedics found her spread eagle on the bed.
They had gotten there just too late, so the official story said.
But other theories differ and will we ever know.
What it was that happened so many years ago.
Had she used that telephone, they found beside her bed?
If so, who was the last to hear her voice,

Before they found her dead?
She will always be remembered, as a beauty of her time.
And perhaps, to that memory a plus, by dying in her prime.
It would not have suited Marilyn, growing wrinkled, going grey.
We would much prefer the picture that we have of her today.
Nature overdid its duty by giving her such beauty.
But in every given day, God took something else away.
Did the Kennedy Brothers love her, did the Kennedy Brothers not?
Then perhaps a classic irony, that the Kennedy's both got shot.

"Your Biggest Fan"
"Monroe Three"

Marilyn, Marilyn, beautiful and bothered.
Held onto your looks,
Died before they withered,
Oh how you were used,
Is it any wonder, you were confused.
Passed away abandoned in your bed.
The world mourned, when you were dead.
You'd never think your life, was such a mess.
The way you look in that white dress.
That innocent look upon your face,
Body exuding femininity and grace.
God was good, to your outer shell.
While he sadly made your mind a hell.
There are stories told that you were very bold.

Of your political connections and your Presidential erections.
I think the reports were very mean.
To me you look so squeaky clean.
Envy begrudges looks like yours.
So it put you in every bed like whores.
What was sex to them, I hope for you was love.
As some have joined you, up above.
Would things have been different? It's hard to know.
If you had been happily married to Arthur or Joe.
Your famous movie shot is all I've got.
Your smile brightens up the room.
I never feel alone when I'm on my own.
Even though you're in your tomb.
You remain a Goddess to every man.
Today, I became your biggest fan.

APEX TRAVEL

LOW COST FLIGHTS
Australia , USA , Canada
Far East , Africa
Agents for all Airlines & Tours operators
Member of ITAA & IATA

2 4 1 8 0 0 0
Fax: 6 7 9 1 5 2 8
Email: info@apex-travel.ie
59 Dame Street Dublin 2
The Management and Staff of

Apex Travel
Wish Ned and 'The Novas Showband'
Bon Voyage

As they traverse the globe like real stars

TACTAMOTORS

Dublin Rd, Cavan
Ph: 049 433 1188. Fax: 049 433 1642
Or Email: info@tractamotors.ie

'Just one call solves it all'

Open Mon – Sat – 9am – 6pm
During Lunch . Late Thur 8pm

....

Superb range of CALOR GAS COOKERS
NOW AVAILABLE
Complete range of LIGHTING for inside and outside your home
Including Seasonal Lighting
The Largest Selection in Town

....

For your CAR, LORRY, TRACTOR, BIKE
Tyres . Batteries . Exhausts
Hancook . Kumho . Pirelli Tyres
FREE Tyre Fitting . FREE Wheel Balancing
FREE Valve with all new Tyres Purchased

....

In our BIKE DEPARTMENT
All sizes of Gents, Girls and Boys
Mountain Bikes and Helmets and Bike accessories in stock

....

The AGRICULTURAL MACHINERY
& CONSTRUCTION EQUIPMENT DIVISION
Has
MOWERS. HOPPERS. FERTILIZER SPREADERS.
ROTARY HARROWS.
ROUND BALE MACHINE FOR SILAGE, HAY OR STRAW. CEMENT
MIXERS; All Sizes. LAZER DIAMOND SAW BLADES.
POWER WASHERS.
All At. TRACTAMOTORS, Dublin Rd, Cavan – 049 433 1188
Wishing Jim Smith Good Luck With His New Book.

'NED THE BED'

Velvet Music Presents

3 Great Original CD's & Cassette's
From Jim Smith
The author of
'Ned The Bed' and 'Animal Mountain'

Current satire, good songs & instrumentals
Something for everyone

To contact us –
  Tel.: 00 353 91 792 853   00 353 86 249 1027
          Or, e-mail:
mightyavon@eircom.net   velvetbooksandmusic@gmail.com

Made in the USA